AF424762

Praise for
Kimberly Brighton's Books

EDITORIAL REVIEWS

"Brighton skillfully weaves together a heartwarming romantic comedy filled with alluring chemistry and poignant moments...from the bustling courtrooms of Philadelphia to the tranquil sandy shores of the Jersey Cape, Brighton's tender yet humorous Cape May series explores the power of choice and fate and the complexities of love."

~ Prairies Book Review

"The perfect light romance novel for summer beach reading at the Shore...these Cape May-based dramadies have all the twists and turns to set your heart aflutter."

~ Main Line Today

"This fun read fully embraces its Love Actually-inspired plot, featuring enthralling vignettes which take their protagonists through the ups and downs of love and life."

~ Reedsy Discovery, starred review

"Kimberly Brighton depicts each couple's perspective in vivid detail. The unpredictable plot kept my interest, as every page gave another piece to each puzzle. The Way to Cape May will appeal to romance readers who enjoy stories that give a realistic view of individual progress in love."

~ Readers Favorite

"A heartwarming tale with a strong sense of place and relatable characters, brimming with complicated relationships, delicious romantic chemistry, and a touch of human drama. Brighton's mastery of complex yet endearing characters shines through as the tensions between each couple reach a boiling point before finally simmering down. With her astute understanding of human psychology, she weaves a story that is both heartwarming and full of passion and vulnerability."

~ Prairies Book Review

READER REVIEWS

"Such a cute, light story, following three sisters—their love lives & career ambitions, successes and failures behind all of the characters' stories, the opportunities given and taken away, small town, big city. So many pulls, thought provoking...And ALL the feels as the story closes. A must read."

"Kimberly did an amazing job weaving six perspectives together, along with combining past and present storylines. Each story flowed well and they were cohesive at the end."

"This story was such a fun ride from start to finish and held my interest the entire time...the author did an excellent job writing each character in a unique voice, which made the story flow so well."

"I laughed out loud and cheered on these ladies who have become my friends. This was such a satisfying ending to the trilogy but left me wanting more (hint, hint to the author....)"

"I absolutely loved this book! Such a fun, laid back summer read."

"Keep writing, KB."

BOOKS BY KIMBERLY BRIGHTON

THE CAPE MAY SERIES
The Way to Cape May
A Cape May Kind of Love
Cape May Ever After

STANDALONE
Cape May Christmas in July

Copyright @ 2026 by Kimberly Brighton

Readers Guide Copyright @ 2026 by Kimberly Brighton

Cover design by Mary Ann Smith and book design by Jessica Kleinman

All rights reserved.

The scanning, uploading and distribution of this book without permission is theft of the author's intellectual property. If you would like permission to use material from the book (other than for review purposes), please contact CapeIslandPublishers@comcast.net. Thank you for your support of the author's rights.

Published in the United States of America by Cape Island Publishers

CapeIslandPublishers.com

Library of Congress Control Number: 2026903068

Printed book ISBN: 979-8-9987632-0-5

Ebook ISBN: 979-8-9987632-1-2

This is a work of fiction. Names, characters, places, and incidents either are the product of the author's imagination or are used fictitiously. Any resemblance to actual persons, living or dead, business establishments, events, or locales is entirely coincidental.

KIMBERLY BRIGHTON

☒ My ☒ Summer ☒ Bucket ☒ List

~ To Deirdre and Ellen ~

Oh, how I cherish those Sea Isle summers of our twenties. I always thought my favorite parts of our weekends "down the shore" were sunny days spent on white sand beaches, and cool nights dancing to our favorite bands, laughing until we couldn't breathe. But I was wrong. Turns out, what I loved the most about those precious and fleeting days of our youth was simply being with the two of you.

Rest in peace, sweet Ellen. In a way, you will always be twenty-five to me. I know you're somewhere warm and sunny, driving with windows down, sea breeze teasing your soft blonde hair as you croon to Bruce Springsteen songs. You are dearly loved and sorely missed, but your laughter stays with me. Always.

If once you have slept on an island
You'll never be quite the same;
You may look as you looked the day before
And go by the same old name,

You may bustle about in street and shop
You may sit at home and sew,
But you'll see blue water and wheeling gulls
Wherever your feet may go.

You may chat with the neighbors of this and that
And close to your fire keep,
But you'll hear ship whistle and lighthouse bell
And tides beat through your sleep.

Oh! you won't know why and you can't say how
Such a change upon you came...

But once you have slept on an island,
You'll never be quite the same.

~ Rachel Field

If you're looking for a heartwarming love story, you've come to the wrong place.

You probably picked up this book hoping to find a starry-eyed FMC (female main character, that is), searching for love but going about it all wrong. Along the way, she'll go through all sorts of shenanigans, dreamed up by a crafty author, before finally learning what she needs to do differently. But not before having her heart broken in the third act, because readers love that shit. Or maybe authors are just that sadistic. If they're not, damn straight their editors are.

But what of the FMCs who don't believe in love? Who'd rather be shot naked from a cannon at a country rodeo than get married? Because you're looking at one.

Sorry to burst your bubble, but I'm nothing like the once-hopeful romantics who end up across the desk from me, dabbing at tears after hiring me to undo their marital mess. You see, I'm the person you come to when your marriage tanks. The divorce lawyer you never think you'll need. There are tons of jokes about us too. That whole shark analogy? That's me and my firm-mates, circling our prey, trying to get what we can for our clients. If you've ever been through such an ordeal, I profusely apologize. Truly. It's never personal, it's just that we can be assholes sometimes. A lot of the times. Actually, we suck. If you're a divorce attorney, I'm sure you're the exception.[*]

---

[*] The lawyers made me say that.

At least, that's what I did until this past summer. The summer everything changed. The summer I turned witty (just kidding, I was already witty). What wasn't I? Full of hope and squishy feels.

Strap in, because while I can't promise a love story like no other, I *can* promise it's one you won't see coming. At least I didn't.

It starts one fateful Friday in April, when I'm called into my boss's office. I should've known better than to expect pleasantries. Bosses never have anything good to say at 3:00 on a Friday. Hell, if your boss is anything like mine, they rarely have anything good to say. Period.

Mike gestures to a seat, lowers his rotund body into his chair, and rubs his bald head before dropping the bomb. "We're letting you go," he says.

"Go where?"

"Home."

"As in, early dismissal?"

"No, Kacie. As in, we're letting you go. Permanently."

I laugh out loud for two reasons. One: I think he's joking. Two: I have a tendency to laugh inappropriately. It's one of my special party tricks.

"Not a joke, Kacie," Mike says, eliminating my first reason.

"Do you care to tell me why?" I demand.

"Of course. I introduce Exhibit A," he says, aiming a clicker at the computer monitor on the credenza behind him.

My recently aired TV commercial pops up on the screen. I knew I was taking a chance with it, but that doesn't stop me from beaming with pride as I squirm in my seat from excitement. I'm proud of that ad. To top it off, I was having a good hair day, and my makeup looked fierce. As fierce as it can look when your skin's roughly the shade of printer paper, and you manage to apply mascara without looking like Beetlejuice. I can't pull off what Kardashians can—exotic reds and deep earth tones that complement their beautiful olive skin. For me, only a light brown mascara can frame my pale blue eyes. Anything darker and I look like I'm toe-tagging it up in the morgue. And my lip color can't be any deeper than a baby pink without appearing as if Hannibal Lecter's chewed them off and paired them with a fine Chianti. It's the curse of the fair-skinned.

Before you go thinking I'm a total train wreck, let me clarify. I'm not a gargoyle. It's just in my nature to be self-deprecating. Sue me.

Mike presses play.

"*Hi. I'm Kacie Layne,*" my video begins. "*Some of you may know me as a divorce lawyer for the firm Mazerati Jones. If you don't know me, you probably will soon…if you dare get married. Statistics show that 50 percent of all marriages end in divorce. Trust me, folks—there's nothing more heartbreaking than having to decide who gets that NutriBullet you so lovingly registered for before all heck* broke loose. That's why I'm here with a public service announcement: don't do it. Believe me, you can still have fun just living together. If you do decide to bite the veritable NutriBullet, remember my name, because you'll likely need it one day. Kacie Layne, THE divorce attorney. (PS - I also do custody.)*"

"I assume you can see the obvious reason we need to let you go," Mike says, glaring at me as he stops the video.

"Not really. Isn't truth in advertising the gold standard?"

I expect him to say I'm a buzzkill, that people are falling in love left and right like mosquitoes to a bug zapper. That I have no right to burst everyone's bubbles because we *want* people to fall in love, screw each other (sorry, make love…the other way comes later), and all that happy horseshit so we can procreate and continue the human race. I wait for him to say I'll solely be to blame for our collective demise if people don't tie the noose (sorry, knot) and the planet's taken over by murder hornets.

---

* I wanted to say "hell," but the FCC wouldn't allow me.

But he doesn't say that.

Instead, he says, "Kacie, if people stop marrying, we'll lose business," like the true shyster he is.

"I don't see anything wrong with it. It's funny! Not like the other family law firms' sad and depressing commercials. I'm trying to save people from making a grave mistake."

You're probably wondering what crawled up my ass and died. It's not that I'm *completely* heartless and anti-love. I've just been burned by two Major Love Events, so excuse me if I'm not squealing with joy over the thought of strapping myself to another human for eternity. Maybe it's not so much love, but long-term commitment *(ahem,* marriage) that gives me the creeps. Whatever it is, I think my attitude is realistic.

"My point is, shit happens," I continue. "Life happens. People fall out of love, they cheat on each other, even end up on Jumbotrons in compromising positions. I'm not *making* it happen by talking about it. I'm just calling it out. I'm saying, if you don't wanna deal with someone like me, don't get married. But when they do, and it fails, they'll be like 'sucks that my marriage didn't work out, but how about that funny chick? She seems good.'"

Mike stares at me. "You need help."

I laugh, because number two above.

"I like you, Kacie. You've taken this difficult job we do and made it fun. But *funny* is for stand-up routines, not the practice of law."

"I beg to differ. If you don't find a way to laugh in this ugly area of law, it'll eat you alive."

I know you're probably thinking I should watch it here. But the way I see it, I'm not gonna be employed by this firm much longer anyway, so why not go down in a blaze of glorious humor? My go-to for all things unpleasant.

I also know, on some level, he's about to do me a huge favor. Truth is, I've been looking to leave this firm for a while. He's just holding the door open for me.

More like kicking my ass out of it.

"We don't need to be mocking people for wanting to marry, Kacie. I like you, so we're not gonna call this a firing. It'll be a lay-off, so you'll get severance pay."

My ears perk up. "Is anyone else getting laid off?"

"Yes. Three of you." He pushes a button on his desk phone. "Send them in."

I swivel in my chair with the same gawking curiosity one feels passing a car wreck. I can't wait to see who else is getting the heave-ho. There are a bunch of duds in this firm, and I bet I can name the ones getting the ax.

In walk two strapping security officers instead.

"You have five minutes to pack your belongings before they escort you from the building," Mike announces.

"What's this?" I ask, spinning back toward him. I've seen them do the security-enhanced walk of shame with others, but usually it's one officer—Ernie, the front desk security guy, who even my ninety-year-old grandmother can outrun. With him, I stood a chance. "What happened to Ernie?"

"We've hired a new security company. Nothing personal."

"You can't be serious. Two of them? I'm barely five feet tall. What do you think I'm gonna do, steal pens? Sit on the printer and photocopy my ass? Throw admin staff through floor-to-ceiling windows?"

The guards tighten up, hands on gun holsters. (Gun holsters! Like we're in the Wild West!) (Then again, it *is* Philly). As they move closer, I pick up what they're putting down.

Rising from my chair, I give Mike a double-barreled middle finger show. I've wanted to do this for so long. Damn, it feels good.

"Fuck you, Mike," I say as each guard takes an arm.

"Fuck you right back, Kacie."

Ten minutes later, I find myself on the Broad Street line

heading home, box of office bullshit on my lap. I cannot believe what's transpired. For all my false bravado, I'm now reeling—drunk from a well-shaken cocktail of rage and shame. I would've preferred to resign of my own accord, instead of being escorted from the building like a convicted felon.

I try to cry, but nothing comes out. Sorry, I'm just not a crier. Maybe on some level I know Mike *has* done me a favor. To say I'm burned out is an understatement of epic proportions. I've had enough of the whining and crying on this job, and I'm not just talking about clients. I mean the partners. *Step up your billable hours, Kacie*, they keep saying, as if I don't work a lifetime of billable hours in one week's time. *Pay more attention in staff meetings, Kacie.* Provide cocktails, and you got yourself got a deal. *Stop pranking your coworkers, Kacie.* Right, as if everyone didn't love seeing Mike's face on a Most Wanted poster for consuming the last piece of staff-meeting pizza. Even Mike himself laughed.

My best friend, Amy, seems to think my dissatisfaction stems not so much from the firm I work(ed) for, but from the practice of law itself. Case in point: she found my commercial to be a cry for professional help. In retrospect, she may not be wrong. Spend every day in the trenches of marital trauma, cheating, and despair, and let me know how much you love practicing in this despicable area of law.

The closer I get to my stop, the more my office bravado wanes. Despite this axing coming for a while, self-imposed or not, it sucks. My hands shake, as if I'm nervous. Of course, I am—unless I win the lottery or dabble in felony extortion, I now must find a job.

What if I can't?

I think of all the things I'll have to change, now that I don't have an income. Like stop using the King of Prussia mall as a therapist. Quit the expensive gym I never go to. And ditch plans to trade in my current mode of questionable transportation for a new set of wheels. Living in Philly as I do, I'm fortunate that most of my galivanting for work and pleasure is accomplished via train, but every once in a while, it's nice to escape the city. Which is why I allowed my ex to talk me into buying a used piece of shit in the first place. Not surprising, given that he's one, too, but it seemed to make sense back then. Not now, knowing all the money I spent on repairs could have been used to pay down the national debt. My plan, up until roughly 3:05 p.m. today, was to combine my trade-in with a hefty downpayment, but it looks as if I'll need the money I saved for that to buy groceries for the foreseeable future.

I text Amy and ask her to meet me at McGillin's Olde Ale House, our usual jawn. I don't bother going home first to unload my bullshit box, that's how badly I need a drink and my best friend.

"What's this?" she asks when she arrives, peering eagerly into the box as if expecting it to be stuffed with kittens. Upon inventorying its contents, her head pops up and her eyes widen. "You did it! You finally quit. Kudos!"

"Not exactly..."

"Oh, my God, Kacie!" she exclaims after I tell her what happened. "What are you gonna do?"

"Going out on a limb here, but...find another job?"

"Hopefully you didn't burn any bridges at Mazerati and can still use them for references."

"I didn't burn them," I say, rolling my eyes in exasperation before giving her a cheesy grin. "I blew 'em up."

I fill her in on my parting two-gun salute.

"Oh, Kacie. That's not good. Although, that bridge was already burned with that crazy commercial of yours. Didn't I warn you not to do it?"

No, in fact, she did not. When I first showed her the video, expecting a high five, fist bump, or other physical accolade, she merely shook her head.

"You need help," she'd said.

I remind her now how miserable I was there.

"Yeah, but you didn't have to implode your career on the way out."

I lowkey fear she's right. Suddenly regretting my two-gun salute and snarky response to being "laid off," I wonder if I should've fought a little harder, apologized for the commercial, groveled for forgiveness. Maybe not turn everything into a joke for a change.

"I shouldn't have a problem finding a job, with my experience and track record," I say, not sure if I'm trying to convince Amy or myself. Although it's true. Over the past seven years, I've gained tons of civil law experience, in addition to my specialty area of family law, making me a perfect fit for any firm.

If that's what I want.

"Mazerati is the only place you've worked since passing the bar," Amy reminds me. "How do you expect to get a decent referral from them?"

"Good thing I'm besties with the HR director."

Despite being the person whose job it is to maintain a professional work environment, Harriet Bloom is (or was) my partner in crime, helping me lighten up the workplace with silly, nonthreatening office pranks. After my exodus, she texted to say she'll forge any referral I need and thanked me for all the legal assistance and laughs I provided when she, herself, was going through a messy divorce.

"Maybe this is a sign I should apply to Ben's firm," I add.

Amy smirks. "I'm sure his recent divorce has nothing to do with you wanting to work there."

"It has nothing to do with Ben," I lie.

Of course, it does. Ben is our good friend, who doubles as my longtime crush. I met him on our first day of law school when we turned a corner and bumped into each other. It was like the sun broke through the ceiling of Delaware Law

School's hallway, beaming down on him as if he were the second coming of Perry Mason. He was beautiful, dark, mysterious, and I'd never seen anyone rock horn-rimmed glasses like he did. After discovering we'd been assigned to the same section, we became fast friends. Bonding over our studies, it wasn't long before that little love-at-first-sight thing developed into a massive crush.

It wasn't just his looks that had me hooked—dark wavy hair and toned, athletic frame, despite being more bookworm, less athlete—it was his personality that won me over. He was kind, gentle, funny. Emotionally mature and intelligent beyond belief. The whole package. I've often wondered if I'd have made it through law school without his helpful tutelage, encouragement, and support.

Unfortunately, Ben had a serious girlfriend back home, so I had to squelch my romantic feelings for him as our friendship grew, until it gradually developed into an unspoken *more*. At least it was about to, until a life-altering event tripped us up before we could fully explore that possibility. Yet here I am, years later, still intrigued by the idea of Ben as *more*, despite my general disbelief in long-term love. I know it makes no sense, but here we are.

In addition to the perk of working with Ben on the daily, his is the **chef's kiss** of law firms. Anyone with a law degree and a pulse would kill to work there for its renowned prestige. It's really the only firm I'd want to work for if I'm gonna keep doing this law thang.

"Oh God," Amy huffs as her eyes rest upon my collarbone. "Why are you still wearing that thing?"

My fingers instinctively go to *that thing*—a ring dangling from a necklace. It's the "promise" ring my ex, Seth, gave me before he went and broke all his promises.

"To remind myself to watch out for assholes," I say as I pull the ring up to my eye and peer through it like a monocle. "To examine their souls and reveal the player within, so I never make the same mistake again."

"Maybe you should examine Ben's soul with that same laser focus."

"Bite your tongue, woman. Ben is nothing like Seth."

Ben—quiet, reserved. Trustworthy. Safe. Above all, my best guy friend. Seth—charming, gregarious. Edgy, dangerous. And a class-A douchebag. The polar opposite of Ben, and the kind of guy I will never go near again.

"You should hock it," Amy suggests. "I heard they're paying a lot for gold these days."

I shoot a look at my brilliant bestie. "You're absolutely right. With this ring, I'll be led...to a car dealership with a wad of cash."

I know I should probably forgo the new car, but reliable transportation will open up job opportunities outside the city without fear of abandonment on the Schuylkill Expressway, as cars whiz by at 150 miles an hour (15 during rush hour). No doubt this band of gold—along with its diamond embellishments and huge honking emerald—will score me the cash I need to assure a lower monthly bill than what I'm still paying for the lemon. In fact, I can't afford *not* to trade up. I just need to do it before the credit checkers learn I'm no longer employed. Hopefully my excellent credit history will speak for itself without having to confirm employment.

I'm about to tell Amy my plan when she bounces in her seat and gives a little clap.

"I have an idea. Sell the ring and use the money to join me in the shore house. Wendy says there's still an opening."

"Asked and answered," I say without thinking about it. "My resounding no hasn't changed since the last time you suggested it."

Amy's work friend, Wendy, has invited her to join a group rental in Sea Isle for the summer. It's a Philly thing, where groups of twenty- to thirty-somethings rent large houses on the Jersey coast, working in the city during the week and flocking to the shore on weekends. It's a great way to share the cost of a summer by the sea, if that's what you need in your life.

You can exclude me from that tally.

"Come on, we'll have so much fun together," she says. "Partying it up, flirting with hotties...I mean you flirting with them, that is."

Amy, who's been in a long-term relationship for the past five years and circling the drain of perpetual sorrow, is obsessed with finding me someone. I suppose it's so I can join her in pre-marital misery. Or maybe she just enjoys living single life vicariously through me.

"Sounds like fun," I say, sarcastically. "Until they find out I'm an attorney and beat feet."

She shakes her head vehemently. "With your Barbie doll face and banging little figure, you'll easily lure them in, like seagulls to a French fry. By then, they'll be so hooked, they won't care if you're a lawyer or a serial killer. Which, you know, is one and..."

I hold up my hand to keep her from finishing the sentence. I get it.

In addition to the attorney digs (which I can get away with, since I am one), I hate it when she references Barbie in conjunction with my looks. Sure, if I were seven feet tall with triple-E boobies, I'd take it as a compliment. You'll need to take off a couple feet and a whole bunch of letters before you're even close. And that's not just me being self-deprecating. I literally have to avoid wearing light green so as not to be confused with Tinkerbell.

"Appreciate the compliment, but I'd rather just have the fries."

She ignores me. "You may even find the man of your dreams this summer."

I laugh out loud. "There's a greater chance of me finding Bigfoot than the 'man of my dreams.'"

She smiles. "What if he's one and the same?"

"Then I'm better off going to the Poconos. Now, shut up about this shore thing. Let's order another round before happy hour ends and I can't afford to be here."

2

If I thought losing my job would be the biggest travesty of justice that week, I had another one coming. This time from Seth.

Not Seth himself, but the man who shows up on my doorstep to serve me with legal papers. He's here *on behalf of* Seth who, it turns out, is suing me to return the promise ring.

You read that right. If you're like me, you're probably wondering—is that even legal? Also like me, you're probably incensed, although your reaction may not be as strong because you don't know the whole story. Here it is...judge for yourself.

I met Seth six years ago, at a time when I was feeling particularly needy. It was an insta-love kinda thing, which, in retrospect, was probably part of the problem. I allowed myself to get sucked into a false belief in love at first sight, soulmates, and all that happy horseshit, despite my growing distrust of marriage after witnessing what my clients had been through. Seth made it easy—his charming adoration was intoxicating. On our third date, he told me he loved me. A month later, we moved in together. Five months after that, he gave me the promise ring, a placeholder for a future engagement ring.

When he later asked if I wanted a more official proposal, I declined. He'd already spent a fortune on that ring, and I loved it. Up to that point, I had no reason to believe he wasn't in it for the long haul. Seth made loving easy, and commitment not so scary. It wasn't long before all my reservations about marriage dissipated, despite what I do for a living. That's how much I trusted him, and the promise his beautiful ring had symbolized. I truly thought Seth and I could beat the odds.

Was I wrong.

Last year, just before our fifth anniversary of dating, I found out he was cheating. We were in the kitchen making dinner when his dog came traipsing into the room with a thong in his mouth.

Now, hear me out. I'm not talking flip-flop thong, I'm talking undergarments of the ride-up-your-ass-until-it-almost-comes-out-your-mouth thong. A pair that didn't belong to me. And I know that because I don't own any. Excuse me, but your girl can't stand something splicing her undercarriage in half. No anal floss for me, thanks.

"What the hell is this?" I demanded, pulling the string of fabric from Rufus's mouth. Holding it up, it took me a minute to realize what it was.

"Gross!" I yelled as I flung the panties at him, which landed on his chest.

He jumped around as if I'd tossed a boa constrictor at him, screaming as he peeled it off his sweatshirt and threw it across the room.

Rufus, in turn, dutifully fetched it and returned to me, thinking it was some sort of game.

"Where in the hell did those come from?" I hissed, pointing at the disgusting garment, now hanging from Rufus's snout.

"I have *no* idea," Seth said, his tone of bewilderment matching his baffled expression. An absolute, stellar, Oscar-worthy performance as *Guy Who's Just Been Falsely Accused*. Until he gave his next line. "He must have brought them in from the yard."

I cocked my head at him. "Is there a lingerie shop back there I'm not aware of?"

"Oh, um, I mean—you know, maybe someone's laundry blew into the yard..."

I may have bought it, until the smoking gun of his twitching eyelid gave him away. It was then that I knew.

"I think you're full of shit," I challenged, staring him down. "What's the real story?"

And that's when he spilled it. He'd met a woman one night in a bar when I was out of town for a work conference. He brought her back here, but they "didn't have sex—just fooled around" and she must've left without them.

"I swear, it was just a one-time thing, Kacie. It meant nothing to me. I promise."

"Well, it means something to me." My tone was eerily quiet, as if on some level I'd known. "The end of us."

I ripped the lying farce of a ring off my finger and hurled it at him. It missed and skidded across the tile floor, clinking with the echo of empty promises.

Quietly, calmly, he picked it up and set it on the counter.

"Keep this," he whispered. "Sell it. It's the least I owe you."

"The least you owed me was keeping your dick in your pants!" I screamed at his retreating back.

I swept the ring into a drawer, hoping sight unseen would ease my grief. But it only got worse when I discovered he'd been cheating on me with multiple women, basically the entire time we were together. I later heard from several mutual acquaintances who'd suspected his infidelities after seeing him out with others. Of course, none of them bothered to tell me when it would have mattered. Needless to say, those people are no longer a part of my life.

When I was finally ready to face facts, I did a complete 180—I put the ring on a chain and wore it around my neck. No longer a promise ring, I wore it as a constant reminder of his betrayal, to keep me from ever falling for another player again.

Then, three months ago, he texted and asked for the ring back. I never responded, nor did he reach out again, so I assumed he dropped it.

I'm jolted to the present as the delivery guy hands me an oversized envelope.

"You're hereby fucked," the man says. Or maybe he says "served"—I'm too flabbergasted to hear straight. Although, points added if he did say that. No matter how alarming this is, I always appreciate wry humor, even at my own expense.

I read the legal papers with disgust. Get a load of this asshole—after cheating on me, he actually thinks he has the right to take back the ring? Before my car issues and job loss, I might have given it back. But now it's about principle. And cold, hard cash.

It's been a damn year since we broke up, and nearly six years since he gave me the ring. There has to be a statute of limitations. The good thing about being a lawyer is you never have to hire someone else to help you out of legal jams.

I call Ben to tell him the news.

"A lawyer who represents himself has a fool for a client," Ben says when I share my plan for self-representation. "Haven't you ever heard that phrase?"

"True, but I can't afford to hire someone."

"Why not just give the ring back? Isn't it cursed anyway?"

"He's already taken so much from me. My dignity. My self-respect. Possibly my reproductive health, which I now get to spend the rest of my life checking for whatever communicable diseases he passed on. Plus, I need the money."

"Alright. I'll represent you."

Gasp. "Really? How much will you charge me?"

"A home-cooked dinner."

Shit. He may as well have asked me to sherpa him up Mount Everest, as I'm better suited for that. Cooking is so not my thing. Nonetheless... "Deal."

The following day, Ben calls back. "Hate to be the bearer of bad legal precedent, but he's got you dead to rights, friend."

"In what way?" I demand. "On what planet does a person

have a right to demand the return of a ring?"

"Planet Pennsylvania. According to law, an engagement ring in this state is considered a conditional gift. Which means—"

"It's conditional upon us actually getting married," I finish his sentence because I'm not an idiot. "But it was a promise ring, not engagement."

"The law includes promise rings."

"Son of a bitch."

"Yeah. Sucks, but you're gonna have to give it back."

"What if I say I already sold it?"

"You just told your lawyer you're gonna lie to get around the law."

"Asshole."

"Me or him?"

"Both of you right now."

Damn it. I really needed that money. I throw a hex on Seth. And the ring.

"You may change your mind when I tell you my idea for how you can satisfy your shitty legal requirement."

An hour later, I watch, horrified, as Ben shovels a hunk of dog crap from his backyard and places it in a box. With gloved hand, he sinks the ring into the guano and places the note he's had me write—*Here's your ring, you piece of shit*—atop the scooped poop.

"While the law requires you to return the ring, it's silent on the method to be employed," Ben informs me as he seals the box.

"Doo process of law, in every respect," I say, my voice filled with pure respect for his brilliant idea. I high-five Ben on his non-shit-touching hand. "Ding dung, this bitch is dead."

Returning home from our dirty deed, I turn to my new favorite pastime—procrastinating on finding a job—but I can't even get into that. I should feel victorious, justified for what we just did to Seth. Instead, I feel deflated. Sad. A whole phase of my life ending in literal shit. I also, on some level, feel bad for Seth having to dig through the dung.

Most of all, I feel bad for the ring. I cherished that thing.

I wish I'd seen this all coming. I wish I'd run from Seth the moment I met him to avoid the pain and humiliation I've endured at his hands. Trusting someone, only to have them plunge a dagger into my heart, killing any hope that once remained there of finding love.

I only have two words.

Never. Again.

I take solace in that thought. As well as this one—my life can't get any worse.

3

Ah, but it does.

I just don't know this yet as I head to McGillin's. Amy has summoned me for happy hour, luring me with the promise of Big Good News.

"Hey girl," she says as she spots me. "I didn't order yet because I didn't know what mood you'd be in. What's your poison?"

"Feels like a cyanide kinda night."

"Red wine, it is."

After getting our drinks, we find a high-top table in the back of the crowded tavern.

"What's this big news?" I ask, wanting to get right to the point. It's weird that I truly have no idea what she's about to tell me. We've been besties since sixth grade and know everything there is to know about each other. I just saw her yesterday for lunch, so whatever it is, it happened recently. I can feel the excitement radiating off her as she raises her glass for a toast.

"You're looking at the new international manager for Global Solutions, carbon capture division. And they're relocating me to...wait for it..."

Dutifully, I wait.

"London!"

It takes a minute for this to sink in. "London, Connecticut?"

"Nope. The UK. Where they're actually doing things to protect the environment."

"Really?" I ask, as if she's joking. "When—how—I had no idea this was even a possibility!"

As if that would stop it from happening. My heart begins to race as the news settles in, hoping this is one big April Fool's joke. Except it's Cinco de Mayo.

"What about Mark?" I ask about her beau. "Is he coming with you?"

"Eventually," she shrugs. "But I'm not passing up a great career move for a man. For now, it'll be a long-distance thing. Good way to see if we stand the test of time. And distance."

That's one thing I love about Amy. As much of a romantic as she can be, she's also grounded in reality. As her bestie, I know Mark is her person, and he'll follow her to the ends of the earth. They'll make it, despite an ocean between them.

Me, I'm not so sure.

She must see the dismay on my face as she clasps my hand. "I know this is a rough time, and I'm sorry to leave you, but it's an opportunity I can't pass up."

Of course, she can't. If the tables were turned, I wouldn't pass it up, either. That doesn't stop me from whining about it.

"What am I gonna do without you this summer?"

Amy's always been my main source of fun. Unless you consider Ben, my only other real friend. But as a single dad, his free time is limited. Sure, I have other acquaintances, but they're about as fun to hang out with as my houseplants (with the exception of my Venus flytrap, which is vastly more entertaining than any human companion).

"You're gonna have a great summer," she says. "I feel it in my bones. I know big changes are coming for you."

"I'm just feeling sorry for myself," I say, setting my misery aside to celebrate her news. "Tell me all about this new life of yours. What will your living situation be?"

"I found a potential roomie on a roommate finder app. I'm gonna FaceTime her tomorrow. Her flat's half a block from my new office, so fingers crossed we get along."

"Fingers crossed," I agree, although my heart isn't in it. I don't want this to happen so quickly.

Stop being so dramatic. Be happy for your friend.

My selfish dismay diminishes when I see the way her face lights up as she talks about her new position.

"And then, on weekends, I can travel to other countries," she says. "Paris is a train ride away. You'll have to visit, so we can go together."

"Not until I find a job," I say.

"Have you heard from Ben's firm?"

"Negative."

"Any luck with the other openings you were considering?"

I shake my head. I don't want to tell her I've only applied to Ben's firm. I know I shouldn't put all my eggs in one basket, but its excellent pay, partner fast-track, and big dick reputation justify my lack of interest in working elsewhere. I was already burning out on the practice of law prior to losing my job, and the only way I'll go back to it is with a firm like Ben's.

She narrows her eyes. "Maybe that's a sign."

"Of what?"

"That it's time to quit law, do something different with your life."

"I spent way too much on a law degree to throw it all away."

"No one says you have to throw it away. Haven't you always said law degrees open doors in areas outside traditional practice?"

"I love it when you use my own words against me."

"Someone has to. No offense, but you've been miserable ever since you started practicing divorce law. That commercial of yours was a major cry for help. What happened to the optimistic girl I once knew, so hopeful for a life of love and roses? She gone."

"I learned that's not how life—or love—works," I say. "And roses have thorns."

How can I help but have such a tainted, hopeless outlook? I've witnessed too many broken hearts, unraveled lives. Held the hands of a gazillion grieving women as I free them from the legal ties binding them to the man they once loved (and sometimes still do, despite that he's been sliding his sausage into someone else's bun). I give out so many tissues to sobbing spouses, I'd be well-advised to buy stock in Kleenex. That, coupled with the heart-wrenching pain I suffered in my own ill-fated relationship, is enough to zap the hope from anyone.

Ignoring me, Amy goes on with her branded optimism. "Why not take a year off from law and do something else? You can always go back to it."

She snaps her fingers. "I know! Come to London with me. Get a job as a barista. Spend a year brewing coffee and traveling with me on weekends."

My ears *perk up*, pun intended. I've always wanted to be a barista. But then, I remember the rules of international employment law.

"Don't I need a work visa for that?"

She deflates. "Right. Didn't think about that. Then, just visit."

"I need to find a job first." I sigh. "I just can't get myself motivated."

"I know you've been through a lot, but you have to find a way to rise up. You know what they say—when life hands you lemons, make Limoncello."

"I appreciate your enthusiasm, but it's not me."

"No shit, Sherlock. You and your 'life's a bitch' mentality. You need to change things up, live a little."

"I fear change. I'd rather rot in a vat of stagnant status quo."

"Being unemployed and single?" She raises an eyebrow to underscore her point. "Hating your career and miserable 24/7?"

"Touché."

"Maybe if you visit me, it'll give you the inspiration you need. Sometimes you need to get away to gain better perspective."

"When does this big move go down?" I ask, hoping it's not soon.

"June 1."

"That's less than a month from now," I whine. I need more time to get used to this.

"I know. So much to do. Oh! Just thought of something else." She pulls out her phone and begins dictating as she types. "Storage unit. Get boxes. And—oh shit." She stops speaking into her phone and looks up at me. "I still have to find someone to take over my shore house share."

Staring me down, her grimace relaxes into a conspiratorial smile. "I have the perfect solution."

Oh, geez. I don't love it when Amy comes up with *solutions*. Most often, they're things I'm not on board with.

"I need a replacement, and you have nothing going on. Why don't you take it over?"

I shake my head. "I have to stay here and find a job."

"Says who?"

"Says my Wells Fargo bank account."

She tilts her head in disbelief. She knows I spent the majority of my twenties in a doomsday state, living frugally while furtively stashing away most of my earnings for the rainy day I *just knew* was coming. Well, aside from those occasional splurges at the KOP mall, but those are more like medical expenses for all the good they do my mental health. Still, that's the beauty about being a pessimist...you're always prepared and never disappointed. In fact, there's a sick kind of twisted joy that comes when you predict something disastrous and it happens. Thanks to my healthy savings account and the severance package the assholes gave me, I should be fine financially until I find another firm to hire my ass. Assuming its soon. If not, Seth's ring won't be the only thing deep in doo-doo.

In addition to having no extra funds to support it, the thought of doing a shared rental makes me cringe. All those happy singles, looking for love...hex on their hopeful outlooks. They wouldn't feel so happy if I shared some of my clients' stories. Although bummer I can't, thank you attorney-client privilege. Nothing halts cocktail party chatter like a legal prohibition against juicy client gossip.

"Go down on weekends," Amy says. "That's what I was planning to do."

"You're forgetting I drive a piece of fruit. Plus, the gas alone will drain my account."

"Or..." She gives a pregnant pause.

"Or what?"

I know this isn't just about filling her shore house spot. She wants to go to London knowing I'll be okay, and figures this is the answer.

"Sublet your apartment and live down there full time."

"But I need to work."

"Find a job at the shore."

I laugh. "Doing what?"

"Waitressing. You'll make a killing on tips alone."

"Can't stand dirty dishes."

"Clean houses between renters."

"Ditto on dirty houses."

"Work for a summer camp or something."

"You're forgetting I can't stand kids."

It's not that I can't stand them, really. Kids just make me nervous, especially in large batches. I don't understand how someone could be a teacher, surrounded by loud little humans all day long. Hard pass.

"Just...do something. Break out of your miserable comfort zone."

"Why? It's comfortably miserable."

"So, instead of lounging on a beach with sun and sea breezes, you'd rather fester here? Applying for jobs you don't want, sweating in your hot apartment, smelling the rotting stench of summer in the city?"

"How *can* I leave, when you put it that way?" I ask, giving her a Grinch smile. "It's my nature. You know that better than anyone."

"Then it's time to change your nature. Lighten up a bit, Kacie. Turn your Sad Girl Summer into Fun Girl Summer."

The moment I don't immediately object, she misconstrues my silence as agreement.

"I knew you'd come around," she says. "That's why we're BFFs. I'm the yin to your yang. I help balance your negativity with my own brand of—"

"Delusion."

"I like to think of it as optimism." She waves to someone behind me. "Why don't we get his opinion?"

Ben slides onto the stool next to me. My heart quickens and a tingle radiates through me as it always does when I see him. We've only ever been friends—except for that time we almost crossed the line into *more* in our third year of law school. But that was seven years ago, and a lot has happened since then to cement the platonic nature of our relationship. Then again, there was that night in my office a couple months ago when it felt as though the dynamic between us was shifting...

I shake off a fresh batch of tingles. I can't let my imagination run wild over that night because it was probably just that—my imagination. I need to cease with thoughts of *more,* at least until his divorce is well behind us.

"Hey, girl." He looks at me with those dark chocolate eyes. "Ames told me you'd be here. I wanted to stop in and see how you're doing."

He wraps an arm around my shoulder, pulling me in. The familiar scent of his aftershave wafts into my nostrils like a charmed snake as he plants a kiss on my cheek.

"What can I get you guys?" he asks, gesturing to our empty glasses. "If you don't mind me joining you for a drink."

"Of course, we don't. Where's Leo?" I ask. After a somewhat strange and amicable divorce, Ben earned full custody of his four-year-old son this spring. Thanks to his excellent lawyer: me.

"At my sister's for a cousins' sleepover."

"Nice. Does that mean you can stay awhile?" I'm hoping he says yes.

"Just got time for one. Gotta get back to the office, big case going on."

After taking our orders, Ben saunters to the bar. I watch, mesmerized.

"Stop it," Amy says.

"I can't," I say. Old habits die hard, especially when they've recently resurfaced.

"Besides, he's old news."

Instead of responding, I let her think that. She doesn't know about that night in my office. I didn't tell her because Amy doesn't like Ben for me, and she takes every opportunity to remind me of that, despite him being her good friend, too. I guess because Amy's the type of person who doesn't easily forget the crushing blow of a friend's unrequited love, especially after years of me draining my tear ducts on her shoulder.

"Seriously, Kacie. You need to move on."

"But he's finally divorced…" I sigh as he turns back toward us. His eyes catch mine and he winks.

"I don't think I can," I whisper.

"You can, and you will. If he hasn't come after you by now—what's it been, a decade since you've known him?—he won't. Time to find someone who cherishes you. You can't make that man feel that way about you."

"Watch me," I say under my breath.

You may be wondering how I can be so down on relationships, yet so Team Ben at the same time? Easy. He's safe. He's a one-woman man, and I know he'd never hurt me. My love for him preceded the Seth debacle, and in some ways survived it. I know if Ben and I ever got together, it wouldn't involve marriage, but instead, a peaceful coexistence between two consenting adults. It's about all either one of us can handle right now.

"Drinks for my girls," Ben says as he slides glasses of wine to us. "What are we dishing about tonight?"

"Kacie's taking my spot at the Sea Isle house this summer," Amy blurts out.

"No, I'm not."

"Come on, Kace!" Ben exclaims as he turns to me. "You have to. Leo and I will be there all summer."

What, now?

"Since when?" I ask.

"Since my parents asked us to house-sit. They'll be traveling this summer," he explains.

"What about work?"

"Two days in the office, three days remote. I've hired a nanny to watch Leo on my office days. I figured a summer in Sea Isle will do him well, considering what he's been through this year."

Before the ink on their divorce papers had even dried, Leo's mom moved to California in hot pursuit of the man she cheated on Ben with. Fortunately for Ben, revelation of the affair wasn't shocking. After years of trying fruitlessly to make their marriage work, Ben had realized Angi wasn't his person and was all too eager to let her go. I could have told him that years ago, if only he'd asked.

Ben gained full custody of Leo, and Angi agreed to visitation rights throughout the year, consisting of several week-long visits alternating between here and California. She *just couldn't* with the whole mom thing, apparently.

"Wow, nice work arrangement," I say. Another reason I'd love to work at his firm—the partners are super cool, their work week flexible.

But let's go back to this plot twist. Suddenly, spending summer at the shore seems a lot more interesting.

"See, Kace?" Amy asks. "Ben's even going."

She must really want me to go if she's dangling Ben—who she's been encouraging me to "get over" for years—as a carrot.

"A chance to turn your 'life's a bitch' mentality into 'life's a beach.' The summer of sunny outlooks and beachy-keen vibes."

"Yeah, Kacie," Ben says, slapping my hand playfully. "Do it."

Biting my lip, I twist my ponytail around my finger as I consider her words.

Under normal circumstances, I'd never agree. Kacie Layne isn't that impractical. But knowing Ben will be there all summer, Kacie Layne may just have to...how did Amy put it? Change things up. Live a little.

Perhaps a Sea Isle summer is just what I need.

4

Three weeks later, Amy and I meet up again at McGillin's, this time to say goodbye. She's leaving for London on Thursday, and it'll be the last time I see her until she visits for the holidays.

"Here you go," she says as she slides a house key across the table. "I can't believe you're actually doing it."

I can't believe it either, quite frankly.

By the time the drinks had worn off after our last meeting, I'd completely dismissed the idea of spending the summer in Sea Isle, despite the promise of Ben being there. It just felt too risky and whimsical, especially after admitting to myself the only reason I'd even consider such a move was because of Ben. It wasn't until a series of fortunate events occurred that everything seemed to fall in place, as if the universe was begging me to toss all caution to the sea breeze and shoobie my ass down the shore.

It started when an acquaintance from college, who was moving to Philly, asked if I could recommend good neighborhoods for her apartment search. I gave her a list, including my own, and after a tour, we ended up in my apartment for drinks. She went apeshit over the place, saying it was exactly what she was looking for. I heard a distinctive voice in my head (later echoed by Amy through AirPods) telling me to sublet it to her for the summer. Doing the math, I discovered I'd be spending significantly less on the summer house than my city rent, so that was a no-brainer.

I'd also applied to three law firms in areas of law I could tolerate, but all three were busts. This, of course, thrust me right back into my "law is an ass" mentality. I still haven't heard back from Ben's firm, which has me fantasizing about the type of career I might consider outside of law. Since award-winning author (a dream I've never shared with anyone) and stand-up comedian (a dream I've shared with everyone) aren't immediately achievable options, I found myself applying for a job at the last place one would expect of a laid-off attorney who once made six figures.

Starbucks.

I'd been holed up there, working on my CV and searching for open positions, when I saw a sign that they were hiring. Knowing I was overqualified, I nonetheless gulped down the rest of my mocha latte (along with my pride), filled out the application, and waited while Barista Brandon read over my application.

"Any other qualifications?" he asked after a quick skim.

"Not to brag, but I can misspell names like nobody else."

He tossed my application on the counter. "Sorry, we need someone with more experience."

Gloves off, I went unemployed-attorney-ballistic on him.

"How fucking difficult can it be to make coffee?" I demanded. "I've been drinking the shit longer than you've been alive."

With the flick of his wrist, Brandon summoned the security guard. Needless to say, I won't be returning to that location anytime soon.

The final straw came when a man approached me on the subway platform, dick in hand, and proceeded to pee on my brand-new Jimmy Choos. *Check, please!*

I texted Amy that night to inquire if her shore rental share was still available. It was.

"Well, lotion me up and call me a shoobie," I say now. "I just hope I'm not making a mistake."

"Spending a summer down the shore can never be a mistake. As long as you keep it platonic with Ben. In fact, I'm gonna help you meet someone new."

"How will you do that from London?"

"You'll see."

Whatever that means.

"What if I hate the roommates?" I ask, Pessimistic Patti still lurking.

"Who cares? It's just for the summer. I don't know the others, but Wendy's cool."

I've met Wendy on a few occasions over drinks. I agree with Amy's assessment of her coworker.

"It helps you're female," Amy continues. "Wendy said the organizer of the house was worried I'd find a guy and throw off the male/female ratio."

"Wait—did I sign up for a shore house, or *Perfect Match*?"

"No *Perfect Match* for you, friend. Hooking up with a housemate is actually the worst thing you can do in a summer share. Meet your men elsewhere if you want a drama-free summer."

"No need to worry about that. I'm not hooking up with anyone. This is Single Summer for me."

After spending five summers locked down in coupledom, the last thing I need is to take on another ill-fated relationship. I need to focus on myself, my life. Figure out what I'm doing with it. I gotta use my time wisely and figure out next steps, and I can't do that if I'm swooning over a boy like some sort of heart-eyed emoji.

Then again, with Ben here for the summer—

Stop it, Kacie. This summer's about you.

According to Amy, there are fourteen housemates, but only two of us will be living there the whole summer. The rest have full-time jobs in the city, so they'll only be down on weekends. Since I don't have a job or an apartment to return to, I'll be staying in Sea Isle for the entire length of the rental—which runs Thursday before Memorial Day to Labor Day.

"You sure I don't have to pay more, being there all summer?" I ask.

"Nope. Everyone's welcome to come down whenever they want and aren't limited to weekends, so they agreed to pay equal shares. They're just grateful the two of you will be there during the week to take out the trash and watch the place while they're away."

I'll have to find a way to earn my keep, beyond trash-hauling and house-watching. Maybe I'll offer to play Happy Hour Hostess with the Mostess to welcome them home on Fridays.

"According to Wendy, the organizer is happy someone else will be staying all summer. He thought it would just be him there during the week."

"When you say 'the organizer,' is that a formal title?" I joke. "One I should capitalize in my mind, as if he's Sea Isle's answer to *Jersey Shore*'s The Situation?"

"I forget his name," she says, chuckling. "It's something like Spencer or Wadsworth, or one of those finance bro names."

Great. Sounds like I'll be cohabitating with a blowhard this summer.

"I'm gonna miss you." She sighs, clasping my hand. "I can't..." Her words give way to rapid blinks as she staves off welling tears.

"Oh, Ames." I laugh as I squeeze her hand.

She's going soft on me, wallowing in sadness about our impending separation.

"I'll see you at Christmas," I remind her. "Remember, you're doing this for career advancement. It's gonna be great."

"I know," she says, wiping her tears.

"And you'll be fine without me," I assure her. "More than fine. If anyone should be crying, it's me, having to live in a house full of strangers without you."

"Speaking of which…" She pulls a gift bag from the seat next to her and slides it toward me.

I give a guilty chuckle. "Why are you giving me a gift when you're the one going away?"

"Open it. You'll see."

In the bag is a beach bucket filled with all kinds of summer nonsense—sunscreen, aloe, lip balm, and more. Nestled in the middle is a journal featuring a beach on the cover, with a hand-written title: *My Sea Isle Summer.*

"That's for you to record all the wonderful things you'll do this summer, so you don't forget any details. I expect a fully filled journal when I return."

I flip to the inside cover where she's artfully drawn a beach bucket, inside of which she's written a list of items. The title reads: *My Summer Bucket List.*

"What's this about?" I ask.

"To guide you on your Fun Girl Summer. Ten things you must do to loosen up, live a little, have fun. Who knows—with any luck, you may just fall in love."

"I thought you knew me," I tease. Skimming the bucket list, I chuckle. "Nice try, Ames…"

"Yeah, I know. Bucket lists are too optimistic for a person dead set against change."

Something about the way she says it makes me feel like a forehead "L" loser. Having recently lost my job, my relation-ship, and now my humble abode, I've been forced into change. I'm lowkey here for it, especially since I seem to have shed the things that had been making me unhappy. Maybe I'll have to give this bucket list bullshit a chance to show her I'm not a complete lost cause.

"One more thing…" she picks up her phone. After scrolling, she taps the screen. "I'm adding you to the house group chat. I don't have everyone's names in there, but at least you'll have everyone's numbers."

My phone alights with Amy's incoming text.

> Hey everyone, I'm adding Kacie to the group chat so you have her number.

I tap on the group chat to see a long list of phone numbers, with Amy's at the top. She was right—aside from Wendy and a couple other names, the rest are just phone numbers. Except for one.

"The Organizer," I say, chuckling. "I'm glad you capitalized that."

"I've been racking my brain trying to recall his name. Something prep schooly." She shrugs. "You'll learn it soon enough."

My phone dings in succession as several responses come in, all from unnamed sources.

> Hi Kacie!

> Welcome to the group, Kacie!

> Can't wait to meet you KC!

As more texts pop up, I feel welcomed by my new house-mates. Maybe this little coastal detour isn't the worst idea Amy's ever had.

We finish our drinks and head outside to part ways. I'm simultaneously sad over my friend's impending departure, and excited. For us both. Big changes ahead, indeed.

But am I ready?

5

And the correct answer would be...hell no.

Sitting on the debris-scattered floor of my apartment as I pack that night, the shrapnel of my imploded life surrounding me, panic sets in. Not just over the upheaval of my life, but over finances as well. I can't stop running numbers in my head, hoping I haven't made a grave mistake—perhaps I didn't carry a digit, or I put a decimal point in the wrong place—and I really can't afford to be doing this. I'm terrified I'll have to dig into my savings to finance this (now seemingly ridiculous) summer folly. Going to the shore instead of staying in the city to find a job—what's wrong with me?

Once again, trademark pessimism sets in.

When my subletter texts an hour later to inquire if I have any leads on a used car, I hear *cha-ching!* Sea Isle's a walkable town, and as long as I have a bike, I'll have no need for a car this summer. Before I allow myself to get too excited, however, I give her disclaimers about its many issues, along with a detailed list of the repairs it's had. She doesn't care about any of that, she says. All she wants is something she can use occasionally until she finds a permanent place to live (hopefully not the shoulder of the Schuylkill Expressway), at which time she'll get a new one.

It makes me feel better, knowing I have a little extra fiscal padding. Not enough to live like my mom, a Lady Who Lunches, but enough that I won't have to worry if the only job I can find this summer pays minimum wage. Perhaps it means

I won't have to work every day, either. I could use some downtime to plot my future.

But now I need a ride to the shore.

Enter Ben, who learns of my carless status and offers to drive me, since he's also heading down that Thursday. With Leo still at his aunt's house, it'll be just the two of us.

"So, Kacie Layne is joining a party house this summer," he says as we sit in bumper-to-bumper traffic on the Ben Franklin Bridge. "It's about time you took Amy's advice. You need a lifestyle upgrade, girl."

His words sting, but I know he means them in good fun.

"What else was I going to do?" I ask. "No job, no apartment, no Amy. With you only being in the city two days a week for work, I would've rotted to death this summer." Realizing I'm sounding like a real downer, I borrow Amy's words. "I'm turning my 'life's a bitch' attitude into 'life's a beach.' A.k.a., Fun Girl Summer."

"I'm glad. You're too young to be so miserable. Maybe you needed to lose your job in order to change your perspective on life."

He's probably right, but I hate that he sees me that way.

"How's work going?" I ask, hoping to deflect focus from my pathetic life. In truth, work isn't what I want to talk about. There's been something brewing between us, and I'm wondering if now would be a good time to bring it up—to discuss what happened in my office a few months ago. Or if that's even something I want to do. As much as I love dealing in facts, I'm not one to easily talk about my feelings.

Before I can decide, Ben launches into a discussion of his most recent case. I flash back to law school—the two of us huddling in the library, digging deep into case law, scrutinizing judicial opinions and discussing legal philosophy. I honestly believe those deep dives into precedent and theory were what sparked my keen interest, sharpened my brain, and honed my ability to navigate complicated legal cases. Not that the cases I'd handled now were that complicated factually or legally. Just emotionally.

Ben's area of practice involves business law. As he discusses this particular case, my attorney brain takes over, hailing back to the days before I started exclusively practicing family law. It's refreshing, dealing with cases devoid of personal attacks, threats, and cheating. And that's just the lawyers.

Before I know it, we're crossing the bridge over the bay into Sea Isle. I thoroughly enjoyed diving into Ben's world of business law and brushing up on concepts I'd long ago forgotten. Good use of my time, in case his firm decides to hire me.

"Thanks for the ride," I say as he pulls up to the first light on JFK Boulevard. I glance at the Fish Alley banner hanging over Central Avenue, welcoming guests to dine at one of Sea Isle's bayside restaurants. It gives me an idea. "Can I treat you to dinner tonight to thank you?"

"Sorry," he says. "I'm heading back tonight."

I shoot him a look. "Did you come down just to give me a ride?"

"Of course. I couldn't bear the thought of my bestie hitching down the AC Expressway with all her shiz."

"How sweet of you!" Right? I mean, there has to be something going on here. "What about work?"

"Took the day off. Plus, this'll give me a chance to check out my parents' house, make sure it's ready for when I bring the little guy down on Monday."

Okay, so it wasn't just about me. Still, he didn't have to do that. My heart does a little dance.

"Can I take a raincheck on dinner?" he asks. "Maybe some day next week?"

Maybe someday. Not the first time I'd heard those words from him.

As we proceed down JFK, my mind takes me back to the

spring of our third year of law school. Ben had just broken up with his longtime girlfriend, leaning heavily into our friendship in the process. We'd sit for hours over coffee or drinks, talking about it. The relationship had run its course, he'd said, but it was still difficult. He couldn't stop thanking me for being there for him.

A couple weeks later, we attended a law school party on the banks of the Brandywine, where the beer flowed stronger than the river. Ben and I became cozier than we'd ever been, as night fell around us and a bonfire glowed before a silhouette of trees. He lent me his Delaware Law School sweatshirt, wrapping me in a warm cocoon against the cool April air as we snuggled by the crackling fire.

And that's when he leaned in and kissed me.

An all-too-willing participant, my head and heart simultaneously combusted as the guy I'd crushed on for the past two years kissed me in a way my wildest dreams couldn't have imagined.

"Wow," I finally said when we came up for air. Laughing inappropriately, of course. "What was that all about?"

"Sorry," he said, sheepishly. "I've been wanting to do that for a long time."

My heartbeat thrummed in my ears as a tempest of thoughts swirled. Wondering if he meant it. Wondering what he'd meant by that.

Wondering what it meant for *us*.

He was only two weeks out from his breakup, so it couldn't have been *that* long of a want on his part. Unless, like me, his feelings had grown over the course of our friendship. I was dying to ask for details, but romantic-me was still in shock over the kiss. Meanwhile, practical-me knew I should be careful. I was desperately disinterested in being someone's rebound, their consolation prize because someone else hadn't worked out. Or presuming the kiss meant anything beyond two friends getting caught up in a moment under the influence of a swoony setting.

Worse, conjuring a false reality that this was heading somewhere beyond friendship if it wasn't. He was my friend, and I didn't want our relationship to be strained if my imagination took this further than he intended it to go. Most importantly, I didn't want to get hurt.

A sudden rainstorm broke the spell. We scrambled to help our classmates put out the fire, grabbed our belongings, and headed for our cars. I'd driven with some friends—we were having a post-party sleepover—and as Ben and I headed in separate directions, he told me he'd call me tomorrow.

Crammed in the backseat, I took a deep breath and calmed my racing heart, telling myself not to rush to judgment until we had a chance to talk in the sober light of day. We'd had a lot to drink, and I wasn't certain if the kiss was the result of beer or feelings.

"Sorry about last night," he said when he called the next morning. "I shouldn't have kissed you like that...you know...our friendship..."

As I had thought—the kiss was nothing more than a drunken thing, with the convenient excuse of a friendship to keep it from becoming more. I was proud of myself for not getting too tingly over it. I suspected it had to be the drinks, the cozy setting, loneliness on both our parts, the anticipated nostalgia of our law school days soon coming to an end.

In other words, the kiss had nothing to do with *me*.

"I know," I blurted out, wanting to take the onus off him having to mansplain things. I also didn't want him thinking I expected a different outcome. "Our friendship means the world to me, as I know it does to you. Don't worry, I'm not making more of it than there is."

"I wasn't saying that...I mean...maybe there's *something* there..."

My heart skipped a beat, taking my breath with it. I could almost picture the lopsided grin tugging at his lips as he tripped over his words. Maybe I was wrong. I reminded myself to proceed with caution, make a joke. Say something to keep him from knowing just how much was already there on my end.

"But..." he said, drawing it out before I could respond.

My heart sank, his reticence telling me everything I needed to know. Just one little word, but it hung heavy in the air, laden with uncertainty. I decided not to wait for what came after the *but*.

"We were drunk and you just got out of a relationship," I said, then cued up the humor. "Newsflash: I'm not out here trying to be someone's rebound chick."

A joke, maybe, but also the truth. I wanted to be someone's first choice. Like Amy once was, when she started dating her college crush, until he went back to his ex two weeks later claiming he wasn't over her. I wasn't about to take that chance. My feelings for Ben were exactly where they belonged, protectively nestled into the folds of a cherished friendship, guarding me from potential heartbreak if something similar were to happen to us. No need to expose them now, with his *but* hanging out there.

I continued rambling. "Besides, we have a lot coming up, with graduation and the bar exam, finding jobs, and everything...gotta stay focused."

"True," he said after a pause. "Maybe someday..."

"Someday," I said, trying to sound aloof.

To this day, I don't know why I pushed him off like that, why I didn't just ask what he meant when he suggested there might be *something there*. I'm haunted by the thought that what happened in the following weeks wouldn't have, had I simply asked. Had I expressed my feelings for him then.

My concerns about the bar exam were legit, until they weren't. I just wish future-me could've told then-me it was all going to work out—that I'd pass with flying colors, and I didn't have to avoid life, possibly love, to make that happen. I'd just put way too much into my legal education to get tied up with a boy with a wobbling heart right before the biggest test of my life. A test not only of the last three years of my studies, but also my cognitive ability, credibility, and deservedness of a license to practice law. Despite the grueling nature of the exam, my dad and brother had passed on their first try. I couldn't embarrass my family—or let myself down—by failing.

In my defense, I thought Ben and I would have all the time in the world to explore a possible relationship after the turmoil of those crazy few months subsided, when we could continue that kiss and discover what lay beyond it *for us*. But that time never came. Turns out, the bar exam, finding jobs, and getting over exes weren't the only challenges we'd face.

I'm brought back to the present by a phone call from Amy.

"Today's the big day!" she exclaims. "Are you on your way?"

"Ben's driving me down as we speak. Did you make it to the airport?"

Amy's flying out of New York this morning on a daytime flight to London, to avoid having to sleep overnight on the plane. Brilliant move on her part.

"Yes, hopefully boarding soon. Anyway, there's something I forgot to tell you. The three cardinal rules of summer house shares."

I smile at how she always has my back. She knows how much I love rules, especially those deemed *cardinal*.

"One, always clean up after yourself."

"Not a problem. You know me." Spoken like a true neat freak.

"Two. Cause no drama."

"Okay..." A little vague for my liking. I'm the polar opposite of a *pick me* girl, but just in case... "Can you elaborate?"

"Don't participate in gossip, don't join cliques if they emerge among the housemates. And for God's sake, don't go after someone else's man."

"That's it, I'm out."

She laughs. "I'm serious. That shit'll tear a house apart more than anything else."

"They're lucky, because I'm not here for any man. Free or taken." Unless that man is the one sitting two feet from me. I shoot him a glance to see if he heard me, but he's too busy crooning a Bruce Springsteen song. "I'm here to dwell peacefully among a group of strangers. My only goal is to get a tan and turn this pasty pale skin of mine a darker hue, like—"

"A Band-Aid?"

"Shut up, you olive-skinned bitch. Not all of us can refrain from glowing in the dark."

"And stay away from Ben," she says, as if she knows where my mind just went. "This is your summer to meet new people, crawl out of your comfort zone, try new things. Did you bring the journal?"

"Yes, Mom," I say like an impatient pre-teen. "What's the last rule? I think you said there were three."

"There are, and it's the most important one. Don't hook up with anyone in the house."

"You've already told me this."

Again, Amy should know better. I'm not here for *Perfect Match*, and I'm the furthest thing from *Girls Gone Wild*. I'm here to reset, feel the sun on my skin, figure out my life. I don't have bandwidth for anything more. Except a job. And maybe Ben, if what happened in my office that night —a near repeat of that law school party—is an indication he's coming back around.

I assure her she has nothing to worry about. After we hang up, Ben and I shoot the shit about Amy's Big New Adventure.

Turning down the street toward my summer abode, Ben clasps his hand on my knee. "So excited you're doing this, Kace," he says, shooting me his brightest smile. "I cannot wait to hang out with you down here. Leo's over the moon, hoping the three of us can do some fun things together."

I give him a smile. "That sounds wonderful."

I may look cool on the outside, but on the inside, my heart is racing over the fact he wants to hang out with me. And Leo, of course. I definitely made the right move, coming to Sea Isle.

As we pull in, I notice a Jeep in the driveway—likely belonging to The Organizer, who I was told had already moved in. I gather my belongings, and Ben helps me lug them to the front door. He offers to help me take them in, but I know he needs to get back on the road soon.

"I've got it from here," I say. "But thanks again. Don't forget, I wanna take you for dinner when you get back."

"Great. I'll be in touch, and we can figure out a night."

He kisses me on the cheek, and I'm about to turn away when he grabs me in a hug, holding me for longer than he usually does. I can feel his heart beating through his polo shirt, and mine instantly falls into rhythm. I cannot be imagining the shifting intimacy between us.

Finally, he tears himself away and jogs to his car.

Watching him, I sigh, knowing this is the summer I either get with this man, or get over him. There can be no other resolution to this dance we've been doing under the guise of friendship.

I'm just hoping I'm not the only one dancing.

6

I'm surprised how modern the shore house looks from the outside. I thought a group rental would be an older unit. As I open the door, a blast of air conditioning greets me, carrying with it that musky-salty-sea-air scent characteristic of many Jersey Shore houses.

Aside from The Organizer, I'm the first to arrive, as my weekender housemates won't be down until Friday evening. Room assignment is on a first-come basis, with the exception of the primary suite, which goes to The Organizer as a perk for doing the organizing. Otherwise, I'm to go ahead and pick a room on the first floor where the girls are staying. Thankfully, Wendy offered to room with me since I don't know the others.

In standard Jersey Shore fashion, the bedrooms are on the first and third floors, with the main living space on the second floor to maximize views. Leaving my bags at the door, I wander through each of the first-floor rooms, consisting of three doubles and a triple. I do the fingertip dust test as I try to determine which room would best suit my needs in terms of space, bathroom proximity, and least likely to let in the vicious morning sun. I Goldilocks the hell out of each bed, flinging backwards and rolling around, until I find the one that's *just right*.

I snap a few photos and text them to Wendy for approval before going upstairs to check out the rest of the place.

The second floor boasts an open-concept living room, dining room, and kitchen with stainless steel appliances and a large island with several stools. To maximize views, the living room is two stories tall with huge windows. A wall of sliding glass doors leads to a large deck which, combined with several skylights, lets in abundant sunshine. A loft-like third floor hosts the remaining bedrooms in the back of the house. The place is spotless, with seemingly nothing out of place. It doesn't appear as if anyone has moved in yet, despite the Jeep in the driveway suggesting otherwise.

"Hello?" I call out and wait for a response. When none comes, I decide The Organizer must be out somewhere.

I make my way to the third floor, peeking into a dorm-style room with four bunk beds. Next to it is the primary suite, featuring a California King. The bed is fully made and the room appears empty, except for a display of men's products neatly nestled on the far corner of the dresser. Between the Barbasol, Old Spice, and a straight-edge razor, I'm wondering if The Organizer isn't my grandfather himself. Next to the products is a stack of books—all classics, like *The Old Man and the Sea* and *Catcher in the Rye*. Giving more old coot, making me wonder if the guy is north of fifty.

The open closet door suggests a more youthful resident, with its neatly hung Hawaiian shirts (giving party boy), a light blue Oxford (giving finance bro), a pink polo (giving manhood security) and...what's this?

A tux?

Odd, for someone working at the shore all summer. Without knowing anything about this dude, I decide he must have a summer job as a maître d' for one of the posh restaurants. Although, come to think of it, Sea Isle's mostly comprised of family-friendly Italian restaurants, breakfast joints, and sandwich shops—none of which require an Armani tux.

Oh, no. Another thought springs to mind, a thousand times more horrifying than if I'd discovered severed heads in his closet. He's some sort of cheesy entertainer. Or—God forbid—a magician.

Great. Exactly what I want to do with my summer—play captive audience to someone who demands we pick-a-card-any-card while he pulls coins out of our ears.

Rudely (yet abundantly curious) I take a quick look in one of his drawers, where pristinely folded t-shirts are stacked neater than a Hollister store on opening day. I pause before peeking in the top drawer, where I assume underwear dwells. I'm torn between respect for one's privacy and burning curiosity, but the latter wins out. Undergarments say a lot about a man, and for some reason I've decided I need to know.

Inside, I find stacks of folded boxer briefs. Nice. Not that I would ever be seeing them on him. Not with a magician's getup hanging in the closet, and certainly not after he shoots me in the eye with a water-squirting boutonniere. Wait—that's a clown, not a magician. I think. Is there a difference?

My phone dings with an incoming text, startling me. I slam the drawer shut, realizing I have no right to be here, Nosy-Nellying up his skivvies. Glancing at my phone as I scurry from the room, I see the text is from Wendy, who agrees with my room choice for us. Amy told me she was easygoing. A great quality in a roommate.

Back downstairs, I lug my stuff into our room and begin setting up, until a sunbeam shoots directly into my cornea from a slot in the blinds, reminding me I'm wasting prime beach time. The rest of the unpacking can wait until tonight.

I pull out a pale blue bikini, a perfect shade for my practically translucent skin. Turning to the side, I check the mirror to make sure none of my bits are falling out—which is silly, since I don't really have any bits to keep in. I'm basically built like a piece of plywood. Being slight of frame also means I have "petite features, with delicate bone structure, high cheekbones, and almond-shaped eyes," according to an AI missing persons app I shared with Amy in case I ever go missing.

I dig through my beach bag in search of my SPF 100

sunscreen, also known as "shade." Until I develop a base tan, which for me is roughly the hue of a well-done baked potato (inside, not out), shade it is.

Wait! This is supposed to be Fun Girl Summer. Strap in, folks, Kacie Layne's about to go rogue! I lather on some SPF 50 and go in search of a golden tan.

I'm amazed how crowded the beach is for a Thursday morning in May. Schools must be off for the upcoming holiday weekend, judging by the number of kids here. Great. I was hoping for a few days of relaxing beach time before the weekend crowd descended upon us. It's not that I despise kids or anything. I'm just not ready to have my beach day ruined by ear-piercing shrieks, meltdowns over Fudgy Wudgy, and foot-flung blanket sand. And that's just from the parents.

The closest spot to the water, and far away from kids, is behind the lifeguard stand, which provides a double benefit. One, no one will sit directly in front of me. Two, if I decide to take a dip, I won't have to walk far. The only useful advice my parents ever gave me was *always swim in front of the lifeguards.* Being the rule follower I am, I do that to this day, even though I've outgrown the other perk of swimming in front of the lifeguards—checking them out.

"Whoa!" I exclaim as a whistle pierces the air.

A lifeguard jumps from the stand, red float in tow, and jogs into the water. I watch, mesmerized, as Mr. Baywatch swims beyond the breakers and pulls a shrieking kid and his boogie board back to shore.

Okay, maybe I'm not quite over checking-out-the-lifeguard phase just yet.

My phone vibrates with an incoming call. It's Amy. Ruh-roh. Her flight was supposed to leave two hours ago.

I swipe to answer, bracing for a tirade. "Don't tell me—"

"Delayed," she confirms in a deadpan tone.

She sounds calm. Must be having drinks.

"How's the house?" she asks. "Are you living your best life? How many things have you accomplished on the bucket list?"

"I've been here an hour, Ames."

In truth, I haven't looked at the list since she gave it to me, although I did put the journal in my bag in case there was something beach-themed I could knock off right away. I flip it open now and read aloud.

"*Number one. Kiss a hot guy on the beach.*" I guffaw. "You know that's not happening."

Amy knows I've never kissed a guy I wasn't totally into, and only after several dates. One, to establish I'm not up for one-night stands. Two, because I require a full health screening to rule out such atrocities as syphilis or other diseases before swapping spit with a person.

"You said you were gonna make changes this summer," she reminds me.

"Did I say that?"

She humphs as I read on.

My Summer Bucket List

1. Kiss a hot guy on the beach

2. Do something completely out of character

3. Make some girlfriends

4. Get out on the water

5. Learn a new skill

6. Do something charitable

7. Wear a fancy dress

8. Go on a boardwalk ride

9. Just say no (to something you'd normally say yes to)

10. Fall in love (with someone who's not Ben)

There's a greater chance of Sea Isle freezing over in July than there is of me achieving these things. Get out on the water? How—by commandeering a yacht? Wear a fancy dress—to what, sit on the beach?

Nope! This reads more like a "fuck it" list.

"We're gonna need a different list. Or at least change that last item," I inform her. "Not happening. I don't know why you're out there trying to marry me off."

"Because that's what I want for you. To find someone who's worthy of your greatness."

"Bad news, kiddo. Ain't gonna happen. Find another friend to try on bridal gowns with."

"I'm waiting for you. I know it's gonna happen, Kace."

"Hex on marriage," I retort. "Hard pass."

In truth, there's only one person I could ever see myself doing that with.

Let's say, for the sake of argument, I had the cold end of a long-barreled shotgun shoved into my ribcage, and the only way out alive was to get married. Ben would be my only choice, but not until his divorce was years behind us and Leo was off to college. I'm not out here trying to raise someone else's kid. Or my own, for that matter. It's not that I hate kids, I just don't want any. I only want to *date* Ben, not marry him. Lucky for me, he's told me on a number of occasions he's never going to remarry, which is why this scenario works for me. Another thing that makes him a safe bet.

"I know that's your narrative, but it doesn't have to be. Look at all the people who are happily married."

"Like my parents?" I punctuate my question with a raised eyebrow, even though she can't see it. Sarcasm fully intended.

"Your parents are...your parents. There's no explanation. But history needn't repeat itself. You need to get over this man and find your person. Ben has chosen not to be that man for you. If he'd wanted to be, he would've dated you in law school.

Or when his divorce was final."

"He's still getting over it."

"That's bullshit and you know it. I think that's why your crush has lasted for so long. He's safe. No chance of getting your heart broken, because, deep down inside, you know he's never gonna engage with you in that way."

Her words reach a pit in my stomach. One that's been there for quite some time, despite that night in my office. It wouldn't be the first time I felt it—I just haven't been ready to acknowledge it. I hope she's wrong, but on some level, I fear she may be right.

7

Amy's words conjure the pain I felt that summer after law school, waiting for that *maybe someday* to happen with Ben—once we passed the bar and got far enough beyond his breakup that I wouldn't feel like a consolation prize.

That someday came for Ben a month after our kiss, but it wasn't with me.

His proclamations of *something there* between us didn't keep him from sleeping with another one of our classmates. Angi was gorgeous, flirtatious, and an absolute guy magnet. She made it no secret she wasn't in law school for a degree, but for a man. As much as you'd think no guy would be interested in someone so shallow, they all clamored for her attention. Except Ben, who (without trying) became the object of her desire in our third year. When I heard they'd been seen leaving a party together, I was relieved—if he was going to rebound with someone, let it be her. I knew she wasn't his type, so I didn't feel threatened that they'd become something long-term.

Was I ever wrong.

One night in June, Ben asked me to meet him at Stanley's Bar for a drink. That's when he broke the news.

"Angi's pregnant."

"Who's the father?" The buffoonish question poured from my mouth before I had a chance to consider it.

He answered me with a look that said, *Who do you think?*

"Oh, shit."

"What am I gonna do?" he pleaded.

His truth bomb detonated my heart. I wanted to scream at him for being so careless. Pregnancies don't just happen. People make them happen, intended or not. This, on the heels of telling me he didn't want to start something with me. That *something* wouldn't have involved an unwanted pregnancy, I can tell you that. I wouldn't have slept with him until we were in a committed relationship. Even then, I would've made sure we were careful, knowing I'm no more ready to become a mother than the captain of a Bering Sea crab boat.

"I'm so sorry, Kacie," he said, his expression begging forgiveness. "I never wanted this to happen. I always thought it would be..."

When he stopped talking, I leaned in with an abundance of snark. "Be what?"

He dropped his forehead to his palms. "Just...not this."

Suddenly slammed with a zero-fucks tsunami, I shrugged like a heartless motherfucker. "Shit happens, I guess."

His head shot up, surprised by my reaction. He wasn't the only one. I would've thought news like this would gut me, take me out at the knees, but there I sat—stoic, and stingingly sarcastic. I'm not sure what he expected me to do—burst into tears? Lead a cheer? Launch into a discourse on disposable diaper brands? Instead, I went stone cold, waiting to feel something. Sadness. Anger. Anything. But I completely shut down.

"Say something. Please."

"Something," I said, getting up from the table, my ill-fated attempt at a joke landing as awkwardly as the twenty-dollar bill I threw down on the table. I walked out, not turning back once, not even when he called my name. It was as if someone had stolen my soul.

I threw myself into my studies and eventually got over the shock. In time, I even began feeling sorry for Ben, knowing fatherhood was the furthest thing from his life's bucket list. I did care about him—beyond my romantic feelings, he was a good friend, and I empathized with his situation.

As a show of getting over it, I invited Ben to study with me. What choice did I have? I wasn't about to spend precious weeks before the bar exam boo-hooing over a guy. It was almost as if I needed to do that, to prove to myself I was over him as a romantic prospect. He'd always been a solid study partner, helping me do better. I couldn't afford to change that up now, on the near eve of the exam. Selfish, maybe, but also self-preservation—if I'd let his situation impact my study habits, much less end our friendship, that meant I was giving all my power to him and not me, where it belonged.

Besides, he'd been there for me throughout the years—sharing compassion when my Nana died, bringing soup when I fell ill, giving piggyback rides when I broke my foot and couldn't walk to class. Whenever I hit a rough patch, Ben was there. The least I could offer him was the normalcy of our study sessions.

Then came the ultimate test of our friendship. It was the night after the bar exam, and we were celebrating the end of the nightmare over drinks.

"I couldn't have gotten through this without you," he said, his soft tone matching the look in his eyes. "You're the best friend I've ever had."

His words warmed me, even though they shouldn't have. But friendship was what we did best, and all we'd ever share, so I took comfort in his words.

"No one knows about the pregnancy," he said. "Angi hasn't told anyone, and you're the only one I've shared it with."

I wondered where he was going with this. If he was about to ask if I'd be the kid's godmother, I was going to have to throat-punch him. Not that I condoned violence, but I felt he had it coming.

"So, will you?" he asked, his expression eager.

I must have blocked out his question as I imagined his come-uppance. "Will I what?"

"Be our witness."

"Our witness for—"

And then I realized what was happening. He was going to marry Angi.

"It's before a justice of the peace," he said. "We're thinking next Friday. You free?"

"Free?" I repeated, giving a sardonic laugh, as if he were asking me to join him for drinks. But no. He was asking me to play a starring role in helping him create a life with someone else.

Once again, fatalistic friendship took over.

"Do you love her?" I asked.

"I guess I'll learn to. I mean, I'll have to once we're married. Right?"

I should have delivered the throat-punch then. But I didn't. Ben was only proving why I'd crushed on him for so long—he was a decent guy. Of course, he wouldn't impregnate a woman and take off, even though he could have. He didn't necessarily have to go so far as to *marry* Angi, but that was between the two of them.

I had to remind myself it simply wasn't meant to be between Ben and me. Aside from Amy, he was my closest friend. What kind of a friend isn't willing to stand up for someone who's trying to do the stand-up thing?

So, I did it. I stood up for the man of my dreams so he could marry someone else.

A month later, she miscarried.

"I'll help you get it annulled," I offered eagerly when Ben told me over drinks. I'd just landed a job as a law clerk for Mazerati Jones, one of Philly's top family law firms. "I worked on a case and learned the ropes—"

"Not so fast there, friend," he said, giving a chuckle. "I can't leave her now. She was in the second trimester, and it's been traumatic for her." And then he drove the final nail into the coffin of our *someday*. "It's been traumatic for *us*."

I felt like a fool, assuming he'd only married Angi because of the pregnancy. As the months rolled on, Ben and I grew apart while they grew together. I dove into my work and, when not in the office, hung out with Amy. She, too, had recently been burned by a guy, so together we forged onward, arms linked, doing the things we longed to do with a significant other. We tried new restaurants, scoured farmers' markets on Saturday mornings, cuddled in darkened theaters sharing popcorn over the latest horror flick. Up until then, Amy was the best boyfriend I'd ever had.

Until, one autumn day, Amy and I decided to check out a fall festival at a local pumpkin patch. We'd lost each other in the corn maze and were playing our favorite childhood pool game to find one another.

"Marco!" I'd called out, awaiting her response.

Silence. I yelled it again.

Finally, "Polo!"

Except it wasn't Amy's voice. It belonged to a man who careened into me as I turned a corner. He grabbed my elbows to keep me from falling. His touch was magic, his eyes were dreamy, and his laugh was contagious. Later, sipping hot cider around a bonfire, Seth asked me out for our first date. It didn't take long for him to whisk me away on a whirlwind romance.

Amy believes I only dated Seth as a rebound from Ben. She's probably right. Seth was appealing because he was the complete opposite of Ben. I just didn't realize how much of a schmoozing, charming player Seth was, until it was too late.

Ben and Angi stayed together, their next pregnancy going to full term when Leo was born. Just after his third birthday, Angi met and fell for another man, also a lawyer. Ben found his way back to me, this time seeking my legal counsel to file for divorce. I'd often been teased by friends and family for being a homewrecker, but this time I used my law degree for good—to untangle a legal web that never should have been woven to begin with.

Amy's voice on the line brings me back to the beach, and the present. "I'm assuming your silence is you mentally agreeing with me—that you're off Ben, and opening your heart to someone new?"

"Hardly," I say.

"Well, at least indulge me in the Summer Bucket List experience and let me know when you start checking things off," she says.

"Already have. *Number 9: Just say no...to this list!*"

"Bye, bitch," she says. "Got a plane to board."

After we hang up, I return the journal to my beach bag. Cute of Amy to think I'd use it for its intended purpose, but I'm so not a journaler. Not an introspective thinker, not a boo-hoo-is-me girl, no therapy mumbo-jumbo for this chick. Maybe because I was raised by parents who were disciples of the tough love movement. None of this gentle parenting stuff for them. They believed children should (a) be seen and not heard—which posed some challenges for me and my four siblings; (b) only come crying to them with a gaping head wound or detached limb; and (c) do something worthwhile with our lives, so we wouldn't embarrass them at cocktail parties when talk turned to children's professions.

Case in point: I'm a lawyer. Same with my oldest brother, Gary. My sister Robin is a pediatrician. My brother Nate's an investment banker.

And then, there's Maverick, a professional skateboarder. What did they expect, naming him that? From birth, he was destined to either be an extreme sports figure or a fighter pilot. The only thing keeping him from humiliating my parents is (a) he's world-renowned in his field; (b) his earnings outweigh the rest of our salaries, between product endorsement and wins; and (c) he's the youngest—and arguably the cutest of us all, if you were to ask our mom.

Maverick came along six years after my younger brother

Nate was born and eight years after me—an *oops!* baby, no matter how hard my parents tried to pretend he wasn't. That didn't stop the rest of us from taunting him. Or loving him as our collective favorite. Fortunately, his good nature inspired him to turn our teasing insult into his skateboarding moniker: Oops McGee[*], the nickname we'd given him as kids.

The thought of him makes me smile. Oops is also staying in Sea Isle for the summer with a houseful of his friends, in between skateboarding gigs. Another reason I'd wanted to summer down here—to spend some time with my baby bro.

Amy's been hounding me for years to seek therapy to deal with my parent issues, the cause (she believes) of my inability to land a relationship that doesn't end with my face in a tub of Ben & Jerry's ice cream. It's not that my parents were serial killers who stalked my prom dates and buried their bodies in our backyard. But they may have something to do with the fact I don't think I want kids of my own. Because as much as it pains me to say it, the day I turned thirty and looked in the mirror, I saw my mom staring back at me with her "delicate bone structure, high cheekbones, and almond-shaped eyes."

At least my blonde hair doesn't come from a box.

---

[*] Not our real last name, just the fake one we gave him because it sounded funny.

8

The sound of crashing waves lulls me to sleep, despite being surrounded by shrieking children. It's an act that easily qualifies for bucket list item #2: *Do something completely out of character.* I cannot, for the life of me, take a nap on a beach without jolting into consciousness like a shock therapy recipient. Must be my subconscious alerting me that I'm one nod away from becoming a *20/20* episode.

Nonetheless, I drift off for a while, until I'm awakened by a revelation. Maybe Amy's right—this is my summer to challenge myself, change things up. Languishing on the beach for the summer with no job, no significant other, and no responsibilities is likely something I'll never experience again. I should use this time for soul-searching, deciding what needs to change.

Challenge: accepted.

I pull the journal out and dig for a pen. Being the funny gal I am, I address the journal to Amy. Starting with:

If you're hoping for a heartwarming love story, you've come to the wrong place.

Wait, that sounds like the old Kacie Layne. Under that I write:

Captain's Log. Star date 0527...

Alright, Layne. Get serious. What to write about?

I hear my creative writing professor's voice. *Just start somewhere.*

Before long, my pen scurries across the page, dropping ink about all that's going on around me. The sound of the ocean, the laughter of gulls, the cries of the Fudgy Wudgy guy heralding ice cream. It awakens my childhood desire to become a writer (and eat a Choco Taco). I spent much of my youth drafting humorous short stories, but it's been a minute since I've written anything creative. Law school cured me of that, as it required so much technical writing, I would rather have streaked through a sold-out Eagles game in the dead of winter, than write in my spare time.

Finally, I find my happy place. Not just the beach itself, but the experience of putting pen to paper. So much so, I lose myself in the moment. Even the sound of children doesn't bother me anymore. I'm filled with such uncharacteristic joy, that when a football falls from the sky and lands smack dab in my lap, I just laugh it off and toss it back.

Really? Usually I'd be so pissed, I'd spin a tapestry of obscenities and lob the offending pigskin into the Atlantic like a fourth-quarter Hail Mary. If being on the beach for a few minutes has turned me into a nicer person, imagine what a whole summer will do?

"Nice throw," I hear someone call out. "The Eagles could certainly use you."

I look up and spy with my widening eyes what appears to be The World's Most Gorgeous Man, in the form of a lifeguard, on a slo-mo jog toward me. This is not the same man who saved the boogie-board kid. This one's a thousand times more gorgeous.

His chestnut hair is sun-kissed and tousled from the sea breeze. As he gets closer, I note his eyes are the color of the Caribbean, an intriguing combination of blue and green. His body is perfectly tanned, toned, and glistening in the sun as if he'd been physically anointed by God.

I gasp as he stops before me. Truly, he was—*Just. That. Fine.*

"Hey there," he says. I literally feel my heart stop as he gives me a slow smile. "Got a huge favor to ask of you."

His deep voice ignites a spark in my groin that smolders its way up to my brain. I feel myself melting from the inside out, turning my insides to rubble. Including my prefrontal cortex, which means I can't take responsibility for what I do next. From somewhere within the deep recesses of my soul emerges a coquettish flirt I didn't know existed. I tilt my head and give him a demure smile. The way he's looking at me, I know what he's about to ask.

"Sorry, I don't give my number to just anyone," I proclaim. My voice, cute and coy, doesn't sound like my own. So convinced am I by my own acting chops, I add an element of tease. "But I could break the rules for you."

"I'm honored," he says, laughing as he places his hand over his heart. "Actually, I was just gonna ask if you could move your chair over a bit. Tide's coming in and we have to move the stand back."

Instant mortification slams into me as I wonder what in the name of Pete has come over me. I'm not a flirt! What's going on here—am I suffering sun stroke? Am I on some sort of sea air high?

He's right, though. The lifeguard stand is becoming immersed in the Atlantic and the only thing separating it from the deep blue sea...is me.

"Of course," I say, trying to keep it light. "I was only joking about my number. I'm already taken."

Jogging backward, he gives me a half-smile, tossing this breadcrumb my way. "That's a damn shame."

His voice is like honey as his aqua eyes drink me in. I stare back, lost in his gaze. I slowly rise from my chair on jellied legs and relocate as requested.

"Thanks, ma'am."

Oh God. He's ma'amed me. Does this mean he's in college? He looks older than that, late twenties, maybe, but what if he's not? What if he's in *high school*? I'm wondering if I should I call the Cape May County Prosecutor's Office and turn myself in for child luring.

No...the more I look, the more I'm convinced he's not *that* young. He's at least old enough to get into bars.

He and his partner tip the stand, lean it on their backs, and drag it back a few feet. I'm now directly to their right with a much better view. Thanks, high tide!

I try to get back into my journal, but for some reason I can't. Listen to me, *for some reason*. I know the reason. As fascinating as writing has been, ain't nothing going on between these pages as riveting as what's going on fifty feet to my left, where Hot Lifeguard is now doing standing push-ups against the side of the stand. His back is to me, treating me to a gorgeous display of well-defined back and arm muscles. Rhomboids, lats, and traps...oh my! Let's not forget the tightest, most scrumptious ass I've seen in a very long time.

Make that *no* time. Never have I ever seen such a fine set of guy glutes.

He is an absolute perfect specimen. A bona fide 3D version of da Vinci's Vitruvian Man, only a thousand times hotter. And real. Points added for his ability to put his arms down. I bite my lip to keep my tongue from protruding, as a tingle rumbles up from my nether region and escapes my mouth as a growl.

"Mmm...*mmm*."

What is happening? This is not who I am. I'm not some lecherous she-wolf who ogles men in the wild. Nor am I on the hunt for a man—especially one who may have recently rushed a fraternity.

Then again, just like with fine art, there's no crime in looking. As long as you don't take, right? I have no idea if I'll be back on this beach during guard duty hours to witness such perfection, once I find a job. Might as well soak it up while I can. I scootch my chair around to gain a better vantage point as I sign up for a full-time membership to the Museum of He-So-Fine Arts.

After Hot Lifeguard finishes his one hundred push-ups (I know because I counted), he picks up an oar. Hoisting it onto his shoulders, he dangles his forearms in front and twists at the waist, which slants skyward in a graceful V, ending with broad, perfectly sculpted shoulders. His tight abs give a whole new definition to *six pack*. Meanwhile, below, another V dives deep into his lifeguard shorts as if pointing to his prized treasure. And what a treasure it is, assuming board shorts don't lie.

Whew. I need drink. Or a cigarette.

I recline my chair a notch and pull my sunglasses down over my eyes lest the lust shoot from them like lasers. My mouth goes dry as he drops the oar, puts a hand on either side of his waist, and leans to the right. Muscles strain against the leg of his shorts, which he hikes up.

I need to look away. Against my will, I do just that. I must find something else to focus on, or else—

I hear a voice call out. My head swivels back the direction of Hot Lifeguard. He's smiling at me.

"Enjoying the show?"

Usually, I'd be so mortified I wouldn't answer. Or I'd babble incoherent nonsense about why I was looking in his direction—dolphins, a passing sailboat, a lost nephew. Even scoping out Fudgy Wudgy would be better than the truth: it's *his* goodies I'm visually snacking on. Yet there's a certain whimsy to having shed all the other bullshit in my life—cheating boyfriend, shitty job, lemon-mobile. I feel free from the binds that tethered me to my boring, celibate life, and with that, social appropriateness. I am, after all, a Fun Summer Girl with a daring bucket list.

"Eight out of ten," I call back. "How 'bout some squats?"

I am going to hell.

I delight in the teasing grin he shoots my way, just as a kid walks up to him and saves me from making a further ass of myself. I take this as my opportunity to put an end to my voyeuristic activities. Pulling out my journal, I continue writing about the things I'm observing. Mostly him.

I think I'm suffering heat stroke. That, or I'm losing my mind. I'm not acting like myself and it's all because this guy over here has me thinking and feeling things I've never thought or felt. All based purely upon physical observation. I have no idea how old he is, if he's a good person, or who he voted for in the last election. Assuming he CAN vote...

I stop and cross that part out. No need to create evidence.

This doesn't mean anything, right? We're all human, we have needs, we find beauty in things (and people) that can't be explained. I don't know because I've never had this reaction to a person before.

A bead of sweat descends from my forehead to my journal, blurring the ink. It's hot as fuck out here. I've held out this long, but my organs are on the verge of well done. Time for a dip.

Passing the lifeguard stand, I suck in my stomach and thrust back my shoulders, trying to look as tall and smooth as I can, all while pretending to ignore him.

Look how precious I am as I step into the ocean! Turning to the side when a wave crashes around me, I catch him watching. Before his very eyes, I metamorphosize into the hot girl frolicking in the water of a Sandals Resort commercial. Hesitation gives way to abundant joy as I toss handfuls of water in the air, giggling and squealing to the doubtless delight of all who are watching (that's you, Hot Lifeguard). I frolic in the waves as if—

Wait. I haven't frolicked a day in my life. Not even when I was three and it was considered "cute" to frolic. Thank God no one on this beach knows me. Otherwise, I could count on a strait-jacket intervention once I emerge from the water.

I'm so hot (not just that way, but heat-wise, too) the water around me nearly reaches boiling point before it finally wins out, cooling my skin to slightly below sun surface temps. Deciding I've had enough frivolity for one day, I turn to make my way out of the waves, à la slow-motion bikini model. I feel all the eyes of the beach on me, including his, and I know what they're all thinking, *damn, look at—*

"Arrgggghh!"

I'm suddenly taken down by the most intense pain I've ever encountered in my life. It's my right ankle and, although I can't see it, I know I've been attacked by a shark. The pain quickly spreads through my leg, assuming it's still attached. And then it goes numb.

"What the *fuck*!" I cry out as I plummet into the ocean like an airshow disaster. It *had* to have been a shark as I can no longer feel anything below my right knee. Fucker must have taken half my leg with him. Sharks are dicks like that.

And then a huge wave smacks me in the ass, faceplanting me onto the bottom of the ocean. Spewing sand and sea water, I turn to get up but realize (too late) that I'm now facing the rushing tide as another jerk of a wave smacks me in the face and sends me ass over teacups, both legs flailing in midair.

Well, one and half legs, considering the other half is on its way out to sea à la Jaws's jaws.

I'm now rolling around in the surf, scrambling to find my bearings, trying to defy gravity and the sheer power of the ocean, but I can't seem to get my feet (rather, *foot*) beneath me. Listing like the Titanic, I go down again.

This is it. I'm gonna die. Right here and now, in two feet of water, as children point and scream with laughter. Why, God, why? What did I ever do to you, to cause me to spend my precious last moments on earth rolling around in the surf like a beaching marine mammal?

"Shark!" I sputter as loudly as I can, hoping someone hears me so they'll render aid.

Oh, they hear me alright, as evidenced by the fact that all within earshot are running for the beach, screaming bloody murder. I try to join them, but another wave takes me down, forcing a metric ton of sea water to enter my lungs.

Suddenly, I feel a hand grasp my arm and pull me straight up from the surf. Must be God—He's had His folly, and now He's lifting me to heaven.

"I got you," He says. The strong arms of the Lord embrace me as He helps me to stand.

I open my eyes to find it's not, in fact, God. It's Hot Lifeguard.

"Calm down," he instructs. "Take a deep breath."

Good thought, if my lungs weren't filled with the Atlantic. I go to speak but cough instead, a gallon of water projectiling from my mouth, all over his chest. Unfazed, his arm still around me, he navigates me to the beach, where I crumble to the sand. I sense my leg is still attached, which means the shark asshole must've only taken a chomp—albeit a big one. I know I'm about to bleed out right here on Thirty-eighth Street beach. I can't open my eyes, or I'll faint if I see it.

Now Hot Lifeguard is kneeling next to me, running his smooth fingers down my leg. I wonder why he's not calling for a medic or making a tourniquet of beach towels.

"I...was...attacked," I mutter between clenched teeth, in case they can't figure it out. "Shark."

He...laughs in response?

"Sit up," he instructs.

"Can't," I say, flinging my forearm over my eyes. "I faint at the sight of blood."

"Then it's a good thing you're not bleeding."

"What do you mean?"

"It's only a jellyfish sting," he announces.

Jellyfish, Great White—seems to me there's no difference, judging by how my leg hurts like a son of a bitch.

Then...a miracle! The pain stops. I look up to see him holding something with both hands at groin level. A gush of warm liquid splashes down on my wound. The abatement of pain is nearly orgasmic, until it dawns on me.

Jellyfish sting. Hot Lifeguard standing above me. Warm liquid flowing down.

OMG. He's—

"*Stop peeing on me!*" I yell as I shoot up to a sitting position. And then...it's lights out.

9

I'm floating, ears ringing, when I slowly become aware of someone far away calling for me to wake up. It's hard to hear what they're saying over the buzzing in my ears. Fuzzy at first, it finally gets louder as someone squeezes my hand. When I open my eyes, the spinning sky comes slowly into view.

With it, the ruggedly handsome face of a man. Two men. Shirtless. I have died and now I'm surrounded by hot male angels. Oh wait—no wings, just whistles around their necks. Right. Lifeguards. The hot one who—

"...wasn't peeing on you," he says.

"It was water," the other man explains, holding up a jug. "Best antidote for a jelly sting is hot saltwater. We fill a jug, and the sun warms it."

"Oh. It's just—I thought—" I sputter as I fully come to. "Aren't you supposed to pee on jellyfish stings?"

"Old wives' tale," the hot one says. "But you're not the only one who thinks so. You don't know how many people ask if that's a thing."

I chuckle, pretending I already know this. "I was just kidding."

Slowly sitting up, I look at my leg to find my ankle bone has been replaced by a huge red welt.

"Where are the teeth marks?" I ask.

Laughter once again.

"What?"

The guys exchange a look of profound amusement.

"They don't have teeth," Hot Lifeguard says. "They sting with their tenacles."

"Excuse me for not being the Discovery Channel."

"There is no excuse."

Now this here, I can deal with. Daring ocean rescue with a side of sarcastic banter? Sign me up. As I struggle to come up with a snappy comeback, I get lost in his aquamarine eyes, glimmering with sunshine and a dash of humor.

"I'm gonna give you this." Other Lifeguard ruins the moment as he breaks open a hot pack and hands it to me. "You're gonna want to keep this on the affected area."

"Don't I need some sort of antidote to remove the poison?"

They exchange a glance, failing to mask their smiles. "No. But you do want to monitor for signs of severe reaction, like trouble breathing, chest pain, swelling of the face or throat—"

"You sound like a prescription drug commercial," I joke.

"Here." Hot Lifeguard pulls a card from a bag on the stand. He jots something down before handing it to me. The card, titled *Jellyfish Sting Warning Signs*, contains a bulleted list of things to monitor. I skim the list, combing for symptoms. None so far, of those listed. Apparently, they forgot to add *exhibits gross misunderstanding of marine science*.

At the bottom is a phone number.

"Is this Poison Control?" I tease, because I would imagine it would start with a 1-800, not a 484 area code—a typical exchange for cell phones in our area.

"My number," the hot one says as a sheepish grin crosses his face. "Unlike you, I *do* give it out to 'just anyone.' Especially one who's suffered a life-threatening jellyfish sting."

A wave of terror washes over me. "How long must I monitor for these symptoms?"

"The rest of your life, honestly," he says but the glimmer in his eye tells me he's joking. "Twenty-four hours. If you experience any of these, shoot me a text and I'll get an ambulance right over to you."

"Right, since I'm not sure I know the number for 9-1-1."

He laughs. "Okay, you got me there. I'm just thinking—you know—if you're not sure, and all, you can—you know, call me and like run your—um, symptoms—"

I smile as he stumbles over his words. *How freaking cute are you?* Instinctively, I twirl my ponytail around my finger. I can't help it. This guy was already swoony to begin with, and then he had to go and get tongue-tied over the whole here's-my-number routine.

But then I remember myself. I'm a grown-ass woman, not a hormonal teenager. I'm not here to encourage, solicit, or otherwise engage in flirtatious behavior with a lifeguard, especially one who looks as if he may still wear a backpack to class. He *has* to be in college, right? Who else is free to spend their summer guarding Sea Isle beaches, besides college kids?

If I'm going to flirt with any man, he's going to be in his thirties, like me.

I hear the devil on my shoulder—a.k.a. Amy—telling me to loosen up, live a little. *Fuck Ben (not literally,* she laughs) *and go for the cute lifeguard.*

I guess there's no harm in flirting. "What if a symptom emerges after twenty-four hours? Can I still call you?"

"There's no expiration on that number, ma'am."

I tuck it away in my beach bag. You know, in case I'm ever moved by the cougar spirit.

10

I'm meeting my brother and his housemates this afternoon at Ocean Drive Bar for "no-shower-happy-hour." Ignoring the "no shower" rule like a renegade, I hop in the outdoor shower, keeping the water on cool so as not to scald my injury. An utterly delightful breeze whispers through gaps in the wooden wall slats, telling me this is the only place I should shower this summer. Alfresco all the way, I decide.

Twisting my hair into a messy bun, I put on a fresh bathing suit and cover-up, hoping I look as if I've just strolled off the beach without putting any effort into it.

I find my brother and his friends gathered at the Sandbar, OD's outdoor bar.

"There she is," Oops calls out as I make my way through sandy bodies. After rounds of hugs, one of his friends goes off to procure drinks.

"How's the house?" Oops asks.

"If you mean the structure itself, it's fine. Pretty nice for a group rental. There's a huge deck, and if you lean over the railing and squint, you can almost see the ocean."

"How 'bout your housemates?"

"They're not coming until tomorrow."

"Sweet. You'll have the house to yourself tonight."

"Except 'The Organizer' will be there. He's also here for the summer, but I haven't met him yet."

Oops laughs. "Why are you air-quoting The Organizer?"

"Amy can't remember his name, so that's what we call him."

His friend returns with drinks and someone raises their glass in a toast to summer. Someone else passes around shots. I'm not usually one to do them, but figure what the hell—it's what Fun Summer Girls do.

Oops and friends begin joking around about things they did in high school while I stand there feeling like petrified wood. They're all around Oops's age, twenty-four. I'm reminded that, at our current stages of life, eight years is still a huge age gap. I'm already embroiled in my career (well, *was*) while most of them still dwell in parents' basements, cohabiting with Xboxes and living for the weekend. Yes, I'm aware I'm casting ironic aspersions, knowing that if no real job offers come my way before fall, I may end up living in my parents' basement as well.

I drain my drink and decide to go unpack before I turn into a nursery rhyme-spouting Mother Goose. Oops has disappeared into a sea of friends who are all doing another round of shots. I wave to get his attention to let him know I'm leaving when I hear a voice behind me.

"Hey, Jellyfish."

My mouth hits the floor as I turn to find Hot Lifeguard standing there. No longer beach-haired and shirtless, he's sporting a turquoise polo shirt and white shorts.

I'm literally dead.

"Glad to see you're still alive," he says, grinning.

"Thanks to your brilliant rescue."

"All in a day's work." He nods toward my empty glass. "What's your pleasure?"

"Oh, I'm good. I'm about to leave."

Although the night, like my brother and his friends, suddenly seems young.

"Night's young," he says as if reading my mind. "Let me treat you to a drink."

The look he gives me makes my knees weak.

"Is that standard protocol?" I tease. "Save someone's life, buy them a drink?"

"Usually it's save someone's life and *they* buy *you* a drink. But I'll let this slight breach of etiquette slide. This time."

"Mighty nice of you."

"That's me, classic nice guy. Allow me, I insist."

Who am I to disobey a lifeguard? If he started waving a flag and telling me to move to the other side of the bar, I'd happily go.

Instead, he flags down a bartender and gives him our order.

"What's your deal?" he asks me. "You down for the weekend, the week..."

"Summer. How about you?" The question escapes my lips before I realize how ridiculous it is.

"Just the day," he teases.

"As I suspected. You're not really a lifeguard."

"You got me. What clued you in?"

"The way you almost peed on my leg."

"If it's any consolation, I'm like that with everyone."

I pout. "You mean, I'm not special?"

"Oh, you're special, alright," he says. "The way you exited the ocean today was nothing short of poetic. Graceful, elegant—like an interpretive dancing queen. I've never seen anything quite like it."

"I work hard at it. I wanna make sure I grab the attention of everyone within eyeshot."

"You certainly got my attention."

The gleam in his eye gives me chills. In a good way, not like he's about to ax murder me or anything.

The bartender hands me my wine and Hot Lifeguard raises his beer.

"To jellyfish stings."

"And daring lifeguards. Thanks again for saving my life."

"The pleasure was all yours."

I laugh out loud as another shiver goes down my spine, this one landing in my panties where a spark's beginning to ignite.

Suddenly, unpacking is the last thing on my mind.

"You down here with friends? Family?" he asks.

I don't want to admit the truth—that I'm spending my summer with complete strangers, as if I don't have a group of friends of my own. I don't, but that's beside the point.

"Friends," I lie. "How 'bout you?"

"Same. What's your real name, Jellyfish? If you don't mind my asking."

"Whitney," I lie. It's a thing Amy and I do with guys in bars, just in case they're weirdos. "What's your name?"

Before he can answer, the crowd around us parts and Oops approaches with a huge grin on his face. I smile back to let him know I'm okay and not here against my free will. And give a silent prayer he doesn't blow my cover and say my real name.

But instead of me, Oops makes a beeline for Hot Lifeguard.

"Oops McGee!" HL exclaims as he grasps my brother's hand and pulls him in for a man hug.

"Chase, my dude!" Pulling back, Oops adds, "I see you've met my sister."

HL shoots me a look, followed by a smile. "Sister?"

I nod through my confusion, wondering how they know each other. Points are immediately deducted for HL's familiarity with my skateboarding brother, confirming his suspected youthfulness. He must either be a skateboarder himself, or one who follows the sport. Meanwhile, I left my *sk8rboi* era long ago—oh, let's just say about the time my braces came off.

"Good to see you back," Oops says, turning to me. "We worked for the same summer camp last year. He had the kids in the morning, I got 'em after lunch."

I recall Oops coaching future skateboarders last summer. No surprise there—despite his illustrious career, he loves working with kids and plans to go into teaching when he retires from the professional circuit.

"How was your school year?" Oops asks HL.

Yep, I knew it. Still in school. Any flames still smoldering are instantly doused.

"Had a pretty good one, thanks for asking."

"What year are you?" I ask. *Please say senior year, so I don't have to secure legal counsel.*

"Fifth," he says proudly, in all seriousness. I wait for him to clarify he's a fifth-year engineering student or something.

"More power to ya, dude," Oops says.

"Ah, it's not all bad. I love that age. Still somewhat innocent and not yet snarky."

I burst out laughing, almost spraying both men with Sauvignon blanc as it dawns on me.

"You good, Toots?" Oops asks, thankfully calling me by my nickname and not my real name as he hands me a stack of cocktail napkins from the bar.

Laughing, I dab the wine off my forearm. "Sorry. I thought you were in college. You're a teacher, I presume?"

"I am," he confirms.

He's suddenly more interesting to me. Teacher means graduated from college, with at least a year under his belt, which makes him north of twenty-three. The age gap's beginning to close.

My brother gets pulled away by one of his friends.

HL turns to me. "I can't believe Oops is your brother. The kids loved working with him last summer."

"He's good with the little dudes. How about you—where do you teach?"

"Philly School District."

Duly impressed. Points are added. It's one thing to teach in the 'burbs, but much tougher in the city, where kids even as young as fifth grade are already dealing with the pressure of future gang involvement, according to my clients who are parents.

"What do you do for a living?" he asks.

This is the part I hate the most about meeting new people,

particularly guys. Once they find out I'm an attorney, I can almost see the hair on the back of their neck rising, as if anticipating I'm a bitch. Followed by a discernible instinct to flee, lest I start suing them for something.

But he doesn't react like the typical guy when I tell him.

"What kind of law do you practice?"

"Family law." Putting it that way is a lot safer than admitting my job is to help rip people from their once-loving bonds and thrust them into an ugly tug-of-war over children and china sets.

Instead of making a joke about it, like other guys, he merely nods. "I've heard that's tougher than criminal law."

"It is!" I exclaim. More points added for his understanding of the difficulties of my specialty area. "In criminal law, clients know they fucked up. Oh, sorry—" I clasp a hand over my foul mouth.

He laughs. "No need to apologize. I've heard worse. Let the F-bombs fly."

Points are racking up, considering my mouth is as clean as a turnpike restroom. I can't stand guys who judge women for saying the very same shit they do.

"In criminal law, there's an understanding as to why they're in the predicament they're in, even if they're trying to convince everyone of their innocence. Not true of family law. No one anticipates, on their wedding day, that they'll end up with someone like me, fighting to make sure they get what they deserve out of it. It's ugly work."

"I'll bet it is. But not uncommon these days. I can't tell you how many divorced parents I deal with every year. And that's just the ones who've married. Many couples don't, and judging by the comments they make about one another, there's good reason."

"That's why you'll never see me getting married," I say.

"Is that so?" he chuckles, as if in disbelief.

"Fifty percent of marriages end in divorce. Not giving up

my freedom for those odds."

"That also means fifty percent don't," he points out.

"Don't *officially* end, but how many of those intact marriages are miserable?"

"You're definitely in the wrong field," he says, laughing as he shakes his head. "You should be writing for Hallmark."

"Oh, I could infuse a dose of reality into those stories."

"So you don't believe in marriage. Does this mean you also don't believe in love?"

Good question. As I ponder it, I gaze up into his turquoise eyes, mesmerized by the way they twinkle when he smiles.

"It's not so much that I don't believe in it, it's just that, seeing what I see on the daily, it...makes you a little jaded, I guess."

"I could see that," he says, nodding. "But what if, tonight, you meet the man of your dreams? What then?"

I shrug. "Sucks to be him."

He gives a hearty laugh. For the first time, I notice his dimples. He even has that chin thing, you know, the dip. It complements his chiseled features—high cheekbones, strong jawline. Although, chiseled makes him sound like a hard-core gym dude. While his features are perfectly shaped, there's also a softness there, the juxtaposition of which makes him criminally handsome.

Somehow, we've drifted away from the bar. He leans with his shoulder against the wall, facing me. There's an undeniable pull between us. I feel it down to my core, and I can tell he does too. Weird thing is, I've never felt this before, so I'm not sure how to name it.

"Super impressed you're an attorney," he says. "There was a time I considered going to law school."

"What stopped you?"

"Life. My dad got sick when I was in college. Early onset dementia."

"Oh. That's awful."

"Yeah, it was. I left school and moved back home to help my mom. They'd just moved to the Philly area from North Jersey, so I transferred to Drexel and commuted. After graduating, I went to work right away to help my mom with the medical bills. He died a year after I graduated."

"I'm sorry to hear that," I say, touching his arm.

"They say everything happens for a reason. I don't know that I'd have ended up teaching, at least not in Philly, but I love it. I wouldn't have it any other way. Except, I'd prefer to have my parents still here."

"That's impressive, taking something tragic and turning it into something positive. What happened to your mom?"

"She passed a year after he did. From a broken heart."

I don't know what to say. I've never bought the whole "dying of a broken heart" thing before. I know it's a way to soften death, but there has to be a physiological reason behind her passing. Heart attack, maybe.

God, what an ass I am. No wonder guys don't want to date me. I'm the OG Debby Downer.

"It sounds like you were close to your parents," I say.

"I was." His adorable smile makes my heart melt. "They had something really special. It's why I *do* believe in love. And marriage."

My heart does an involuntary flip, like this is news I was hoping for. I certainly didn't come here looking for this. It has to be the most intriguing and intimate discussion I've ever had with a guy in a bar, and it fascinates me that our conversation naturally flowed to this level.

"It's never too late to go to law school, if you ever change your mind," I say.

"Nice thought, but I love what I do. I'm over that dream now that I'm in my thirties."

Ding! Ding! Ding!

"I'm thirty-two," I blurt out. "Well, I'll be thirty-two on June 23rd."

"That makes us the same age," he exclaims, holding up his beer.

I clink my glass with his. "Wow. You look so young," I tell him. "I thought maybe you were still in college."

"I wish," he says, taking a sip of his beer. "Actually, I don't. I'm happy with my life."

I'd love to be able to say that about my life. I'm not sure there was ever a time I felt that way.

I look up at him as I take a sip of wine. The deepening of his gaze, his proximity to me, is unmistakably intimate. Perhaps it's because the crowd around us has thickened, smushing us closer to each other. Or maybe it's because we're obviously attracted to one another in a way that's hauntingly familiar, as if we've known each other forever.

His forearm rests on the wall slightly above my head, and every time I speak, he has to lean in to hear above the music and chatter. At one point, a lock of his hair brushes against my forehead, tickling me with its softness. As people move around us, we're pushed even closer together. The narrowing space between us frizzles with electricity, and I'm literally trembling from our outrageous chemistry. It's all I can do to keep myself from going up on my toes and kissing those succulent lips of his.

The vibe feels so mutual, I'm not surprised when he reaches for my hand and weaves his fingers with mine, pulling me closer. Our mouths are mere inches from each other. I can't believe we're about to kiss right here in the middle of the bar. Even more so, I can't believe just how *here* I am for it. All my earlier protestations against kissing a stranger are gone like the bubonic plague.

But instead of kissing me, he whispers in my ear.

"I hope this isn't too forward but...you're beautiful."

I'm about to thank him as he pulls back and smiles, but he continues. "It's not just your looks that captured my attention. There's...something about you. When I first saw you, I was like I *have* to get to know her. And now that I'm getting to…" he shakes his head and smiles in disbelief. "I'm hoping it can continue."

Just the tone of his voice turns my legs to jelly. Coming from any other guy, it might have sounded like a pick-up line, but he sounds genuine. Almost…vulnerable.

His eyes go soft. "Sorry if that was too much. I'd just love to keep getting to know you. Would you like to go somewhere else, where we can talk?"

Normally, given the choice between becoming a murder victim and not, I'd go for the latter. I make it a rule not to leave a bar with someone I've just met, in case their intention is to Ted Bundy my ass. In fact, it's never come to this. Usually, guys take off like bats from hell, the moment they discover I'm an attorney.

He's smiling down at me as the crowd pushes against us. A woozy blend of clean aftershave and sunscreen overcomes my olfactory senses, making me want to do something crazy. Like leave a bar with a stranger.

"I'm not trying to be a creeper," he says. "It's just really crowded in here. I'd love to go somewhere we can talk easier."

Points added for the fact he's not a *complete* stranger. He knows Oops, and he did save me from certain death-by-asphyxiation as I tumbled around in the unrelenting surf. That should count for something.

I nod my consent, praying I haven't misjudged him.

Still holding my hand, he leads me through the crowd, which parts easily as we make our way to the door.

I turn on my Life 360 to make sure Oops knows where I am. With one thumb, I text him.

> Going for a walk with…

Shit, I can't remember his name.

"What's your name again?" I call out, but he doesn't hear me. Shrugging, I go back to the text.

…the lifeguard guy.

11

"Where shall we go, Jellyfish?" he asks once we're outside. "We can go to the Dead Dog Saloon for a drink, where it's probably quieter. Or grab a Wawa coffee and sit on the promenade. We could also walk on the beach..."

"Let's walk on the beach," I say, even though the lawyer part of me is internally screaming *Don't do it!* like I'm watching a horror movie where the girl's about to enter a room where the murderer's hiding.

If I was behaving like Kacie Layne, *the* divorce attorney from Philly, I would never (a) leave a bar with a stranger, (b) agree to walk on a darkened beach with him, and (c) be so excited by the prospect. But that's where we are right now. I have no earthly idea where my easygoing attitude is coming from, whether this is the effect of wine or just this man. He's putting me at ease and giving no red flag warnings whatsoever. I'm enjoying our banter and don't want the night to end.

He's also a lifeguard—sworn to protect and serve. True, his doppelgänger Zac *did* once play Ted Bundy, luring people in with his charm and good looks. But I figure, if he wanted me dead, he could've just let me die from embarrassment when I was rolling around in the surf zone like a piece of flotsam.

He holds my hand all the way to the beach. I'm amazed at what an easy communicator he is as he chats away, pointing out the various houses where his friends are staying this summer, giving the Instagram bio of their lives.

"Luke, phys ed teacher, college buddy. Brian, sous chef,

friend from home." And so on.

I listen intently, wondering if there'll be a quiz at the end of it. After all, he is a teacher.

Once at the beach, I kick off my flip-flops and sigh when my feet sink into the cool, velvety sand.

"Best feeling in the world, right?" he asks.

I agree. "Nothing in the world like Sea Isle beach sand at night."

We walk to the water's edge, where the ocean, black and ominous, hurls long lines of frothy white waves at us. I feel safe as he regales me with tales of his teaching experiences. It's cute the way he's trying to fill the silence, as if he's nervous.

"This year, there'll be twenty-eight kids in my classroom instead of the usual twenty-four. Good kids, though, if the fourth-grade teacher reports are accurate. I'll be starting a whole new lesson this year on astronomy and—" He turns to me. "Are you into astronomy at all?"

I quickly have to think about what he's asking me, as I often confuse astronomy with astrology. Hopefully it's the former—the study of the universe—and not "avoid making important life decisions while Mercury's in retrograde."

"Yes. I'm blown away by it all, this vast universe of ours," I say, hoping I guessed correctly.

"Me too!" he exclaims, dropping my hand as he jumps in front of me, facing me. "It's amazing to think about all that's out there."

He thrusts his arms out like the Vitruvian Man he is and spins around, taking it all in. I giggle at his childlike awe of our universe. It's the cutest thing—this hot man acting like a kid drowning in wonderment. Moved by his enthusiasm, I join in on the twirling skygazing activity.

"So many stars out tonight," he says as he continues to turn, taking it all in. "Let's count them!"

We both start rapidly counting, spinning around, until we

accidentally crash into each other. Laughing, he grabs my waist to keep me from toppling into the sand. My heart races as he gazes down at me, his face lowering. His lips are almost on mine when he suddenly pulls back.

"Sorry," he says, giving me a shy grin. "I promised I wasn't gonna be a creeper."

"You're not being a creeper!"

I'm a bit shocked at my adamant tone. Seriously, I wouldn't have minded a little tonsil hockey, especially with him. Isn't that what Amy wanted me to do—kiss a hot guy on the beach? There's something exciting about the prospect, knowing I may never see this guy again. I haven't dialed back on my desire for Single Summer, but a little make-out sesh on the beach with Hottest Man in the Galaxy wouldn't be the worst that could happen. Maybe *I'm* the creeper.

"I'm not like that," he says, running a hand through his hair, then laughs. "Actually, I am like that. I just don't want to...you know—"

"Don't want to kiss me," I say, teasing, but with a touch of disappointment.

Wait. What does he mean by *I am like that*? That he kisses girls on the beach regularly?

Oh no. It must mean he's a player.

"It's not that I don't want to kiss you," he says. "I just—really like you and I don't want to do anything to give you the wrong impression."

"Oh, you already have."

"No way!" He jokingly stumbles backward, grabbing his chest. "What did it?"

"The way you lured me out here to count stars," I say. "Probably the most romantic thing anyone has ever done."

"And that's the wrong impression?"

"Yes." I give him a sobering look. "I'm just not looking to start something this summer."

What I really meant was, I'm not looking to fall for someone like him...again. He *has* to be a player. He's smooth, just like Seth was in the beginning. Not going down that road again.

"Good," he says. "Neither am I. But this is okay, right? Just two people hanging out on the beach, getting to know each other?"

"Right."

That's a relief. Knowing he's as disinterested as I am in something that goes beyond tonight makes him that much more attractive.

He takes my hand again. We walk in ankle-deep water as cool, frothy waves lap at our feet in comfortable silence. Before long, we make our way away from the water to the dunes, where a lifeguard stand is lying on the sand.

"We do this to dissuade kids from climbing on these when we're off duty," he explains as he hoists it to an upright position. "But at thirty-two, we're above the rules."

"Good to have old friends in high places," I joke as he helps me into the stand.

We settle in, and he gazes up at the sky, ablaze with stars.

"Tell me about the constellations, Teach," I say.

"There's Cassiopeia." He points to a W-shaped cluster of stars. "Andromeda's next to her and, over there, Perseus. One of the greatest love stories ever told, if you were to ask an Ancient Greek."

"What's the story?" I ask. "In case I ever get quizzed by an Ancient Greek."

"It all started when Queen Cassiopeia declared her daughter, Andromeda, to be more beautiful than the sea nymphs. That pissed off Poseidon, so he sent a sea monster to ravage their kingdom in retaliation. The only way Andromeda's parents could save it was to sacrifice their daughter by chaining her to a rock as an offering to the monster."

"Wow, I thought my parents were bad."

"Perseus, flying by on another mission, took one look at Andromeda and fell in love with her. But in order to be with her, he had to battle the monster."

"And they say dating apps are dangerous."

"Right?" he says, laughing. "But Andromeda had already been promised to another dude, so poor Perseus had to fight him too. Perseus won, and now their love is immortalized as constellations in the sky. The moral of the story is, sometimes you have to face your fears and battle your demons before you can fall in love."

I let this sink in, wondering if that's what my problem has been. Maybe my beef isn't with love and marriage, but with my own internal demons and fears. Perhaps, as Amy has hinted at throughout the years, the reason I'm either falling for unattainable guys like Ben or allowing myself to be duped by players like Seth, is because on some level I don't think I'm worthy of something better. Maybe I need to face these demons head-on, label and conquer them, instead of denouncing a universal human emotion, and an entire institution. In addition to spending the summer figuring out my next career moves, I may want to set aside time for personal introspection, so I can learn how to open myself up to find healthy love.

Wait—who said anything about love? That's not what I want. This summer's supposed to be about me, no men. Love is the last thing I'm looking for. I just want...

I'm actually not sure what I want. I guess not to be hurt again. Is that so much to ask?

I don't know if it's the wine, or something about this guy that's getting me all up in my feels, but I better put the kibosh on it.

I decide to put my own spin on the story's ending. "And then Andromeda ran off with the pool boy, leaving Perseus to drown his sorrows in goat's milk and the warm embrace of a strapping farmhand named Hans. And they all lived happily *never* after."

"No, I'm pretty sure Perseus fell for the Amazon delivery dude. At least that's how the legend goes."

"Right, I forgot about him," I say. "Thanks for setting me straight."

I look over to find him gazing at me, as if he's peering into my soul. I don't hate it. His eyes sparkle in the moonlight and the expression on his face is so sweet, a lump forms in my throat.

"Wow," he whispers, summing up in one word all the crazy emotions I'm feeling right now, as all of universe's cosmic forces combine to pull us closer.

I can't hold back. Leaning in, I hear his breath hitch, his unrelenting gaze reflecting the passion coursing through me. Time stands still as my lips instinctively part. The subtle scrape of his teeth against his bottom lip nearly sends me over the edge.

"Kiss me," I say, my voice gravelly like the devil.

Gravelly, yes, but barely a whisper. He hears it alright, judging by the way his lips crash down on mine, no longer able to resist the powerful magnetic forcefield between us. His fingers loop around the back of my neck, his thumbs along my jawline, and he pulls me even closer into him, his mouth devouring mine. With a guttural moan, his lips and tongue swirl and dance in a way that sweep my ovaries into motion. Flames of passion shoot through me to the point I fear my bathing suit bottoms may spontaneously combust.

We kiss for what seems like hours, both of us moaning occasionally as if we're starving and haven't eaten in weeks. His tongue has a way of stroking every fiber of my being, making my whole body tingle with desire in ways I didn't know were possible.

Finally, we come up for air.

"My God," he exhales as he rests his forehead against mine, his voice raspy with desire. "That was...incredible."

Trying to calm my racing heart, all I can do is nod.

"I've never—" Our words come out simultaneously.

"You go first," I say, giggling.

He shakes his head in disbelief. "I've never met someone I instantly hit it off with like this. And that kiss...my God. Talk about out of this world."

Coming from any other guy, it may sound like a line. But he's looking at me with such adoration, I believe his words because I'm feeling the exact same way. I've never had this type of reaction to a kiss before. Not with Seth. Not even Ben's law school kiss—which, by comparison, may as well have been from Betty White. Nothing like this rip-roaring wildfire spreading through me, blazing into my nether region, threatening to set this wooden lifeguard stand on fire. I'm not sure I'm going to make it home on these legs of mine, as weak as they are from the passion still smoldering.

"What were you gonna say?" he asks.

My head is so swimmy, I'm literally incapable of coming up with something more poetic than, "I feel it too."

He laces his fingers with mine. I rest my head on his shoulder, and he kisses the top of my head.

"We fit together," he says, his tone awestruck. "It's like we were meant to meet."

"Mmm," I hum in agreement. It's as if he's taken the words straight from my own mouth.

Wait, no! No no *no*! This cannot be happening. I cannot be falling into some love trap. *Remember your demons.*

I'm about to make a joke when he squeezes my hand.

"What are you doing for the rest of my life?" he asks.

So smooth. Spoken like a true player. Good—I needed the reminder.

"I'd tell you, but I don't have my planner with me," I joke.

"How 'bout the rest of the night?"

Ooo-kay. Here we go. I can practically see the F-boy within, peeking out from his cheesy grin. Of course he doesn't want this to stop at just a kiss. He *is* just like Seth, with whom I made that mistake—sleeping with him the first night I met him, causing me to develop immediate feelings for him. It was the first and only time I've ever done that. Despite how Fun Girl Summer I'm trying to be, this guy has danger written all over him, and I can't afford to fall for someone who will only break my heart.

"My bartender buddy is having an after-hours party," he goes on. "Would you like to accompany me?"

Oh. That's a different story—at least it isn't an invitation to go home with him. He's redeemed himself somewhat. A party sounds fun, but as much as I wish I could say yes, this whole thing is scaring the shit out of me. Any further time spent in his company will likely lead to more, and I need to stick to my resolve. This is the Summer of Me. All joking aside about the Fun Girl stuff, I need to focus on myself and not give it up this easily to a complete stranger. Especially with Ben being down here this summer. I have to see if what happened in my office that night means there's the possibility of more between us, or if I'm just delulu. I owe that to myself.

Unless Ben is one of the demons I need to get rid of. In which case, even more reason to see that through, and close the chapter if so.

"I'm sorry, I can't," I say, trying to come up with a reason—not only one he'll understand, but one I will too. I go with a quasi-truth. "I'm...kinda seeing someone."

He flinches so hard, he almost topples from the lifeguard stand. "But...you just..."

I know what he's thinking—what a skank I am for kissing him if I'm seeing someone else.

"Okay, not entirely true," I say, hoping to paint a better image of myself with a brush of truth. "There's this guy..."

He shakes his head. "You don't have to explain."

"It's just..." I think twice about sharing such intimate details of my life. So, I end with, "Complicated."

"Gotcha."

"I'm sorry—"

"No worries, girl," he says. "I totally respect that. At our ages, life comes with complications. I've got some too."

I nod, although this sends a wave of disappointment through me.

"How about this?" he says. "If things ever get *un*complicated for you, let me know. I'll make mine uncomplicated too."

He leaps from the lifeguard stand and offers a hand to help me down, which he continues to hold as we cross the sand to the steps. We're alone on the darkened promenade, which is lit only by occasional street lamps. As we walk, I try to figure out how I can ditch him before we get to my street. Lifeguard or not, seemingly nice man aside, I don't need some rando knowing where I'm staying for the summer. And rando he is, given I've known him less than twenty-four hours. Even if he did save my life earlier (and thankfully didn't take it tonight).

"Thirty-eighth Street, right?" he asks.

Oh God, that's right. He was the lifeguard on my beach, so of course he knows what street I'm on.

"Thirty-fifth," I lie. I feel bad, but it's for my own protection. Leaving a bar with a guy is one thing; showing him where you live is quite another. "I...decided to hang out on Thirty-eighth today. You know, to be closer to the bathroom. My house is back by the bay." A harmless little lie.

"Okay. At least let me walk you home."

"I'm good. I appreciate your offer, but I'm a city girl. I can handle it."

We continue walking north on the promenade toward Thirty-fifth.

"Do you guys always guard the same beaches?" I ask, wondering if this is going to turn into an awkward summer if he's on our beach every day.

"No, we're randomly assigned to different ones each day."

Which means I could go the rest of the summer without

seeing him. I can't help but feel a twinge of disappointment.

When we get to the entrance to Thirty-fifth Street, he turns to me, lifting my hand to his mouth. His lips, soft and full, rest on my skin, sending sparks through me as I get lost in his gaze.

"I don't want this night to end," he finally says, clasping both my hands. "You sure you don't want to go to the party with me?"

"I'm sure. Besides, there's something...what's the word? Oh, that's right. *Romantic* about spending a night like tonight with a total stranger you'll never see again."

"Never?" He winces in jest, clutching his chest.

"Who knows if we'll run into each other again..."

"You have my number. Feel free to use it."

"Don't hold your breath," I tease.

He gives me a half-smile. "Complications?"

"Yeah..." Among other things.

He sighs. "Then I guess it's possibly goodbye forever, stunning woman I may never see again."

Blowing him a kiss, I jog down the ramp to the street. Suddenly, I'm struck with whimsy. He's still standing there, watching me, as I turn to him.

"I have an idea," I call out.

"Does it involve accompanying me to this party?"

"No, but it could involve dinner."

"Intriguing," he says. "Go on."

"I plan most of my life down to the last detail. But my friend is trying to get me to be more spontaneous. Believe in things like magic and destiny. I've agreed to try."

Did I? Or is Amy's spirit channeling me to say all this? It must be the wine talking, or the pheromones coursing through me.

"That's part of why I'm here this summer," I explain. "To make some changes."

"I like that."

I can't believe what I'm about to say, but I'm not willing to be so practical and fear-driven I potentially miss out on something good. Because one thought has been nagging me ever since I decided he's a player: What if he isn't? What if he's the furthest thing from Seth?

"Let's see what destiny has to say about it," I say. "If our paths ever do cross again, I'll let you buy me dinner."

There. Done. Nothing more uncharacteristic than me acting like a dreamy-eyed soothsayer.

"You'll *let* me?" He laughs. "I'd love that. You got a deal."

I nod. "Good."

I hear him call out as I turn to walk away.

"It was nice getting to know you, Whitney. I look forward to buying you dinner."

Oh shit, that's right—I never corrected my name. Too late now, without looking like a lying asshole. "We'll see."

I can't help but grin, feeling him watching me as I walk away. I turn and wave, hoping to send him on his merry way, as I don't want him seeing me pretend to go into a house. I can't afford a breaking and entering charge right now.

He waves back, shoves his hands in his pockets, and walks away.

Once he's out of sight, I head to my actual street and let myself into the house. Exhausted from the day, I get ready for bed, but sleep eludes me. I can't stop thinking about that kiss.

Throwing back the covers, I rummage through my beach bag and find my journal. I fill in the rest of the story—about running into him in the bar, the way we instantly fell into a repartee that felt cozy, familiar, and exciting. The way his hand felt wrapped protectively around mine. Gazing at the stars, the way his eyes lit up when he talked about the constellations. And that kiss. Hands down, the best I've ever had. In fact, my mouth is still zinging with the feeling of his soft lips on mine, the way his tongue worked its magic.

Ugh, I can't keep thinking about this. I need perspective.

I'm not some starry-eyed optimist seeking summer love. I'm a grown-ass woman with a mission: stay away from charming guys. Keep my legs together, and my heart intact. No matter how tempted I may be after our night together to give Hot Lifeguard a holler, I'm not gonna do it.

Even better—I tear the pages from my journal and ball them into the trash. Tossing the book on the nightstand, I turn just as the cover flips open to the front page where Amy's bucket list stares me down. I chuckle as I read the first item.

Kiss a hot guy on the beach. I put a check next to it.

Okay, girl. You've done it. Now move on.

12

I'm up with the sun, filled with nervous energy. I go for a run to work some of it off, which helps, but only slightly. Despite my resolve from the night before, I still can't get my mind off that kiss. Or the man behind it.

Chase. I remember his name now.

I run until the only thing I can think about is the burning in my legs. Finding myself at the southernmost tip of the island, known as Townsends Inlet, means I've run fifty-something blocks from the center of town where my house is located. A record for me.

I let my mind wander as I gaze across the narrow channel between Sea Isle and Avalon, where the Atlantic rushes in to fill the bay separating the barrier island from mainland Jersey. Reckless waves crash into one another from different directions, feeling much like my life. Turbulent, being between jobs as I am, without the safety net of income or a 401k. Oppositional, as my head tells me to stay with the tried and true and dive back into law, while my heart tells me to tread water, lay still, let the current take me in new directions. Yet amidst the churning waves, round pools of stillness create pockets of calm, where the current pauses to catch its breath. Like the water, there's a sense of peace within me as I pause to catch my breath this summer, knowing the season represents...

Actually, I have no idea what summer represents in terms of the seasons of our lives. I know spring is for renewal, winter is utter bullshit, and fall is for pumpkin spice. But what of summer? I pull out my phone and google it.

Summer is the season of growth and fruition, when the peak of nature's cycle occurs, symbolizing the manifestation of efforts from earlier seasons.

Hmm. Perhaps getting fired from a job I hated is a chance to manifest new growth, building upon all the efforts I put into my career up to now. Of which there were many.

I let this sink in before reading on.

Summer also represents joy and freedom, a season of vacation from work and school. A time for youth and innocence, when new experiences occur. It's also a time for love and passion. The sun brings its boldest light and energy in summer, making more time for deep and intense emotional experiences.

Certain words jump out at me. Freedom. New experiences. Passion. That last word, of course, leads me to recall last night and that kiss. Talk about deep and intense.

I tilt my head upward. "Thanks a lot, Sun."

Sarcasm aside, I let its rays dance upon my face, warming me from the outside in. Much like the warmth I felt under Chase's gaze...

Suddenly, I'm slammed with a tsunami of the past, drenching me in heartache, reminding me that Seth once looked at me that way too. I can't forget that. Instead of falling into another charm trap, I need to move forward, figure shit out, decide how the story of my life will play out. The only distraction I'll allow myself is to finish the chapter I'd somewhat started with Ben, who doesn't stoke the type of fear guys like Seth, and possibly Chase, do.

As I watch the wild, churning inlet, I recall a dolphin-watching cruise we took when I was a kid, coming through this channel on our way out to sea. It was exhilarating to be tossed and thrown about as the boat fought the current—until Oops threw up on me, and I cried for the remainder of the cruise. The memory makes me smile, despite the experience resulting in lifelong vomit-trauma.

Returning to town in great need of caffeine, I stop at Red White & Brew, my favorite coffee shop in Sea Isle, and take my iced latte to go. Crossing Landis Avenue, I'm suddenly filled with the type of euphoria one feels on their first day at the shore. It's exciting to think it all lies before me—that in this moment, I have no idea what will happen this summer, but it won't be long before I know how it ends. I'll know what job I took (*mental note*: find one). What friendships were made. What surprises I'll experience, along with the letdowns. Hopefully not many. Most importantly, I'll know whether Ben and I finally get together.

And whether I ever see Chase again.

Nope! Not going there.

It's almost eleven by the time I return home. This time, the place is filled with the smell of bacon. The Organizer lives! I go upstairs to meet him but...presto-change-o! The place is empty. The scent, a ghost of breakfast past. I find a note on the island.

Hello, Kacie! Welcome to our shore rental. Sorry I keep missing you, but hopefully I'll catch up with you tonight. Enjoy your day!

It's starting to feel like a game, wondering how long I can go without meeting Houdini in the flesh.

You'd think after a vigorous run and life-affirming java, I'd have all the job-hunting mojo I need to go forth and find employment. But I don't. Besides, it's Friday, when the businesses I'd be applying to are likely gearing up for the Memorial Day holiday. I'll take the weekend for myself—with twelve housemates moving in tonight, it's going to be very people-y around here. I'll hit the ground running on Tuesday, once the weekend crowd has flocked back to the mainland. I'm thinking I'll go for something in retail. I have my sights set on Beachy Keen, a cute boutique shop in town, or Book Nook, the quaint bookstore on the promenade. Maybe both.

Donning a new peach-colored bikini, I check myself in the mirror to make sure it doesn't clash too much with my winter skin. Despite being on the beach for hours yesterday, it still gives cadaver. I pull my long hair into a high ponytail, noting it's slightly blonder today. I'm thankful at least one part of my body knows how to react to sunlight. I then go to work on my sunscreen application, forgoing SPF 50 and lathering on 30 instead.

I know I'm obsessing over how I look. Blame a certain lifeguard, whose lingering gaze I still cannot get over, despite all my protestations. I find myself hoping destiny is a thing, and she'll bring him back to my beach.

As I put the tube back in my beach bag, something catches my eye. Chase's phone number, written on the back of the jellyfish card. For a brief second, I contemplate faking one of the symptoms until realizing that may only result in an ambulance ride. I *could* just call and thank him for the daring rescue. Perhaps he'll offer up where he's stationed today and I'll just happen to—

No, Kacie, *no*! I am *not* chasing a guy this summer. Especially someone who likely has women crawling all over him like lobsters to a baited trap. Didn't he mention he, too, has "complications?" That's the last thing I need this summer, a dangerous guy with complications. Not after what I went through with Seth, whose rizz bears a striking resemblance to Chase's. Handsome. Charming. Smooth. But also...heartbreaker. Dangerous. A total dick. Presumably, Chase isn't much different.

Fueled by those thoughts, I rip up the card into tiny shreds and dump them in the trash can at the curb. There. Done with that.

I'm caught up in the gorgeousness of the day as I head to the beach. The sky's high and blue, as a light bay breeze blows puffy clouds out to sea. I delight in the laughter of the gulls swooping overhead and even smile at the man standing beside a hot dog cart emblazoned with the words *Lou's Dogs*. He tips his baseball hat as I approach.

"Good day to you, miss," he says as I pass.

"It *is* a good day, isn't it?"

Usually, when I pass street vendors in the city, I put my head down and scuttle by to avoid making chit-chat. In less than twenty-four hours on the island, I feel like I'm a better person as my tension eases away. The hot sand beneath my feet reminds me that, after a grueling, dream-shattering winter, summer hope has finally arrived. It's a feeling I haven't felt for a long time.

Nor does it last long. I'm overcome with SPF regret as the sun bakes my skin and the sand starts to feel more like hot, flowing lava. Fortunately for me, there's an umbrella rental shack to my left, where a twenty-something woman paces as she squeals into her phone. I leap into the shade cast by an open umbrella to spare my feet from searing.

"I can't tell you how long I've been waiting for your call!" the woman exclaims.

She shoots me a look, the only nearby audience, her mouth dropping open in obvious excitement. Her enthusiasm makes me smile.

"Absolutely," she says, returning her attention to the caller. "Of course, I can start Tuesday." She ends the call, turning joyfully toward me. "I just got offered my dream job. I applied two months ago but never heard anything until now!"

"Congratulations!" I say, hoping her luck rubs off on me.

Her face falls. "Except...I signed a contract for this job, agreeing I'll be here until Labor Day weekend. I'm afraid they'll sue me for quitting."

She's lucky I'm a lawyer.

"New Jersey is an at-will employment state," I inform her. "It doesn't matter if you've signed a contract or not. You're free to leave this position at any time. Don't sweat it."

"How do you know this?" she asks.

"I'm an attorney."

"You don't think there'll be ramifications if I quit?"

"Not legally."

"Do I have to give notice?"

"Generally yes, but it sounds like you'll be starting your new job on Tuesday..."

"Yes!" she squeals again, then laughs. "I'm sorry. You're not here to give legal advice. What can I help you with?"

"I'd like to rent an umbrella."

"Absolutely. It's on me, to thank you for the advice."

She hoists the umbrella onto her shoulder with ease and asks where I'd like to sit. I point to an open spot slightly behind and to the right of the lifeguard stand. Sue me.

"Good choice," she says with a teasing tone. "The guards this summer are drop-dead."

I laugh out loud. "I noticed that yesterday."

She digs a hole and expertly twirls the pointy end of the umbrella until it stands upright. After she opens it, I tip her a five-spot and wish her luck in her new job. She walks away but returns a few minutes later.

"Do you mind if I ask another question?"

"Fire away."

"The contract also says if I leave before the end of the summer, it's my responsibility to find a replacement."

"Nice try on their part, but that's not enforceable. Finding a replacement is never an employee's responsibility."

"Thank God. I wouldn't know who I'd get. My friends are in the city working real jobs."

After she leaves, I set up my chair, trying not to be obvious as I glance over at the lifeguard stand to see if my friend is there.

His partner from yesterday is, but he is not. Despite trying to block him from my mind (epic fail), I'm disappointed. It would have been nice to thank him for yesterday, but this is what I get for trusting destiny. And throwing away his number.

A plan begins to materialize of its own accord. If the trash hasn't been picked up by the time I get back—

"Get ahold of yourself," I chastise myself aloud. "You're not dumpster diving for a man."

That being settled, I adjust my chair to lounge position and lay back. Just as my eyes close, another idea comes to me. This one legit. I make my way back to the shack.

"What are the qualifications for this job?" I ask.

"Why? Are you interested?" Her humorous tone suggests she's joking, but it changes when she sees my expression. "You *are*?"

"I'm between jobs," I explain. "I'm down for the summer and looking for something. What's the pay like?"

"Pretty decent. Eighteen an hour, plus tips. Which are usually generous, thanks to vacationers' good moods. You also get a pro-rated bonus if you rent more than two hundred dollars a day."

"How much do you typically rent?"

"Weekdays, around that. Weekends double, if not triple. You'll definitely want to take the weekend shifts. Especially in this stretch of blocks, because of them." She gestures to the nearby twin high-rises. "Thanks to the Spinnaker Condos, these beaches are the most crowded on the island."

Is this really what I want to do this summer? I thought I'd end up working a cushy job in an air-conditioned shop, but this job offers bonuses.

"What are the hours?" I ask.

"Typically, ten to five, depending upon the weather. You'll have off most rainy days, and when storms blow in, you close early. Truly, it's the best job. Bonus—you get to wear your bathing suit to work."

"Hey, Gina," a man behind me says.

I turn to see Other Lifeguard jogging by, waving to Umbrella Girl (whose name, I gather, is Gina) before he does a double-take at me and stops. "Hey, you! How's your leg?"

"Good," I say. So good, in fact, I'd forgotten all about it. I ponder asking where Chase is stationed today but think better of it.

"Excellent. Excuse me, ladies. Duty calls."

"Double bonus about this job," Gina says as she watches him jog away, "your office comes with a view of *them*. Triple bonus, they switch beaches every day, so there's always fresh eye candy."

Hmm. Handsome lifeguards are definitely a nice bonus, but something tells me nobody could beat Chase's tasty treats. I'm tempted to ask her if she knows him but stop myself. *Pick a damn team already, Kacie.* One minute I'm drooling over thoughts of the man, the next I'm throwing a hex at him. See? This is the problem with players. They make you second-guess yourself—you know you shouldn't indulge, but they always leave you wanting more. Like a fine piece of cheesecake.

"I'll do it," I say before I have a chance to ponder it further.

"You will?" she exclaims. "Wait, but aren't you a lawyer? Wouldn't you want something more...prestigious?"

"Nah. I'm looking to do something fun. This seems perfect."

"You'll love it!" she says, giving a little clap. "My boss will be stopping by later this afternoon. I'll introduce you. She's cool, around our age. You'll like her."

It tickles me that she thinks I'm around her age, but I don't bother to correct her. She plugs my info into her phone, and I return to my chair. After a few hours alternating between baking in the sun and cooling in the shade of my umbrella, Gina returns with a woman she introduces as her boss.

I stand and shake her hand.

"I hear you're interested in the job?" the woman asks.

"Absolutely."

She tells me I must fill out an application as a formality, but if I'm able to start tomorrow, the job's mine. "As long as you don't mind the summer heat, informal dress code, and a job dependent largely on the weather, I'm sure you'll be fine. How good are you at putting up umbrellas?" she asks.

To be honest, I've never put one up. I'm not sure how to answer this, other than to point out I passed the bar exam on the first try, which means I can do anything.

"I'm sure you can," she says, laughing. "Gina will still be here tomorrow, so she'll train you. It's a pretty chill job."

Exactly what I'm looking for. No shade to Beachy Keen and Book Nook—both would have been great places to work—but this way, I can remain a loyal shopper and avoid mixing business with pleasure.

She texts me an application link, telling me she'll call later with a formal offer and instructions for tomorrow. After they leave, I fill out the application, not wanting to lose the opportunity. Working on the beach from ten to five every day with bonuses and tips? Possibly ending up on a beach with a certain lifeguard?

Stop it, Kacie. Remember the hex.

Just as I think it, a text comes through from Ben.

> Hey beautiful - looking forward to our dinner.

Ben has called me a lot of things in our day, but never beautiful. I'm not sure what it means, him calling me that, but it makes me tingle.

> Me too. Where would you like to go?

> Wherever your heart desires, but I'm treating.

> You don't have to do that!

> After all you've done for me, I owe you a thousand dinners.

> In that case, let's go big. I'm sure there's a Michelin-starred jawn around here somewhere.

> Nothing but the best for you. <3

Note the heart, gentle reader. See? It can't just be me. I have to be on to something here. I can't be imagining it.

My mind goes back to that night in my office a few months back. We were sharing a bottle of wine to celebrate the final resolution of Ben's case when he took me in his arms. It isn't unusual for us to hug, but this one felt different. Longer, tighter. The way he stroked my back felt new as well.

Pulling away, he looked deep into my eyes. "I love you, Kacie."

The words weren't new either, as he'd often uttered them throughout the course of our friendship. But that time, it sounded less like friendly love and more like something else.

Something *more*.

His lips brushed the side of my cheek as he whispered in my ear. "You're so special to me."

I fought the urge to pull him toward me and kiss him, excited yet not surprised we were about to repeat history. Working together on his case had brought us even closer than we'd been in law school. Something about going through the real-life trauma of a failed marriage in his case, and a cheating ex in mine, bonded us in a way our carefree youth hadn't.

His mouth moved closer to mine as he breathed my name. My lips tingled in anticipation of us reliving that night in law school until, at the last minute, he pulled back and enveloped me in another hug.

"Thank you so much for everything you've done for me," he said, his voice husky. "Not just with the case, but throughout our entire friendship. You mean so much to me."

"I'd do anything for you," I whispered. Despite everything that had happened over our ten-year relationship, I meant it.

You'd think I would have been long over Ben by then, given he'd gone and made a whole family with Angi and Leo, and I'd been in a years-long relationship of my own, but the old familiar strains of unforgotten love still tugged at my heartstrings. He was a good friend, a trusted ally, the habit I couldn't break. But that night, just like in the past, he was coming off a freshly broken relationship—this time a biggie. His divorce may have been in the works for some time, but I'd learned from previous client reports that healing doesn't truly begin until the final resolution. So, once again, I swallowed my feelings.

I don't think I'm imagining that something between us is changing. Why else would he so enthusiastically encourage me to spend the summer in Sea Isle, knowing he'd be here too? I'm dying to know where his head is at where I'm concerned. It's been a few months since that night in my office, so maybe the time has come to share my feelings with him.

Yikes! The thought is terrifying. I'm just not sure I'm ready to put my heart out there like that, and potentially ruin our friendship, if this is all just my wishful thinking.

13

My housemates are expected to arrive this evening, so I head back to the house at 3:00 to shower and prepare a happy-hour welcome. Once again, The Organizer is nowhere to be found. He's definitely nailed his disappearing act. I arrange a couple charcuterie boards, bowls of chips and salsa, and homemade guac. I'm setting them out just as Wendy arrives.

"Hey, roomie!" she says, giving me a hug. "Wow, this place is pretty nice."

I pour us each a glass of wine and we toast to summer when two women come in. I soon learn the tall blonde is Diane, and the shorter brunette is Rachel. I pour two more glasses, and we sit around the kitchen island, chatting. I quickly learn Diane is outgoing, with a killer sense of humor, while softspoken Rachel possesses a more subtle wit. I can tell right away we're all going to get along.

One by one, more housemates arrive, many still dressed in work clothes. Everyone seems friendly and grateful for the happy-hour spread. It's overwhelming, trying to keep all their names straight. For some reason, I have no problem with the women, just the men. I employ my time-tested memory device—matching each guy's name to a physical feature.

There's Hazel-eyed Harry.

Rex Has Pex has quite the sculpted torso, noticeable through his tight shirt.

Jasper is very fair-skinned, so Friendly Ghost it is.

Regrettably, Aardvark Mark bears a striking resemblance to his namesake.

"Wherever did you get this cheese, Kacie?" Bob the Builder asks. What would you expect me to name him when he's wearing jeans and work boots when it's eighty degrees outside? Turns out, he's actually in construction.

"Acme," I say. "It's called Artigiano."

"I nominate Kacie to be in charge of happy hour every night."

Bob's announcement is met with a chorus of agreement. I'm warmed to know my housemates appreciate my efforts.

Everyone spreads out, some going to the deck while others remain huddled around the food on the kitchen island. I drift between groups as hostess, butlering appetizers and refilling drinks. It makes me feel good to have a role in this group of strangers, even though I won't plan on doing this all summer without pay or some commensurate quid pro quo. The truth is, other than Wendy (who's been in a one-on-one convo with a guy I call No-sleeve-Steve), I don't know anyone well enough yet to feel comfortable sliding into their discussions.

I only count thirteen of us—seven girls, but only six guys. I wonder if The Organizer is one of them, but none of these guys appear to be the cheesy entertainer type I've been envisioning. He must not be here. Probably off sawing a woman in half at a casino somewhere.

When my phone jingles with an incoming call, I recognize the number as my new shack boss. I take it downstairs for privacy, and she informs me I've been officially hired. My hours will be Friday through Monday, which makes me happy because Gina said she makes more on weekends, and it will give me three consecutive days off during the week. I'm to report tomorrow at 10:00 a.m. to the shack on the Thirty-eighth Street beach, where I'll be stationed for the weekend with Gina. Once I have a couple shifts under my belt, I'll be randomly assigned to one of twenty different shacks, spread every three blocks.

We chat for a good half hour about the payment system, pricing, and the types of equipment available for rent.

After our call, I pull up the house's group text to see if I can match missing names to numbers. Seeing Amy's name at the top sparks sadness. I wish she could be here with me this summer. Scrolling through the texts, I see someone has responded to Bob and Rex by name, so I'm able to match their numbers. The rest remain a mystery. In due time.

I head back upstairs, where the music's blaring, drinks are flowing, and conversations are getting louder. So is my bladder, screaming for a potty break. I head for the powder room and whip the door open when—

"AAAAH!" The scream comes from a man, standing before the toilet, doing his business.

"AAAAH!" I shriek in kind, slamming the door before he has a chance to turn and see me.

I don't know who has it worse in a bathroom barge-in scenario—the barger, or the bargee. Either way, it's hella awkward and I'm not sticking around to find out.

Glancing wildly around, I assess my escape route, noting the stairs are too far away for me to reach them before he emerges. With no one else in the near vicinity, it would be a case of guilt-by-proximity, and I'd be collared in an instant. Meanwhile, a group of housemates standing in the kitchen offers an attractive option—other bodies to hide amongst, rendering detection nearly impossible. I'm pretty sure he didn't see me, nor did I really get a good glimpse at him (that's how fast I slammed the door shut), so he'll never be able to finger the true barger without conducting a full-fledged lineup.

With no more time to spare, I hightail it to the kitchen and leap into their conversation-in-progress. They're laughing, so I start laughing, too, although I have no idea what we're all laughing at.

In my periphery, I see a figure emerge from the bathroom,

but he's silhouetted by the sunlight beaming through the sliding glass doors. It appears that he's making his way over to us. Shit! I dodge behind Rex's bulging Pex and turn away, lest he see the guilt splayed across my face.

But then, I hear his voice.

"Jellyfish?"

Turning to the man who's just approached, I'm met with aqua eyes. My chin drops to the floor in utter shock.

"What are you doing here?" His incredulous tone matches my confusion. "Are you—friends with someone in our house?"

"Wendy," I say, my brain scrambling to understand how destiny has not only brought us here under the same roof, but made sure I barged in on his bathroom session. My heart races over seeing him again. "What about you? Who do you—"

Oh.

God.

His words echo loudly in my ear.

Our house.

The room spins as I realize who he is. He's not just Hot Lifeguard, the man I kissed as if my life depended upon it. The man whose tongue I've longed for since he slipped it between my hungry lips, the one I was never supposed to see again. Instead, he's magically reappeared in my life. As none other than...*ta-da!*

The Organizer.

14

This. Can't. Be.

Yet the longer we stand here, staring at each other, the more it becomes clear to me that destiny is a bitch with a sick sense of humor. I don't think he realizes who I am, my reason for being here.

Judging by what I'd found in the primary suite, I'd have bet both kidneys The Organizer was going to be some old-ass, tux-wearing, cheesy stick-up-his-ass weirdo. Not a beach-guarding Adonis who got me so hot he sparked a bonfire between my legs. I suppose it's possible he could still be a magician on the side. I wouldn't doubt it, the way his tongue worked me like a magic wand. I'm just hoping he can abracadabra me into a top hat and make me disappear. Because here I am, less than twenty-four hours into summer, and I've already broken the first cardinal rule of shore house rentals: no housemate hookups.

Not that a kiss is a true hookup, but it certainly felt like it.

He's gawking at me just like he did that night. He definitely hasn't figured it out. Laughing, he clasps my hand. "Talk about a small world."

Dude, it's about to get a whole lot smaller.

"I can't believe this—how do you know Wendy?" he continues rambling before I can respond. "She's one of my housemates."

Mine too, buddy.

"Listen, there's something—" Before I can get the words out, the door slides open and in comes Bob.

"Kacie, I swear to God, I can't get enough of that cheese. Thanks again for setting this up."

My eyes dart to Chase as his expression clouds over in confusion.

"I thought your name was Whitney?"

"Sorry," I mutter to my once-harmless-fling-turned-house-fixture. "I'm—"

"Kacie...our new housemate?"

"Yeah," I say, my stomach sinking. "I'm Kacie. Sorry. I don't usually give out my real name when I meet someone at a bar. It's just a...protection thing."

Back me up on this, girls. Giving a fake name is one of the many tools in a woman's survival toolkit. I realize it makes no sense that I gave him a fake name yet allowed him to lure me to a deserted beach at night, as if begging for my own *Dateline* segment, but my reasoning was clouded by Sauvignon blanc and a heady mix of pheromones.

That same spark begins to ignite again, almost immediately—as though it can't help itself—but I try to douse it with a hex. I have to. I can't be living in the same house with this man in such close proximity and hope to escape the summer with my heart still intact.

"Nice to officially meet you, Kacie," he says, suddenly all stiff and formal.

His reaction has me stiffening too. I'm not sure whether he's mad I lied, or because he just realized we're going to be living together all summer after our steamy beach kiss. Either way, his reaction isn't ideal.

I do my best to avoid him for the rest of the night. He seems to do a good job of ignoring me, too, except for the few times I catch him looking at me from across the crowded deck. I can't tell whether it's a good kind of look, as in *wow, she's hot,* or a bad one, as in *where can I hide her body?*

Other people begin showing up, friends of various

housemates and neighboring shore house residents. Among them is a woman with a blonde, bobbed hairstyle who seems to have Velcroed herself to Chase. I know she's not a housemate, yet wherever he goes, there she is. Her interest doesn't seem reciprocated, though. He's certainly not paying her the same kind of attention he paid me last night on the beach. I wonder if she's part of his "complicated" situation.

I recall our parting words as we left each other on the promenade last night, that if we were to meet again, I'd "let" him take me out to dinner. Well, that ain't happening now. His housemate status renders him untouchable, putting the kibosh on anything more happening between us—thanks to the cardinal rules of shore house rentals, and my desire to avoid messy summer flings.

Unable to stand the awkwardness, I excuse myself and head to my room, where I flop face-down on my bed.

This is not good. It would be one thing if we kissed and it was no big deal. But it *was* a big deal. I was so frazzled by it, I came up with the stupid *let's let destiny decide our fate* scheme.

Oh, she did alright. The meddling bitch.

My first thought is to text Amy, but it's the middle of the night in London so that'll have to wait. Instead, I lay there ruing every decision I've made since getting canned. Especially joining a shore house. My plan was to keep to myself. Have fun, but without a man (unless it was Ben). I never planned to hook up with a housemate and definitely didn't plan to cause drama. I'll have to pull him aside tomorrow and tell him my new plan: (a) pretend it never happened and (b) never do it again. (c) Obviously.

I must fall asleep at some point before sunlight awakens me, exacerbating my already-pounding headache. Wendy's bed is still made, and I'm guessing if I searched the house right now, I'd find her in No-sleeve Steve's room, wearing the same clothes she had on last night. There was definitely a hookup vibe going on there. I wouldn't be surprised if they'd spent the night breaking rules.

Hey, if *they* can...

Stop it, Kacie.

I text the only person I can share this horrifying turn of events with. Amy.

You're never gonna believe this.

No response. Since I can speak faster than type, I decide to just send an audio text. I press record and start talking.

"Hey, girl. Remember that stupid summer bucket list you gave me, and your brilliant idea that I should 'kiss a hot guy on the beach'? Well, I did it! The hot lifeguard who saved me from death-by-jellyfish. Long story short, we ran into each other in a bar, flirted, and went for a walk on the beach where we played tonsil hockey. Who am I kidding? It wasn't just hockey. It was the fucking Stanley Cup. Like I was the last woman on earth and the only way for him to survive was to stick his tongue so far down my throat it came out my vagina. Amy, I've never been so turned on in my life, I almost decided to fuck Ben...I mean, not fuck him literally, but kick him by the wayside. Because... damn. It was *the best kiss of my entire life.* He wanted to walk me home, but I refused in case he planned to Gary Heidnik my ass, and also because I'm not about to have a stupid summer fling just because some guy has awakened in me a mystical sex goddess I had no idea existed. Instead, I suggested we leave it up to quote-destiny-unquote, like I'm sort of saucy minx, and if she brings our paths together again, I'll let him take me out to dinner. I'm glad I didn't let him walk me home, because if I had, it would have been...wait for it...to *his* house. That's right! Ta-da, abra-fucking-cadabra, and all that happy horseshit—he's not only my housemate...he's The Organizer! BTW his name is Chase. You were right, major preppy name, but my God, you gotta see this fucking guy."

My heart flutters, thinking about that kiss. I go on, desperation in my voice.

"What am I gonna do? How am I going to live this summer under the same roof with this yum-yum tasty treat? How can I keep my hands off him? I need your advice. Call me!"

I fling my forearm over my face and hit Send with my free thumb.

A couple minutes pass while I pray for her to respond. Instead of a text, my phone rings.

"Aaaamyyy!!!" I whisper-scream into the phone. "Can you believe—"

"Kacie." Her voice comes across the line like a guttural groan.

I go on. "How am I ever gonna get through this summer—"

"*Kaaaaace...*" She sounds like she's crying, like she's about to tell me my parents died in a fiery crash. Now she has me panicked.

"What? What?"

"You just sent that message to...*The. Entire. House.*"

15

"No, I didn't!" I croak in utter disbelief as I pull my phone away from my face. There's no way I could be that ridiculously dense or moronic.

My eyes dart to the screen, and...

Ohhhhhhhh ffffuuuuuuuuugh!!!

She's right. I accidentally sent my audio message to the group chat, thinking I was in my text chain with Amy. I recall pulling up the chat last night to see if I could plug in the missing names, and with Amy's name at the top of the list I must have...

Shit. Now everyone knows every juicy detail of our kiss. The way it made me feel. My fear of not being able to keep my hands off him this summer.

"Help me!" I hiss into the phone. "Is there a way I can recall the text?"

"I don't think so but I'm googling it right now."

I wait for Amy's response. I think I'm gonna vomit. Or pass out.

"You can't," she reports, her voice sounding as defeated as I feel.

Oh, God. My heart sinks to my feet, taking my entire blood supply with it. I'm either gonna faint, or—

Flee like a felon.

Pulling out my luggage, I start throwing things in. I have to get out of here. Bye-bye, Sea Isle. So long, Fun Girl Summer.

Amy's babbling on the other end, trying to come up with ways for me to save face. There *is* no way. I basically hang up on her in favor of getting out of there. I had no business coming to this place to live with a bunch of strangers, thinking that somehow my life was going to get better. I'm an idiot. And now, I'm going to leave.

As I zip my last bag, the door flings open. It's Wendy, still in last night's fit (as predicted), eyes the size of dinner plates, Rachel and Diane right behind her.

They're here because of the text. They know what a loser I am, and they're about to eject me from the house. I'm literally shivering with gut-wrenching humiliation. Before I can register what's happening, they surround me in a hug.

"I know, I know," Wendy coos as she tightens her embrace. "It happens, girl."

Rachel strokes my back. "It sucks, but we've all been there."

"*All* been there," Diane echoes, chuckling. "I accidentally hit *Reply All* to a company-wide message, thinking I was forwarding it to my friend, complete with comments about what an asshole my boss was. Needless to say, I'm no longer employed there."

"I once texted my friend Sara about how disgusting my boyfriend's mother's house was," Rachel says. "I even attached photos of dust bunnies and baseboard grime as evidence. I accidentally sent it to his mom, who's also named Sarah, but with an H."

I giggle through my tears. "Are you still dating him?"

"Hell no. Sarah-with-an-H broke up with me on his behalf."

Wendy jumps in with her own confession. "I thought I was forwarding a dick pick from a guy I was dating to my friend, along with commentary about how small it was and how he shouldn't be waving it in front of cameras without enhancement. Unfortunately, I also made the mistake of hitting reply instead of forward."

We all laughed at that one.

"I feel like such an asshole. I should move out."

"You'll do no such thing," Diane insisted. "This is a cool

group of people. We'll all have a good laugh about it before the mimosas are even poured."

"What about Chase?" I groan. "I'm completely mortified."

Rachel laughed. "Chase is my cousin. He's the coolest guy around, with the best sense of humor. I'm sure he'll be flattered at your glowing review of his prowess. And I'll bet the other guys will be lining up to find out how he managed to get his tongue to emerge from a woman's hoochy-cooch."

Oh *God*. I'd forgotten all about that crass comment.

"I've learned the best way to deal with a cringe moment is to laugh about it," Diane suggests.

"I guess I should apologize to everyone first," I say.

"No worries. We got you," Rachel says. "Let's go consume cocktails for breakfast."

Upstairs, several housemates are scattered about the living room in varying stages of consciousness. Most looking at their phones, all avoiding my eye contact. The only one not here is Chase.

My instinct is to follow the girls to the kitchen and slink into an island stool, hoping to make myself invisible. Instead, I pull a classic Kacie and call out the pachyderm traipsing through the room.

"Did y'all enjoy that voice text I sent?" I ask the room at large. "Obviously, it was meant for my grandma."

My announcement is met by a smattering of polite chuckles, mixed in with what sounds like a collective gasp of relief.

"I was gonna ask if anyone was up for some hockey," Rex says, sounding serious. "The Flyers are *this close* to winning the Stanley Cup."

"No, but I'd take a yum-yum tasty treat," Jasper says.

Harry winks at Jasper. "You saucy minx, you."

"He can't help it," Wendy joins in. "It's his quote-destiny-unquote."

Everyone laughs, including me. Grateful for this opportunity to not take myself too seriously, I join in with self-mockery of my own. "At least you're not parading around like a mystical sex goddess, like some of us."

"Nice one, Kacie!" someone calls out, and everyone applauds.

I take a bow, my heart swelling over the fact that my housemates are this cool, helping me laugh off my embarrassment.

Jasper approaches and holds out a fist bump. "Way to go, kiddo. Our first faux pas of the summer. Rest assured, there'll be thousands more, even by the end of the weekend."

I breathe a bit more easily, hearing that.

"Speaking of hockey," Rex says. "Here comes the Jersey Devil."

We all look up to see Chase descending from the top floor, jogging down the steps with a big grin on his face. Whatever respite from embarrassment I was beginning to feel instantly evaporates, as my heart nearly leaps from my chest. Not only from sheer humiliation, but because I've never seen a man look so fine in the morning. His hair is tousled once again—this time not from the sea breeze, but from what appears to be a restful night's sleep. The rising sun cascading through the large sliding glass doors lights up his face, and I swear I hear angels sing. He's shirtless, wearing nothing more than his green SICBP shorts, apparently heading to work.

"Top o' the mornin'," he greets us at large.

"Abracadabra! The Organizer's here!" Harry exclaims.

Chase looks confused. "I don't get it."

"Sorry, I was being *tongue* in cheek."

"Still don't get it." Chase shrugs and goes to the fridge and begins packing a cooler.

Does this mean he hasn't listened to my text? I would think, if he'd heard it, he'd be acting very differently.

It's only a matter of time, though.

His phone dings with a notification. As he looks at it, his eyes widen. "Whoa."

Oh God, here it comes. I fight the urge to grab it from his hand and chuck it off the deck before he can play the message.

"Phillies went three extra innings last night," he says.

The guys start discussing the game as Wendy, Diane, and Rachel huddle around me at the kitchen island.

"He must not have heard it," Wendy whispers to me. "Yet."

"Should I steal his phone when he's not looking and delete it?" Rachel asks.

"Delete what?" a deep voice says.

I jump as Chase chomps into an apple beside me.

"Why's everyone acting so weird?" he asks.

"We're just wondering if you—" Rex begins, but he stops speaking as a woman with a blonde bob glides down the stairs. The one who was hanging all over Chase as he masterfully ignored me. She's wearing an oversized SICBP t-shirt, her legs bare.

My heart sinks.

"My man," Rex says as he claps Chase on the back. "Two in one weekend?"

Blonde Bob takes the apple from Chase and bites into it. Keeping the apple in her mouth, she twirls toward Chase like a pig on a roasting pit. I gasp out loud when Chase leans in and bites into the apple from the other side, visions of Adam and Eve dancing in my head.

Rex laughs. "Hey, Chase—can you make your tongue—"

"Worm!" Wendy shrieks, as she bats the apple from their mouths in Rex's direction, who jumps back like he just wandered into an ax-throwing contest.

"What the—"

"Sorry, guys, there was a huge worm coming out of that apple," Wendy says as she rushes to pick it up and slams it into the trash can.

Chase's gaze locks on me for a moment, and I try to decipher his expression, wondering whether he's heard the text and is pissed about me outing us, or whether he's flattered at my outrageous drivel about our kiss. If I were to wager a guess, I'd say he hasn't heard it.

At least he's looking at me today, after avoiding me last night.

"What time are we rallying tonight?" someone asks.

"Six," says another.

Just like that, the group begins discussing the party we're throwing tonight. I'm relieved they've moved on from my blunder, but I get no relief from impending doom. I'm waiting for the other shoe to drop on Chase's phone, alerting him he has a pending text from yours truly.

My ears do perk up when I hear No-sleeve Steve say we can invite whomever we want to the party tonight. Maybe I'll invite Ben, who said he'd be back down today, sans Leo. That way, I'll have someone familiar to hang with to help dispel the myth I've created about longing for Chase, who no doubt will be entertaining the enchanting Eve and her apple-tempting ways.

I know I shouldn't care who he spends his time with. Being with another woman last night only confirms my player suspicions. Even if I'd been interested in pursuing something with him despite that, his status as my housemate serves as a preemptive strike against anything more happening between us. Which also means the jealousy I feel creeping through me is unwarranted. And uninvited. I'm in control here, not my libido.

Despite wanting to drown my conflicted emotions in mimosas, I only allow myself one, as I'm to report for my new job at ten.

I'm in the garage applying sunscreen when I hear a familiar voice behind me.

"How's it looking, Jellyfish?"

I'm startled by his presence. My heart races, thinking he's going to confront me about the text, tear me a new asshole, tell me I'm the biggest jerk on the planet for divulging our hookup.

Instead, he squats down. "Let me take a look."

He rubs his thumb over my sore, his fingers wrapping around the back of my calf. The very touch of his hands shoots flames up my leg.

"Looking pretty good there, Kacie," he says. "I think the jelly spared you."

"It was the first aid response that did it. Jelly didn't stand a chance with Chase the Lifeguard on hand."

He smiles politely. "Glad to be of service, ma'am." He stands. "Off to work. Enjoy your day."

While I'm relieved at our pleasant exchange, something seems off. He's not exuding the same warmth and friendliness he did when we met the other night. Then again, who can blame him? I lied to him about my name and where I was staying this summer. Protection defense aside, it pretty much makes me an asshole. At the very least, a liar. Not a great first impression.

Or...maybe he *has* heard the text. I consider saying something but don't want to alert him to it if he somehow missed it. I know messages sometimes get lost in an avalanche of notifications, so if his inbox is anything like mine, it's possible it got buried somehow. I also consider making a joke, but I'm not sure how it will land. Or if he'll find humor in the way I outed our kiss in such a crass manner. It was one thing to laugh off my faux pas with the housemates, but Chase may not find it so funny.

I stand there indecisively. Do I apologize? Make a joke? Grab his phone and throw it into oncoming traffic in hopes a set of Goodyears crushes it to smithereens?

Before I can decide, he's rolling down the driveway on his bike, giving a dismissive wave over his shoulder.

Shit. With no other choice, it's off to work I go—impending doom in tow.

16

Gina wasn't kidding when she said the shack does well on weekends. On my first day of work, we rent over $400 in equipment. Bonus: only one of the umbrellas I install blows away. Fortunately, all beach-going humanity is spared.

Double bonus: Chase isn't assigned to our beach today. I don't want to be there when he finally hears my text.

I watch as my housemates trickle down to the beach, one by one, forming a large circle with their chairs and coolers. Throughout the day, several come over to talk to me, which helps me feel more connected to them.

During a lull after the morning rush, Gina goes off to grab us something for lunch, and I text Ben about the party. He responds to say he'll be there. I'm thankful I'll have a companion tonight.

Before I know it, it's five o'clock, the official end of my first day of work. After taking an outdoor shower, I go inside to help with party prep. Already, the kitchen and deck are filling up with people. While I was hard at work, wrestling umbrellas and gathering abandoned beach chairs, the guys rigged a tiki bar on the deck. Fairy lights zig and zag from the roof to a pergola I swear wasn't there last night. The handiwork of weekday workers who get to spend their weekends sitting on the beach, drinking from red Solo cups, and building party pergolas.

I'm relieved when Ben finally arrives. Wendy has been all over No-sleeve, and Diane and Rachel are entertaining friends from home. Chase is nowhere to be found, so I spend the better part of that first hour wandering around, trying to look like I belong.

"Hey, Kacie," Ben says as he leans down and kisses my cheek. "You look amazing."

It's not the first time he's seen me in this sundress, but I'll take it. He wraps his arms around me and kisses the top of my head just as Chase enters the kitchen. Awkward, because it's just the three of us.

"Ben. I'd like you to meet my housemate, Chase," I say, untangling myself from him. "Chase, Ben."

"Nice to meet you, Ben," Chase says, shaking his hand. He looks from Ben to me, and back to Ben again, as a look of enlightenment crosses his face.

"Ohhh. *Ben!*"

Ben seems oblivious, but in his defense, he has no idea what's transpired since I arrived here. He knows nothing about the jellyfish sting, the heroic save, or the kiss between me and the guy who continues to stare him down. Or the barely perceptible dismay that flashes across his face before he turns to walk away.

I'm struck with a horrifying realization. I never told Chase the name of the guy I referred to as my *complication*. The only way he would've heard Ben's name is from my group text.

Does this mean...?

I'm internally freaking out, trying to recall if there was any other time I would've referenced his name, but my thoughts are interrupted when Ben asks to see the house. Relieved for the distraction, I take him on a tour that ends in my bedroom.

"Nice room," he remarks as he looks around. "Cozy lair you got here."

He sits on the end of the bed, leaning back on his elbow. When he pats the space next to him, I dutifully sit.

"How's it going so far?" he asks. "Happy you joined a shore house?"

"Yeah," I say, trying hard not to focus on the way he's rubbing his hand up and down the small of my back. We've given each other backrubs before, but tonight, his touch seems different. More intentional or something. And it feels *amazing*.

I think about bringing up that night in my office, but with a raging party upstairs, it doesn't feel right.

"How's Leo doing with the new custody setup?" I ask instead.

"He seems okay. He's only cried once about missing his mom. My sister's keeping him busy. Being with cousins definitely helps."

"That's great."

"I'll be bringing him down Monday for the summer. His surf lessons begin on Tuesday."

"Wow, at four years old? They certainly start 'em early."

"You forgot he just turned *this many*," Ben jokes, holding up five fingers.

That's right, I forgot about the party they had for him before his mom moved to California. He'll be heading off to kindergarten in the fall.

"His surf lessons are on Tuesdays and Thursdays from seven to nine," Ben continues. "Which works out perfectly, because I'll drop him off before I head to work. The nanny will pick him up after his class and entertain him till I'm home for dinner." He looks up at me. "I'm really pumped for this summer, dialing back a bit on work to spend time with Leo. And you, of course."

"I'd love that." Including me in their summer plans? I'm definitely not imagining the shifting sentiments between us.

"I'm still childless tomorrow night," he says, "if you'll let me take you out to dinner."

My heart flutters over the invitation, even if I'm the one who suggested it to thank him for driving me down here.

"I think I'll let you."

"Good. I've been looking forward to it."

Ben lies all the way back and pulls me with him so I'm lying next to him, his arm under my neck, his fingers now trailing up and down my forearm. My leg instinctively bends over his. We've lain like this plenty of times throughout our friendship, so the physical proximity is nothing new—again, it just feels different. Especially the way his fingertips brush softly against my skin. I feel an instant rush go through me, followed by a dash of trepidation. The thought of getting involved with someone again, even someone as safe as Ben, is nonetheless terrifying.

"This is nice," he says.

"Mmm," I murmur in response.

We lay there for a moment as silence falls between us. My heart races as he nuzzles his head against mine, still stroking my arm with the lightest touch.

Suddenly, Wendy appears in the open doorway. We both jolt upright, as if we've just been caught doing the nasty.

"Sorry. I'm just here for my jacket," she says as she shimmies toward the closet, hand over her eyes.

I laugh. "It's okay, Wendy. This is Ben, my good friend."

"Hey, Ben," she says sheepishly as she holds out her hand for a shake. "I'm just gonna grab this and I'll be outta your hair."

As she heads for the door, she asks if she should close it.

"No, that's fine," we both say simultaneously, then laugh.

"I'm ready for another," Ben says, shaking his empty beer bottle. "How 'bout you?"

Back upstairs, we refill our drinks and join others on the deck where we get pulled into a heated discussion of the Eagles' recent draft picks and their likelihood of winning yet another Super Bowl. The drinks have been flowing, and my housemates are letting their true colors fly, allowing me to get to know them a bit more. I learn Rex is a football coach for one of the city high schools, Harry is a distant relative of the Kelce brothers, and Builder Bob is a closet Cowboys fan, but hasn't come out yet to his Eagles-loving coworkers, lest he take an ax to the head when he's not looking.

I hear the laughter of two people racing up the outside steps to the deck. It's Shaniya, one of our roomies, and her boyfriend, Tyler.

"Hey, guys," Shaniya says as they stand before us. "So...this just happened." She thrusts out her left hand, where a simple band of gold rests on her third finger. "We're engaged!"

The girls erupt in squeals of delight. As everyone jumps in to congratulate the happy couple, I refrain from spouting my TV commercial script. Yet, for a nanosecond, I'm captivated by the look of joy on their faces, something I've not witnessed before. (See? I'm already evolving into a more positive person, and summer's barely begun.)

Ben leans over and whispers in my ear. "Sucks to be them."

"I'll say," I whisper back, but for some reason, I don't quite believe myself.

Shaniya informs us they'll be married on July 31 in a simple beach ceremony. "Just our immediate fam, a few friends, and you guys, if you wanna join us."

Great, just what I need. Yet another wedding to attend, after a batch of coworkers all got married this year. No joke, it was as if someone had laced the water cooler with some sort of love potion. I count nine weeks until their wedding—plenty of time to talk her out of it. (Relax! I'm only kidding.)

Ben announces he has to get going. "Got some work to do on this case tomorrow, before Hurricane Leo hits on Monday."

I chuckle at his reference to the energetic boy. I'm not surprised he's working on a holiday weekend, given we're cut from the same work-obsessed cloth. Well, at least until this summer.

After he leaves, I'm helping myself to a Corona from the cooler on the deck when Chase appears.

"So that's the illustrious Ben?" he asks, with a teasing gleam in his eye.

I twist open the top and take a huge swig. "That's him."

"*Hmm.*"

His proximity has my heart racing. I don't know what it is about this man, but there's some sort of magnetism between us. The deck is crowded and getting more so by the moment, to the point where we're jostled up against a railing, our faces inches from one another, just like that night in the bar.

"What's going on? Why is the deck suddenly so crowded?" I ask.

A loud boom sounds above us, followed by the crackling of falling fireworks.

"Memorial Day celebration," Chase says, smiling down at me. "Happy first weekend of summer, Kacie. Kinda makes me want to...I dunno...*create a bucket list.*"

He turns and disappears into the crowd as I feel the color drain from my face.

There's only one way he could know about the bucket list.

He's heard the group text.

17

I spend most of the night tossing and turning, waffling between being sure Chase heard the audio text, and harboring false hope he hasn't. Could I have mentioned Ben's name at some other point? Could the reference to the bucket list have been coincidental? Amy certainly didn't invent the concept when she created mine. I know I'm grasping at straws, but still…if he heard it, he's acting very cool about it. Which is weird.

When morning comes, I roll over to find Wendy already awake.

"Good morning!" she says. "The girls and I are grabbing coffee. Wanna join us?"

"That sounds wonderful."

Diane, Rachel, Wendy, and I head to Red White & Brew, snagging the last open table. We spend the next hour chatting about our lives. I already know that Wendy works as an analyst for Amy's environmental firm, which is how they know each other. Rachel is an accountant, and Diane is an associate professor of nursing at the University of Pennsylvania.

"Wow, that's impressive," I say. "How do you like it? I've often thought about teaching one day, after I retire from law."

"I love it. Great schedule, love the subject matter, and it's fun to work with college-aged kids now that I'm in my thirties. Keeps you young, for sure."

I learn Diane and Rachel are both in serious relationships. They each met their boyfriends in Sea Isle last summer—Rachel at a party, and Diane standing in line at the Ocean Drive waiting to get in.

Diane regales us with her story. She was with a male friend the night she met her boyfriend, who mistakenly thought she was taken, so he didn't ask for her number. She was disappointed, thinking he wasn't interested. Weeks later, she was at The Point—Sea Isle's tropical-themed outdoor bar—when he walked in. He was supposed to be at a golf outing, but it had rained that morning. He finally worked up the nerve to ask if she was still with her boyfriend, and they had a good laugh over his misunderstanding of her single status.

The rest was history.

"They were destined to be together," Rachel swoons.

"Wish me the same luck," Wendy says, informing us she's single but hoping not to be by summer's end. I'm guessing No-sleeve is her intended victim, judging by the way they've been hanging all over each other. I wonder if she knows about the housemate rule, or whether she simply doesn't care. I'm dying to ask, but don't want to sound judgy.

"Who's the hottie you were with last night, Kacie?" Diane asks.

"Ben—my good friend."

"You sure he's just a friend?" Wendy teases.

"He seems really into you, the way he kept giving you puppy dog eyes all night," Rachel says.

"I think they were Corona eyes," I joke. I don't know why—it's not as if he drank any more than the rest of us. It's just in my nature to deflect someone's compliment with a joke. Still, my heart thrums with satisfaction that they've noticed what I've been feeling. Maybe I'm not crazy after all.

"I'm sure he's a much better catch than my cousin," Rachel says. "I mean, Chase is a great guy and all, but...just a bit of a ladies' man."

Ah-*ha!* Just as I suspected. Good thing I put the kibosh on going any further with him.

Back at the house, I pull out my bucket list and put a check-mark next to *#3: Make Some Girlfriends.* It's been a long time since I've hung out with women who aren't Amy, and I'm amazed at how easily we bonded. I'm happy I get to spend the summer with them and hope to soon get to know the other women as well. Becky, Shaniya, and Celeste share the triple on our floor. So far, they've kept to themselves, but hopefully that changes. I record my thoughts in my journal before heading off to work.

If you can call it that. Work once consisted of sifting through the rubble of imploded marriages, trying to salvage whatever I could for my clients. Threatening opposing counsel, begging judges for favorable rulings, writing my clients' unhappy endings. Now, it consists of flinging beach chairs and umbrellas at vacationers. I think I prefer this type of work, but not for long. I'm too much of an overachiever to have my brain stay dormant. I'll soon need to restart the career I spent a fortune on for schooling (or start a new one), but each time I think about practicing law again, I find something more interesting to do. Like stare into the abyss, wondering if there's literally anything else I'm qualified to do.

When a summer storm rolls in later that afternoon, Gina teaches me how to close the shack in preparation for a storm. It's her last day, so after this, I'm on my own. Just as we finish, the skies open up and fat, cool droplets plunk down in a lazy cascade. We take cover in the shack.

"Are you happy you've taken this job?" Gina asks.

"Absolutely. It's different than anything I've ever done, which is exactly what I needed this summer."

"I'm glad." She gives me a curious smile. "I hope everything works out with that cute lifeguard."

Her comment takes me by surprise. What does she know about the cute lifeguard?

"I saw you guys that day you got stung by a jelly."

"How did you know I got stung?"

"News travels fast on the beach. Anytime guards come off the stand to help someone, it's a spectacle. Especially when it involves a rescue."

"It wasn't exactly a rescue…"

"Girl, I saw you rolling around in the ocean."

"Okay." I jokingly roll my eyes. "Rescue it was."

"I also saw the way he kept looking over at you when you weren't looking. I don't know him personally, but he does have a bit of a rep on the beach as being—well, very friendly with the women."

See? Even without my promise ring, I can spot a player from a mile away.

"But he seemed—I dunno. More interested in you than I've seen him with others. Even before the rescue, that's why it drew my attention. I think I even saw sparks."

I laugh out loud, trying to slow the pounding of my heart. Then again, what does it matter what she thinks?

"He's my housemate this summer," I confide.

"Oh, no! Not good. You should never fall for one of your housemates. If it doesn't work out, it can ruin your whole summer."

"Trust me, that's not gonna happen."

Gina eyes me. "By the look on your flushing face, I'd say it already has."

"No, really. I'm not here to—"

Suddenly, the rain picks up. Laughing, we dash to the promenade where we give each other a quick hug.

"Thanks for hooking me up with this job," I say. "Good luck with your new adventure."

"Enjoy that summer love!" she calls out as she takes off.

I stand there, letting the rain fall on me. It's refreshing, wiping away the humidity that's blanketed my skin all day. Beneath it, a layer of career-induced permafrost begins to melt away as I think about the summer that lies ahead. It feels…hopeful.

Struck with uncharacteristic giddiness, I twirl around, arms wide open, trying to catch raindrops with my mouth. It's only my second full day of summer, but it feels like the weight of my despair-filled life is slowly lifting. The drops are still light, playful, as I close my eyes and revel in the moment.

In the distance, I hear laughter. Wondering if I'm the cause of someone's merriment, embarrassment takes over, causing me to suddenly halt my momentum.

In physics, there's this thing: for every action, there's a reaction. And the reaction to my sudden stop is my bare foot slipping on the sole of the rubber flip-flop, causing me to lose my balance and careen sideways—headfirst—across the promenade.

Right into an oncoming bicyclist.

"Watch it!" he shouts as he stops, but not before I topple backwards onto my ass.

I probably don't have to tell you who it is.

"What was that all about?" Chase asks, his eyes twinkling with amusement. He leans his bike against the railing and offers me a hand. Hoisting me up, I come within inches of his bare chest.

He's still shirtless and tan, his skin glistening from the rain. I'm rendered breathless for a second, but I'm not sure if it's because the rain has picked up and is now dripping into my (unintentionally gaping) mouth, or because the storm has sucked the oxygen from the island. Perhaps it's the vision before me. I can protest all I want about this man, but there's something raw and animalistic about the way I feel drawn to him. I fight the urge to snake my arms around his waist and rest my cheek against his perfectly sculpted chest.

"Auditioning for *Interpretive Dancing with the Stars*?"

"Already made it," I say, trying to catch my breath. "This is just practice."

"Doesn't surprise me, with moves like that. Where's your partner? What's his name again—Baryshnikov? I'm guessing he's a guy with two left feet, but a big you-know-what."

"No, I don't know what," I teasingly challenge. "Enlighten me."

"A big *brain*," he says. "God, Kacie, you gotta get your mind out of the gutter."

"Why, when it lives there rent-free?"

It feels good to be bantering with him again, the other day's awkwardness washing away with the rain.

It's pouring now, and Chase grabs his bike. "Here, get on. I'll give you a ride."

Every aspect of personal injury law springs to mind, wondering how a grown-ass woman can jump on a bike with a grown-ass man and not end up in the grown-ass ER, along with a law school study in contributory negligence.

"The handlebars," he yells over the roar of the downpour.

"You won't be able to steer," I object.

"You're basically the size of a Barbie doll. I can handle it."

I jump on, hoping he knows more about physics than I do, because I can't imagine a way in which this doesn't end in years of litigation. Sure enough, he glides us down the promenade ramp and coasts us into our open garage.

"Made it just in time!" he exclaims after a crack of thunder booms above.

We find our housemates in varying stages of shore exodus, all packing up their cars to beat the scary-Sunday return-to-Philly-traffic, despite that tomorrow is Memorial Day. I think its weird that everyone's leaving tonight when tomorrow is the holiday, but I'm told a bunch are attending a mutual friend's wedding in the city, and the rest have hometown parties.

After the last stragglers leave, I get ready for my dinner date with Ben before heading upstairs to grab a water bottle. The house, now emptied of its occupants, is eerily silent—but for the running of the shower upstairs, coming from Chase's primary suite. As excited as I am to be having dinner with Ben tonight, I'm having a tough time blocking my mind from envisioning what's going on up there in that shower. I'm half tempted to run in and sneak a peek, but being booked on charges of voyeurism isn't on my bucket list for tonight. I think about the preview I got earlier in the rain, and I'm finding it hard not to imagine how Chase looks up there with water cascading down that rock-solid body, now uninhibited by clothing—

Get a freaking grip, Kacie. I remind myself I'm about to have dinner with my years-long crush who, recently, has given me more-than-friends vibes in a way he never has before. Gotta keep my head in the game, my eyes on the prize.

"You clean up nice, for a jellyfish."

His voice startles me. I turn to find Chase wearing nothing more than a towel around his waist.

Goddammit! I struggle to keep my tongue from rolling out of my mouth, across the floor, and knocking him off his feet.

"Oh! Uh—" I sputter, as if I've been caught red-handed doing something I shouldn't. Like gawking. I bite my tongue for good measure.

"Looks like everyone's taken off by now," he says, joining me at the windows as he stretches, leaning back, arms splayed at his sides. If he's trying to showcase what's going on under that towel, he has my full unwitting attention. Talk about eyes on the prize.

"Did you enjoy your second day of work?" he asks.

"I did." I casually shift away from him before that magnetic pull gets ahold of me.

He gives me a sexy half-smile. "Maybe destiny will work her magic and assign us to the same beach one of these days."

"May the odds be ever in your favor," I tease, quoting a line from *The Hunger Games.*

"May they," he says. "But we don't have to wait until that

happens to hang out, right? Kinda awkward if we're the only two living here all week and we're not."

"If this is your way of getting me in the sack, you can forget it." A warning, carefully packaged as a joke.

"Who said anything about a sack?" He laughs. "I was thinking Chinese and a movie. Perfect night to watch some eighties rom-coms."

Oh.

"I'm not a rom-com kinda gal."

Yeah, like that's the biggest reason for turning down his request. Not the tingling of my nether region, despite him being the poster child of players, or the fact I'm going out with someone else tonight.

"No, not you!" he mocks. "You can't be serious."

"Deadass. It's a question they ask as we're getting sworn in to practice law. *Would you rather spend a Sunday night watching a romantic comedy or sue someone?* And the correct answer is..."

"*When Harry Met Sally* it is."

Another good reason for turning down his request, beyond the obvious—that I already have plans—is because such a night sounds fabulously appealing and dangerously risky. If the way my body hums with electricity in his presence is any indication, I have a feeling we could easily find ourselves back in a lifeguard stand sitch, despite my three reasons not to: (a) player, (b) housemate, (c)...

I know there has to be a third reason. Oh, right...(c) Ben.

I cannot allow Chase's half-clad appearance to derail me from my plans with Ben. I've waited too long for that man to be enticed by another. Chase is displaying a key tactic of a seasoned player—coming on strong, making you think you're the most desirable woman on the planet, evicting thoughts of other men from your mind like non-paying tenants.

Been there. Done that. Not again.

"Sorry, I can't. I'm going out to dinner tonight."

"Ooh, with Boris?"

His reaction makes me chuckle. "Yes."

"Where are we going?"

"Not sure. What, are you my mom now?"

Funny thing for me to say, since my own mom never bothered to ask where I was going. She didn't have to. In a seven-member family, people knew what you were doing before you did.

"Hey," he says.

I glance over, unable to tear my gaze from his eyes, which have gone soft.

"We should probably talk about—"

I jump as a doorbell ring interrupts him. I hadn't even noticed Ben coming up the street. I shoot Chase an apologetic look and head to the stairs.

"Be home by midnight!" Chase calls out behind me.

"Okay, Mom!"

18

Ben and I end up at Carmen's Restaurant, lucky to score a waterside table. The rain has let up, and we have a great open-air view of the boats docked across the bay. I slide onto the bench of the thick wooden picnic table as he opens the bag he brought in.

"BYOB," he announces, pulling out a bottle of wine and presenting it to me on his forearm as if he's a sommelier. "Jessie Creek Winery, Sauvignon Blanc. I recall you loved this wine when we did that Cape May wine tasting tour with our law school friends."

I can't believe he not only noticed, but remembered. That was a long time ago.

A server appears with an opener and glasses. After telling us the specials, she gives us a few minutes to review the menu. He pours the wine and hands me a glass, announcing he has good news.

"My firm's going to be hiring later this summer."

"That's good to hear!" I'm excited, at least I think so, considering it's the only application I still have pending. I ignore the little voice in the back of my mind, asking if this is truly what I want to do with my life. "Put in a good word for me?"

"Already have." He slides his hand across the table and gives mine a squeeze. "It'll be fun to work together again."

Fun wouldn't begin to describe it. I'm warmed by the memory of good times we had in law school, clerking for the same firm in our third year, before his life eventually exploded into a family of three.

Just then, I hear someone say my name. I turn to see a familiar-looking woman approaching our table.

"I thought that was you," the woman says. "It's Mary Applegate. You represented me a couple years ago."

"Of course I remember you, Mary," I say, relieved she introduced herself. While I may have been able to place her as a client, I'd forgotten her name. "How have you been?"

She steps aside and gestures to the man standing next to her. I'm pretty sure it's her ex—the man I helped free her from.

"Remember my hubs, Robert?"

"Uh, yeah..." I sputter, as I shake his outstretched hand.

I stand there, my mouth gaping like the crab traps lining the dock, wondering what on God's green earth brought these two back together. If I recall correctly, their divorce was hella contentious.

"We're on our honeymoon, part two," she explains, hooking her arm with his. "Who would've guessed it, right?"

Robert gives her googly eyes. "Happier than ever."

My first thought, even before *WTF*, is how much they spent on their complicated divorce case. I hope they're not here to demand their money back.

"We finally realized we're meant for each other," Robert says.

"Turns out, marriage takes time and effort, as does anything worth cherishing," Mary adds. "You have to be willing to put some work into it. Which we weren't, first go 'round."

"Not every marriage can be fixed," Robert adds. "Some just aren't meant to work out, no matter how hard the couple tries. We both had a lot to learn about how to communicate better, really listen to each other, have patience..."

My focus shifts to Ben in my periphery, who's raising his personally informed eyebrows in mockery.

"Your husband?" Mary asks, gesturing to Ben, who quickly replaces his smirk with a smile.

"Oh, no!" we both object, probably a bit too vehemently.

Robert chuckles. "Never say never. Look at us!"

"Look at you!" I exclaim, not sure what else to say. I wonder if I should remind Mary of her parting words after we left court that final day, something along the lines of, *That bastard stole the best four years of my life, and I'll never forgive him as long as I live.*

Yet she's back for more. There's no accounting for love.

After they say goodbye, I sink back down in my seat. "Well, that's the surprise of a lifetime."

"It's gotta be about sex," Ben says flatly. "That, or money."

"I dunno, they seemed pretty much...in love. Maybe they just weren't in the right headspace the first time around to make it work."

"No one who marries is ever in their right headspace."

"Watch it, you're sounding like me now," I tease.

While that's our usual banter about the Institution of Perpetual Sorrow, for some reason I believe in this couple. I think of Chase's parents, how happy he claimed they'd been. Perhaps it does work out for some. Look at me, giving marriage its props.

"Trust me, it's the worst thing ever," Ben says, taking a swig of wine with a twinkle of amusement. "Beyond the hefty divorce fees bloodthirsty attorneys suck out of you."

"Haha," I deadpan.

Now seems like a good time to bring up the subject of us. I'm not dissuaded by his attitude about marriage. This is the way he and I have always talked about it. Like I said before, that's not what I want with him. I just want to peacefully coexist in a committed relationship, fearing anything beyond that.

"How've you been doing since the divorce?" I ask. I want to know this before I plunge into a discussion of us, to gauge if he's moving on or still traumatized by the finality of it.

"I'm doing okay. Good days and bad. At times, I'm sad it didn't work out, but mostly I'm fine."

I'm not surprised by this. A period of mourning, even for those who initiate a divorce like Ben did, is typical. People say divorce is the hardest thing you can go through, which is why you'll never see me promising to love anyone "'til death do us part."

See, that's the problem with marriage. It's so terminal. Why not give people an option to renew after five years, much like a car lease? Let's be real—most people marry in their twenties or thirties, when they barely know themselves. How can they possibly know what they need from another person? We change a lot throughout our lifetime, especially during those formative years. Removing the onus of staying together forever would lessen the burden, allow couples to grow as individuals without dropping guap when they grow in different directions.

"How's Angi doing with it all?" I ask from a place of genuine concern. While all's fair in love, war, and divorce court, I generally don't wish ill will on my clients' exes. Despite that she and I were never that close, she was once a fellow classmate and, more recently, the wife of my good friend. Which means I probably violated some rule of ethics in representing Ben against her, but I only agreed knowing their ultimate split was amicable. By the time he hired me, they'd already had the fights, the sobbing meltdowns, the burdensome weight of finger-on-trigger before they pulled it. It's probably more of an ethical violation that I've been secretly in love with him for years. But if you don't tell the Attorney Disciplinary Board, I won't either.

"Angi's doing well," he responds. "Seems we parent better from different ends of the country than in the same house."

That's good to hear, for Leo's sake.

"Have you started dating yet?" The question escapes me before I can stop myself. I'm not sure I want to hear his answer, but I'm trying to get around to the topic of *us*. If he says yes, I'll bury it as proof he's not interested in dating *me*.

"Nah." He waves me off. "Not now, at least. I just want to enjoy Leo this summer before he starts school, give us time to bond and make sure he's in a good place with this upheaval."

Before I can respond, he raises his glass and continues.

"Maybe, then, you and I can talk about exploring...you know...this." Giving me a poignant look, he sips his wine without taking his eyes off mine. "At long last."

My pulse quickens with joy over confirmation of his interest. At long last! But what does he mean by that—how long? I'd ask, but my heart is beating so fast I can't catch my breath.

Putting the glass down, he takes my hand. "Look at us both being single for the first time since law school. Kinda crazy, isn't it?"

Breathless, I can only nod.

"I'd love to take you out on a real date, once I get Leo here and settled in. Hopefully the nanny will agree to watch him one night. Not that this isn't a date," he quickly adds. "But you suggested this dinner, and I want to extend an invitation of my own."

The server appears just then to take our order, and I can barely remember what it is I wanted—king crab legs or a king-sized suite? Maybe both, a bottle of chilled champagne, and some fluffy robes to go with it...

The server gives me an odd look. Did I just say all that out loud?

"She's asking what sides you want?" Ben prompts.

"Oh! Uh...side salad with ranch dressing and a baked potato. Sorry."

After she leaves, talk switches to other topics—his case, Leo, our observations of the people coming in from the boats tied up at the dock. The setting sun casts a rosy glow on Ben's beautiful smile, dances off his mocha hair, casting his otherwise dark chocolate eyes in a lighter shade of hazel. He's never looked so good to me as he does right now.

Our small talk continues until after we finish our meal, when Ben slides his plate away and takes my hand.

"Thanks for dining with me tonight, Kacie. Like I said, it's my treat."

"If you insist," I say, smiling.

"I do. Whoa!" He looks up at me and laughs. "Those are words you're never gonna hear from me again. How 'bout...I don't?"

"How about 'no fucking way'?" I joke, but for some odd reason, it strikes an off chord with me. I don't know why. We've bonded over our mutual disdain of marriage, but for some reason, it makes me feel a bit sad. Perhaps seeing my client and her former ex reunited, hearing about Chase's parents, and seeing Shaniya and Tyler's post-proposal glow, has somehow gotten under my skin.

"I should get you home," Ben says. "I need to be up early to get back to the city and fetch Leo, but I'm looking forward to doing this again."

I'm filled with joy knowing I haven't imagined the shift between us. The *more* I've been waiting for. As we get up to leave, it takes everything I have to keep from melting into the wooden floorboards of the old bayside restaurant.

Out on the street, he takes my hand in his. It feels warm, safe. Protective. We've held hands before, but this feels more intimate.

"Is this okay?" he asks.

"Yes." I sound cool enough, but inside, I'm struggling not to scream it out and break into an end zone celebration dance.

We take our time walking home, our conversation turning to the new shops and restaurants we discover as we head to my house. On my front porch, he turns and takes me in his arms.

"I'm excited to spend time with you this summer. It feels like the start of something new. Something I've wanted to explore for some time now."

If words could knock one down, consider me walloped. Those last four words deliver a total KO. For a sharp-witted, wordsmith-happy, snappy-comeback attorney, I can't think of anything to say in response to his parting comment. Other than, "Me too."

He kisses my forehead with a promise to call me tomorrow. I'm lowkey disappointed, wishing for more, but I remind myself to be patient.

Inside, music is blaring upstairs, which means Chase is still awake. I'm happy to have company, knowing I'm only going to toss and turn and mull this night over in my head to the point I can't sleep.

I stop dead in my tracks when I see he's with someone. Eve, of blonde bob fame. They're sitting close together on the couch, bottle of wine on the coffee table before them. They don't see me, so I back down the steps and retreat to my room.

Good for him. Two nights in the same week with the same woman. Maybe his cousin is wrong about him and he's finally settling down with someone. Perhaps now the two of us can go about the business of just being friends and housemates without tantalizing temptation tugging at us. Knowing Ben's all in, I'm confident I can ignore the dangling carrot that is Chase.

Sorry. *Was* Chase.

19

I t's a gorgeous Memorial Day, cloudless with considerably less humidity after yesterday's showers. The beach is busy with the holiday crowd, but by three, it empties as people prepare to return to the city.

You'll be happy to know that my first day flying solo at work goes well. Despite a few moments of uncertainty, I'm reminded how lucky I am to be here instead of arguing in court over who gets the linen tablecloths that no one uses but suddenly can't live without.

As five o'clock nears, I begin packing it in when a man approaches.

"What time do we need to return the equipment?" he asks.

"I close at five," I tell him.

"Okay..." He looks back at his family. I remember them from earlier, when they rented chairs, umbrellas, and boogie boards. "We're waiting on pizza to be delivered, but I saw you packing things up. I guess we can wait up on the promenade and have our pizza there."

I feel bad not offering to stay later, but I was planning on going for a run after work before meeting up with Oops and friends for happy hour.

"It's my son's birthday," he continues. "He once saw someone order pizza on the beach and thought it was the coolest thing. We're from Erie and don't get to the beach much."

Now I really feel bad, especially when a kid, presumably Birthday Boy, runs over to us. "Dad, can we boogie board while we wait for the pizza?"

"I'm afraid we have to wrap it up, buddy," he says, squatting down to the child who must be around Leo's age. "It's time to return everything. If we try to eat on the beach without an umbrella, the seagulls will fly away with our pizza."

I think of Ben, how he can't wait to spend time with his child at the shore this summer. I look into the apologetic eyes of the dad and my heart flops. I have two hours before I'm due to meet Oops. I can skip the run (points added for thinking about taking one). Surely their beach picnic won't take that long.

"I can stay a little longer," I say. "Why don't you guys enjoy your pizza and when you're all done, I'll pack everything up for you."

"You'd do that for us?" the dad says. "It would mean the world to him. To us. It's been a tough year. We could only afford one night's stay, not a week like we usually do."

My heart lurches, knowing this is the plight of many American families—no longer able to afford a simple week at the beach.

"It's my pleasure," I assure him.

As father and son walk away holding hands, a smile forms on my crusty divorce lawyer heart. Their gratitude over something as small as extra beach time is so Western Pennsylvania of them. Being from Erie means they're geographically closer to the kindhearted Midwest than we are in Philly, where our preferred greeting is a middle finger. I'm happy to do them this solid. This could be the charitable action required of my bucket list.

I pull the journal from my beach bag for confirmation. Yup, right there—*#6: Do something charitable.* Not entirely sure giving up a run I didn't want to take in the first place counts, but it should.

Upon further inspection, I note I've already accomplished the first four bucket list items. Go me!

I text Amy, but not before ascertaining I'm *only* texting Amy. Don't need to relive that trauma again.

> Bucket list update: Four days in, four bucket items accomplished. Kissed a guy on the beach. Did something out of character. Made some girlfriends. And now, did something charitable.

> Okay, rewind. What did you do out of character?

That's right, she doesn't know I've become a paid beach bum. She knows about the first item...thank you, group text. I also told her how I've bonded with the three women. But she doesn't know about the job, or this selfless act of charity.

I take a selfie with the beach shack behind me and send it along with this message.

> My summer job. From divorcing couples to mounting beach umbrellas, I'd say that's pretty uncharacteristic.

> Agreed. What have you done that's charitable?

I text her the story about the guy and the pizza picnic, and how I've given up going for a run so they can stay and enjoy their time.

> LOL Kacie, that's being a decent person. Doesn't rise to the level of "charitable" I'd intended.

> So sorry Mother Teresa. What shall I do instead?

> Something that truly helps another. Human, or creature.

Save a manatee. Assist the elderly. Something bigger than forgoing a run you know you weren't going to take anyway.

Touché.

So, I've accomplished *three* things on the bucket list. I still consider that a win, having been here less than a week.

I purposely don't tell her about my date with Ben. I don't want her pointing out he only wants to *talk about* exploring options with me. Which is fine by me—I'll let the slow burn, friends-to-lovers anticipation percolate in the background while I go about the business of fixing my life.

Settling into a chair, I pull out a pen. I'll take this time to update my journal so I can show Judge Judy over there in the UK all the effort I'm putting into this silly project of hers. In the distance, a delivery guy heads toward the family with a stack of pizza boxes. Good, won't be long now.

I get lost in my writing for a while, until suddenly I feel a presence behind me.

"Gotcha!" the presence yells as he grabs my shoulders, scaring the living shit out of me.

I scream, toss my journal into the air, and lose five years off my life. "What the *fuck*!"

The presence starts chortling. It's Chase, still in his lifeguard trunks, still without a shirt. Still hot AF.

And...still not for the taking.

"I was riding home from my shift and saw you're still here," he says. "It's after five, which means you're currently in violation of one of the major house rules."

"Oh yeah?" I ask. "Which rule?"

"The *Happy Hour Begins at Five Sharp* rule, where *all work must cease and drinks must flow*. Obviously, you haven't read the house handbook, a prerequisite for group living. The rule can be found in Section 1(a)2."

"Oh, but you're wrong. I've not only read the handbook, I've memorized it. Might I remind you of Section 2(b)3? *Thou shall not prohibit a fellow housemate from performing her Very Important Job in the name of alcohol.*"

"I scoff at your assertion you've memorized the handbook. Because if you had, you'd recall Section 3(c)4 states, *No rule contained herein shall trump the happy hour rule.*"

"Shit, I'd forgotten about that."

"Looks like you've got some reading to do. Speaking of which..." He retrieves my journal from the sand where it landed—bucket list face up—and glances at the open page. "*Number 1: Kiss a hot guy—*"

I grab it from him so hard I nearly rip his hand off. His eyes twinkle with amusement as he steps closer, smelling of sunshine and sunscreen. His proximity threatens to take over more than just my olfactory senses, as it did the other night.

"I can make that happen right now, you know," he teases as he lightly bites his bottom lip.

"It says, 'kiss a *hot* guy.'"

"You're right." He gives me a sexy half-smile. "Not for nothing, but there's a checkmark next to that item. I'm assuming the other night covered it?"

"I have no idea what you're talking about," I say, turning to hide a smile.

A voice comes from behind me—Birthday Boy's father. "Miss? We're done with our party. Just wanted to thank you for staying late. I can't tell you how much this means to us. Hopefully, this'll show you."

He presses a hundred-dollar bill into my hand.

"Sir, I can't take this from you," I say, thrusting it back at him. "I appreciate it, but I'd rather you use this to treat your family to something special tonight."

He holds up a hand in refusal. "We're going to the board-walk, the tickets are already purchased, and you've allowed us to enjoy our dinner before we go. Thank you, but I won't be taking that money back." He gestures to Chase. "Why not treat your boyfriend to something special?"

I'm about to object, but he's shaking Chase's hand. "Thanks for keeping our beaches safe. I appreciate all you lifeguards do."

After the man leaves, I show Chase the C-note. "That was generous of him."

"As it was for you to allow them extra time. Well-deserved, Kacie Layne."

Once the family leaves the beach, I head over to pack away their rented equipment.

Chase follows. "Let me help you."

Breaking down the equipment, I laugh as Chase straps four beach chairs to his back and hoists two umbrellas on his shoulders.

"You're hired," I tease.

"Don't let this brawn fool you," he says. "I'm all brains too."

"As big as Ben's?" I throw a raised eyebrow at him as a callback to his statement from yesterday.

"Bigger." He gives me a smile as he stops walking. "Because mine's devoid of complications."

"I thought you had them too?" I ask as I keep walking. "Certainly looked like it the other night."

"Not where you're concerned."

Thank God he's behind me and can't see my involuntary facial contortion as my brain screams, *OMG!* If that isn't a blatant come-on, I don't know what is. Thank God we're back at the shack, and I can distract myself with putting things away.

"Thanks for your help," I say after locking up. "You made that much easier."

"My pleasure, but now you owe me. And I know just how you can repay your debt."

"Oh, boy," I say, bracing myself for a raunchy suggestion. "I can't wait to hear this one."

"Come sailing with me."

Not what I expected. I laugh out loud as the theme song from *Gilligan's Island* plays in my head.

He points to a line of small fiberglass sailboats shored along the beach. "The Sunfish with the rainbow sail is mine. I was about to take it for a spin."

"I don't know..." While I'd love to go sailing with him, time's creeping closer to when I'm supposed to meet up with Oops and friends at O'Donnell's Pour House. Not that they'll miss me.

"Come one, Kace. Just you, me, and the setting sun. There's nothing like being out on the water at this time of day."

"Okay," I acquiesce. "As long as you promise not to *Gilligan's Island* me."

"I make no such promises, Mary Ann," he says.

I love that he gets my reference to the old sitcom, one I used to binge with friends in college as we placed bets on whether Mary Ann and the Professor ever got together.

"Just a three-hour tour," he says, then drops his voice to a deep baritone and sings, "*A three-hour tour.*"

20

Chase helps me onto the Sunfish and pushes us until we're out of the breaker zone before effortlessly hopping on. He settles in next to me and maneuvers the sail as we bob over gentle swells. I'm awestruck over how silent it is beyond the waves. I marvel at how the setting sun has cast its spell, turning the clouds an orangy-pink and transforming the usual murky green water of the Atlantic into a sea of sparkling emeralds.

It strikes me as interesting that, back on land, Chase and I have nearly constant banter between us, but out here, we're silent. As if finding comfort in each other's presence and the nature surrounding us.

"This is beautiful, Chase," I finally say. "Thanks for inviting me."

"I figured you'd enjoy it. I love being out here. It's where I do my best thinking."

We're silent again. I dangle my hand in the water, trailing my fingers back and forth, my thoughts drifting along with the Sunfish.

"Lemme know if you see our jellyfish friend," he says, his voice sounding different. Husky, almost. "I'd like to thank him."

"Thank him for what?" I ask, even though I know where he's going with it.

"For this."

Feeling his soft touch on my leg, I turn to find him lying next to me, propped up on an elbow. The setting sun illuminates his smile and his aquamarine eyes sparkle like the sea. Just the light touch of his thumb on my sting site has my head spinning.

"It's how I got to meet you."

He's gazing up at me with a tender look that ignites a spark in me. He's absolutely adorable and handsome at the same time. The spark quickly ignites a raging fire in my soul. I have no idea what is happening—I've never had this physiological reaction to a man simply by the way he looks at me. Not even Ben, who I'm obviously also attracted to...but nothing like this.

Wait. I have had this reaction before. With Seth.

Fuuugh.

And that's when I remember—Chase, like Seth, is a world-class player. And I'm about to be world-classed played.

I'm so not suited up for this game. While I love our good banter and witty repartee, that's about where my player prowess ends. I'm not someone who can flirt and fuck and move along as if nothing happened. Not that we've done the latter, but if eye contact could be considered penetration, consider my soul fucked.

Quick, I need to think of something funny to say. Nothing comes to mind so, instead, my mouth releases one big ass run-on sentence.

"You should thank Amy, my friend, the one who ditched the shore house for a work gig in London, because she's the reason I'm in the house, so we would've met anyway, even if it weren't for the jellyfish—no shade on the jellyfish, but he's rather spineless so..."

I realize I'm babbling like the non-player I am, but it breaks the spell.

Chase turns to the horizon, cups his hands around his mouth, and calls out, "Thank you, Amy!"

I give a nervous laugh, grateful for the distraction.

He looks back at me with a playful grin. "Yes, we would have met eventually. But if I'm being completely honest with you, the first time I saw you, I couldn't look away."

Oh. My. God. He has my insides jiggling like a Jell-O mold in an all-terrain vehicle. I can't be going down this bumpy road again.

Quick—make a joke. "Thanks to my awesome impression of a beaching whale."

"No, before that." He laughs. "Gotta hand it to you, though. I've never seen a creature look so cute trying so hard to stand up in knee-deep surf."

"It was rough!" I defend.

"I know, that's why I give you an A for effort. It's just—I felt something when I pulled you from the ocean."

"A slap on the back from the almighty heavens?"

Here I go again, unable to set humor aside when things veer toward intimate. All thanks to my experience with Seth, which taught me to use humor as a shield, my tongue as a sword, to keep someone from getting too close and being burned again.

Remember your demons. At least, remember Ben.

While Ben may not elicit all the zinging feelings in me Chase does, I know he's trustworthy. Devoted. Let's not forget he married a woman after knocking her up and hung in there with her until she cheated on him. Ben doesn't possess the player capacity to win women over and screw them (literally and figuratively) as guys like Seth and Chase do.

"I did it because you're someone worth saving." He looks deep in my soul again as my pulse picks up its pace. "And because I'd lose my job if I hadn't."

Okay, he's redeemed himself with the truth.

"What's up with Eve?" I ask, not only to deflect his attention but also to remind myself that he's playing me.

"Eve?"

"Yeah, that woman last—" I stop myself from admitting I saw them together last night. "The other morning. The one who took a bite of your forbidden fruit."

He laughs heartily. "Eve. That's a good one. Now I'm not going to remember her real name."

"But you've been with her—"

"I'm kidding," he says. "Her name's Francine. She's a friend of a friend, and we're just casual...friends."

"Hmm. Does she know that?"

"Absolutely," he says without hesitating.

That's not what it looked like to me, but I hope he's right. For her sake. Not for mine, of course—it has nothing to do with me.

"How about you and that guy?" he asks. "What's his name, Bubba?"

I laugh at his continued attempts to suggest Ben's insignificance. "Also just a casual thing. For now."

"Hopefully more, someday?" he asks. "I'm assuming he's the complication you referenced the other night?"

"Yeah. We have—history."

"I get it." He rolls onto his back and gazes at the sky. "I just have one question though..."

I can tell he's hesitant to pose it. Drumming his fingers on his chest, he turns his head and gives me a shy smile.

"Did you mean what you said in your text? The way our kiss made you feel?"

I groan and clamp both hands over my face. "You heard it." So much for the foolish hope I'd been grasping.

"Yeah, I heard it. Sorry," he says, giving a soft chuckle. "I know it was wrong of me to listen after realizing it wasn't intended for the group."

I feel him sit up. He peels my hands from my face.

"Don't be embarrassed," he says, looking deep into my eyes before pulling me in for a hug. I melt against his sunbaked chest and feel the beat-beat-beating of his heart. "We've all done something like that."

"Hands down, *the* most humiliating thing I've ever done," I say, pulling away. "Thank God for the girls—they rallied around me, told me to laugh it off, even helped by making jokes about it."

"I felt so bad for you."

"Yet you've been acting as if you didn't hear it. Why?"

"Because I didn't want to make you feel worse. I'm sorry for even bringing it up now."

"I'd rather address the elephant than not."

He's silent for a moment as he regards me pensively. "It also kinda scared me, if I'm being honest."

"Oh God," I groan again, dropping my head into my crossed arms, cradling my knees, trying to make myself as small as possible.

I'm instantly taken back to fifth grade, when I passed a note to a boy I liked. It read, *I really like you! Will you be my boyfriend?* The kid shrieked out loud, tossed the note in the air, and ran down the hall, nearly knocking over our math teacher. Another kid grabbed the note and read it aloud to the crowded hallway. News of my romantic faux pas spread so fast through Martin Van Buren Middle School that the entire student body knew about it within the hour. Including my seventh-grade sister, who got wind of the scandal and practically tackled me on the playground.

"Don't *ever* tell a boy you like him before he says it first!" Robin scolded. "You only make them scream and run away when you do that."

It's advice I've taken to heart (*see:* why I've never told Ben how I feel about him). That is, until I recently passed the adult version of a crush note via household group chat.

Chase's voice is serious. "What's scary is...I feel the same way about our kiss."

My head shoots up, meeting his gaze.

"Although I don't have a vagina for a tongue to emerge from, I do have something else in its place, and it certainly likes to replay that kiss. Like...all the time."

Holy fuck. My heart is thundering in my chest. I swallow to keep it from breaking through my ribcage as all thoughts of Ben's Future Exploration Plans blow away in the breeze.

"Sorry to be so graphic."

"No more so than I was." I cringe again over the words I spoke into that group text.

"Sooo...what are we going to do about it?"

"About what?" I know what he's referring to, I just want him to put *it* in words since I don't know what the hell *it* is. I should be struck down for encouraging this discourse, but I can't stop myself.

"This..." He waves his hands between us. "Chemistry, or whatever this crazy feeling is I get when I'm around you."

His comment sucks the breath right out of my chest. I'm relieved he's called it out, so I know I'm not the only one feeling it. Am I being played, or is this for real? It's hard to tell. I just know I've never had such chemistry with another human, especially one who's just admitted he feels it too. Not even those first days with Seth felt this strong.

And that scares me shitless. So, what do I do? I punt the ball into the humor zone.

"I think we need to consult the handbook," I say, my mouth so dry I'm surprised actual sparks aren't shooting from my mouth.

"What section would contain that rule?" he asks. "Is there one for when you're so turned on by the very thought of your housemate you don't know how to behave around her?"

Jesus. The intensity of his words strikes like a landfalling hurricane. I have to hold on to something to keep from being swept from the boat.

"Yeah, I'm pretty sure that can be found in Section 4(d)5," I croak out. "*No fraternizing with housemates.*"

"God, I love it when you talk law," he teases. But the look in his eyes, the proximity of his lips to mine, is no joke. "How do you suppose maritime law factors into this?"

I giggle as I know where he's about to go with it. "If what you wanna know is whether the laws of the Almighty House Handbook apply offshore, the answer is..."

As I speak, his lips begin to descend on mine. Any concern I have about the rules and his player status get swept away with the tide as I render my ruling.

"They don't."

I close my eyes, waiting for those succulent lips to touch down on mine, when suddenly I'm plunging face-first into the Atlantic. I flail about as water engulfs my entire being, trying to determine which way is up. A strong arm pulls me from the death grip of a strong undercurrent and into the boat.

"What was that all about?" I sputter angrily, as if he pushed me in on purpose.

He laughs. "Rogue wave. You okay?"

"I'm not sure," I say, spitting out a gallon of water. "Let me check my ego."

"I'm so sorry. I didn't see it coming or I would have grabbed you sooner," he says, still chuckling.

"It's not funny!"

But soon I'm laughing along with him as water continues to erupt from my mouth like the Trevi Fountain. He, too, was doused but apparently had the wherewithal to hang on to something to keep from plummeting twenty-thousand leagues under the sea.

"I guess we should probably take that as a sign?" I ask, now that the icy waters of the Atlantic have doused the flames of desire. "All joking aside, Amy warned me of the three cardinal rules of house shares. Handbook rules and their application to maritime law aside, the first rule is there shall be no hooking up with your roommates."

"What are the other two?"

I lowkey don't remember so I make shit up. "Always

remember to flush. And if a housemate's horrific sailing skills cause you to go overboard, he must prepare your meals for the remainder of the summer. Section 5(e)6."

He gives me that half-smile. "I think I can make that happen."

My eyes glaze over thinking about having my own personal chef.

"But only as friends." He pauses, eyes steady on me. "Right?"

I force a nod. "Right."

"Fucking complications."

"Yep."

We stare at each other for a moment before I break the silence. "As I said that night we met, I have some things to work out this summer, and I'm not interested in starting something."

I don't mention my one exception: Ben. Grandfathered in by past history, I have to see that through before I can think about anyone else.

"Especially someone I'm living with," I add. *Someone who reminds me so much of the man who cheated on me.*

"Hundred percent agreed."

"Yup."

"And there's Ben..." The tone of his voice suggests he's prompting a positive response.

"And Francine..."

"Like I said, she's just...a friend."

With benefits, I add in my head. I've seen him with her twice now since I got here, so what else am I to think? He's also hinted about having complications, plural, which means there could be more than one Eve lurking in his garden.

Duh, Kacie. Isn't this the exact definition of a player? He's got more than one woman clinging to his fig leaf. Don't be one of them.

"So, platonic friendship it is," he says.

I nod my head vehemently. "Absolutely. Nothing more."

"Okay," he says, laughing. "Good. I really enjoy your

company and don't want to fuck it up."

We sail on in silence as the sun makes its final descent, its last burst of glory matching the spark in my heart over this new-found friendship and our resolve to keep things safe.

Until I make the colossal mistake of looking at him, fading sunlight shimmering in his aqua eyes, sun-kissed locks being tossed about in the sea breeze. He's propped on his elbow next to me, the contour of his biceps revealing his strength.

And I know.

We can sit here and pretend we're only going to be friends all we want, but by the look on his face as he gazes at me, I know this isn't over.

21

It's Tuesday morning at 7:30 a.m. when I'm startled awake by an incoming call from Ben.

"Hey!" I answer, hoping to sound like I've been awake for hours.

"Are you working today?" he asks.

"No. Why?" Excitement mounts. Maybe he's decided to skip work and play with me instead.

"I have a huge favor to ask of you."

Shit. I hate it when people lead off with that—confirming you have no plans before laying the whole "huge favor" thing on you, leaving you defenseless and without access to a bogus excuse.

"What is it?" I ask.

"The nanny had a stroke last night. Her family called to tell me this morning after I'd already dropped Leo off for surf lessons."

"I'm sorry to hear that."

"It was mild, fortunately. But that leaves me without childcare for Leo, and I'm expected in court in an hour."

"And you need my help...how?" *Please don't ask me to watch him.*

"Can you watch him today?"

I laugh out loud, wondering if this is Ben's idea of a joke. I've spent time with Leo over the years, so the kid knows me. But Ben also knows this fun fact about me: I don't exactly love kids. Don't hate them, just don't love hanging out with them.

Certainly not for a whole day. Which could cause complications if Ben and I get together, but I'm sure I'll learn to deal with it. Him. The kid, that is.

"I know what you're thinking," he says. "You hate kids and the last thing you'd wanna do is watch one today."

"I don't hate *Leo*." It's true. Ben's kid is sweet, but that doesn't mean I want to spend my first official day off with him. I was planning to go for an extra-long run (repenting for the one I didn't take yesterday), get my nails done, maybe do some shopping.

"Good," he says, taking my proclamation as consent. "It's just for today."

"But—"

"Asshole!" he grits.

"Well, now you can forget it."

"Sorry, some dick just cut me off on the parkway. What was I saying?"

"You were saying you'll pay a hundred an hour."

"Right. Oh...ha-ha. Maybe not, but I *will* make it worth your time."

"How?" I ask, as if I'm considering it. I'm not, I just want to hear an offer I can't refuse.

"I'll be back in time to treat you to dinner. In addition to paying you. How about a hundred dollars for the day?"

"Make it two hundred, and you got yourself a deal."

"Dude! That's more than I was paying the nanny."

"She's not here, is she?" I just can't help the lawyer in me—if there's a negotiation to be made, I'm all in.

Nor can he. "A hundred twenty-five."

"How many hours are we talking?"

"Eight. He's at surf camp until nine, and I'll be back by five."

I do the math. "Dude. That's almost three dollars less than I make per hour babysitting beach chairs, and yet you expect me to guard his safety, feed him, wipe his snotty nose, and potty train? A hundred seventy-five."

"Where have you been? Leo's been fully potty trained for three years now. A hundred forty."

"Might I remind you, you're trusting me with your most prized possession. A hundred fifty. My final offer."

He sighs. "You drive a tough bargain, counselor. But...deal. Way to take advantage of a desperate man."

"Yes!" I pump the air in victory, until it dawns on me what just happened. I got so hung up in the thrill of negotiation, I bartered my way into nanny-hood.

The only saving grace is the promise of seeing Ben at the end of his workday, and that dinner he mentioned.

He recites my instructions: pick Leo up from surf camp at the Fortieth Street beach and take him home for his morning snack, where I'll find a box of his fave cereal on the kitchen island. He'll need lunch around noon, and there's plenty of sandwich-making ingredients, fruit, and cut-up veggies in the fridge.

"Naptime after lunch?"

Ben laughs. "He gave up nap time when he traded in his diapers. He'll be going full bore all day. Endless energy, that kid. It's enviable."

Damnit. I was hoping for some downtime.

"He loves to read, so if you take him to the beach, have him bring a book. All his beach stuff is in the cart in the garage."

I wonder what he means by *all his beach stuff*. Aside from a towel and a book, what more can a five-year-old need?

"Just don't forget, he's allergic to peanuts. We don't have any in the house, but make sure no one gives him anything that can trigger a reaction."

He goes on to tell me there are two EpiPens in the kitchen, and two in his beach bag.

We hang up, and I glance at the time. I have a little over an hour before I have to pick up Leo. Plenty of time for a run.

But...first I have to get dressed, stretch, and of course, I should allow time for coffee afterwards. I'll need copious amounts of caffeine to keep up with Ben's offspring. And I don't want to be late...

Oh well. Points added for considering a run.

Upstairs, I glance at the third-floor landing (casually, of course) and note Chase's bedroom door is open. His cooler is gone, meaning he's left for work. Good. I don't want to spend precious energy pretending I'm not checking him out as he moves about the kitchen, shirtless, gathering his sustenance for the day.

Relax. Handbook rule 6(f)7 states: *It's okay to look, as long as you don't touch.*

I take my coffee to the deck where I think about last night, how we returned to the house as if nothing happened on the boat. Turns out, being tossed overboard was just the comic relief we needed to break the spell and ease the sexual tension between us. We wrapped ourselves in towels to dry off, as the setting sun conspired with a cool sea breeze to chill the evening air. We chatted about everything as we bobbed over waves—our current lives, our college experiences, our childhoods. He told me he grew up in Spring Lake, a coastal community in North Jersey. We even got into the ever-raging Jersey processed meat debate. It's rumored that somewhere in Central Jersey lies the Mason–Dixon line of ground pork products—where those of us below the line refer to it as "Pork Roll," while those above, call it "Taylor Ham." I won that debate, of course, because #southjerseyrules.

The waning dusk and a rising full moon lit the way as we navigated to land. Back at the house, we went our separate ways to shower. It wasn't until almost ten when we both appeared in the kitchen to grab something to eat.

"Is this where the housemate-of-the-first-part invokes her right to a home-cooked meal after the housemate-of-the-second-part tosses her into the Atlantic?"

"Wasn't me. Blame it on the rogue wave."

"Which I never saw."

"That's what makes it rogue." He gave me a lopsided grin. "Besides, I'm not sure that's an official rule."

"House handbook Section 7(g)8." I shrugged. "Don't blame me, I don't make the rules."

"I think you just did."

"What can I expect to dine on this fine evening?" I said as I rubbed my hands together in anticipation. "Let me guess. Filet, medium-well, lobster tail, sautéed asparagus? Perhaps with a full-bodied pinot?"

He opened the fridge and dug around. "How about leftover charcuterie and a beer?"

"Sold."

He pulled out the charcuterie spread from the other night, and we snacked on that as we downed a couple beers before heading to bed. Separately.

Other than that, we behaved as mature, respectable house-mates, abiding by the handbook Section 4(d)5.

22

Surf camp is still underway when I arrive at the beach to retrieve Leo. I watch as sunlight glimmers on the water, making silhouettes of the surfers. From what I can make out, there are three adults and six students in the water. I easily spot Leo, the smallest boy out there, his wetsuit making him appear even tinier than he is. I'm surprised Ben's approved this activity for such a little squirt, as he typically errs on the side of helicopter parent with a few layers of bubble wrap. Ben grew up surfing in Sea Isle, so maybe it's a generational thing.

I watch as one of the instructors holds the board Leo is lying on, waiting for the right moment. As a swell approaches, the man thrusts the surfboard forward. The wave takes over as Leo paddles like his short little life depends upon it before jumping to a standing position. Wobbling, he thrusts his arms to his sides and, with the unwavering confidence of a five-year-old, maintains balance like a pro as the board glides him to the shallows.

I let out an involuntary, "Whoo hoo!"

A figure emerges from the waves and jogs toward Leo.

"Way to go, little man!" a familiar voice calls out. "I knew you could do it!"

Blinking, I squint harder and lower my sunglasses, allowing me to see why the guy looks and sounds so familiar.

It's Chase. No wonder he's out the door so early each morning. I had no idea he's a surf instructor.

Leo's laughter is carried by the sea breeze as Chase scoops up the boy before setting him down, offering him a high five.

Together, teacher and student swim back out, and Leo catches another wave. I'm super impressed. No other kid is able to get up and stay up, despite appearing to have years on Leo.

Finally, the lesson comes to an end, and everyone gathers on the beach where Chase gives the kids a pep talk.

"You guys did great today," he said. "Don't worry if you didn't get up, just keep trying. I was almost fourteen before I mastered it. You'll get there."

Chase high fives each kid and speaks to them individually. I can't make out his words, but I can tell by their smiles he's giving them encouragement. I head to the water's edge to claim Leo when Chase looks up and our eyes meet.

"Excuse me, guys," he says to the group and jogs toward me. "Section 8(h)9," he starts, sounding so serious I can't hide my smile. "The housemate-of-the-first-part shall not stalk the housemate-of-the-second-part."

"No worries, second-part. I'm not here for you. I'm here for a kid."

"Just any kid, or one in particular?"

"Hmmm. Which one would you recommend?" I ask, happy he's playing along.

"If it were up to me, I'd take that one," he says, pointing to Leo.

"Good, because that's the one I'm here for."

He grins, taking it as a joke. "What *are* you doing here?"

"I'm an inspector with the US Department of Surfing, Imposter Division. I'll need to see your license and credentials to know you're legit."

"Busted," he says, laughing. "Never surfed a day in my life."

"It shows."

From the corner of my eye, I see Leo scanning the beach, looking for someone. I give a wave.

"Kacie!" he yells as he sprints toward me.

Chase shoots me a look of surprise. I'm so busy gazing at

him I don't realize, until it's too late, that Leo's jumping into my arms, expecting me to catch him.

I don't. Instead, the little guy knocks me clean onto my ass.

Chase offers his hand to help me up.

"Thanks for the assist," I say, brushing the sand off my backside.

"That's four times in a week, Jellyfish," he says. "Don't let it become a habit."

"I'll try not to."

"You weren't joking when you said you were here for a kid."

"Actually, I *was* here to stalk you, but now that you've pointed this one out, I think I'll take him."

This one was now jumping up and down, his arms wrapped around my waist. "Did you see it, Kacie? Did you see how I rode that wave *alllll* the way in?"

"I did! I was afraid if you didn't stop soon, you'd end up in Pennsylvania."

"Actually, it would be the Delaware Bay," Leo corrects me.

Chase and I both do double takes.

"He's right," Chase says under his breath.

"Yeah. He's a bit of an underachiever that way. It's embarrassing to think it took him until he was *this many*—" I hold up five fingers "—to understand geography of the eastern coastline."

"I'm still not convinced you should take him. Leo, do you even know this woman?"

"Sure. It's Kacie." Then he adds, "My dad's girlfriend."

"Friend," I quickly correct. "Your dad and I are just friends."

The last thing I need is for Ben to hear Leo say that word and think I put the idea in his head.

Leo shrugs. "But you're his friend and you're a girl."

"Ah," I say, laughing. Chase smiles too. I'm happy we cleared that up.

"I don't have any girlfriends...yet," Leo says. "I'm planning on getting a few when I get to kindergarten."

Chase and I share a snicker over his moppy head of dark curls. Leo runs off to join the other kids as they chase seagulls.

"So, Leo is Ben's kid," Chase says, making the connection. "I was in charge of getting the boards down here this morning and missed parent drop-off so I didn't know. But why are you—"

Another surf instructor approaches us. "Debby, is it? Leo's nanny?"

"No, I'm Kacie, a friend of Leo's dad. The nanny wasn't able to make it today, so I'm here in her place."

He nods. "Will you be picking him up every day?"

"Hell no!" The words are out before I can stop them. "Just today."

"Got it," the man says as he scribbles something on a clipboard and walks away.

Chase turns to me with a teasing look. "Funny, I don't see you in a nanny role."

"Why not?" I ask, feigning indignance.

"Well, your reaction just then kinda tipped me off that you're not really the kid type."

"Kids love me," I say, defending my non-reputation in the kid department.

"I'll bet they do." The gleam in his eyes reveals his disbelief. "Well, I'd love to sit here and banter all day, but I need to get the equipment back to the shop and report for work."

"What beach are you on today?"

"Ours," he says. "It's your lucky day. Maybe I'll take you up on your destiny-inspired offer for dinner tonight. I'm assuming your promise still stands."

"Sorry, the housemate status renders the offer null and void. Besides, I have plans—"

He raises his eyebrows. "Bend It Like Beckham again?"
I nod.

"Sounds like it's getting serious."

I shrug, not sure how to answer that. "It's a thank you for

watching Leo today."

He smiles. "Too bad. Your loss."

As I watch him saunter away, the devil in me wonders if he's right.

Leo returns. "Where's the nanny? I only met her once, but I don't see her here."

"She's sick, Leo. Looks like you're stuck with me today."

"Yippee!" he says, bouncing as he grabs my hand. "I didn't like that nanny. She didn't seem fun. I know you're fun. What are we gonna do today, huh? Can we come back to the beach? Will you help me build a sandcastle? Can we boogie board?"

I laugh at his exuberance. "Let's take it one step at a time. How about we go home and have your snack first."

We return to the house where Leo insists on pouring his cereal and milk into the bowl. When he's finished eating, he goes into the living room and brings back a box.

"Game time," he announces. "Have you ever played Trouble?"

"Have I ever played Trouble," I say in a tone suggesting his question is the most ridiculous one ever posed. "I'm the reigning Trouble champ of all time."

"Well, you've met your match," he informs me.

I laugh. "We'll see."

In the end, he was right. He beat me badly.

"I hope you didn't just let me win," he says as he packs up the game.

"Hell no."

I instantly regret my words, forgetting I'm with a five-year-old. He's so well-spoken, he has me thinking he's a mini-adult. I'd better watch the language.

Leo takes his bowl to the sink, steps on a stool, and starts washing his bowl. "Gotta clean up after ourselves if we want to go to the beach."

I'm amazed at his maturity. For all the dysfunction between Ben and Angi, they certainly raised their kid right. He's bright—no surprise there, being the offspring of two attorneys, even if one has never practiced a day in her life. At five, Leo's vocabulary is already more evolved than many of the adults I know. He's also a pleasant child, well-behaved.

Leo puts his clean bowl away and announces it's time for the beach. I throw my bag over my shoulder and head for the door.

"Not that way, silly girl," he says. "We need my cart."

That's right, the cart with *all his beach things*. Heading to the garage, I'm expecting to find Cat in the Hat's Thinga-ma-jigger.

It's worse than that. I peer inside the cart in abject horror, as if it contains skeletal remains. Inside are two chairs—one child-sized, one adult. A CoolCabana. A mesh sack filled with beach toys. A pouch containing sunscreen and bug spray. First-aid kit. Minion-shaped backpack labeled LEO (in case there's confusion about whose bag it is, I guess). A stack of towels. Paddleball set. Another mesh bag filled with toys. Two boogie boards.

Holy beach shit, Batman. Bearing witness to the sheer amount of equipment a five-year-old requires for a few hours on the sand sets me even further away from family planning possibilities. I'm not ready to be lugging all this crap across the beach like some sort of soccer mom.

"Should we bring this too?" I ask, picking up a bucket from the ground.

"Hell no," he says, all straight-faced. "It's broken."

I deserve this. I curse myself.

"That's a bad word," I tell him. "You shouldn't say it."

"But you did."

"That's because I'm an adult. I get to do things you can't until you're older."

"Oh," he says, nodding. "Like fuck?"

"Leo!" I shriek his name so loudly, the little guy jumps a foot in the air. How on earth does he know that word, much less what it means? I take back everything I said about Ben and Angi's child-rearing skills.

I'm trying to think how I should respond when he continues. "My dad fucks a lot," he says.

Oh God. What have I gotten myself into? I'm praying Leo is referring to the usage of the word, not the act itself.

He continues. "It's not fair adults can say things kids can't."

"It isn't, but that's how it works. Life's unfair, and the sooner you grasp that concept, the easier it becomes. Capisce?"

He giggles. "Am I allowed to say that word?"

"Yes."

"Okay, capisce. I'm putting that one on my word-of-the-day list."

"What's that?" I ask, even though it's pretty self-evident—just not coming from a kid who recently crawled out of Pull-Ups.

"Whenever I hear a word I don't know, I add it to my list. I pick one each day to use. Dad says it's a good way to 'span my 'cabulary.'"

I stifle a giggle. "How about we make a deal? I won't say bad words, and you won't say bad words. If we go all day without saying a bad word, I'll treat you to ice cream. Sound good?"

I hold up a hand for a high five and he reciprocates.

"Fuck yeah!" he says. "My dad says that one too."

"Welp, you just broke the rule," I say, folding my arms and squeezing tight to keep the laughter in. "No ice cream for you today."

"I didn't mean it. I thought it would be funny. I'll take it back." He sucks in his breath and makes nonsensical sounds. "That's me, pulling the bad words back into my mouth."

I turn away, trying to hide a smile. I don't want him to know how amusing I find all this, especially since I'm supposed to be a respectable babysitter today.

Fuck yeah.

23

I let Leo pick our spot on the beach. I don't hate that he has us parked near the lifeguard stand. Chase is already there, guarding all us beach-going souls.

"Which chair is mine?" I tease as I lift them both from the cart.

"You're being silly again," Leo says, pointing to the child-size chair. "Obviously that's yours."

Even his sense of humor is highly evolved for his age.

"Okay, if you insist." I flip it open and squat down, pretending to sit.

He doubles over in a fit of laughter.

"What?" I ask in feigned seriousness.

"Goldilocks, your chair's too big!" He drags the adult chair next to me and opens it. "Try this one."

I settle into the chair. "Just right. Thanks, Big Bad Wolf."

"You're confusing your fairy tales," he informs me. "We're gonna have to work on that."

My heart can't help but swell over this kid. I'd forgotten how adorbs he is. I'm growing to like him more and more by the second.

He pulls a book of fairy tales from his bag of many tricks and brings it over, surprising me when he climbs on my lap.

"We should get to work on this right away." He opens the book to the Three Little Bears story. "This is the big bad wolf. He torments the piggies. He's what my dad calls a homewrecker. Just like my mom's new boyfriend."

I'm taking a sip of water when he delivers that last line, and I spew it all over the sand.

"What's that all about?" he asks.

Good God. I can't believe Ben would be telling his kid about the affair, let alone explaining what *homewrecker* means in the context of human relationships. If I didn't know better, I'd wonder whether I helped the wrong parent gain custody—one who drops frequent F-bombs and disparages his coparent's significant other. Not that I blame him, but maybe don't bring Leo into it. While I may not be super familiar with kids, I do know messy divorces and traumatic custody situations. Sharing details with kids, even if true, only traumatizes them further.

"If you mean he's a guy who demolishes houses, that's incorrect," I say, hoping to do some damage control. "I think he's a lawyer. Like me and your dad. And Mom."

Leo tilts his head and looks at me. I can tell his little brain is working to decode the situation.

I change the subject. "What do you want to be when you grow up?"

"Chase," he says, with a sigh.

"You mean, you wanna be like Chase? A surf instructor?"

"Yes, and a lifeguard." He looks toward the stand like a heart-eyed emoji. "They save people."

"They do." I follow Leo's gaze to see Chase standing on his seat, blowing his whistle and gesturing to swimmers to move in front of the stand.

"Today was my first day of surf camp, but I know I love it already," Leo says. "And I'm good at it. You could probably see that."

"Oh, absolutely." I try to choke back a giggle. Oh, to be five, and call out your strengths unabashedly without worrying someone will think you're bragging. "I can't believe you've never surfed before."

"I've surfed. My dad's been taking me out when he can. But this is the first time I met a lifeguard in person." Once again, he gazes at Chase adoringly.

As if on cue, Chase turns to us and waves.

Leo's little hand grabs mine. "He just waved at me," he whispers excitedly, like a teenage girl with a major crush. "Come on, let's go say hi."

"I don't know if we should, Leo. He has to keep his attention focused on the water."

But Leo is already holding out his hand to help me up. I really shouldn't let down this chivalrous little guy. Especially since I'm sporting a flattering new bikini. Sue me for wanting to look my best in public.

We head to the stand, Leo bouncing all the way.

"Hi, Mr. Chase! It's Leo, your student."

Chase laughs. "Yes, Leo, I remember you. Hang ten, dude!"

"Hang ten!" Leo does the gesture.

"Hey, Kacie," Chase says, and I wonder if I imagine his grin widening. "Hang ten to you too."

"Hang ten," I say. But instead of giving him the traditional greeting, I form my fingers into the Bloods gang signal.

He laughs.

"Kacie, you have to teach me how to do that," Leo says.

Goddamn. This kid doesn't miss a trick.

"Maybe not," I say.

"And you, Mr. Chase. Can you teach me how to be a lifeguard?" Leo asks. "That's what I want to be when I grow up."

"That's an awesome thing to wanna be. I can't invite you up here during work hours, but maybe later. What do you say, Kacie? Maybe after my shift someday?"

"How about today?" Leo asks.

"Dad says he'll be home by five for dinner," I tell Leo. "Maybe another day."

"Ohh, that's right. Dinner again," Chase says, flashing

his eyebrows, clearly mocking me. "Sounds serious. When's the wedding?"

I hope Leo didn't hear that one, but he's already behind the stand, asking questions of Other Lifeguard, who's adjusting oars on the wooden rowboat.

Chase's attention returns to the water.

"Hey," I call up to him.

When he looks, I surreptitiously flip him the bird. "Hang one."

He laughs even more, and I have to admit it does something to me. He has a great laugh, and it warms me to know I'm the cause of it.

I go behind the stand to pry Leo off Chase's partner. When he sees me coming, he kangaroos toward me. I'm coming to understand hopping is Leo's preferred mode of transportation.

"Kacie, Kacie, Kacie!" he calls out. "Can we go boogie boarding?"

I assume such water activity is permitted, judging by the fact Ben has outfitted the beach cart with two boogie boards. With Chase in the stand, I'm confident he won't allow anything to happen to the little dude.

We take both boogie boards to the water—his legit, mine a prop. I have no intention of boogie boarding. I'd rather be water boarded.

"You coming?" Leo calls back to me after I stop at water's edge.

"I wanna take videos of you so we can show your dad!" Points added for my creative avoidance tactic. "Just stick to the shallow part, okay? No going in higher than your waist."

"You're no fun," he says, looking me square in the eye.

"You're right, I'm not. There's no way you're getting swept out to sea on my watch. Safety first."

I take a bunch of videos as the little guy rides the tiniest waves to shore, the ones already broken up in the surf zone. I'm impressed how well he follows the rules, despite not being accustomed to taking them from me. His excitement over riding the smallest of after-waves is adorable.

After several rides, Leo dashes over and wraps his arms around me. "I think we got enough videos. It's lonely out there. Can you come in with me?"

Interesting question, Leo. Let me introduce you to the concept of legal reasoning, which views the words *can you* and *will you* as two very different things. Yes, I absolutely *can* (physically) go boogie boarding. But *will I* (willingly) go is quite another story.

He looks up at me with that cute little freckled face, big blue eyes pleading. "Please?"

How can I say no? He's Ben's mini-me in every way, except for his eyes, which he got from his mom.

"Okay," I acquiesce, tousling his wet curls.

I ditch my phone and follow Leo into the surf zone. With a boatload of trepidation and jellyfish-inspired PTSD, I laser-eye the water for signs of the jerks. None so far, thankfully.

I'm about to take on my first wave when I hear Chase call out to us.

"Don't worry, Kacie. I've got the Coast Guard on speed dial."

With no one in our direct line of vision, I place two middle fingers on the side of the boogie board facing him.

"Hang two," I call out.

Again, his laughter dances across the sand before reaching my ears. I can't help but smile.

Just before I get broadsided by a huge wave.

24

Coming up for air, my first thought is of Leo, hoping the wave didn't get him, too. Wiping water from my eyes, I glance wildly about to find he was not only spared, but is now bent over, cracking up.

"That was so funny, Kacie!" he says, laughing. "Do that again!"

"Hard pass," I sputter, water cascading from my mouth as I struggle to breathe.

My second thought is whether Chase saw my wipe-out, but there's a group of bikini-clad twenty-somethings gathered around the stand, talking to him and his partner. I'm guessing I could set myself on fire and he wouldn't notice.

"Okay, ready for this?" I ask, as I try to reclaim my dignity.

"You go first," Leo says.

Dutifully, I wade out farther as I recall the day my older brother taught me how to boogie board.

"Feel the energy," he'd said. "The ocean's telling you when it's the right time to release."

Before long, I understood. I'd wait for the ocean to pull away from land as it prepared to release its shore-bound energy, and that's when I'd push off. I got so good at boogie boarding as a kid, I'd often end up on dry sand. No cap.

Turns out, boogie boarding is like riding a bike, as this is what happens during my first demonstration. I execute such a perfect ride, I almost end up in the middle of town. So proud of my run, I wait for the applause as I jump up. Instead, I see a grimacing, wild-eyed Chase yanking at his chest. The sea of women around him has parted and they're all looking at me. I give WTF arms.

"Why the charades?" I ask aloud, even though we're far enough away he can't hear me.

A woman next to me steps in. "Honey, your top—"

I look down to find my bandeau-style bikini top is around my waist. I yank it up so fast, I almost scrape off my nipples. Thank God Leo's still in the water behind me, unaware I've just flashed the entire Thirty-eighth Street beach and all its Spinnaker-dwelling beachgoers.

Back in the water, humiliation tucked between my legs, I try to impart my brother's lessons upon Leo. I take him out far enough where he can experience what I'm teaching him, but not so far he's in danger of ending up in Portugal. I push his board forward as I ride mine beside him. I'm surprised by how much fun we're having as we complete our rides, laughing and high-fiving one another.

Before long, Leo announces he's ready for lunch. We emerge from the water, fist-bumping each other as we pass the lifeguard stand.

"Way to go, *bosom* buddy," Chase says, not taking his eyes off the swimmers.

"*Bust*-ed," I punt back. Leo dashes ahead of me so I add, "I feel like such a *boob*."

"Just tryin' to help. I like to keep *abreast* of the swimmers."

"Thanks for *nippling* it in the bud."

There's that laugh, again.

Leo's already digging in our cooler by the time I meet up with him at our chairs. After a delectable two-course meal of PB&Js and apple slices, I suggest we sit and dry off, let our bellies settle. That lasts about thirty seconds before he's up rolling around on the sand, asking me to bury him. I refuse, as I don't feel like getting out of my chair, so he amuses himself by burying my feet. Next, we build a sandcastle, search for seashells, take another dip in the ocean, and play beach paddleball. I must be getting old, because I almost stop for a nap on our way back to Leo's house, a whopping block from the beach. I'm relieved to find Ben's car in the driveway when we get there.

"Hey, there's my peeps!" Ben calls out as he meets us in the driveway.

Leo jumps into his arms and regales him with details of all we did today in one big, run-on sentence.

"Wow, it sounds like you had a great day," he says when Leo finally stops to take a breath. "Who's in the mood for pizza?"

Leo jumps up and down. "Me! Me!"

"Good because I got us one," he says as he waves us in. "Kace, you in for pizza?"

My heart sinks. Ben must have forgotten his earlier promise of treating me to dinner. Or maybe I took it the wrong way, and he didn't mean it would be just him and me because, duh...of course, Leo would be with us too.

That's life with a kid, I guess. Question is: Could I ever get accustomed to it? Do I even want to?

We sit at the kitchen island enjoying our pizza until Leo jumps off his seat. "Well, kids, I'm off to play a game on my tablet. Enjoy your meal."

We snicker as he leaves the room.

"Hey, listen." I lean toward Ben, speaking softly so there's no chance the little guy can hear me. "Leo dropped a few F-bombs today. You gotta watch your language. He can't be doing that in school."

He laughs. "Says the queen of F-bombs herself."

"Yeah, but I'm not five."

"I know," he says, sighing. "I think he may have heard me say it a few times."

"*May* have?" I tease. "Says the king of F-bombs."

"I've talked to him about it, but I'll do so again. Any other incidents of bad behavior?"

"No, that's it—wait, there is something else." I glance over my shoulder and drop my voice to a whisper. "He referred to Angi's boyfriend as a homewrecker. Did he get that from you?"

"I've never said—" He cuts short his defense with an eyeroll. A grin spreads across his face. "Hold that thought."

He calls to Leo.

"No!" I hiss. "Don't tell him I told you."

He shakes his head, still smiling. "Come show Kacie that yellow crane Mom and Calvin gave you."

Leo appears moments later, holding a toy crane with a sign on the side, *Demaris Demolition Company.*

I recall Angi's boyfriend's last name is Demaris. "He owns a demolition company?"

"Looks that way."

I'm so confused. "I thought he was an attorney?"

"He is, but he and his brother own this company on the side. They basically tear down houses. So..."

"Homewrecker," I say, nodding. Still, that hits a little too close to home, even for this hardened divorce attorney. "And you're okay with this?"

"With what?"

"With Angi and the guy she cheated on you with, giving Leo a toy with his name on it?"

He shrugs. "Demaris gets her, I get Leo. A win-win for me."

"Still..."

"They're officially together, and Leo will be staying with them when he visits her in California. I have no choice, I have to be fine with it. Like I said when we filed for divorce, it'd been over between us for a long time. The guy's done me a favor."

I wonder why his words aren't landing easily on me. I've always blamed their first pregnancy for the reason Ben and I never got together. When he stayed with her after the miscarriage, I assumed he'd fallen in love with her. To hear him tell it now, he's discussing the breakup of his marriage as dispassionately as if he's talking about switching banks.

"Thank you for doing this today," Ben says. "You saved my ass."

"My pleasure."

I wouldn't go so far as to say that's the truth. It was a lot of things, but pleasure wasn't one of them. It was fun (at times). Draining (always). Exhausting (no cap). But not as awful as I'd expected.

I'm afraid to ask, but I do. "How's your nanny doing?"

He grimaces. "She's okay, but she won't be able to babysit at all this summer. I'm not sure what I'm gonna do."

"When are you going back to the office? Can you take him with you?"

"Thursday. And no, I'll be in court all day."

"Take him to court? Play him off as an intern?"

"Funny, but no. It's too late to find someone else for Thursday. I like to interview babysitters and have them come over to play with Leo first, to see how they do."

I remain silent so as not to invite what I know is coming.

"Yeah, so..." He rubs his hand up the back of his head, scrunching his face. "Whatcha doing Thursday?"

I quickly scan my brain for possible excuses. Root canal. Jury duty. Driver's license renewal at the DMV. None of which are true, all of which would be less painful than having to spend another day with a kid. Not that Leo's a bad boy, he's just...a boy. Overflowing with boy vim and vigor. It's too much for this thirty-two-year-old chick to handle, especially twice in a week.

I know what you're thinking...what if Ben and I get together? What will this chick do with this vim-and-vigor boy? We'll worry about that when it happens. And anyway, that's what other nannies are for.

I'm about to decline, but the look on Ben's face melts my heart. Before I can stop myself, I agree.

"Thursday. That's it," I say. "Enough time for you to find someone else."

"You're the sweetest." He hugs me. I breathe in his woodsy jasmine scent, and it overpowers me. "Next time, I'm taking you out for a real dinner date, as promised. Just the two of us."

He pulls back and gives me a soft peck kiss, but as soon as his lips land on mine, they take off again, reminding me we're still in the friend zone.

Ben calls out to Leo that it's bedtime. Little dude comes bounding over and gives me a fist bump. "Take care, polar bear."

"Peace out, silly trout." I hold up a peace sign, and he bends over in a fit of laughter.

"Thanks again for today," Ben says as he walks me to the door. "I'll be in touch about Thursday."

Whoopee. Another day off to spend entertaining a five-year-old.

Sucks to be you, cockatoo.

25

I wake up earlier than expected on Wednesday morning but still can't find the motivation to go for a run. Don't judge. It's my first day off since getting here and yesterday wore me out.

I make coffee and head to the deck for an early morning dose of vitamins D and Sea. I contemplate everything I plan to do on my glorious one-day vacation. My nails are in desperate need of a new polish. I'd be remiss if I didn't check out the swimwear sale at the promenade surf shop—now that I'm working on the beach, my wardrobe needs enhancement. I know I shouldn't be spending money, but after Ben Venmo'd me for babysitting, I feel nouveau riche. I should probably treat myself to something after being so charitable with my time yesterday.

That's right—I was charitable!

I dash back inside to retrieve my journal and refill my coffee. Settling back down on the deck lounge chair, I review my bucket list. Not only did I *#6: Do something charitable* by nannying yesterday, I'd also accomplished *#4: Get out on the water* when Chase and I went sailing. I draw a big fat checkmark next to both items and revel in the glory of having completed five of Amy's ten stupid bucket list items, before summer's even a week old.

Three hours later, I'm the proud owner of two new bikinis, a fine set of French manicured nails, and a red cloth bag of beach treats from Wawa. Two for the price of one hoagies*,

---

* For those of you not from Philly, a "hoagie" is a submarine sandwich. AKA: sub, hero, grinder, torpedo, wedge, Blimpie...call it what you will,

compliments of Wawa's Summer Hoagiefest.

It's a beautiful day, and I feel like taking my lunch to the beach. It'll be the first time since I arrived that I'll get to just sit in a chair and read a book instead of slinging umbrellas, boogie boarding with preschoolers, or becoming prey to marine invertebrates. I'm about to stash the second hoagie in the fridge for tomorrow when, once again, my cup overflows with charity with a brilliant idea: I should make an offering to the Lifeguard Gods. Chase told me he was working our beach again today, and a gratuitous lunch offering seems like a great way to show him just how good a friend I am. I cut the sandwich in half and wrap each individually, one for each lifeguard. I pack them in the Wawa bag with two water bottles, a bag of chips, and frozen grapes.

I settle in my usual spot, to the right and slightly behind the lifeguard stand. Just as I finish setting up, the bells of St. Joseph's chime the noon hour, heralding lunchtime. I head to the stand with my offering. Chase is with his partner from the day of the jellyfish incident. Good. He'll likely regard me as a thankful rescuee, and not a groupie.

"Hey, guys." I hold up the bag. "Thought I'd treat you to a little lunch to thank you for saving my life the other day."

"Wow, that's mighty nice of you," the partner says as I hand it to him.

Chase gives a playful smirk. "Bribery will get you nowhere."

I laugh. "What would I be bribing you for?"

"So you can climb our rowboat."

Is there a double entendre there?

"People bribe you for that?"

"Kids try. Not actual bribes, just attempts," Chase explains.

"True," Other Lifeguard says. "We're always chasing kids from the boats."

---

but when you're here, it's a hoagie.

"I promise I'm not here to climb your boat."

"Shame." Chase gives me a half-smile. He turns to his partner. "Don't believe a word she says, Jeff."

"She does seem pretty sus," Jeff says as he unwraps his sandwich.

Chase snaps his fingers. "I know what she wants. To swim outside the perimeters, hoping we'll turn the other cheek."

With a surrendering shrug, I agree. "You're onto me."

"I imagine you'll expect us to save you, too, if you get swept away in a rip current," Chase adds. "You know, the typical 'I'll grease your hand if you grease mine' routine."

"It's a hoagie," I say, laughing. "Hardly bribery material. And anyway, I'll do all the above with or without your assistance."

"See, didn't I tell you?" Chase elbows his partner. "That accent. So Philly."

"What?" I object. I don't have an accent.

"What do you call this?" He holds up his sandwich.

"A hoagie?"

Chase laughs as Jeff nods. "Yep, I hear it."

"Hear what?" I ask.

"The way you draw out the 'ho' and give it a little twang," Chase says. "Like, *hoew*."

"That's right," I say. "I forgot you're from North Jersey. But you're in the south now, friend, where Philly/South Jersey/Delco accents rule."

Jeff nods as he swallows a bite of his *hoew*-gie. "You were right, man. It is a cute accent."

I shoot a look at Chase. He must have been talking to Jeff about me, or my accent at least. I feel a flutter in my belly as his cheeks blush from behind his tan.

"I never said it was cute," Chase insists.

"Oh, that's right," Jeff says, elbowing Chase's arm. "You said *she* was cute."

I try to hide my smile. "Thanks, Chase," I say as I turn to

walk away. "You're not so bad, either."

Returning to my chair, I'm buzzing over the fact that Chase talked to his friend about me. So bamboozled am I, all common sense goes out the window as I pull out my *hoew-gie* and chomp into it without remembering the cardinal rule of eating on the beach.

Which is: don't. At least not without an umbrella.

One minute, I'm sitting there with a sandwich in my hand. The next—*gone*, snatched by an avian asshole. I scream as every seagull currently scouring the Jersey coastline swarms my personal space. The swiper must lose control of the sandwich because somehow it ends up in my lap. Bird talons pierce my thighs as their wings slap me in the face, pulling at the sandwich from all ends, while feathers, sandwich bits, and F-bombs fly. I clamor to get out of my seat, away from these flocking, squawking, shitting seagulls, but they overpower me. My screams of bloody murder have alerted everyone in the tristate area (including any seagulls not already engaged in the food fight).

"Shoo!" A male voice calls out, and the sea of gulls parts to reveal a man waving a boat oar. Not just any man. My hero, part deux (or cinq for anyone who's counting).

The gulls give chase to the victor, now flying over the Thirty-eighth Street beach with my *hoew-gie* hanging from its mouth, dropping turkey-and-cheese shrapnel on unsuspecting beachgoers.

I look down to see I'm covered in sandwich parts and bird shit.

"Ever heard of an umbrella?" Chase asks as he tries to hide a smile. "I believe you can rent them here."

"Fuck off."

"Fair enough. Before I do, come with me."

He leads me to the ocean where he splashes water on me. "Go ahead, if you wanna swim beyond the stand, I'll let you. Just this once."

I dive into a wave, hoping to cleanse my body of turkey, shit, and embarrassment. I come up, turning to thank Chase, but he's already back in the stand. I tread water, enjoying the freedom bestowed upon me to swim outside the acceptable perimeters. Rule-breaking feels pretty liberating.

My fellow beachgoers have cleaned up the murder scene, I note when I return. Several check in with me to see if I'm okay, reminding me how kind people can be when they're on vacation.

Later, back at the house, I'm getting ready to meet my brother and friends for happy hour—this time, not to be waylaid by a hot sailing lifeguard—when I remember today was Amy's first day at work. I ring her to find out how it was.

"Great," she says. "Overwhelming, meeting all my new office mates and finding out which projects I'll be on. But enough about me. How's Fun Girl Summer going so far?"

I regale her with tales of the past week, starting with the seagull incident. She laughs so hard it hurts *my* stomach.

"I wish I could've been there to witness it," she says. "I miss you. I need you to come visit me. I'm lonely and bored."

"How can you possibly be bored? You've only been there five days."

"We're in the middle of a heat wave and lots of places don't have air conditioning, especially the Tube. Or elevators. They don't believe in ice, either."

"You're in London!" I exclaim.

"But it's not the Jersey Shore. Lucky bitch."

I guess she's right. I am pretty lucky to be spending a summer here.

"London is awesome," she continues, "but I'm also dying to travel—to the Amalfi coast for cool sea breezes and sunshine. Take silly pictures holding up the Leaning Tower of Pisa. Share a baguette and wine on the banks of the Seine."

"That sounds fabulous," I sigh, imagining how much fun

we'd have doing all the above.

"Let's do it!" she exclaims. "They're so generous with time off here. I get five weeks' vacation right off the bat."

"You're shitting me!"

"No, girl. They know how to treat their workers over here. Plentiful time off. Generous family leave. Amazing benefits, including free health care. Nothing like the US where it's work-till-you-die-oh-but-here's-two-weeks-off-for-the-next-ten-years."

"But for now, that's where I'm stuck," I remind her. "If I get a job, I'll likely only have two weeks off until I retire."

"That's why you need to visit this summer, before you find a job."

"I don't have the money, dude."

"How much are you making at the beach shack?"

"Eighteen an hour, which is only enough for spending money. I'd need to make a shit ton more if I wanna travel."

"Get another job, then. Aren't you only working four days at the shack? Why not pick up a waitressing gig? I know you hate dirty plates, but it could be worth it. I bet you'd clean up on tips alone."

"Hard pass. I don't want to spend my whole summer working. I wanna have fun too."

"What could be more fun than a trip to London and a jaunt around Europe? At least consider it."

She's right, it would be amazing. I just can't justify digging into savings, not knowing when I'll get a paycheck next.

"How's the bucket list coming along?" she asks.

"Halfway through already."

"Impressive. What have you added since we last spoke?"

"*Number 4: Get out on the water.* Also, *#6: Do something charitable.*"

"Tell me about the water experience. What did you do?"

I tell her how Chase invited me out on his sailboat, and how

I plummeted into the depths of the ocean. I strategically leave off what I was doing immediately before that—waiting for him to kiss me. I don't want her to get excited thinking there's a potential love interest. More so, I don't want her to be mad that I almost broke the cardinal cohabitation rule. She gave me a pass for the first incident, not knowing Chase was my housemate at the time. This time, I do.

"How about the charity thing? Please tell me you did something truly benevolent this time."

"I did!" I exclaimed. "I hope you're sitting down, because I spent my first day off babysitting a kid."

"Wait, I thought I was talking to Kacie!" she exclaims. "How did that happen? More to the point, who would trust *you* with their kid?"

"Ben."

"Of course. Should've known."

"Leo's nanny had a stroke. Ben asked me to step in, so I entertained him all day."

"Oh, that sucks," she said. "Both for the nanny and you. But mostly Leo. How was it?"

"Not bad," I admit. "He's a cutie. Very well-spoken for his age. Ben's asked me to watch him again tomorrow while he finds a replacement."

"Anything for Ben, right?" I can envision her smirk from across the pond.

"He's my friend, he's in a bind, and I happened to have a day off."

"So why not step in and be his hero?" She pauses, before adding, "Again."

"It's not like that," I say, despite knowing it's exactly like that. If some rando came up to me on the street and asked me to watch their kid, I'd laugh all the way to Children and Youth Services to report them.

"Sure, I believe you," Amy says, sounding as if she doesn't.

"Is he paying you at least?"

"A hundred and fifty for the day."

"Sorry, friend. It's not charitable if you're getting paid for it. Wait—did you say a hundred and fifty? You're basically gonna be raking in three hundred this week alone? Tax free?"

"Yep."

"Dude, fuck waitressing. You need to keep nannying— that's how we're gonna get you over here. Did you say he's still looking for a replacement?"

"Yeah, but—"

"Do it!" she encourages. "There's still ten weeks left of the summer. That'll give you plenty of money to visit. You have a free place to stay here in London, and travel between countries is relatively cheap."

The wheels start turning as she speaks. She's right—I can finance a European trip without having to dip into savings, simply by playing with Leo two days a week. Hell, since I'll be doing Ben a massive favor, I may even barter for higher pay.

"I dunno..." I say, even though I'm pretty sure I know what I'm going to do.

Alert the press: Kacie Layne's about to become a nanny.

(May want to alert Children and Youth while you're at it. Just sayin'.)

26

As a seasoned divorce attorney, I've become somewhat of a master negotiator. Which is why I not only feel confident in what I'm about to do, but certain I can name my price.

After hanging up with Amy, I call Ben. Let the negotiations begin.

"Any luck with the search today?" I ask, knowing he'd planned to interview several prospects.

"No. I thought I'd found someone, but my cop friend ran her name and discovered she has a rap sheet as long as a CVS receipt."

"Yikes. It's not gonna be easy to find someone who can watch that precious little guy. You can't take chances with strangers."

"Tell me about it."

"You really should have someone you know well. With his peanut allergy, you'll definitely need someone who knows what to do in case of a reaction."

"No shit. That's one of the first questions I ask. You'd be surprised at how many people have no idea. I thought allergies were more prevalent."

"I know what to do," I say. "I'm allergic to bees."

"That's right, I forgot." He sighs. "I'm lowkey panicked I won't find someone."

Shoot your shot, girl.

"You know...I have to think about this..." I pause for effect, given I already have. "But...maybe I could watch him for you.

That way, you have someone you trust—who's law abiding, knows her way around EpiPens, and fun to be with."

He laughs. "You almost had me, until you got to that last attribute."

"What? I'm fun!"

"Okay, if you say so." I know he's teasing by the tone of his voice. "Actually, Leo said so. I was like, 'You sure we're talking about the same woman?'"

"Haha."

"Are you seriously offering to spend your summer watching a kid?" he asks incredulously.

"It's only two days a week, right?" I cannot all-day-every-day with a kid. Even Leo.

"Yeah. At a hundred and fifty a day, that means three hundred a week for you. Not a bad gig."

"Hmm. I do want to help you out..." I pause again for dramatic effect. It's the art of negotiation—I can't let him know I'm already in. I need the leverage to up my price. "I dunno. I need to make bank this summer, because I don't know how long I'll be without a job. I was planning on picking up a waitressing gig. Vacationers are pretty generous with tips, and I need every cent I can muster."

"Didn't you once say you'd rather turn tricks in Kensington than waitress? Something about people's gross, dirty plates?"

"That's how badly I need to make money this summer. I'm even willing to risk dysentery—"

"I'll up the pay," he snaps. "One seventy-five a day?"

"Two hundred, and you've got yourself a deal."

"Four hundred dollars a week for childcare?" he exclaims. Then, "I guess that's about what it would be at home."

"And you're getting someone you know you can trust."

"Who's just negotiated her way to an extra Franklin per week."

I smile smugly. "You can't cut corners when it comes to childcare."

And just like that, I become a nanny. I'm kinda excited for it, not just because my awesome negotiation skills have earned me four grand, but because it means I'll get to hang out with Ben in the evenings when he returns. I call that a win/win.

Now I just have to suit up for the kid game. Yikes.

"I can't believe I've been out-negotiated by my friend," he says.

"Tell it to your law firm," I suggest. "They'd be well-advised to bring me on."

He chuckles. "That, they would."

27

On my first official day as a nanny, my little buddy and I basically repeat our routine from Tuesday. Surf lesson, followed by cereal (followed by washing out his bowl—gotta love this kid). Slather him with sunscreen, go to the beach, do all the things: paddleball, sandcastle building, boogie boarding. It's never ending with this guy, but now that I've given up (half-baked thoughts of) running, I'm happy to be getting some physical exercise.

I just can't wait to get to work tomorrow so I can relax.

We're eating lunch—under cover of an umbrella, thank you traumatic avian attack—when Leo looks up at me.

"Hey, Kacie. Apparently, I have some questions for my lifeguard friend. Is it okay if I go talk to him?"

Chase is back guarding our beach again. Seems sus, when their beach assignments are allegedly "random," but who am I to question fate?

"Sure, just ask him if it's okay, first. They're supposed to be guarding the swimmers so you can't distract him too much."

"I'm aware of that, apparently," he says, and I fight hard not to crack up. "I should probably bring him a treat to thank him. Is it okay if I give him my Oreos?"

"Whatever you want to do, Leo."

I watch as the little guy runs toward the lifeguard stand, guarding his prized cookies with his life after I warned him to watch out for seagulls. Not only for the sake of his treats, but his entire being. He's so small, he could easily be scooped up and carried out to sea by the jerks.

I give Leo a few minutes to chat before I go rescue Chase.

"Hey, Leo, let's let them do their jobs," I say as I take the boy's hand.

"Apparently he's doing his job," Leo informs me. "He apparently can watch and talk at the same time."

Chase and I look at each other and chuckle.

"Is that new?" he asks. "I've never heard him use that word before, but he's dropped it seven times since we started talking."

I laugh. "Yep. *Apparently* that's his word of the day."

"He certainly has the gift of gab," Chase says as Leo runs to the water to splash sand off his legs.

"He comes out with the funniest shit sometimes. He's also advanced beyond his years, especially with electronics. I think he's headed for a job in IT."

This morning, while he was having his cereal, Leo showed me a PowerPoint he worked on last night when he heard I was babysitting him again, detailing all the things he wants us to do together. It almost reads like my bucket list, but instead of such chicanery as *kiss a hot guy on the beach*, his consists of making a rocket ship-shaped sandcastle and beating me at paddleball.

"Why don't we go build our sandcastle," I suggest when Leo returns.

I'm not exactly sure how to build a sandcastle that looks like a rocket ship, so I let Leo guide us in the planning and execution. He does an admirable job.

"This is so fun, Kacie," Leo says as he pats a mound of sand-turned-Apollo-13. "I think we should build one every day. How many sandcastles would that be?"

"How high can you count?" I ask, not sure if he's even able to count to ten. Sue me for not knowing the cognitive abilities of five-year-olds. It's my first rodeo.

"I can count to infinity!" he says, puffing out his little chest.

"I'm sure you can, but I'm only here for the summer. Let's

find something we can count out so you can visualize how many castles you can build."

I find a stick and draw three calendar pages in the sand, starting with today and ending Labor Day.

"These are all the days left in summer. Wanna count them?"

I sink into my chair as he drops to his knees. Scooting along the sand, it takes him a while to count the squares. I'm thankful because I need a damn rest.

"Is that the Fudgy Wudgy guy?" I call out as he's about to finish counting.

He jumps up and scans the beach.

"Sorry," I say. "Just a guy with a beach cart."

He slaps his hand on his forehead and proclaims he lost count. Now he has to start all over.

I'm thrilled my evil masterplan worked. You're right, I'm probably the worst, but I'm enjoying sitting down for a damn change, and hoping we can make this last for another hour or so.

"I have ninety-five days left of summer!" he finally exclaims. "That's bigger than infinity!"

Returning to sandcastle building, I summon my inner child and soon become obsessed with making drippy fins on the rocket sandcastle. Leo's found a friend, and the two of them split their time between bringing me buckets of water and hanging out with the kid's mom.

I'm hard at work squeezing sand through my hand when a shadow passes between me and the sun.

"Impressive," Chase says. "I had no idea how talented you were in the sand sculpting category. What else don't I know about you?"

"Stay tuned."

"Fully tuned, housemate."

I don't look up at him for fear I'll give away the tingle going through me. Instead, I joke, "Wait till you can see what I do with a shovel."

"Hopefully it doesn't involve the disposing of bodies."

"Keep mocking me and you'll find out," I say, sitting back on my heels.

"I come in peace." I look up to see him holding a seashell mold. "So he can make designs in his castle."

"How sweet. Are you sure it won't make you sad, parting with one of your toys?"

"I have a lot more where this comes from."

Leo, who must've noticed Chase's presence, comes bounding back to us with something in his hand. He takes a bite of the thing which is shaped like a—

"Peanut!" I scream, batting the thing from his hand.

Leo gives me a terrified look as his lower lip begins to tremble.

"EpiPen! EpiPen!" I run to the cart and frantically dump out bags in search of the lifesaving device. "Where is it? Where is it?" I whimper as I maniacally search. It's not here. No! Leo cannot die on my watch. I grab my phone to dial 9-1-1.

Spinning back around, I see Chase and Leo staring at me with eyes the size of soccer balls. What am *I* doing? He's the first responder.

"Don't just stand there!" I yell at Chase. "Get an EpiPen!"

"I don't think that's necessary," he says calmly as he bends over and picks up the offending allergen, holding it up. "It's a circus peanut."

"But he's allergic!"

"Dude. It's made of marshmallow. No peanuts involved."

"Are you sure there's no peanut flavoring?"

Leo is now doubled over, laughing his tiny head off. Chase too.

"Stop laughing!" I say, trying to reclaim my breath from sheer terror as Chase hands it to me.

"I've never seen one of these." Holding the orange squishy thing, I now see it's candy.

"I know who I wanna be with when I go into anaphylactic shock," Chase jokes.

I'd tell him to fuck off, but we have a G-rated audience. Who's still doubled over in laughter.

Sue me for not wanting the kid to die.

"You're lucky you're alive," I tell Leo. "Circus peanuts have been known to kill people."

Chase hands Leo the seashell mold. "Now that we've sorted that out, I came to give you this."

"Wow, what is it?" Leo asks.

"One of my discovered treasures. Kids sometimes leave their toys behind, which could pose harm to sea life if they get swept out to sea. I like to come out early in the morning, before the beach rakers, and pick them up. That way, I'll have them in case the owners of the toys come looking for them."

"Can I do that with you someday?" Leo begs. "Apparently I get up early enough."

"How about one day before surf camp?" Chase asks, turning to me.

"I'll have him again on Tuesday. I'll see if I can get him earlier."

"Yay!" Leo exclaims.

Ben texts at lunchtime to say he and Leo have reservations to play laser tag in Ocean City that night. He asks if I want to come along, but I decline. There are fewer things I'd hate to do more than play laser tag, even if it involves Ben. I have to draw the crush line somewhere.

After dropping off Leo, I head home where I'm greeted by the distinct scent of seafood. Chase is in the kitchen, wearing nothing more than an apron and his guard shorts. I hate this for me.

"I scored some lobster tails and filet," he says, giving me a huge grin as he takes a sip of wine. "Care to join me?"

"To what do I owe this honor?"

"Simple math. There are two tails, two steaks, and two of us."

"You sure I'm not interrupting something?"

He follows my gaze to a second glass of wine, already poured. "That's for you."

"Oh. I thought maybe you were expecting someone else."

He smirks. "Who would I be expecting?"

"Uh, Francine?" I tease, unable to refrain from poking the player bear. "Seems to me if you've been shacking up with her, the only respectable thing to do is treat her to dinner."

"I already gave her an apple. Isn't that enough?"

"Depends on what you want from her."

"How about nothing?"

"Right. I guess you got what you wanted the night of the party."

"The night of the—oh." His brow furrows. "Nothing happened between us that night, so you know."

My disbelieving guffaw echoes off the stainless steel appliances.

"I'm serious. She had too much to drink that night and threw up on her dress. I gave her a shirt, and we had her stay over so the guys could keep an eye on her."

"Is she the complication you referenced earlier?"

"No," he says. Then, "Not her."

His response suggests there's someone else. I wait for him to offer up details, but he doesn't.

"No need for *this* to be complicated, though," he says. "Just one housemate treating another to a fine dining experience. Section 9(i)10 states, and I quote, '*If the housemate-of-the-first-part is bestowed upon him a feast, he shall share it with the housemate-of-the-second-part.*'"

"They really did think of everything for these rules," I say, trying to hide my smile.

"They had to. Without rules, there'd by anarchy."

"Especially in a summer shore house."

"Oh, you have no idea. Wendy said you've never been part of a shore house before?"

"My first."

"I've been lucky, so far. Most of my housemates over the years have gotten along well. But man, you should hear some of the stories other guards tell about shared-space living. All the drama."

"I'll get the popcorn."

"Here, take this instead," he says, handing me a glass of wine as he raises his for a toast. "To a peaceful summer, filled with rules."

"To rules."

We stare at each other for a long moment, and my skin prickles with goosebumps. Why do I get the feeling that we're both thinking the same thing?

That rules are made to be broken.

28

The last thing I want to do is treat this as a date, so I ditch my idea of wearing a sundress for dinner and instead err on the side of casual. Nothing says *look how chill and unassuming I am* like a tank top and baggy sweatpants.

Chase serves us and we dine on the deck below a lavender sky as the sun creeps toward the horizon. The food is amazing, and he regales me with tales of the house drama he hinted at earlier. Wild shit, like two women in the house vying for the same guy, the other housemates choosing "teams" and getting into near brawls over it.

"This is delicious," I say as we eat. "Thank you."

"My pleasure."

With the sun now tucking itself in for the night, the air has become considerably cooler. He must see me shiver because he pulls off his sweatshirt and hands it to me. "Here, it's clean."

It's warm and cozy and smells like Chase.

I shiver again when I realize he's just cooked the exact dinner I made a joke about yesterday when I suggested he should cook for me after "pushing" me off the sailboat.

"I know I asked this before, but I don't feel I got a direct answer. Why did you cook this delicious meal for me?"

He shrugs. "I enjoy your company. Seems pointless for the two of us to be living in the same house but not sharing meals together. It's what people who live together normally do, or so I'm told."

"You've never lived with someone? Not even a girlfriend?"

"Nope."

I realize through all our bantering, friendly talks, and that steamy kiss, I don't know much about his romantic background. But I want to. A friendship is developing here, after all, and I like to know about my friends' journeys. Especially since we'll be living together all summer.

"No serious relationships?" I ask.

"I had a semi-serious relationship in college, until I returned home to take care of my parents," he says. "She broke up with me shortly thereafter. Since then, there's been nothing serious. It's hard to date while watching your parents—well, you know."

I place my hand on his. "I'm so sorry."

His eyes meet mine with a smile. "Life happens. At first, I was hurt that she left while I was going through the worst experience of my life. Especially seeing the way my parents were there for each other, for everything, up until the very end."

I think of my own parents, and how I never experienced that. Mine have always been in it for themselves.

"But we were young, and I know now she wasn't my person. Once I wrapped up their estates, I threw myself into teaching and coaching. Now, I'm too busy. I'm not looking for a serious relationship unless I meet someone worth it."

"I feel you," I say. "I've put my career before all else. When you're working late nights and weekends, there's not much free time left. Especially for bullshit relationships."

"Uh-oh. Sounds like you speak from experience."

"Yep. My ex cheated on me—multiple times, it turns out. After I found out about the most recent one, people couldn't wait to tell me they'd seen him out with other women on occasion. When confronted, he always had a convenient excuse. An out-of-town cousin. A coworker assigned to the same project."

"But no one told you at the time?"

"Nope. None of them were good friends of mine, just mutual acquaintances who either believed his lies, or didn't want to get involved."

I can't believe I'm telling him all this, but here we are. The cool night, the cozy sweatshirt, and a good listener—all makes me feel like I'm in a safe space.

"That's pretty shitty no one said anything, at a time you could've done something about it."

"Yep. People suck."

"I get how you'd feel that way," he says, nodding pensively. "But not all people do."

"Just the sucky ones."

He holds out his wine, and I clink my glass against his as our eyes meet. It's the first time I've shared my history with someone who didn't already know about it. It's cathartic.

"So, no serious relationships for you," I say. "Does that mean...just hookups?" I know I'm being forward, but if we're gonna be friends...

He gives me a half-smile. "Occasionally."

I roll my eyes. "Tell me you're a player without telling me you're a player."

"Guilty as charged."

"A-*ha*! I knew it!" I exclaim as I leap to my feet and point at him like he's the accused at a Salem witch trial. When no one comes to burn him at the stake, I calm the fuck and sit back down. Narrowing my eyes at him, I add, "You're a dichotomy."

"How so?"

"The first night we hung out, you're all *ooh, love is real* and *I can't wait to meet my soulmate.*"

"I don't believe I ever said those words," he says, smiling.

"Fair. But you were definitely all *I believe in love and marriage.*"

"Because I do."

"Yet you're not interested in settling down. Why is that?"

He levels a look at me. "I just prefer to keep things casual..."

His admission, combined with his expression, serves as a red flag. The kind lifeguards fly when the water's too dangerous to go in. Not that I was planning on wading any further into this pool of temptation, but at least he's confirming my belief. He's charmed—and extremely dangerous.

"...until I find my *soulmate*," he continues, air-quoting my word.

His statement throws me off balance for a moment. Not that it should. What do I care whether he's casual or soulmate-seeking? We're friends, so I should support whatever he wants to do. "I get that."

"My friends say I'm too picky."

"You too?" I laugh out loud. "Sorry I'm not willing to derail my life for someone who may not be worth it in the end."

"Exactly! Thank you, someone who gets it. I love my life and what I do. I don't need to fill it with something that's only going to cause drama and heartache in the end."

"Facts."

"What my parents had was beautiful. I've vowed to never settle for anything less. It's my way of honoring their lives—even if it means I'm single for the rest of mine. It would kill them to know their only child, born from such love, ended up with something less than what they had."

"Aww," I say, clutching at my shriveled heart, which has now grown a half-size bigger at his words.

"I guess that makes me weird, being a guy," he says, giving me a shy half-smile. "Hopeless romantic, here."

"A self-admitted player with a romantic side. As previously stated, you're quite the case study."

"Or...maybe I'm just a romantic, playing it out for now, until I find her. Ever think of that?"

I squint, regarding him closely. "Interesting."

"How about you?" he asks. "How did you get so bitter about love? Other than your ex, what about your other relationships?"

"Aside from a high school boyfriend, that asshole was my only relationship."

"That sucks. How about your parents? Do they have a

good relationship?"

I laugh out loud. "They get along about as well as our two political parties."

"Oh," he says, grimacing. "Sorry to hear that."

"Yeah. Not a good sitch."

Without warning, I open my soul and vomit more of my backstory all over the wooden deck table.

"I found out several years ago my dad's been cheating on my mom. Something about us Layne women must attract it. Except my sister Robin—her husband's a peach. Looks like one, too, but no shade. Anyway, it was apparently going on for years before Robin stopped by my dad's law firm one day, unannounced, to take him to happy hour. Found him kissing his coworker and threatened that if he didn't tell our mom, she would. So they went home—as Robin put it, 'with the gun of truth to his head'—and he confessed."

"Oh no."

"It gets better," I inform him. "According to Robin, our mom laughed out loud. A nasty laugh, as Robin described it, and said, 'You must think me a fool to not know this.'"

"Whoa! Not what I would've expected."

"Right? According to legend, she turned on her heel, took her glass of wine to the patio, and called a friend to discuss their Mahjong tournament as if nothing had happened."

"Wow."

"Not exactly the reaction my sister had expected, so she dug further. Turns out my mom had known and turned a blind eye to the affair because she didn't want to humiliate the family or upend her life by seeking a divorce. She consciously decided to trade love for a lavish lifestyle. And because she was willing to let my dad carry on with his affair, she basically got whatever she wanted."

"Like what?"

"BMW, country club luncheons, endless spa sessions.

Shopping high-end boutiques and an exclusive membership to an upscale gym. Oh, and private tennis lessons with a pro half her age. Rumor has it, they've been seen out together quite a bit."

Chase is silent for a moment. "I have two thoughts. First, I'm sorry for your experience. Must've been hard."

I wave him off like it's no big deal, even though my parents' backstory has significantly informed my feelings toward marriage.

"Robin was so afraid how we would react, she waited until I'd taken the bar to tell me and the boys. Over time, we each developed our own take on it. My oldest brother, also a lawyer, stopped talking to my dad other than when we're all together for holidays. Robin and Oops sided with my mom, and my other brother defended my dad every chance he got. We later discovered why—he, too, had cheated on his longtime girlfriend."

"What team were you on?"

"Neither. I was referee," I say, shrugging it off as if we'd been divided over what color to paint the living room. "One of us had to stay neutral. Given my chosen profession, that was me, the one least surprised by it."

It was my role, as a typical middle child, to play mediator between all the moving parts. A skill that paid off in my professional career. Perhaps it was my factual approach to law—and love—that allowed me to see both sides and view the situation without emotion. Or maybe I was just accustomed to seeing marriages in shambles. Either way, it's no wonder I ended up a family lawyer.

My parents' dysfunctional marriage has fed into my own distrust of the institution, for sure, but I also have to admit it has been refreshing to see my parents doing this weird, self-centered dance—together but separate, living parallel lives. Somehow, they make it work. Both became happier as a result. Proving that love may not all be what it's cracked up to be, if two people can be happier in an unloving marriage than in a loving one.

Or maybe my parents are just whacked.

"It makes more sense to me now, why you're anti-marriage. It certainly hasn't been modeled well for you."

"Facts. What was your second thought?"

He smiles and shakes his head. "You should write a book, girl. That's some great fiction there, if it weren't actually non-fiction. You have quite a talent for humor. I think you'd be a great comedy writer. No, I know—romance. Since you're such a big proponent of it."

The twinkle in his eye tells me he's joking.

"Now who's the funny one?" I ask. "I'm guessing you have to *believe* in something in order to write about it. But you are right about one thing—I've always wanted to be a writer. Just not romance."

"What would you write about?"

"Human tragedy, horror, and grisly murder, to start."

"Oh, geez. Sorry I asked."

"Enough about me," I say. At the risk of sounding like I'm interviewing him, I turn the questions on him. I want to know more about my new friend. "What sport do you coach?"

"Middle school football in fall, mini-hoop basketball in winter, and surf camp in summer."

"No wonder you're in such great shape," I blurt out.

He gives me a shy smile. "Thanks. I'm flattered."

"Is it called mini-hoop because the nets are little?"

He chuckles. "No, the players. Preschool to elementary. It's the most fun one can have coaching, teaching basic skills."

"Random question but...how do you spend your Wednesday nights, off-season?"

I ask because Amy once told me about an article she'd read that suggested if you really want to know a man, ask what he does on a Wednesday night. Allegedly, it gives you info about how he spends his free time, which in turn is supposed to tell you about his values. Not that coaching kids in various sports, at varying levels, isn't value-revealing in itself. Still, I'm curious.

"Throughout the school year, I volunteer at the youth center's after-school program—"

Of course, he does.

"—helping with homework, curating their interests, being an adult they can talk to in a safe space. You'd be surprised how many kids want to be there instead of going home at night."

Who *is* this guy?

"What do *you* do on Wednesday nights?" he asks.

I'm at a loss. Other than work, I have no idea what I do any night of the week.

"I used to work," I say. "Now, not so sure. Got any ideas?"

"Do you surf?"

"The internet, yes. Ocean, no."

"You should come with me. I'll teach you."

I'm reminded of the bucket list, and Amy's directive to learn a new skill. I can't believe the next words that come out of my mouth.

"Why not?"

29

It's two weeks later on a Wednesday when Chase and I finally align our schedules for surf lessons. I hesitated to do it on a day when I'd have Leo, as Ben was starting to arrive home later each day. Not that I minded. I was enjoying Leo's company and helping another attorney do their job. I was also scoring points with said attorney—teaching his kid how to use the outdoor shower, getting him ready for bed, and learning how to pull kid dinners out of my ass (apologies for the visual). As one who rarely cooks for herself, I'm proud to say I'm becoming somewhat of a Kraft Mac & Cheese connoisseur and a whiz at microwaving Dinosuar nuggets.

I find Chase waiting for me on the beach after work, suntanned and smiling, holding two boards.

"Ready to learn how to surf, Jellyfish?" he asks. "Conditions are perfect tonight."

If someone had told me a month ago that I'd be standing on a beach about to risk life and neck bone, I would have told them they were full of shit.

"First we need to learn how to get up," he says, laying the boards on the sand.

He teaches me how to go from a supine position to a crouch, to a stand. The moves require muscles I didn't even know I had. Once I somewhat-nail that, he takes me into the breaker zone. He holds the board while we wait for the right wave to come along and then thrusts it forward.

We practice a few times with me just lying on the board

to get a feel for the wave action. Then, he has me get up to a crouch. The first few times I try, it's on wobbly, uncertain legs, and only for seconds at a time. When I finally stand, my legs are shaking so much they nearly give out on me. Fear grips my chest as I picture the tip of the board impaling the sandy bottom—assuring a ride on a backboard to the ER instead of a surfboard back to land.

"I can't do it," I plead, ready to quit. "I tried. It's just too hard."

"Kacie, don't let fear guide you. Tell yourself you got this. Makes all the difference in the world."

I picture Leo and manifest his five-year-old confidence. I'm surprised the difference it makes. I still suck and spend most of my time toppling into the drink, but soon I stay up longer. The more I do it, the more natural it feels.

"You're getting it," Chase says as I finally make it to the shallows standing upright. He jogs toward me through the surf and offers two high fives. "Ready to go out a little farther?"

"I guess?"

He heads inland to grab his board. Here's the moment I've been lowkey dreading—going out beyond the breakers, becoming one with unseen creatures lurking below. I'm experiencing a bit of post-traumatic sting syndrome, but Chase keeps reminding me to take deep breaths as he shows me how to paddle over the swells until we're out beyond the surf zone.

He sits on his board and I follow suit, overcome with a feeling of peacefulness I've never experienced before.

"I'm starting to get why people do this," I say.

He looks around before his eyes lock with mine. "Beautiful, isn't it?"

Something about the way he's looking at me makes it feel as if I'm part of the scenery he's referencing. A tingle goes through me, but I have to remind myself we're just out here as friends. Surf instructor and student.

"You good if I ride a couple?" he asks. "You won't be tempted to run off with another jellyfish?"

I laugh out loud. "No, I'm good. Do your thing."

I'm mesmerized as he executes several perfect rides, his tan, muscular body glistening in the setting sun. I'm enjoying this moment of solitude, watching him in awe and admiration. His movements are graceful, powerful, and his vital strength is no match for the tumbling waves. Or my rising libido.

After his last set, he paddles over. "And that, my friend, is how it's done."

"Nine outta ten."

He laughs. "Only nine? How can I improve?"

"Help me become as good as you are, Mighty Surf God."

"Okay, Spineless Sea Creature. Strap in."

Chase shows me how to pick the right wave by feeling the energy of the ocean, calling upon my supreme boogie boarding skills, as well as how to set up and paddle my way to standing. Each time, I go a little farther but always end with a clumsy dismount.

"I had no idea marine invertebrates could surf so well," he says as I paddle back out to him.

The sun is getting closer to slipping below the horizon. We go out again and bob over the swells as we lie on our boards, facing one another.

He finally speaks. "I realized what it is about you that's so attractive."

"It's my surfing prowess, isn't it?" I ask, laughing.

"That. Right there," he says, giving a shy smile. "You have the cutest laugh that lights up your whole face. You're quite fun to be around, Jellyfish."

"Flattery will get you everywhere."

A beat, and then a whisper. "Promise?"

His hand, still underwater, reaches toward mine. I dip my hand under the surface and take it.

"Just two friends, holding hands after experiencing something fun," he announces. "And it's underwater, so it doesn't count."

"Don't make me bring out the handbook."

"Aren't we in maritime jurisdiction now?" he asks. He looks so adorably vulnerable right now.

"We're not far enough offshore."

I'm teasing, because fuck the rules. This feels so nice, bobbing on the water with Chase, holding hands and existing in this space together with no intention of making it more. The fact that our hands are clasped underwater feels symbolic of the mutual attraction I can no longer deny, bubbling just below the surface of our friendship—attraction that doesn't need to be acted upon, and won't be. For once, my brain's not scrambling to figure out what we're doing, where we're going with it, how it's all going to work out, pondering what the future holds... I'm just in the moment, enjoying the way his hand feels in mine.

I think of Ben and wonder if I should feel guilty, if not more conflicted, especially now that he's showing interest in exploring *more*. Something I've been wanting for so long. But isn't that the beauty of being single? The prerogative to explore options? I'm not doing anything wrong. I'm just here to enjoy my summer. I don't have to explain myself, or my waffling feelings, to anyone. For once, Kacie Layne gets to enjoy the feeling of two men showing her attention, with no shame.

"Okay, one more run," Chase says, breaking the comfortable silence. "It's gonna be dark soon. How 'bout you take the next one?"

The last ride proves to be my best. I finally feel like I'm in my element, being one with the board and the wave, my strong legs holding me steadily confident as the wave carries me forward.

Chase follows with a perfectly executed ride of his own, expertly careening to where I'm standing in waist-deep water.

He dives in and swims over, rising to his feet when he reaches me. For a second, I'm lost in his aquamarine eyes, beads of water sparkling on his eyelashes. His smile is so bright it's almost blinding. He pulls me toward him and lifts me up.

"Great job today," he says.

The huskiness in his voice compels me to wrap my legs around him as he holds me. Our chests are touching, skin on skin as cool water swirls around us. Our boards, strapped to our ankles, float upon the surface just beyond us as he looks deep into my eyes.

His grasp around me tightens as he pulls me closer and grunts. "God, girl..."

"What?" I give a shy giggle. I know what, but the devil in me wants him to say it.

"You have no idea what you do to me."

"Unless a narwhal just joined us, I have a pretty good idea."

Chase laughs out loud and releases me, then sinks beneath the surface. When he comes up for air, crimson creeps across his cheeks in the most adorable way. "Busted."

I cup my palm and thrust a wall of water toward him, splashing his face.

Folks, I'm sorry. You're probably hoping for a juicy scene here but, as I've stated, humor is my go-to for these types of situations. Like I warned you in the beginning, I'm not your typical FMC. Apparently, I'd much rather act like a fifth-grader than a grown-ass woman when faced with a hot-ass man.

"Just for that," he says, then sweeps both arms through the surf, drenching me with a wall of water thrice the size of mine.

Not one to ever turn down a challenge, I do the same. Before I know it, we're engaged in a water battle royale until, finally exhausted, I struggle up onto the sand with my board and collapse. Chase follows and stands above me.

"Don't ever think you can take me on in a splashing contest and win. I was captain of our varsity team in high school."

"Wish I'd known that sooner," I say, panting. "That should be the first thing you disclose upon meeting someone."

He extends his hand and helps me up. Picking up his board, he begins walking back to the house. I follow suit before he turns to me.

"Oh, hi!" he says, pretending he didn't realize I was there. He extends his hand. "I'm Chase Maddox, Worldwide Splashing Champion. And you are?"

I take a breath and swallow all the flirty, suggestive things I want to say. Instead, I go with, "Gonna beat you to the house!"*

And then I beat feet.

---

* I don't.

As another week gets crossed off the calendar, my summer begins to feel routine. I don't mind—I'm a routine kinda gal. Fridays through Mondays, I work the shack, and Tuesdays and Thursdays I'm with Leo. Wednesdays belong to me. I try not to schedule anything routine for that day so I can enjoy flying by the seat of my pants. Something new for me.

Since our surf lesson, my friendship with Chase has developed. During the week, when we have the house to ourselves, we often spend evenings on the deck, talking over a bottle of wine or a bucket of beer. Mornings, we ride bikes on the promenade until we split ways toward our assigned beaches. One rainy day, we found a closet filled with board games. Chase ran to Wawa for their two-for-one hoagie deal, and we had a board game marathon. For dinner, we ordered Chinese, and he forced me to watch romance movies. Three of them: *Dirty Dancing, When Harry Met Sally*, and *Titanic*.

"Doesn't this make you swoon?" he begged after Harry gave his New Year's Eve speech.

"Meh," I teased, even though I did feel a bit misty-eyed. This summer's turning me into a softie, but I must keep up appearances. "Sorry, romance is still not my thing. Now give me a grisly murder movie..."

He shook his head and laughed. "You need help."

Today, we're doing something out of the ordinary. Chase has a day off, so we're taking Leo to the Wetlands Institute for a turtle release. I've already confirmed with Amy that such activity indeed qualifies as *doing something charitable.*

It all started one morning when Leo and I helped Chase search for abandoned beach toys. The first one Leo found was a plastic turtle.

"Look, guys!" he exclaimed as he came running to us. "My dad and I love to read about turtles. Did you know they travel all the way from the wetlands to the beach to bury their eggs? The mom takes off, never to see her kids. Kinda like..."

He swallowed hard as his little face went pale, and I knew he was thinking about his mom moving to California.

"Let's see that turtle," Chase cut in, obviously trying to deflect the situation. I'd given him the SparkNotes, non-violative version of the Ben and Angi story, so he knew about Leo's mom sitch. "Wow, dude! This is way cooler than any toy I've ever found. What shall we name him?"

Leo giggled. "It's a toy, Mr. Chase."

"Yeah, but he's real to me. What about Snyder?"

"Silly man, this is a girl turtle."

Chase slaps his hand against his forehead. "You're so right. I *am* silly. Okay, how about Sandy?"

Leo smiled. "I like that name."

"Ever meet a real turtle?" Chase asked.

"No."

"We need to change that. We should visit the Wetlands Institute someday for a turtle release."

According to Chase, the Wetlands Institute hosts a family-oriented program every Tuesday to educate visitors about diamondback terrapins, a species found only in New Jersey. Visitors help release baby terrapins, whose eggs were rescued and hatched, to return them to their natural habitat.

So here we are on Turtle-y Tuesday, strapping Leo into the car seat Ben dropped off that morning. It cracks me up that a kid so wise beyond his years has to sit in one, but rules are rules.

It's a beautiful day, so Chase drops the top as we cruise down Ocean Drive, through Avalon and Stone Harbor, to the Wetlands Institute.

I wasn't sure a lecture on turtles was up a five-year-old's alley, but Leo is fully engaged in the lesson. When it's time to release them, he names each of his turtles, wishing them luck in their new home. When he gets to the last one, he's quiet.

"What's wrong, buddy?" I ask, noting a tear streaming down his cheek.

He heaves a sob. "I don't want to say goodbye. I love him. Can't I keep him?"

I look around for a volunteer to ask if I can buy one, because I can't stand to see him broken up about this. But Chase steps in.

"I'm sure he'd love to live with you, but he'd miss his family."

I fire a warning look at Chase, hoping he doesn't say anything about the turtle needing to find his mom.

"All those turtles you released?" he continues, nodding his acknowledgment of my warning. "They're his cousins, and they're waiting for him so they can swim together."

I breathe a sigh of relief. Points are added for referencing cousins, which he must know means something to Leo.

"Are they gonna go find the Eastern Australian Current, like in *Finding Nemo*?" Leo asks, smiling through his tears.

"They are."

Leo blows a kiss to the tiny turtle nestled in his palm. "I love you, Tommy Turtle," he says as he crouches down and submerges his palm until the turtle swims away. "Go find your cousins and tell them I said hi. Capisce?"

On our way home, Ben texts to say he's running late and asks if we can give Leo dinner. I show Chase the message at a red light and tell him he can drop us off at Ben's if he doesn't want to partake.

"I'm *turtle-y* in," he jokes.

I turn to Leo. "Hey, buddy, your dad's running a little late. What do you want for dinner? Your choice."

"Pizza!" Leo cries out.

Chase turns to me. "You heard the man. Pizza it is."

"Homemade," Leo adds.

I glance at Chase. "Any idea how to make homemade pizza?"

"No, but I bet Chef Google does."

We're fortunate to find premade pizza shells and fixings at Acme. We take Leo back to our house and are constructing our individual pizzas when Chase suggests we make it a movie night.

"Let's make a picnic in the living room and watch *Finding Nemo* in honor of our turtle release," he says.

Chase cues up the movie and I set up a picnic with blankets and pillows on the floor, while Leo jumps from pillow to pillow, pretending the floor is lava.

"Guys, this is the coolest thing I've ever done!" Leo exclaims as we settle in for the movie.

Ben texted earlier to say he'd be back around nine, but I'm hoping he'll be later. At least after Nemo's found. It's so cozy—the three of us sitting on the floor eating pizza and watching the movie—even more so with a summer storm now raging outside. Chase and I are leaning with our backs against the couch, thighs touching. Leo's curled up next to me. It's feeling really intimate, and I'm not ready for the night to end.

During the jellyfish sequence, Chase whispers to me. "Were any of your family members cast in this movie, Jellyfish?"

"That one there," I say, pointing.

"I see the resemblance."

I laugh and punch his thigh.

Ben arrives two minutes after the movie ends, apologizing for his tardiness. "Wow," he says, taking a gander around our living room, where blankets are spread on the floor, pillows propped against the couch, empty pizza plates strewn about. The lighting is low—Chase's idea, to make it feel like we were at an old-time drive-in movie.

"This looks cozy," Ben says. I'm not sure if I imagine the tension in his voice but it definitely sounds...different.

"It was fun, Daddy," Leo announces. "We even made our own pizzas."

Chase cleans up while I walk Ben and Leo out to his car. The storm has passed, leaving behind the scent of rain and a lingering layer of humidity.

After he gets Leo fastened in, Ben turns and puts his arms around me. "Thank you for today," he says. "You don't know how much it means that I can rely on you to keep Leo for so long. This case is taking up more time than I thought."

"No worries," I assure him. "He's a delightful little boy, and I love spending time with him."

Who would've guessed this plot twist? But it's true. Leo is easy to be with—dare I say, even fun. I could see myself doing this more regularly.

"Let me make it up to you," Ben says, his voice low and suggestive as he pulls me in. "I'd like to finally make good on my promise for an actual date. A nice dinner tomorrow night. If I recall correctly, it's your birthday."

He remembered! While we've been through ten years of birthdays together, he isn't always the best with dates.

"I'm dropping Leo off at my sister's tomorrow for a sleepover, but I'll be back late afternoon. He'll be staying with them in Philly for a few days, so it'll just be you and me."

"I would love that," I say, even though I suspect I'll miss the little guy.

"I can hardly wait." He grasps my waist and pulls me in closer, giving a low, sexy groan as his lips descend toward mine.

A tingle of passion zings through me, excited because we're finally going to kiss, the first time since law school—at long last.

Instead, he moves his lips to my cheek and whispers in my ear. "I want to kiss you so badly, but little eyes are watching..."

My gaze follows his to the car window, where Leo is peering out at us. I give Ben a friendly hug like the respectable nanny I am.

Later that night, I write in my journal about the day and how fun it was, watching Leo release his turtles, the rapt attentiveness he showed the instructor as we learned about diamondback terrapins. Also, how kid-friendly Chase is, and how I think he'll make a great dad someday, once he finds that person he deems "worth it."

I write about my upcoming date with Ben, and the expression on his face when he asked me out on our (finally official) date. A chance to talk about our future.

I'm putting a check beside *#6: Do something charitable* when #7 on the bucket list catches my eye.

Wear a fancy dress.

I didn't bring a fancy dress, but a special birthday dinner with my longtime crush tomorrow sounds like the perfect occasion for a new one.

31

I don't just find the perfect dress. It finds me.

Chase has lent me his Jeep for the day, and as I cruise over the Townsends Inlet bridge, I'm thankful my birthday falls on a Wednesday this summer. I don't think I've had a day off on my birthday since I graduated college. It feels liberating to have the sun shining on my skin and the sea breeze blowing through my hair as I croon along to my Down the Shore playlist.

Once in Stone Harbor, I grab a mocha latte at Coffee Talk, where Taylor Swift once performed as a kid. Strolling down 96th Street, I find a boutique with fancy-ish dresses. When the owner notices me searching racks in bewilderment, she asks what I'm looking for.

"I'm having a special dinner tonight and looking for something a little fancier than what I'd normally wear."

She pulls a selection from the racks and sets me up in the dressing room. After I model several dresses, she gasps when I emerge wearing a turquoise maxi dress with cutouts on the sides.

"That's the one!" she exclaims, clapping.

Even I have to admit a bit of stunning-ness, a first for me.

After my successful shopping spree, I treat myself to a margarita and nachos at Buckets, a bayside Mexican cantina, and splurge for a facial at The Reeds hotel's swanky Salt Spa before heading home. Birthday perfectly spent.

Ben had planned to pick me up at seven-thirty, but he texts to say he's still at the office and running late, and could we meet at the restaurant instead? He scored a hard-to-get reservation at the Deauville Inn for 8:00 and doesn't want us to lose our table. No biggie, especially when he offers to pay for my Uber.

I'm standing on the porch of the shore house waiting for my ride when Chase turns the corner and jogs up the stairs, still in his lifeguard uniform. He's halfway up the steps before he looks up and sees me. Stopping dead in his tracks, a smile spreads across his face.

"Wow," he says, with an exhale. "You're...stunning."

My heart quickens as his eyes drink me in. I'd be lying if I said I didn't love his reaction.

"Hot date?" he asks. "Don't tell me...Benswali?"

"Yeah."

He shakes his head. "He's a damn lucky guy. You look gorgeous."

"Thank you," I say, smiling at his compliment. "I appreciate you allowing me to use the Jeep today. If it weren't for you, I'd be wearing a trash bag."

"You'd still rock it. And it was my pleasure." He jogs up the rest of the steps and turns back. "I hope it's his too."

You and me both, buddy.

When I arrive at the restaurant, I'm seated at a prime table along the water, perfect for watching the sun set over the bay. I wonder if Ben requested this table specifically. The server presents me with a chilled bottle of wine, explaining my dining guest preordered it. A chill goes through me. He's pulling out all the stops. This has to be it, the day our *maybe someday* starts.

I take small sips of wine, watching as kids play on the beach next to the dock. Adults chat animatedly, drinking cocktails as they enjoy a beautiful summer evening. As the minutes creep beyond eight, I begin nervously glancing at my phone. No messages from Ben. When my phone finally dings with an incoming text, I assume he's here.

But it's Wendy, checking in. I'd told her about my date with

Ben when we were texting last night. She understands the significance of this outing, having told her about my past with Ben during one of our drunken late night deck talks.

> Hope you're having fun, and all your birthday wishes come true!

> Thanks. He hasn't arrived yet.

> Held up in traffic, I assume?

> That's my guess.

A few minutes later, another text comes through. From Ben, at last.

> Hey, girl. There's a huge accident at the 42 Freeway merge, and I've been sitting here for half an hour. Even if we started moving now, I wouldn't get there until after nine. I don't want to keep you waiting. Can we do this another night?

Tears sting my eyes as I read his message again. I don't bother texting him back. Instead, I text Wendy again.

> He canceled.

> OMG why?

> Stuck in traffic and claims he won't get here in time.

I know how long it takes to get from his office to the merge point of the freeway. He should have been well beyond that point by now, if he left when he needed to in order to make it in time for dinner. I play the route out in my head now, trying to figure out what time he actually left. Even giving him the benefit of the doubt—a Mummer's Parade breaking out in front of him unexpectedly as he navigated Philly's congested streets—he still left late enough to almost ensure he wouldn't make it here on time.

The reality hits like a pie to the face.

Blinking away tears, I look down at my beautiful dress and chastise myself for thinking tonight would be special. And for crying about it. Like I said, I'm not a crier—but this time, tears are warranted. That's what I get for getting my hopes up where men are concerned. I should know better by now.

I turn away from the diners seated around me, hoping no one can see me sitting here blubbering like an idiot. I surreptitiously swipe and dab at my tears, which continue to well and tumble down my cheeks despite my will. Staring out at the happy people, laughing and yucking it up, I wonder if any of them have ever been stood up on their birthday. The thought only makes me sadder, so to keep my mind off it, I pour more wine and take slow, deliberate sips to wash away the anger and disappointment.

When the tears finally subside, I pick up the menu. It's my birthday, and I'll be dammed if I'm gonna sit here wallowing in self-pity. It's time to celebrate my life with a fancy meal splurge, even if I'll be enjoying it alone. Residual tears still blur my vision, and it takes several minutes for me to make sense of the words.

I'm trying to decide between filet and lobster when the server returns with a glass of champagne.

"From the gentleman at the bar."

Great. Just what I need—some creep hitting on me when I'm down in the dumps about Ben. Can't I just sit here in pitiful solitude? I'm about to decline the drink when she steps aside and gestures across the deck.

Leaning on the bar, one foot perched on the rail, a man in a tux lifts his glass in a toast to me.

Chase.

I laugh out loud as he approaches.

"I didn't know they served jellyfish here," he says, giving me that sexy half-smile. "Just my luck, 'cause I was hoping to dine with one tonight."

My lower lip descends into a pout as tears begin flowing again, this time with gratitude. "Are you really here for me?"

"Of course. Who else would I be here for?"

Sniveling, I laugh-snort through tears. "How did you even know?"

"A little birdie told me what happened. No one should spend their birthday alone."

"You wore a tux," I point out. It's the same one I saw hanging in his closet, that first night I arrived and snooped around his room.

He shrugs. "A tux was in order after seeing how stunning you look tonight."

The breath is literally sucked from me. But not the humor.

"Please tell me you're not a magician," I say, straightening his lapel.

"No presto-digitation here, ma'am. Just me."

"Is this your side hustle—hired gigolo for damsels in dateless distress?"

"What tipped you off?"

I point to him. "Gigolo." Then, I point to me. "Damsel in *this dress.*"

"Nice," he says, laughing at my play on words.

I hold up my glass for a toast. "Maybe you do have a little bit of magic in you. Thanks for alakazaming your way here."

"My pleasure." He clicks his champagne with mine. "To you, and the day the world got a wonderful person."

As we sip, our eyes meet.

"I promise to make your night special," he says.

And boy, does he. We order a bottle of champagne and

the most expensive items on the menu. While the sun sets, we watch, enthralled, as a man on the dock below holds a hawk on his heavily gloved forearm, demonstrating how hawks keep seagulls away.

"I know what I'm getting you for your birthday," Chase says, chuckling. "A hawk of your very own, so you can dine on your beach *hoew*-gie without an umbrella."

"Don't make promises you can't keep," I tease.

"How's your bucket list coming along?"

I almost choke on my shrimp cocktail but recover quickly. "Pretty good." To save face, I add, "Just so you know, that wasn't my idea. Amy made it, hoping to inspire me to try new things."

"Is it working?"

"You got me on a surfboard, so..."

"What would be on a bucket list *you'd* make?"

"I dunno. Travel, I guess. And you?"

"Travel for sure."

"Where would you go?"

"First stop, Paris," he says. "But only if I had someone special in my life. My parents went there on their honeymoon and kissed atop the sparkling Eiffel Tower at midnight. Hearing them talk about how special it was, I want it for myself."

I cannot believe this man. He has me tingling in places I didn't know I had. Before meeting him, Amy was always the most ooey-gooey romantic I knew. Chase definitely has her beat.

But then I remember how Seth would wax poetic in the same way, making lofty statements intended to woo me. In the aftermath of our relationship, as I tried to figure out how I didn't see the signs, I deemed this trait the mark of a true player: someone who can easily chameleon themselves into a romantic main character.

"Where's the first place you'd go on your travel bucket list?" he asks.

Determined to keep some emotional distance, I lean

on my usual crutch—sophomoric humor. "Willy Wonka's Chocolate Factory."

As previously noted, I need help.

His eyes twinkle. "Something tells me life with you would never be boring."

Just as we finish our meal, a group of servers approach our table with a slice of cake lit with a candle. I turn crimson as everyone sings to me.

My gaze meets Chase's over the flame. "You're too much," I whisper. No one has ever treated me this special on my birthday, certainly not a guy.

"I'm just getting started."

After we've shared the piece of cake, I reach for my purse. "Thank you for showing up and making this one of the best birthday dinners I've ever had. It's my treat, to show my gratitude."

"Already taken care of, my lady," he says. "I gave my credit card to the server when I came in."

"You didn't have to do that!" I object.

"I wanted to."

"But—"

"If you don't stop arguing with me, I'm gonna take back that hawk I got you."

I giggle. "Okay, but next time's on me."

He gives me that smile. "What makes you think there's gonna be a next time?"

32

By the time we leave the restaurant, the sun has fully set into the bay. We're crossing the gravel parking lot, about to summon an Uber home, when we notice a huge pink moon rising above the narrow barrier island.

"Strawberry moon," Chase says. "That's what they call June's full moon."

"Why does it look so pink?"

"Because of its low position in the sky, combined with atmospheric effects."

We stop and marvel at it—so huge and surreal. Chase pulls out his phone and checks something.

"Low tide," he says, taking my hand. "Come on, Jellyfish. One more treat for the birthday girl."

We cross Ocean Drive and navigate beyond the houses huddled at the tip of Ludlam Island to a beach path. We leave our shoes at the wooden railing, and Chase rolls up his pant legs. He holds my hand as we trudge through thick sand to the water, out to a sand bar pointing across Corson's Inlet toward Ocean City on the other side. We go to the very tip where water rushes by to get into the inlet. It feels scary and exciting all at once.

"Are we safe like this?" I ask.

"You're always safe with me."

He looks down and squeezes my hand, and I believe him. For once, I totally forget the potential dangers lurking around me—swirling ocean, a romantic full moon, the man who's just wrapped his arms around my waist. All threatening to sweep me off my feet, but fear has completely eluded me.

"Happy birthday, friend," Chase says as he pulls me closer and begins swaying back and forth.

I giggle as he takes one of my hands in his, cradling it against his chest.

"Need I remind you of the rules?" I tease.

"Fuck the rules." He looks down at me, his face so close I can feel his breath mingle with mine. "They don't apply on birthdays."

Okay, then.

"We're dancing...by the light of the strawberry moon." He starts crooning to the tune of "Silvery Moon," exchanging the word *silvery* with *strawberry*.

My heart swoons at his low, sexy tone. The reverberations of his baritone voice dance upon my chest and tickle my heart.

It's almost too much for me to take. Him in a tux. Me in a fancy dress. The moon sprinkling a trail of pink glitter across the water, leading right to us. This has to be the most romantic thing that's ever happened to me.

His voice gets huskier as he comes to the end of his song. We stop swaying and now it's just moonlight, me, and this incredible man gazing at me, his mouth, breathless with anticipation, coming closer.

"I can't stop myself this time," he whispers in a throaty voice as he cradles my face with both hands.

Neither can I. Screw the rules—the house ones, and my own.

"Then don't," I say.

His lips crush down on mine as we both emit involuntary moans. Like our first kiss, I'm transported to another world. I don't care about housemate drama. I don't care about player avoidance. While we're at it...Ben, who?

All I care about is this kiss.

It goes on for a long time, getting more and more intense as the moments swirl by. I can picture us as if we were in a movie.

He's leaning into me like his life depends on it. His hands are now grasping my waist where my skin, exposed by the cutouts, tingles from his touch. He pulls me in tight, kissing me with everything he's got. It's the stuff of Amy's rom-coms, and I can't believe this is my life right now.

Screw it all. For the first time in a long time, Kacie Layne is falling in...

To the Atlantic.

At least it feels that way as water splashes over my feet just as Chase pulls away. We look at each other in amazement and start laughing as we simultaneously exclaim, "The tide!"

Chase lifts me, throws me over his shoulder, and takes off running. I'm so high from our kiss and giddy with feels, I almost don't care if we end up in the drink. Fortunately, Chase is faster than the tide and we make it back to the main beach in time, splashing all the way, just before a wave takes over the entire sandbar.

He must have been bit by the same giddy bug, because we laugh all the way back to the main road where we summon an Uber. Silence fills the backseat as we hold hands all the way home.

Climbing the stairs to our house, I'm trembling with anticipation over what comes next. Despite my resolve not to repeat history, I'm ready for whatever's coming.

Once we're inside the foyer, he takes my hand. "There are so many things I'd love to do with you right now, but I'm not going to take advantage."

"You won't be..."

He shakes his head. "I want this night to be the story we tell our kids someday."

For a second, I cannot breathe.

He lifts my hand and kisses it ever so softly, not taking his eyes off mine. "Happy birthday, beautiful girl."

33

My phone is buzzing on my nightstand, waking me from a passionate dream about a certain magician. Rolling over, I tap the screen to see Ben's calling me. At 4:00 a.m.

"What?" I croak, sitting up in a panic, hoping nothing's wrong with Leo.

"Hey, Kace," he says, his slurry tone filled with remorse. "How was your birthday?"

"How was my birthday?" I give a sardonic laugh. "You stood me up, that's how."

"I'm so sorry. That's why I'm calling. Please let me make it up to you."

I roll my eyes. It's the middle of the night—he couldn't have waited until morning?

I'm pissed at him, but it did turn out to be one of the best birthdays ever. No thanks to him, but also thanks to him. Still, that doesn't make what he did right. I get traffic being beyond his control. That route can be brutal, but leaving as late as he did makes me feel like an afterthought. Not the first time.

For ten years, I've given him all the power—waiting for him to reciprocate my feelings, make room for me in his life, take me on a date. It burns knowing how excited I was to start a new chapter in our whatever-ship, only for him not to show up. Amy's right. He hasn't made himself available to me—physically or emotionally. I've always blamed it on the circumstances, but it's clear I'm simply not a priority for him.

Chase makes me feel like a priority. Last night, he opened my eyes to what a romantic experience truly is. I'd never experienced anything like it.

I want this night to be the story we tell our kids someday.

The memory of his words sends a shiver through me. It was such a sweet sentiment. It may be not what I want, what I'm looking for, but it made me feel special—even if it sounded like it was plucked from the pages of the player handbook on how to make women swoon. I wouldn't be surprised, the man is that smooth.

These are the things I'm telling myself to keep from getting carried away. He's a first responder and rescuing people is what he does. I have to believe he turned on the charm to make my birthday night special and save me from humiliation—the kiss was simply a cherry on top.

I may sound delusional to those of you who picked up this book hoping to read a heartwarming love story, but this is my life. I still have to live with him for the rest of the summer. I can't afford to start drawing hearts around his name in my journal, while trying to protect my own.

"I'll be back tomorrow night," Ben says, interrupting my thoughts. "Can I take you out then, to make up for it?"

Friday night is when everyone returns for the weekend. We've gotten into a groove where I host a welcome back happy hour, and Chase cooks burgers on the grill.

"Sorry," I say. "I wanna be here when my housemates arrive."

"Oh." He sounds disappointed. "Maybe another time?"

"Yeah," I say, then add with a twinge of sarcasm, "*Maybe someday.*"

He's silent, and I wonder if he's picking up what I'm putting down. If so, he doesn't say anything.

I have a hard time getting back to sleep after our call. I'm not sure why it was so urgent he had to call me at four in the morning. Was he missing me? Regretful for blowing me off?

Drunk dialing? I wait for my heart to flutter like it usually does when I talk to Ben. Instead, it flatlines.

Drunk dialing? I wait for my heart to flutter like it usually does when I talk to Ben. Instead, it flatlines.

34

Thanks to Leo still being at his aunt's, I get to sleep in today. When I reawaken at ten, Chase is already at work. Good—I'm nervous about seeing him in broad daylight after last night.

This morning, I don't just think about going for a run, I do it. Running always helps to clear my head, which is exactly what I need right now. Once again, I run to the end of the island and treat myself to an iced coffee at Shorebreak Café.

I'm walking home on the beach when my sister calls.

"Hey, bitch," she says when I answer. "Ready for me and Mom to descend upon you next Thursday?"

"I can't wait," I say. I mean it. I haven't seen either of them for months, and I can't remember the last time the three of us did anything together. I'm grateful Robin's able to get away from her medical practice to spend the July Fourth holiday weekend in Sea Isle.

"When do you think you'll get here?" I ask.

"Probably around six."

"Perfect. I'll have dinner ready."

"Speaking of dinner, how was your birthday? Was it everything you expected?"

"Not exactly."

Robin is the only other person on the planet besides Amy, and now Wendy, who knows about my crush on Ben. And how that dinner was supposed to be "the start of something new."

"Oh, Kace," she says, when I tell her he stood me up.

"But one of my housemates showed up and saved the day."

"That's nice. Which one?"

"Just...a friend."

I know my sister. If I tell her Chase's name, she'll gush all over him when they meet each other next weekend, thanking him for saving my birthday. I don't want anyone else to know about it. The night belonged to us. Even Wendy doesn't know that Chase came to join me after she told him about Ben's blow-off.

"I don't believe you," Robin says. "I can tell from the tone of your voice, it was more than that. I can't wait to get there and suss it out."

"There's nothing to suss."

"We'll see about that."

That's the last thing I need, my meddling older sister investigating whether there's something going on between me and Chase. Because, after last night, I have to admit—there's definitely something to suss, no matter how much I'm trying to deny it.

"Well, Ben...you snooze, you lose," Robin says. "He's had enough time to make this happen. Traffic or not. I think you have to face facts—it's never gonna happen with him, sis."

I change the subject to their impending visit, and we discuss plans before ending our call.

With a Leo-less Thursday sprawling out before me, I spend the rest of the day catching up on me time—lunch at Sunset Pier, window shopping along Landis, zen-ing with Full Moon Beach Yoga. When I return home that night, I find a note from Chase saying he's working a sleepover shift at the summer camp. Good. More time to myself.

Settling on the deck with a glass of wine, I'm relieved to have space and time to process last night, tired of avoiding the significance of what's transpired in the past twenty-four hours. Ben blowing me off. Chase showing up to sweep me off my feet and...*damn*, that kiss. What he said about our future kids, for crying out loud. I'm hoping when we do finally see each other, things aren't awkward or messy between us. I have to admit, there's a part of me that wonders what it would be like to step into the unknown, open up my heart, take a chance on someone new. But the thought stokes familiar fears.

In other words, it pokes the demons.

My conversation with Robin has reminded me that I've spent ten years hiding my love for Ben from him, terrified the truth would leave me exposed, rejected, and heartbroken if he didn't feel the same way. The excuses I gave him after our law school kiss were my way of protecting my feelings, choosing a silent crush over a truth that could crush me. Taking shelter, instead of chances. What if I'd spoken my truth that night? Would it have made a difference?

Maybe not. Perhaps Amy is right—he *is* unattainable to me, and on some deep level I know that. Yet, for some reason, my subconscious feels safer clinging to false hope with him than taking a chance on someone fully available.

Like Seth, who represents the other end of the demon spectrum. The guy so readily available, his enthusiasm made me jump in feetfirst without testing the water. In retrospect, if a friend of mine told me a guy said he loved her after three dates, I would have called bullshit on him, warning that quick involvement often equates to control and other nefariousness. But for some reason, I needed to believe I was *that* alluring to make a man focus so intently on me. Probably because I was just coming off the Ben and Angi ordeal, and my bruised ego wanted—no, *needed*—to believe I was worthy of someone's unbridled, enthusiastic love. I took Seth's always wanting to know where I was, and who I was going with, as a sign he couldn't bear to be away from me. Turns out, he only wanted to know my whereabouts so he could wine and dine other women.

Let's face it—the guys aren't the real problem here. The problem is something within me, causing me to distrust my own ability to be truthful with my feelings, and to love and be loved. Somewhere, between the unattainable guy and the too-good-to-be-true snake in the grass, is the sweet spot. The question is whether I can get to the point where I can (to borrow my sister's term) suss that out for myself. And discover if that guy actually exists. Chase could be in the running, but he still seems just a bit too perfect to be true.

I think of Perseus, how he had to face his fears and battle his demons to find love. One thing is clear. Before I entertain thoughts of "more" with Ben or Chase—or *any* guy for that matter—it seems I've got some work to do.

35

By the time I return to the house after work on Friday, several housemates have arrived, but my happy hour partner-in-crime is nowhere to be found. I know he's not still sleeping off his night shift because his door's open. Come to think of it, his Jeep isn't in the driveway, either.

"Where's your husband?" Rex asks as I join my roommates on the deck.

"Husband?" I ask giving a nervous chuckle. I hope we haven't given the housemates the impression we're an item.

"You know, that tall, good-looking dude you live with all week?"

"Chase?" Becky looks up from her phone and pipes in. "He's in Philly. On a *daa-aate*!"

I flinch so hard, I almost throw my back out.

"Who's the unlucky woman?" Rex asks.

"I think it's some chick he met on the apps," Becky says.

My heart drops. For two reasons. One, I didn't know Chase was actively seeking dates. Not that it's my business, because in this day and age, who isn't on apps? Besides me. I'm not about to meet some online rando IRL so he can drag me to a basement, hogtied, and carve out my organs for sale on the black market. I prefer to meet men organically, so I know I'm not getting catfished into believing he's a hot army dude, stuck overseas, who needs my money to get home.

The other reason, which I'm starting to come to terms with, is...I *like* him. Perseus would be so proud of me, peeling back a corner of fear to acknowledge my truth after my late-night-on-the-deck solo therapy sesh.

I thought he liked me too, but now he's on a date with someone else after telling me he wants to tell our future kids the story of last night? My play-dar goes off again, reminding me of what I already know. He's dangerous. Him going on a date tonight means the kiss meant nothing to him.

Hear me out, my dudes—talking to you, too, Perseus—I am *not* doing the Ben thing again, pining for some guy who's unavailable to me. For whatever reason. Same with the Seth thing, as I've said ad nauseum.

"What are we dishing about?" asks Celeste as she joins us on the deck.

"Chase's date," Rex says. "Some chick he met on a dating app, apparently."

"She's not some Hinge chick," Celeste says as she takes a seat, leveling a look directly at me. "She's my cousin. I set them up. It's their second date."

I almost spew wine all over my housemates as my heart nosedives into my knees. Although, none of this should come as a surprise. His cousin even referred to him as a ladies' man. Chase *himself* confessed that he was a player. Of course, he softened that with disclaimers that he doesn't date much, doesn't have time, not looking for something serious until he finds someone "worth it." I also recall what he said about having complications. Now I wish I'd asked for details because this is the last thing I need—to literally and figuratively be swept off my feet by a guy already holding on to someone else. Someone worth the drive to Philly to see a second time.

Strawberry moon and future kids, my ass. I should have trusted my instincts and not allowed myself to let my guard down, get caught up in his aquamarine gaze, feel his tender lips on mine—

Stop it!

For the rest of the night, as my housemates and I chill on the deck, I carry on like I could give two fucks about Chase. So well, in fact, I'm deserving of an Oscar.

36

On Saturday night, my housemates throw me a birthday party. Wendy insists on leading me to the deck blindfolded, despite the fact I already know it's happening. After a resounding "Surprise!" a little body breaks through the crowd and throws himself into my arms.

"Happy birthday, Kacie!" Leo exclaims.

Well, this part *is* a surprise. I had no idea Ben and Leo would be here.

"How many are you turning?" Leo asks.

Recovering like a pro, I flash both hands three times and add two fingers to signify thirty-two.

"Gosh, that's a lot of many," he says, smacking his forehead. "What is that, like fifty?"

I crack up as Ben joins us. I'm not sure I'm ready to see him again, but I give him props for showing up. This time.

"Hey, Kacie," Ben says, looking woefully apologetic as he gives me a peck on the cheek. "Happy belated birthday. Again, I'm sorry—"

"I know."

I make a conscious decision to set aside my disappointment about my birthday dinner, at least for tonight. I will, at some point, tell him how it made me feel, but now is not that time. Holding grudges takes more negative energy than I'm willing to give the situation, especially during a party in my honor. I won't let what he did, or his presence, ruin my night.

Ben goes off in search of Leo, who's dashed away, as Wendy joins me.

"I'm sorry!" she whispers, grabbing my arm. "I ran into him at Wawa last week before the blow-off and invited him. I didn't have his number to disinvite him."

I laugh. "No worries, you're good. He definitely screwed up, but I'm not ending a friendship over it."

"You're a better person than me," she says before walking away to greet a guest.

Now, watching him out on the deck holding his son, my heart softens. It has to be hard raising a child alone when work is so busy he can't leave the office in time for a birthday dinner with his best friend. Let alone the time he's missing with his child.

"Here are my guys," I say as I join them on the deck. "I brought you beverages."

I hand a juice box to Ben and pretend to hand the beer to Leo. They both laugh before I switch and hand them their age-appropriate drinks.

"Whatcha looking at?" I ask.

"I'm pointing out all the different varieties of seagulls found at the shore," Ben says.

I admire how Ben takes every opportunity to teach Leo about our world, which accounts for why the child is so well-spoken and knowledgeable about things. He's only ever conversed with him as if he were a little adult.

Chase emerges from the deck just then. It's the first time I've seen him all day. In fact, with him working the overnight camp, it's the first time since he left me in the hallway, mouth agape over his comment about our future kids.

"Ben," he says, giving him a handshake before gesturing to Leo. "And who is this handsome man you brought with you?"

"Coach Chase, it's me, Leo. Your student."

"I dunno..." Chase rubs his chin pensively. "I only know

one Leo, but he's a wee bit of a boy. You're more of a grown man. Looking so dapper!"

It's true. The little guy couldn't look any cuter in his tiny khakis and button-down shirt.

"It's for my girlfriend," Leo says, beaming with pride as he takes my hand. "It's her birthday."

"You mean friend who's a girl," Ben corrects him.

He looks up at Ben all wide-eyed and innocent. "Isn't that what I said?"

Someone taps my elbow and wishes me a happy birthday, and soon I'm pulled into conversations with other guests. Wendy brings out a cake and has everyone sing to me. Shortly thereafter, Ben comes over to let me know he and Leo are heading out. I know it's after Leo's bedtime, but the look on Leo's face tells me it's not his idea to leave.

"My fam's visiting early tomorrow," Ben explains.

I'm disappointed but remind myself I wasn't expecting him and Leo to come in the first place. I walk them out.

"Tuesdays and Thursdays are my favoritest days of the week, Kacie," Leo announces as we get to the sidewalk. "Wanna know why?"

I kiss his little cheek. "Probably because they're my favoritest days too."

He gives me a big smile. "Gotta go, buffalo."

"Mañana, iguana."

Back upstairs, I make my way to the deck where a cooler of Coronas awaits. I dig to find the coldest bottle. Standing up, I come face-to-face with Chase.

"Nice of you to include Ben," he says. There's an edge to his faux-sweet tone.

"Wendy invited him."

"Have you reconciled the blown-off birthday dinner? Everything hunky-dory again?"

I'm not sure what bothers me more—his tone, his words,

or his gall. I don't need to explain my complicated ten-year re-lationship to him when he's already on to someone else so soon after our kiss. So, I do the thing I do best. I counter.

"How was your date?" I smile, my tone matching his—grain for saccharine grain.

I walk away, not waiting for his response. I really don't care how his date was. I just want him to know that I know.

37

I took Sunday off in case I was hungover after my party, but I feel pretty good. I was looking forward to hanging out with my housemates on the beach, but it looks like it may rain. Upstairs, I go to put on a pot of coffee, but someone already has. After pouring myself a cup, I head to the deck where I find Chase, wearing a faded Sea Isle tee and sweatpants. Quite the departure from his normal morning attire.

"Mornin', Sunshine," he calls out, a fake sweetness to his tone. "Feel refreshed after that early bedtime?"

"Sure do."

"Why did you go to bed so early? I thought you were a party animal."

I shrug and cue up a lie. "I was tired."

I'm not sure I want to sit here with him, just the two of us. I'm still hurt he went on a second date with someone after our moonlight kiss, but I have to remember our status quo—he's just a friend, free to date whoever he wants. As am I. Acting like a jilted lover and casting him aside is not battling my demons. Acknowledging that disappointment can exist within a heathy relationship *is*. Points are added as I decide to act like an adult.

"What's with the getup?" I gesture to his outfit. His morning fit usually consists of lifeguard shorts and nothing else.

"Day off."

"Me too."

"Whatcha got planned for today?" he asks.

"Hanging out on the beach. That is, if the weather holds out. Looks like it could be a washout. And you?"

"Same. I'm hoping to get a girls-on-guys volleyball game going. Ever play beach volleyball?"

"I make it a habit not to."

"Well, you should give it a try. So I can take you down."

"We'll see."

He leans forward, elbows on knees. "Listen, there's something I—"

Just then, the sliding door opens and Harry leans out.

"Visitor for you, Kacie," he says, stepping aside to reveal Ben.

"Good morning," Ben says, looking between me and Chase.

"Is that what I think it is?" I ask. He's holding a brown box with white *Maryanne Pastry Shoppe* lettering.

"Box of Bismarks for my friend and her housemates."

Ben hands me the box and I lift off the lid to take a whiff. He knows what a sucker I am for Maryanne's Bismarks, the most delectable pastry on the island.

"Peace offering of some sort?" Chase asks, giving him a raised eyebrow.

Ben laughs nervously. "I'm...not sure what you mean?"

"For standing up Kacie on her birthday."

"Chase—" I'm about to tell him to let it go but then he stands up.

"I'll leave you two alone," Chase says.

I see the look he gives Ben as he passes him. Part of me is mortified, but the other part wants to give him a high five.

"What's that all about?" Ben asks, watching Chase's retreating back. "Did you tell him I stood you up?"

"I didn't tell him anything."

Wait. Those old habits of mine are rearing again, as I hear myself wanting to protect Ben's feelings. Maybe it's time for the truth.

"I told Wendy, and *she* told him you stood me up."

"Kacie, that's not—"

"Oh, right. Sorry—she told him you called off our date because you'd left the office too late to get there in time."

"Not entirely true," he exclaims.

"Yep, traffic, I get it. That's why you leave a reasonable amount of time to account for it." I sigh. "I deserved a little more respect, Ben. It was my *birthday*. I even bought a fancy dress for the occasion."

"I'm sorry, Kacie," Ben says, his eyes reflecting genuine sorrow. "You're right. Chase is right too—I'm here with a peace offering. I don't want you to hate me."

"I don't hate you," I say, softening. "I was just really looking forward to it. After going to bat for you, endlessly, during your divorce. Watching Leo so you didn't have to hire a stranger. Feeding him dinner all those late nights. After telling me you want to explore...this." I gesture between us. "I just wish the dinner had meant more to you."

"I'm sorry, Kacie. It did. Does. Please, let me make it up to you. Leo and I would love to cook dinner to celebrate your birthday some other night."

I don't want to let him off the hook so easily, but mention of Leo tugs at my heartstrings.

"Where is the little dude?"

"He's playing with kids whose family moved in next door."

"Nice," I say, happy to hear the kid has made friends down here. We stand there awkwardly for a moment. He seems to be in no hurry to leave. "Can I...get you some coffee?"

He says yes, and I go inside to pour him a cup. I'm passing the powder room when Chase emerges.

"I see we've forgiven him," he says.

"Yes, we have."

"I guess Maryanne's will make one forgive and forget."

"Forgive, maybe," I say, not loving his snarky attitude. "Not forget."

"Good." He moves in closer, smiling down at me, giving a slight flash of his eyebrows. "Because I wouldn't want you to forget the night we had. In fact, I should go thank Ben right now."

He starts making for the door, and I take off like a defensive lineman, grabbing him around the waist from behind, laughing as I try to pull him away from the door.

"What?" He laughs, too, continuing his forward momentum as if he's going for a first down. "Don't you think I should tell Ben all about our night?"

"You wouldn't dare!" I protest. Not because I don't want Ben to know. In fact, it may do him good to know he's not the only guy my pen whispers to my journal about. I just don't want anyone else knowing about that night.

He continues. "The way you mauled me on the beach, how I had to fight you off..."

"Like this?"

I go for Chase's neck and start tickling. His hands immediately pull mine away as he shrieks and melts into a fit of guy giggles.

"Okay!" he cries through his laughter, doubling over. "Stop! Stop!"

I look through the sliding glass door and see Ben watching us with a confused expression.

"I'd better—" I say, freeing my hand from his grasp.

"Yeah."

Ben gives me a smile as I return to the deck. "Coffee?"

"Oh, shit, sorry! I—got distracted."

"Yeah. Looked that way."

Going back in to retrieve the coffee, I find Chase in the kitchen, pouring himself a second cup. Without words, he pours a mug for Ben. Reaching around him for the creamer, I accidentally brush his waist.

"Grope me all you want, Layne, but it's not gonna work this time."

I laugh. "Oh yeah? When have I ever groped you?"

"In the lifeguard stand. On the beach the other night, when you melted right into me." He takes a sip of his coffee, staring at me over the rim.

Oh God. His look liquefies me, makes me forget everything. Ben. His date. My resolve.

I finally find my voice. "I think it was the other way around, pal. I recall you leaning into me so hard, I didn't know where you ended and I began."

I'm shocked by the intensity of our flirtation, but there's something that feels so sexy about having this conversation in the middle of the kitchen, in broad daylight—casual, as if discussing the weather. Apparently, him being on two dates with the same person, and me still considering Ben as an option, doesn't diminish this spark between us. The titillating ebb and flow between lighthearted flirtation and impending danger is almost intoxicating. Especially when he gives me that sexy smile.

"You may be right about that."

My heart is about to beat right out of my chest. I can't keep standing here, threatening to break the rules, when I've got another guy waiting for me on the deck. The one I've been waiting for all these years. Who, yeah, may have screwed up, but he's here to make it better.

I turn away from Chase and return to the deck.

"Thanks," Ben says as I emerge from the house and hand him his coffee. "You look adorable this morning, by the way."

I look down at my sloppy Sunday fit and wonder if he's drunk. I'm a hot mess. In fact, with my hair piled on top of my head, baggy sweatpants, and off-the-shoulder crop top I've had since high school, I'm one broken nail away from being a People of Walmart meme.

"Flattery will get you everywhere," I say as I sink down into a chair. "Even if it's based upon mistruths."

"No mistruths here. You just seem so...happy lately. At peace.

I haven't seen you smile so much since we were in law school."

He's right. Maybe it's being so close to the ocean, or the new friends I've made these past few weeks. Or maybe it's not spending every day actively trying to piece together people's shattered lives. Including my own.

At long last, I feel a sense of peace I haven't felt since the summer days of my childhood. I just hope it lasts.

38

Finally, it's the weekend of my sister and mom's visit. Our schedule is packed with plans, starting with a little welcome-to-the-shore clambake party in the backyard Thursday night, when my housemates will be heading down to beat July Fourth holiday traffic.

The moment my family arrives, my sister grabs me in a hug.

"You look great, sis," she says, squeezing me tight. "Looks like the shore's treating you well. You're almost as dark as a roasted cashew."

"Fuck you," I whisper lovingly into her hair.

"There's my girl." My mom leans in for a hug as well. I know it's mostly for show, in case anyone's watching. She's never this nurturing. Pulling back, she glances around the room. "This place is actually nice. I expected something...I dunno..."

"What?"

"Shabby, I guess."

That's my mother for you. Always ready with a backhanded compliment.

I lead them to the kitchen, where I've set up a couple charcuterie boards, bowls of chips, and dip.

"This is beautiful, but this can't all be for us," my mother says.

"No, Ma. My housemates are coming down tonight to beat the holiday traffic."

I pour their drinks and we go out to the deck. In the backyard down below, the caterers are setting up a clambake.

"What's all this?" my mother asks.

"I'm hosting a little seafood party to welcome you to the shore, and help you guys get to know everyone."

"Aww, how sweet. Are you sure you can afford this?"

"Yes," I say, my tone terse. Now that I've added nannying to my income stream, I decided to splurge a bit, hoping to show my fam a good time. I found the start-up catering company, run by two college guys, advertised in the *Sea Isle Times*. For a decent price, they'll cook various seafood and side dishes right here. They'll even clean up.

"Can't wait to meet Mr. Charming," Robin says.

Shit. I forgot I'd told Robin about my birthday-saving housemate.

"Oh, yes." My mother's eyes light with curiosity. "The mystery man. Is it okay if I join in the fun and try to guess who he is?"

"There is no mystery man," I say, giving an eyeroll. Even though it's nice that my mom's showing some interest in my life, I don't need these two meddling ninnies poking into my business. "Just a platonic friend."

"Mom, get her some wine," Robin jokes. "I still don't know what happened that night, but maybe she'll start talking after a few glasses."

"Nothing happened," I insist. "Drop it."

A sudden commotion comes from downstairs, signaling the arrival of housemates. We go back inside to greet them. As they arrive, I introduce them to my mom and sister. Rex and Harry turn on the instant charm, and the keen interest my mom and sister show them in return cracks me up. I'm pretty certain they think the "mystery man" is one of them.

Shortly thereafter, He Who Shall Not Be Named arrives, shirtless as always, wearing only his lifeguard trunks and a huge grin. The sun, beaming through the skylight, seems to follow him, illuminating his sun-kissed hair and casting his eyes the color of Arctic ice. My sister gasps as my mother clutches her figurative pearls. I try not to stare as he crosses the room and offers handshakes to them.

Why must he be so damn sexy?

My mom—who must think so, too—practically leaps into his arms. There's a reason my sister and I call her Cougar Colleen. She's got a bit of a rep.

"Bring it in, big boy," she says, pulling him into a hug.

I'm instantly mortified.

"Nice to meet you, Mrs. Layne," Chase says, laughing with surprised amusement. He turns to my sister. "And you must be Robin. Kacie's told me so much about you."

I watch my mom and sister transform into flirty teenage girls. My sister wraps her hair around her finger and asks Chase whether he's made any rescues lately. I can practically see the air quotes in her loaded question. Fortunately, he doesn't seem to notice.

After more idle chitchat, Chase heads upstairs to shower, and I go into the kitchen to refill their drinks.

"I have a good guess on the guy who saved your birthday," my sister coos into my ear.

I walk away, ignoring her.

As the house fills with incoming housemates, I enjoy watching everyone interact. Soon, we've all gravitated to the backyard and, before long, the servers announce the feast is ready.

Chase comes down the steps to the yard, all freshly showered, wearing a pink polo shirt and white shorts. This is new. Other than a tux on the night of my birthday, I haven't seen him so cleaned up. Usually, his evening attire consists of shorts or sweatpants, top optional, but if opted for, nothing more than a t-shirt.

The food is delicious, drinks are flowing, and steel drum music blares from outdoor speakers. The string lights, tiki torches, and *Finding Nemo* party decorations I purchased at Sands Department Store in town create a festive tropical atmosphere.

Including several cardboard cutout jellyfish, which I hung on the fence.

Chase appears beside me, offering a Sea Isle Iced Tea.

"Great job, girl," he says. "Mucho impressed."

"Thanks. I thought it would be a fun way to kick off the holiday weekend."

"It's a nice cozy night, just your fam and the housemates." Something behind me catches his eye. "Wait, are those jellyfish?"

"Yep. They insisted I invite them."

"In that case, let's go say hi and get a selfie."

We position ourselves in front of the jellyfish, and Chase leans his head against mine as he snaps a photo.

"Aww, look how cute," he says, showing me the picture. "Jellyfish's family portrait. This'll make a great Christmas card."

It is a nice picture. We both look tanned, relaxed, and happy.

"Send that to me," I instruct.

"Already have."

As Chase walks away, my sister joins me. She gives me a smile. "I'd put money on Chase being the birthday savior."

I chuckle. "How much are you willing to wager?"

"Doesn't matter, cause I know I'd win. I've seen him refresh your drink three times. He follows you around—where you are, sure enough, Chase is there too."

My heart pounds to hear this, confirming what I've noticed myself.

"He's absolutely adorable for you," Robin says. "I fully approve."

"Thanks, but there's nothing going on there. He's kinda seeing someone else."

She looks me square in the eyes. "I bet not for long."

From your mouth to his narwhal. Sorry...ears.

I bite my lip. Part of me wants to tell Robin about that night, but it belonged to us.

"Speaking of men, where's Ben?" she asks.

"I just wanted it to be us and my housemates tonight. He and Leo are coming to the party Sunday."

"How's the nanny thing going?"

I lift up a macaroni necklace Leo made me. "This is how it's going." I smile, adding, "I think I'm in love."

"Wow," she says. "I never thought I'd hear you say that about a child."

"I'm not *that* bad," I insist. "I can't wait for you to meet this kid. He's adorbs."

"He must be if you're still hanging in there with him. I'm proud of you, Kacie. I've been worried about you, especially when you left your practice to come here, but it seems as if it's exactly what you needed to turn your life around."

"I couldn't agree more."

39

I never thought my mom and sister's visit would make me as happy as it has. I've felt somewhat disconnected from them in the past few years, mostly because of work, often choosing it over spending family time together. Some years, I only saw them for Christmas. Even then, I held my cards close to my chest, not sharing much about the details of my life to keep parental inspection to a minimum.

But this girls' weekend is climbing the charts.

I've taken off from work so I can be with them. In the mornings, we meet up for coffee after my morning run, then head to the beach and hang with my housemates. We spend Friday night with Oops and his friends, and on Saturday we dine at Henri's outdoor patio.

"A toast to my beautiful girls," Mom says after the server pours our Prosecco. "I'm having so much fun hanging out with you two. It's been too long."

"It has been," Robin says. "I'm glad we were able to do this. We should make this a tradition, just us girls."

"I agree," I chime in. I mean it. There's something different about my mom that I can't quite put my finger on. She seems lighter in spirit, not as judgy as she often is. Might I say, even fun.

"It looks as if you're enjoying your summer, Kacie," my mom says. "But what are you doing about finding a job? Summer won't last forever."

Welp, should have seen that coming. She's been too quiet about my choices, including the one to spend my summer here.

I lied about being axed, not wanting to face my parents' judgment. Instead, I told them I quit and was taking the summer off before finding something new.

"I know, Mom. I'm trying. I sent out a few applications, but no one's hiring right now."

"Are you *really* trying, dear?"

I can't tell my mom the truth, that I've only applied to Ben's firm, and if that doesn't work, I may leave the practice of law all together. My parents were proud of me when I became a lawyer. I'm afraid to tell them I don't like it and haven't for years, that I'm hanging in there largely to avoid disappointing them. From the time we were little, my parents told us we could be anything we wanted to be, as long as we were the best at it. That's why they were okay with Oops becoming a world-renowned skateboarder. You could plug in anything after *world-renowned* and they'd be fine with it. Pig farmer. Unicyclist. Times Square furry.

But...maybe my fam is deserving of the truth.

"Actually, no. I'm not really trying," I admit. "I need a break from it all."

"What will you do come fall?" Mom asks.

"I'm trying to figure that out."

"Maybe something outside of law is what you need."

I shoot her a look of surprise.

"Don't make the same mistake I did with my marriage," she says, clasping my hand. "I knew it wasn't right for me, and Dad and I weren't right for each other, but I've hung in there longer than I should have. I've spent half my adult life drowning my misery in frivolous pursuits. Tennis, shopping, girlfriend getaways. But, one day, I asked myself, am I *really* happy? Is this how I want to live out my days? The answer is no."

Robin and I stare at one another. We've been saying this about her for years. It's refreshing to hear her mirroring our thoughts.

"So," Mom continues, taking a deep breath, "at long last, I'm ending my marriage."

"It's about time," Robin says, beating me to the punch.

Mom smiles and pats her hand. "I know."

"What happened to make you take the leap?" I ask as the news settles in.

"I've been following this guy on Instagram who talks about up-spiraling your life. He challenges his followers to envision what their best lives look like. For me, that's being in a warm, beachy climate, like Florida. I could never get your dad to even travel there. Or buy a house at the shore, which you know I endlessly advocated for. Living my best life means going back to real estate."

It's what my mom did for a living before kids. With five of us spread over a twelve-year age range, someone needed to be there 24/7. My lawyer dad was no help, staying in the office late most nights as he did, working on briefs (his secretary's, not his own).

"Putting families in homes where they belong made me happy, gave me purpose. Having become accustomed to this opulent lifestyle I created, I need to go where the money's good. Thus, Florida. This time, it'll be *my* money I'm both earning and spending."

"And whatever settlement you get from splitting the estate," I remind her, always the lawyer. I know their worth. She's entitled to a shit ton from my lawyer dad, who's made a killing over the years.

"Actually, I'm doing something different for me. I'm taking the least amount I need to get started and putting the rest into a fund for you guys. I want you all to find a place together—a vacation home—so you can get together on holidays and vacations. Maybe here, in Sea Isle."

"You don't have to do that, Mom," Robin says. "We all make good money."

Well, some of us.

Mom nods. "I know you do, but life happens. I want this money to belong to the five of you. And I want you all to up-spiral your lives." She turns to me. "Especially you, Kacie. I've watched you over the past few years, going from a fun-loving girl to someone who's pessimistic, seeing the world through doomsday glasses. Feeling sad. Hopeless."

"Thanks, Mom," I say sarcastically.

"I don't mean hopeless as in there's no hope for *you*. I mean you're going through life without hope."

"Family law will do that. It almost assures I'll be miserable."

"It doesn't have to be that way. Life's too precious, and time's too fleeing, to waste it on things that aren't working for you. Like my marriage. And your career. I want you to envision your best life. What do you see? I may be wrong, but I highly doubt it involves divorce and custody."

If she'd thrown Prosecco in my face, it would have been less jarring. Once the shock wears off, though, I focus on her words.

"Take back the power," she whispers. "Your life isn't what happens to you. It's what you make happen."

"I haven't been happy for years," I admit. "I didn't want to disappoint you guys."

"You won't, sweetheart. You've worked your ass off. If you choose to flip burgers, we'll still be amazed by you. You have nothing left to prove."

"As long as you're the best damn burger flipper," Robin pipes in.

"Of course," Mom jokes.

My heart swells upon hearing that. My parents must have gone soft in their older years. At least, my mom has.

"What if I decide to do something outside of law? Do you think Dad will be disappointed?"

She levels a look at me. "Fuck your dad. I mean that in the kindest of ways. If he wants to practice law, let him. He doesn't get to decide what you do with your life. Only you do."

"Good, because I haven't exactly been honest with you. I didn't quit my job. They let me go."

She flinches as if I've slapped her. "They let you go? I thought you willingly quit."

"Nope. Sorry for lying. I didn't want you guys thinking I'm a loser."

"They're the losers. How could they let *you* go?" She shakes her head. "When you told us you'd left your job and were coming here for the summer, I thought you'd lost your marbles. But honestly, Kacie, your decision inspired me. Once I got over the shock, I thought, *You go, girl.* I shouldn't be afraid to upend my life, either."

I can't believe her words. Me? The Switzerland-neutral middle child? An inspiration?

"In my opinion, they've done you a favor," she continues. "Sometimes, when God closes a window, he opens a door."

I laugh. "I think the saying is—"

"I know what the saying is, but I stick by my version. We cling on to this little portal of happiness, a window, thinking it's all we have. When it closes, we're often presented with a much larger portal of possibility, a door, allowing us to step into a bigger, better world than we'd been living in."

Wow. I never took Cougar Colleen for someone so wise and reflective. Must've been all the spa zen.

"What does ideal life look like, Kacie?" my sister asks.

I think about the happiest people I know and what they're doing with their lives. Amy's saving the planet. Robin's helping the sick. Chase's teaching children. All I've done is dismantle lives.

I think about my summer and all I've experienced with the bucket list. Learning a new skill and doing something charitable were amazing. As I think about what's left, particularly *#9: Just say no,* I wonder if it's time for me to just say no to the law.

(Relax...I'm talking about the practice thereof. Not abidance by.)

The *study* of law—its evolution, reasoning, and effect on society—has been my passion since high school. It's the *practice* of law I'm not loving, especially family law. Seeing people at their worst, finding there is no happily ever after for the folks I deal with. It sucks, and I've never realized how much its negative impact has affected my life until this summer. Not just my outlook on love and marriage, but the world itself.

I'm still not entirely convinced I want to leave law altogether, especially with an application pending at Ben's firm. If they offer me a position, I owe it to myself to at least give it a shot to see if a different firm and area of practice makes a difference. But if I don't get the job, I'll consider something new.

For the first time since learning I passed the bar exam, I feel hopeful about my future.

40

Our Fourth of July party is well underway when Ben arrives with his little sidekick.

"Kacie!" Leo yells as he jumps up for me to lift him. I swear, this kid has grown over the past few weeks. "This is my first ever July Fourth party, and I'm excited to be here! Thanks for 'cluding us."

"*In*cluding," Ben corrects, chuckling. "His word of the day after I told him we'd been *included* in your party."

We go off to find my fam, who Ben's gotten to know over the years, and introduce them to Leo. I can tell my mom and sis are charmed by the little dude as he launches into a discussion of his words of the day. I excuse myself to greet other guests. Before long, someone announces it's time for the town's beach fireworks, which we'll have a great view of from our place.

Party guests gather outside. From the deck, I spot my mom and sister on the lawn. As I head for the outdoor stairway to join them, someone blocks my path.

"Where do you think you're going?" Chase asks.

"To find someone enjoyable to watch fireworks with."

"Who's more enjoyable than this guy?" He points a thumb at his chest.

Smirking, I gesture to the general audience gathered on the lawn. "Where do I start?"

As I turn to walk away, he snakes an arm around me from behind and pulls me into him. "How 'bout here?"

The crowd has gathered around us, making it difficult to

get away, so I take the liberty of leaning back against him as he tightens his arms around me. No biggie—just two friends watching the show.

"Kacie! Kacie!" a little voice calls out.

I separate from Chase like he's on fire.

"I wanna watch the fireworks with you," Leo says as Ben joins us, too.

Chase gives a defeated smile.

"Wow!" Leo exclaims as the first firework bursts above us.

"Can you see okay, buddy?" Chase asks.

"Little tough with all you tall people around. Except Kacie."

"Thanks, dude," I say, sardonically.

"Here." Chase hoists Leo onto his shoulders and turns to Ben. "Is this okay, Dad?"

"Absolutely," Ben says, giving his grinning son a high five.

I feel a hand on the small of my back. At first I think it's Chase's, but both his hands are on Leo's knees to keep him steady. Ben then takes my hand and lifts it to his mouth for a kiss. The significance isn't lost on me—he may as well swing his dick around for Chase to see. Still, I don't exactly *mind* the fact they're both flanking me, vying for my attention. It's about damn time I become the star of this show.

After the finale, Chase puts Leo down. "Okay, guys, happy Fourth. I'm off to bed."

I cock an eyebrow at him. "So early? I thought you were a party animal."

"This party animal has to work tomorrow."

"What's a party animal?" Leo asks Ben.

Ben chuckles. "I'll explain in a few years."

"Thanks for coming, guys." Chase shakes their hands and gives me a wave. "See you tomorrow, Kace."

As he walks away, I sense he's disappointed our special moment was interrupted. Or maybe I'm just projecting.

"Okay, kiddo, we better head out too," Ben says.

"Why so early?" Leo asks. "I'm also a party animal."

Ben ruffles Leo's hair. "That you are."

I walk them out and give Leo a fist bump. "Time to squirm, wiggle worm."

"Out the door, dinosaur."

As Leo skips down the sidewalk, Ben turns to me. "My sister's invited Leo on their two-week vacation, so you'll have some time away from the little party animal."

"Boo," I say, thrusting my bottom lip out.

Two weeks? That's a lot of time. I'm not sure what I'll miss the most. The pay—$800 coming out of my Europe fund—or the little guy who's waving an American flag at passing cars, chanting, "USA! USA!"

Ben chuckles as he runs his thumb along my lips. "What's the pout for?"

"I'm gonna miss Baby Uncle Sam when he's gone."

"I love hearing that," he says as he pulls me into a hug. "But this means we can finally go out for that dinner I owe you. Just the two of us."

He gives me a peck on the lips as Leo rejoins us.

We say good bye, and as they walk away, my heart sinks knowing I won't get to see Leo for two weeks. I quickly calculate how much time we have left before school starts. Not as much as I'd like. The summer seems to be slipping through my fingers. Before long, I'll be back in the city, hating my life again.

Or will I?

Maybe not, if my mom's inspirational talk sticks with me. This summer has allowed me to hit life's pause button and assess the choices I've made—like exclusively practicing family law. Crushing on a friend. Forsaking all others in both respects.

I think about my mom's observations of the person I've become. She, like Amy, is correct in their assessment of me. Somewhere along the way, I lost my main character energy and let pessimism take over where hope fell off. Maybe it's time I recast myself in that role, take control of my fears, and forge a new path. As Mom says, up-spiral my life. At this point, there's only one way to go, and it's up.

Thanks, Mom. For all your faults and imperfections, you sometimes *do* know best.

Returning to the party, I go in search of my fam when I run into Chase in the backyard.

"I thought you were going to bed?" I ask.

"Yeah, but I left my phone—"

"AAAHHH!" Wendy shrieks from across the lawn as others let out a cheer.

Peering through the crowd, I see Diane's boyfriend, John, down on one knee. Diane's nodding, crying, as she leans down and kisses him. Even my crusty divorce attorney heart swoons when I see it. Especially when I feel Chase's arm slinking around my waist.

"Wow," he sighs, unable to take his eyes off the happy couple as John picks Diane up and swings her around. Chase wipes a tear from his lashes as he pulls me in closer.

"But...they've only been dating a year," I say, glancing up at him. "Don't you need more time than that to know if someone's right for you?"

"No," he says, peering down at me with misty eyes. "When you know, you know."

As I climb into bed that night, I find myself feeling uncharacteristic joy for Diane and John. I know, right? I'm just as surprised as you are by my squishy reaction. But witnessing my first IRL proposal was surreal. Other than my housemate Shaniya's beach proposal, which I didn't observe with my own eyes, I only ever see the complete other end of the marriage spectrum, the tragic finale of a broken union. Unless you count the scores of weddings I've been dragged to begrudgingly by virtue of association. Even then, I spent most of those ceremonies with my eyes rolled so far back in my head, the only thing I witnessed was the back of my own eyelids.

Maybe I've been too busy focusing on the end of the relationship, and not the front. Maybe it's time I stopped mocking the beginning part of a couple's journey through life, predicting a premature ending, and instead focus on the good parts. The hope. The love.

I never thought I'd find myself saying this, but...I think I'm starting to understand the hype.

41

It's been a week since my mom and sister left, and I'm still smiling about the great time we had. Our discussion had such an impact on me that I've since filled several journal pages with thoughts and, dare I say, feelings. That's right—me, the woman who once claimed she wasn't a boo-hoo, woe-is-me, journal girl. Turns out some self-introspection isn't so bad. It's been fun exploring career ideas, along with thoughts on how to up-spiral my life, hoping to find insight into what that would look like for me.

With Leo away for two weeks, I've picked up extra shack shifts to make up for the loss of nanny income. Chase is back to working summer camp night shifts, which means we don't see each other much.

Tonight, Ben is finally taking me out for that dinner he long ago promised.

He picks me up at six sharp. Not only does he walk me to the car, but he opens the car door like a bona fide gentleman. This is some level of formality, something he's never done before.

Once inside, he hands me a single pink rose.

"What's this for?" I ask, sniffing the rose.

"Pink roses signify the beginning of a new romantic journey later in life," he says, giving me a sweet smile. "Not that we're later in life, so to speak, but definitely later than I'd wanted to do this."

I wonder what he means by *later*, but I'm quickly distracted when he leans over and kisses me on the lips. What starts as a peck soon becomes so much more, and my insides turn to jelly as our kiss intensifies.

"Wow," he sighs as we finally come up for air. "That was a long, long time in coming."

My heart's pounding, and I can't find the breath to speak. I wonder if his reference to time means he's been catching feels for longer than he's let on.

"For you," he says, handing me an envelope. "From our little friend."

Inside is a drawing of two stick figures sitting at a round object, which I assume is a table, surrounded by little hearts. The artist has signed "Leonardo S" at the bottom in shaky preschool font. At the top, he's written a personalized message.

"'Hav fon on yur dat,'" I read, chuckling.

"He's learning to write words by using his letters phonetically," Ben says.

"I just can't with this kid," I say, swooning over his drawing. "I guess this means you told him we were going on a dat?"

"Yes. He was worried I had nothing to do while he was away, so when I told him of our plans, he drew this and sent it to me."

"Do you think that was a good idea, telling him?" I ask before I can stop myself. I'm not the parent here, but maybe we shouldn't be sharing our adult news with the little guy until there's something more concrete to tell.

"He's fine. He knows we're friends, and I don't think he knows what dat means."

Don't underestimate him, I think. Kids today know much more than we did at their ages—thank you, internet and older siblings. Leo probably understands the Dow better than most adults.

Ben tells me it's a surprise where we're going, but as we head south on the Garden State Parkway, I know we're on the way to Cape May. I settle into the plush leather seat of his Mercedes as the sound of chill jazz wafts around us. It's giving major first-date vibes. I've been in his car a million times, but it's never felt so intimate. Especially when he holds my hand.

He takes me to a fancy French bistro where we start with a bottle of expensive wine and a menu with no prices, suggesting we're in for an opulent meal.

"What are you thinking?" he asks as we peruse the offerings.

"I'm thinking I hope you took out a loan for this."

"Nothing but the best for my bestie," he says. "I hear the duck à l'orange is fabulous."

He must see my wrinkled nose as I conjure visions of Donald.

"The filet au poivre, as well," he offers.

"Filet, it is."

Ben raises his glass. "A toast, to us."

"To us."

After taking a sip, he puts his drink down and takes my hands. "Here we are."

"Here we be," I say, feeing shy. I don't know why. We've had thousands of dinners together. It's just never felt so romantic between us, and I'm not sure how to act. Part of me wants to tell him to cut it out, stop with the act, be normal. The other part wants to jump his bones. I like this side of Ben, even if it's completely foreign to me.

I can't wait to see where this night takes us.

A server appears to take our order and silently judge us. At least that's what I'm guessing from the way he peers down his nose.

"For starters, we'll share the escargots de Bourgogne," Ben says. "For the entrée, the lady will have the filet au poivre, and I'll do the duck."

Sorry for what I'm about to do, but as you know, I can't stop myself.

"Lady?" I exclaim as the server walks away, looking behind me and under the table. "Is there a lady here?"

He ignores me as he picks up decadent-looking roll and

butters it for me. I'm not sure whether I should be impressed with his chivalry or go burn my bra somewhere. I've never had someone order for me, and I'm not sure how to handle it.

Cue the humor once more. "Well, butter my biscuit," I say as he hands it to me. "Many thanks, kind sir. Wasn't sure I could do that for my li'l ol' self."

"I can't take you anywhere, can I?" he says, a teasing gleam in his eye.

Maybe I should shut up and be gracious for this beautiful setting, this fancy meal, and this fine man sitting across from me, trying his best to make this night special. It's just...making me nervous. Like there are *expectations* attached to the night. Not just for sex—and you'd think after waiting so long, I'd be DTF. I'm more worried about what happens beyond tonight. I'm not sure what it will be like, me and Ben in a committed relationship. I'm wondering if my hesitation is a case of you-al-ways-want-what-you-can't-have, or if it stems from something else. Some*one* else.

When I return from using the restroom, he gets up and pulls my seat out for me. Again, nothing like the Ben I know, who'd sooner pull the chair out from under me as a joke than treat me like the gentleman he is tonight.

I can't take it anymore.

"Are you my date, or the maître d'?" I kid as he places my napkin on my lap.

You'd think after years of wishing for this, I could just en-joy the way he's doting on me. But it feels...unnatural. Dare I say...forced?

"Hoping for the first," he answers, "and more. How does boyfriend sound?"

Sounds like I need another drink.

While I love that he's trying so hard, this is so not us. It feels like one of those animal kingdom shows where the male birds fluffs his feathers, puts on an elaborate dance, and gives mating calls to impress his would-be mate. *Ca-CAW! Ca-CAW!*

He seems to notice my discomfort. "This okay for you so far?"

I decide to be truthful. "If what you mean is being treated like royalty, it's very sweet. But you don't have to go to such lengths, be so formal about it."

"I feel like I do," he says quietly, looking more vulnerable than I've ever seen him. "It's kinda weird, the idea of going from friends to more. I want to make sure you like me that way."

If only he knew the extent to which I already do, and have all these years. If past me could have seen the way this night is unfolding, I would have spontaneously burst from joy. But I hold back from telling him so, as memories of Robin's playground lecture rattle around in my head. *Don't ever tell a boy you like him until he says it first.* I note that he hasn't said anything about his feelings for *me*, only how *he* wants to feel, the label *he* wants us to bear.

I don't know what possesses me to say what I say next. "I just think maybe we need to talk this out, set some ground rules before we start slapping labels on us, you know? With a child being involved, especially, it ups the ante. At least for me."

"Leo loves you. He's told me that on several occasions. You remember that picture I have of the two of you on the fridge, the selfie you sent me when you guys were boogie boarding? He asked me to print it out so he can sleep with it. Takes it off the fridge at night, puts it back during the day. Honest to God."

"Oh, boy..." I'm not sure what else to say. I can feel my heart growing like the Grinch's. Followed by a mounting sense of responsibility. Even more reason to tread carefully.

"You're awesome with him," Ben continues. "I could see us being a great threesome."

A lump grows in my throat as I ask myself: is that what I want? Because if I encourage this, I better be ready for it.

I change the subject to something more comfortable: work.

He gives a brief update on his case, then informs me the hiring process is moving forward.

"The partners have been asking about you, hoping to make a decision soon," Ben says.

"Wouldn't they have to interview me first?"

"Yeah. I mean they're deciding who to interview. They've received over two hundred applications."

"Yikes."

"I'm going to bat for you, hard, so I'm pretty sure you'll at least get an invite. They do it a little differently—they like to bring new prospects to a social outing to see how they are in a more relaxed environment before being invited for an interview. Applicants are pretty equal on experience and success, so the social thing is how they distinguish who would best fit the firm's vibe. They're big on social events and community outreach."

"That's an interesting way of going about it."

"The first outing is August seventh. They'll do something cheeky for the invite, so keep an eye on the mail. I gave them your address down here."

I'm not sure whether to be excited about this or terrified.

After a scrumptious meal, we head to the car, where he leans in for another long, hard, passionate kiss.

"Would you like to come back to the house?" he asks as our lips part, his voice husky with desire. "Finish what we've started?"

Oh God. As much as I would like to, I don't think I can walk by Leo's room—or the fridge, with the photo of us and his word-of-the-day list pinned to it, his plastic Sesame Street guys scattered about the living room floor—without wondering if we're moving too fast, diving into a physical relationship after a first date. I know that sounds very pious and 1880 of me, especially since I've both known Ben and wanted this forever, but I think we need to be prudent here. Before we jump into bed, we should discuss what *more* would look like for us, how we'll navigate the transition from friends to lovers, how we'll present it to the little man. If we start something but can't finish it, relationship-wise, how will that affect Leo? With his mom in California, I'm the closest thing he has to a mother figure right now, other than Ben's sister and a grandmother in Arizona. I have to be careful I don't blur those lines and be yet another woman to abandon him if it doesn't work out between us.

Huh. In all my years crushing on this man, I've never consciously considered the possibility it may not work out. Or that I wouldn't want it to.

All I know is, I'd better be damn certain before I commit to swapping bodily fluids with this man. I know that's laughable after the many years I've waited for this, but we saw what happened with him and Angi in law school.

"Not tonight," I finally answer. "I want to take it slow. For Leo's sake."

He nods. "Of course. Whatever you want."

I can't tell if he's disappointed or relieved. I'm just happy that, for once, I'm the one to make a decision when it comes to us—even if it's just to slow things down a bit. I owe it to myself to think it through before taking the leap with him.

Something about this summer has made me question all I once knew, all I once thought I wanted. Not just in law, but love as well. I need to make sure my decisions going forward align with the new and improved Kacie Layne.

At least that's the result we're going for.

42

After working seven days in a row—thanks to the extra shifts I picked up with Leo gone—I'm ready for a break so I take Sunday off. I spend the morning sleeping in and going for a long walk. When I finally join my housemates on the beach that afternoon, Chase is regaling the group with an animated tale.

Wendy waves me over to the empty spot next to her chair. I'm glad Celeste is on the other side, as she's the one female in the house I know the least. One I want to know better, since it's her cousin Chase has gone out with...twice. I'm here mostly out of curiosity, but also because she always seems a bit stand-offish. I hate it when people don't like me for no good reason, so I challenge myself to change their attitude. Game on.

"Hey, Celeste," I say, settling in my chair. "How's that book?"

She closes the book to show me the cover. Colleen Hoover's latest. "Not my favorite of hers, but it's still good."

I ask some follow-up questions until I feel as if I'm interrupting her. I turn my attention to Wendy. "Got anything to drink?" I ask her.

Chase, still standing, pauses his story and turns his attention to me. "I got you, babe," he says as he reaches into the cooler.

I give him a double take as he slides a White Claw into a Yeti holder and hands it to me. Warm fuzzies bubble to my cheeks, turning them hot.

"Babe?" Celeste asks, raising her eyebrows.

"Oh, hehe. Just a running joke between us," I say.

Total lie. He's never called me that before, so I don't know why he did it now, in front of everyone.

Chase claps his hands together. "Who's up for some beach volleyball?"

Most of the group responds positively as they get up from chairs. I groan and follow suit, shuffling with dread, as if I'm being led into dental surgery. Chase juggles a ball with his feet like a professional soccer player as we head to the net.

"How about girls against guys?" he suggests.

Being the agreeable group we are, we separate by gender. I'm lowkey hating this because I'm (a) the furthest thing from sporty, (b) vertically challenged, and (c) terrified of flying balls.

After flipping a coin, it's determined guys will serve first. Who else but Chase to start. He takes aim and lobs the ball over the net, right at me.

"Ah!" I scream, ducking to protect my face.

The guys laugh. The girls, not so much.

"Nice," Celeste says, her voice laced with sarcasm. She sends the ball back over to Chase.

I don't know why this girl doesn't like me. Our interactions have been few and far between at best. The next time the ball comes to me, I'm ready. I make a bat out of fisted hands and send the ball flying back over the net.

Fortunately, the ball doesn't come to me much. Except when Chase gets it, he seems obsessed with sending it my way. At one point, I'm at the net, opposite him. He's crouched down like a football player, rocking back and forth like he's waiting for a quarterback hand off.

"I'm taking you down, Layne," he says.

"Keep dreaming, Maddox."

On the next play, Diane sets up a beautiful spike. I slam the ball down, right in front of Chase. The women all give me high fives. Even Celeste, looking as if she was about to touch a live squid. The guys ended up winning, but it was a close game.

Chase comes over and does an end zone victory dance, apparently for my benefit, before grabbing me from behind.

"Remember, Layne—its volleyball, not dodgeball."

"Shut up."

"Here, Chase," Celeste says, as she hands him the ball and gives me the hairy eyeball.

What is it with this chick?

We play a few more games before collectively calling it quits. I'm heading to the water to rinse sand off me when Chase zooms by.

"Last one in buys dinner!" he yells.

The guys follow, taking running dives into the waves. I stay at water's edge, rinsing my legs, laughing as they splash and dunk one another. Chase breaks free and runs toward me. Before I realize what's happening, he scoops me up and carries me in deeper, where he unceremoniously dumps me in. I don't hate it. It's hot today, and the water's refreshingly cool.

"That's for spiking the ball," he says as I come up for air.

"I can't touch bottom," I sputter, treading water to keep afloat.

"I got you."

He wraps an arm around my waist and pulls me into him. Instinctively, my legs go around him—this time, for survival. My eyes dart to the other guys to see if they're aware I'm clinging to Chase for dear life as waves crash around us, but they're already heading back to the beach.

"Hey there." His eyes twinkle in the sunlight as sea water clings to his long lashes. "Good job getting over your fear of flying balls today."

"They've been known to kill people."

"You're adorable," he says, biting his lip.

What is going on? Two guys have referred to me that way this week. I've been called a lot of things before, but never adorable. In fact, a coworker once joked that the only difference between me and a pitbull was lipstick. Naturally, I bit her leg for that.

Chase tightens his grip around my waist, pulling me closer. "This is nice."

It *is* nice. I glance at the beach to see if anyone else is noticing how nice this is.

"Don't worry. I don't think they can see us."

He's probably right. The beach is packed today.

I turn back and notice his face is dangerously close.

"God, girl. What is it about you? This is just—" He bites his lip while mine throb with anticipation.

The narwhal's returned, and it's all I can do to keep from kissing the hell out of him. I bet I can finish his sentence, something about this magnetic force being unreal. If I don't break this up soon, I'm going to open my legs and take all of him, right here and now, like Moby Dick and his breakfast of krill.

So I do what I do best. Act like a juvenile. I throw my head back and make a shrill clicking sound.

"What was that?" he asks, laughing out loud.

"I'm a dolphin. Watch this..."

I push off him and leap into the water. When I come up, he's still laughing.

"You're an absolute nut."

It's enough to do the trick, break the spell. As we make our way back to dry sand, I congratulate myself for not clinging to him like a starfish.

"What's with Celeste?" I ask as we weave between families and their beach encampments. "I think she hates me."

"Bit of a backstory there," he says quietly.

"You think?" I give him a raised eyebrow. "Considering you've gone out with her cousin—what? Twice, now?"

He shoots me a look of surprise. "About that. I want to—"

Too late. We're back with the group and Wendy's handing me a drink.

"Looks like you were having fun," Wendy says as I plop down

in my beach chair and Chase heads back to his. "I guess you guys must be getting close, being the only two in the house all week."

"Yeah, we've become good friends."

"Be careful there," Celeste says, without looking up from her book. I had no idea she was listening to our conversation. "He had quite the reputation..."

I note her use of the past tense. Before I can respond, she continues.

"...until he started dating my cousin." She closes her book and gives me a deadass stare.

I almost spit out my White Claw. I know they've gone on two dates, but that's different than *dating*. *Dating* implies some level of seriousness.

Backstory, my ass. Sounds more like a front story. What have I stepped into?

"Hey, Chase," Celeste calls out to him. "Come over. I'm telling Kacie about you and my cousin."

Looks like I'm about to find out, as Chase obliges, looking like a bad dog whose owner is about to shame him on social media for eating the couch cushions.

"Tell us how your date was the other night," she says.

I try to keep my face from scrunching into my trademark cynical attorney smirk as I await his response.

"Oh, um..." Chase stammers, running his hand through his hair. "It was...nice."

Oh, sure. The same word he just used for us.

"It *looked* nice. I saw her photos on Insta," Celeste continues, obviously relishing this moment. "You make a beautiful couple. Her in a gown, you in a tux..."

Chase's eyes flick to me. "Network award ceremony," he mumbles, which does nothing to clear up my confusion. I'm stuck on him *in a tux*.

"My cousin is Meredith Vine," Celeste explains. "You know, the meteorologist from Channel Six news."

Yeah, bitch. I know who she is.

Also, *Fuck. Me.*

Meredith Vine is the hot local celebrity who prances around the ABC newsroom, charming people with her cutesy weather reports every night at five. She's drop-dead gorgeous, the fantasy woman of basically every man in the tristate area. Including Ben.

"Chase's best friend is marrying our family friend August," Celeste goes on. "Chasey's in the wedding but he didn't have a date, so I fixed him up with Mer so they can get to know each other beforehand and maybe go together. Lo and behold, they hit it off." She gives a swoony sigh. "An awards show and a wedding, all in one summer. By the end of it all, I predict we'll be calling you guys Charedith."

Right now, I'm not sure whose face I want to kick sand in the most. Celeste, for being a total bitch, or Chase for not telling me about this monumental complication. If Meredith were here, I'd probably kick her too. And Charedith for good measure.

Really. Dating someone else but kissing and coming on to me? What a jerk. It would have been nice to know all this, in between tongue thrusts down my throat. I wouldn't have even thought about kissing him had I known he was seeing Meredith Vine.

Then it hits me. I suspected it when I learned he'd been on two dates with the same person, but Meredith Vine? She's the *ultimate* complication.

What is it about you, my ass. I'll tell you what it is. Come within a foot of me, and I'll fling you into the arms of someone else like a flaming shotput. It's my special party trick, and it works on all men. Ladies, looking for a husband? Send a guy my way—he'll ricochet off me so fast, he'll be whisking you into a wedding dress before you can say *yes*.

Celeste turns to me. "Lucky you, Kacie. You'll get to meet

her. Chase invited her to stay with us the week before the wedding, since it's here in Sea Isle."

"Celeste—" Chase says, clearly exasperated.

She shrugs and goes back to her book.

I can no longer look at Chase as he slithers back to his seat. If he'd just owned up to it, that would be one thing. But not telling me about this makes it feel purposely deceitful.

From across the circle, I can feel his eyes pleading with me apologetically. He picks up his phone and a second later, mine dings with a text.

I silence my phone to keep from encouraging additional communication. Turning to Wendy, I ask her how her job's going, as if nothing is bothering me. Another special trick of mine—going stone cold emotionless in the face of disappointment. I can't let Celeste know she's gotten to me. And I can't let Chase know how much it stings that he's played me as well as he has.

Then again, I not only saw this coming, but participated willingly. I, too, came into this summer with my own set of complications. Having Meredith waiting in the wings is no worse than me hoping for developments with Ben. Perhaps if we'd met at another time, when we weren't housemates or entangled with others, it may have been something worth considering. The reality is, no matter how strong the chemistry may be between us, we are simply not free to pursue anything further.

And that is that.

43

I'm finishing up my outdoor shower, trying to wash away Celeste's public humiliation, when I see feet appear outside the stall.

"Kacie?" Chase says. "I can explain."

"Not necessary," I say. Wrapping the towel around me, I open the door and skirt around him.

"Celeste is making a way bigger deal of this than it is," he continues as he follows me to the outdoor steps.

"You don't have to explain anything to me," I say. "I was fairly warned about you being a player."

"By whom?"

I look at him dead on. "By you." Not to mention Rachel, Celeste, and my own women's intuition.

"Oh, right," he says, rolling his eyes. "I was kinda joking about that, but—there's more to the story."

"You don't need to—"

"Yes, I do. Celeste fixed us up on a blind date after she realized both Meredith and I were dateless for my buddy's wedding. The date went well enough, and after I asked her to the wedding, she invited me to the award thing. That's the only reason I was out with her the other night."

"Hey, you don't owe me any explanations." He does, but that makes it sound like I don't GAF. Which I shouldn't, even though I do. "You and I both know this chemistry between us was never going to amount to more than just a fun summer fling. We've had our fun, so let's leave it at that."

I turn away and then hear him scoff.

"How hypocritical," he says, his tone biting.

I turn back. "What's that supposed to mean?"

"Tell me you haven't been playing me, too, biding your time, waiting for Ben to come around. Now that he has, you don't need to pretend with me anymore."

"This has nothing to do with Ben. Or you. It has everything to do with me and why I can't—"

"Hey, guys!" It's Rex, coming in from the beach. He's obviously caught the tail end of my statement, as he looks from me to Chase, and back to me again. "Why you can't what, Kacie?"

"Nothing," Chase says, cutting him off.

Rex thrusts his hands up as if he's being held at gunpoint. "Ooh, excuse me. So sorry to interrupt," he says in a mocking tone. "Don't worry. I'll be outta your way in a sec."

"No worries, Rex. You're not interrupting anything." I turn to Chase. "As I was saying, that's why I can't seem to get out of a rip current. But thanks for the info, Chase. I'll remember that next time I'm caught in one."

As I huff away, I sense Chase wanting to follow, but Rex is bending his ear about rip currents and how he was once caught in one. I know his explanation about the dates was perfectly acceptable, but the reality is, they have another date pending—this time a wedding—and she'll be staying here the entire week leading up to it. There's no way I'm competing with that. Game over.

After getting dressed, I text Oops to see what he's doing tonight. He invites me to join him and his crew at The Point. I'm relieved to have somewhere else to be. Everyone's heading home tonight, and the last thing I want is to be left here alone with Chase. While I knew he was a player and tried to protect myself, the fact I'm so mad about this tells me I failed miserably.

Then again, maybe he's right. I'm just as guilty for messing around with him as he was with me, when we both had side hustles. Regardless, I want to keep as much distance between us as possible.

Celeste must've sensed Chase and me growing closer and worried—

Oh, shit. The group text. Now it makes sense why Celeste has been so standoffish with me since the start of summer. Me and my mystical sex goddess talk.

Well, girl, he's all Meredith's. I'm out. I will never fight for a man's attention. Just like I did when Ben told me about Angi, and Seth when I found out about his affair, I'll tap out and retreat to my sad little single corner.

Just where I belong.

44

Aside from the Chase thing, my mom-inspired hopeful outlook is still going strong. I've missed hanging out with Leo while he's been on vacation, but it's been nice having time to myself to think and plan for my future.

I haven't heard anything yet from Ben's firm, so I've started a job search for nontraditional legal jobs. It's somewhat of a test for the universe, of destiny. If invited by the firm, I'll go for an interview; if offered the job, I'll take it. If not, it's my sign to move on. Diane told me that UPenn's Carey Law School is hiring adjunct professors. I'll be applying there, as well, while I wait to see how things shake out with Ben's firm.

In addition to job searching, Amy and I have used my bonus time to plan our trip. I'll be flying to London on Labor Day, when our shore house rental ends, and staying with her for three weeks. We'll use her flat as our base, and take jaunts to France, Italy, and Amsterdam. I can hardly wait. I just need to get Leo back so I can resume making bank, which is happening today.

I'm beyond pumped, but not just for the pay. I've missed the little dude terribly. I can't wait to hang out with him and hear all about his vacation—which I know I will, down to the tiniest detail. Being with a five-year-old breathes a whole new and refreshing perspective into one's life, making it fun again. Without him, my life has felt boring. His curiosity begs answers to questions I wouldn't think to ask, like why seagulls stand on one foot (to conserve energy). His observations of the world brings into focus things I usually don't pay attention to—like how the moon, in a certain phase, looks like a lemon wedge. I can't wait to learn more about the world from a preschooler's perspective, and maybe 'span my 'cabulary.

I haven't seen Chase in the week since I learned about Meredith. He's been working the overnight shift at the sleepover camp, so we've become ships that don't even pass at night. But he left a note this morning informing me camp is over and he'll be home tonight.

I'm happy about that, because I want to clear some things up. I'm embarrassed about how I acted like a smacked ass over the Meredith thing. It wasn't my right to be mad at him for dating someone else. But I do believe a little more transparency was in order, especially after he came on to me like he did the night of my birthday, saying such a thing about our future kids. I told him about Ben from the get-go, brought him around to our parties even. Not to mention—*ta-da!*—the group text. He could have been more straightforward about Meredith. Date who you want, just be honest about it.

I also haven't seen Ben since our date. We've been texting, so I know he's been in the city working on his case and only returned with Leo late last night.

Ben's absence doesn't mean I don't think about him. My mom's words about reinventing my life, combined with Ben's words about us being a good threesome together, echo in my ears as I try to picture what that life would be like. If anything, this summer has given me a good insight into parenthood, and it's not as horrific as I once imagined. I've grown to love this little guy in a way I can imagine a parent does their own child. His bubbly laughter fills me with joy, and his every disappointment is an arrow through my heart. It's funny to think that, someday, when I look back on this summer and read my journal entries, spending time with a child will account for much of my enjoyment. But here we are.

I arrive at the beach to pick up Leo just as he's riding his last wave to the shore like a champ. When he emerges from the water and sees me, he comes running at me full bore. I'm ready this time. I crouch down to catch him properly when he jumps into my arms and twirl him around as my eyes fill with water.

"I've missed you so much, buddy!" I exclaim. "My life has been boring without you here!"

"Why are you crying, Kacie?" he asks as he wipes a drop from my cheek.

"I'm not crying. This is just—"

What in the name of modern science *is* this liquid flowing from my eyes? As stated, I don't ever really cry, except for maybe that night of my birthday, understandably. Certainly not over "joy."

I am definitely turning into a wuss this summer.

"I'm just happy to see you," I say. "Whatever you want to do today, just say the word."

"I want to do our normal routine, which I thoroughly enjoy."

I laugh out loud. "Word of the day?"

"It's *thoroughly* my word of the day."

Later, as we're sitting on the beach eating frozen grapes, Leo turns to me. "Have you ever heard of a bucket list?"

"I have, as a matter of fact," I say, stifling a chuckle. "Where did you hear about it?"

"When we went to Niagara Falls, my uncle said it was on his bucket list. It's all the things you want to do before you die. I'm thinking I should probably start one, 'specially since I'm starting kindergarten soon."

I laugh out loud as he looks pensively out to sea. Sobering, I ask what he'd put on his list.

"I thought about it the *whole* way home." He splays all ten fingers for emphasis. "Build a sandcastle shaped like a shark. Sit in the lifeguard stand with Chase. Go to the Wildwood Boardwalk. Win that stuffed snake in the arcade so I can wear it around my neck for my first day of school. I think the other kids would like that. And I wanna learn how to blow bubbles with bubble gum."

I nearly melt in my chair after hearing his list, filled with all the innocence and wonder of childhood.

"Is that everything you'd put on your list?" I ask.

"Oh. I forgot the most important. Get a new mom."

I have to swallow hard to keep my heart from leaping out of my chest and onto the sand. "What's wrong with your actual mom?"

"She's okay. I love her and all, but she lives in California with that homewrecker guy. I want a mom who's here all the time."

I literally think I'm on the verge of emotional death.

"Your mom loves you, Leo. Don't ever forget that. Wherever she lives, wherever she goes, you're in her heart. Always."

"Oh, I know. I just want someone to make sandcastles with." He looks up at me with those big blue eyes. "Like you."

Houston, we have a problem. I'm in love, and not just with the dad.

If it wasn't crystal clear before, it is now. If I'm moving forward with Ben, I'd better damn well be sure I'm ready to be a parent, because life with Ben would require nothing less. Leo *deserves* nothing less.

Complicated, indeed.

45

Later that night, I pour myself a glass of wine and tread quietly to the deck, hoping not to wake Chase. I need some alone time to think.

Except he isn't asleep. He's on the deck, drinking a beer. The house was so dark and quiet, I didn't realize he was awake.

"Hey," he exclaims, standing as I approach the table.

"At ease, soldier," I say with a soft chuckle. "What are you doing out here?"

"Just thinking. And you?"

"Came to do the same."

I wasn't expecting to have the conversation we need to have right now. When he pulls a chair out for me, I reluctantly sit.

"Nice night for thinking. Take a look at this." He gestures skyward, where a blanket of stars lights the night sky.

He points out the Big Dipper and other constellations. Looking around, I find Perseus and Andromeda. I think about the love triangle she found herself in—the man she was promised to, and the man who came along and fell for her—and wonder how she felt about the whole thing. I recall Chase saying Perseus had to fight the previous suitor before he could win her heart. I chuckle to myself, thinking we've come a long way, baby. No longer does a woman's fate rest in the hands of the best fighter with the biggest sword (well, I can't speak for all of us). But what if she was in love with the first guy? I wonder whether she was okay with the outcome.

We sit in stillness for a while, surrounded by a cool breeze and the sound of crashing waves. I marvel at how much louder they sound at night, without the daytime din of vacationers drowning them out.

Still gazing skyward, Chase breaks the silence. "It's only a date for a wedding."

"With a beautiful meteorologist," I respond. "Who you've been on two dates with. Who's coming to stay with you for the week."

Careful, Kace, you're not sounding much like a main character.

"I had nothing to do with that." His eyes meet mine. "Celeste invited her to stay with us."

I let that sink in for a moment.

"What about you and Ben?" he asks. "That still going on?"

I'm not sure I want to get into it with him, but before I can consult my inner counsel, I open my mouth and the truth spills out. "Ben officially asked me if I wanted to give 'us' a go."

"Meaning...date him?"

"Yeah. Like boyfriend and girlfriend."

He's silent for a moment. "What did you say?"

"I told him I want to take it slowly. You know, because of the friendship. And Leo."

"That matters to you, doesn't it?"

"Friendship?"

He nods.

"Absolutely. Without friends, we're nothing. As they say, you can't pick your fam, but you can pick your friends."

"Just not their noses," we both say simultaneously.

Without cracking smiles, he holds his hand up for a high five and I reciprocate.

"Why does dating seem so challenging in our thirties?" he asks.

I can't believe for a second dating is challenging for him at any age. Snap fingers, get woman. Even the hot single celeb every man in the viewing area would kill to date.

Nevertheless, I take his question seriously.

"There's more at stake at our ages," I say. "In our twenties, it's all fun and games. By our third decade, we're all too busy—rooted in our lives, accustomed to our habits—and it's harder to break out of our mold. There's more riding on it too. For those who want to marry, it's tough finding someone who's marriage material without wasting your time on those who aren't. Or, so they say."

Listen to me, going on like a relationship guru. Except I kinda am. It may not have been my own experience that's schooled me, but I've learned some things from my clients.

"What is it about Ben you like so much?" he asks.

"He's comfortable," is the first thing that comes to mind. "I've liked him for so long."

Wow. Is that it? I've given more passionate speeches about my UGG slippers.

"I get it," he says. "He's safe, you've known him forever. He's been vetted in every setting imaginable, and he's come out clean. Right?"

I nod at his more eloquent assessment.

"Besides that," he continues, "what is it about *him*?"

"Oh, Chase. You're gonna be sorry you asked."

"Girl, my circadian rhythm is still on third shift," he says, smiling. "I have all night."

Before I can stop myself, I tell Chase the whole ugly truth. My lifelong crush, how he got Angi pregnant, his hanging a "maybe someday" out there, and how I've held on to that for dear life. Waiting for him to realize I was the perfect person for him.

"But since then, I haven't stopped to ask myself: is he still the perfect person for me?"

"Is that the question you're asking now?"

"I guess I'm wondering if the crush I developed at twenty-two is still reflective of what I'm looking for now." Not that

I'm looking.

"That's key, isn't it?" Chase asks, echoing my thoughts. "We're not meant to end up with someone just because there's history. Or they look good on paper."

"Or there's amazing chemistry you can't explain."

The words are out before I can stop them, and his eyes find mine immediately.

"I believe when we meet the right person, we know it," he says.

After a long moment, I look back up at the stars, as does he. I can't be certain, but I swear I hear him whisper softly. Something that sounds like, "Maybe we already have."

46

Summer felt like a slow burn in the beginning, but suddenly the end of July is here. Four more weeks, and we'll all be back to real life. I'm trying to hold on tightly, not ready for it to end, but I feel time slipping through my fingers faster than I can hold on.

Today is the day of Shaniya's wedding. The ceremony is taking place on the beach at sunset, followed by a small, intimate reception in the backyard of her in-laws' home in Sea Isle. I've been to so many weddings in my lifetime I could open a boutique with the party favors I've gathered along the way, but this will be the smallest one I've ever attended. I'm super impressed with Shaniya's lack of hype—no high-end table decorations or cheeky dance routines for this chill bride. She's opting to keep the true meaning of their impending union, the start of their lives together, as the main focal point. I never thought I'd hear myself say it, but I'm actually excited to witness their joining of souls.

Proving, once again, just how much of a wuss one can become, spending summer by the sea.

Thanks to the microscopic size of the wedding, none of the housemates have been invited with plus-ones, but that doesn't stop us women from dressing up like it's the event of the century. I'm happy to have a reason to wear my birthday dress again.

After the roomies get ready together and take our requisite selfies, we head to the ceremony location on Forty-second

Street beach. We're among the first guests to arrive as we shuffle single file down a row of white folding chairs to take our seats. No sooner do I sit than a body appears in the empty chair next to me.

"This seat taken?" Chase sits down without waiting for a response.

"It is, actually." I lean into him and whisper. "My date's sitting there."

"I thought we weren't allowed to bring dates?"

"They only told *you* that."

His laughter tickles my tummy.

I can't believe how hot he looks in a tan suit with an open-collared dress shirt underneath. His hair is tousled and sun-kissed and he looks as if he should be doing a photo shoot for men's resort wear, instead of sitting here next to me.

"Is that so, Jellyfish?" He rubs his thumb along my shoulder strap. "I remember this dress. In fact, the last time I saw you in it, I wished you weren't."

I give an involuntary gasp. Did he really just say that? "If I remember correctly, you were just fine for me to keep it on."

He cocks his head. "Or so I wanted you to think."

My heart starts beating fast over his blatant come-on. "Watch it—you're not gonna be able to tell our 'future kids' about that night if you start rewriting history." I give air quotes for good measure.

He laughs. "That's right. I wanna make sure I can recall the facts exactly. Like how you melted into me in the moonlight..."

Whoo-*wee*! Is it hot out here. But also, I'm not falling for this player's tricks again.

"Make sure you get every detail right for when you tell Meredith all about it," I quip.

"No worries. I did," he says, his eyes sparkling with amusement.

I do a double take, wondering if he's yanking my chain.

He gives me that sexy half-smile. "Or did I?"

From the commotion around us, it appears the ceremony is about to start. We turn to watch Shaniya come down the aisle in a simple white sundress, a halo of flowers in her hair. She's simply stunning. Turning as she passes, I feel my eyes getting misty, especially when I see Tyler's expression of pure adoration. From the corner of my eye, I catch Chase wiping his tears away.

As the ceremony begins, I feel the heat radiating from Chase as he leans back, legs splayed, arm draped across the back of my chair. His dress pants strain against his thighs, outlining his perfectly toned muscles. I don't know what's hotter—him dressed like this, or bare-chested in board shorts. So distracted am I, it's hard to follow the program.

Until the officiant announces that one of the couple's friends would like to say a few words and I feel rustling beside me as Chase rises from his chair. Amused, I stifle a giggle. This should be good.

Buttoning his jacket, he takes long strides across the sand. Points added for the fact he's totally barefoot. When he reaches the podium, he looks over at me and smiles. I smile back and give him the Bloods symbol, which causes him to snicker and blush. It's kinda cute how nervous he looks.

He clears his throat. "Hello, everyone, and welcome. I'm Chase Maddox, friend of the bride and groom. I'm honored to be asked to say a few words. The three of us go back a long way, starting when Tyler and I joined our first shore house together. In fact, I was there the night he met his beautiful bride.

"When I was thinking about what to say today, I kept coming back to one thought. Some people search a lifetime to find what Shaniya and Tyler have found—an undeniable chemistry, the way they bring out a light in each other that's obvious to all around them. I remember well the night they first met. Ty and I were at Kix Lounge when Shaniya walked by. I was droning on—"

"—and on," Tyler interjects, as everyone laughs.

"Guilty as charged." Chase, unfazed, merely chuckles. "I was droning on...*and on*...about Phillies stats as I do, completely oblivious, until he backhanded me in the chest. 'That's all really fascinating, Maddox,' he said, 'but if you'll excuse me, my future wife just walked by.'

"And boy, was he right. I later asked Tyler what it was about Shaniya that made him so certain she was the one from the moment he first laid eyes on her. And he said, 'When you know, you know.' We've all heard that saying before, but what does it really mean? Asking for a friend, of course..."

Everyone laughs again. I'm impressed with his delivery, he's such a natural. Then again, he is a teacher.

"In preparing this speech, I thought about my own parents, who shared a love like nothing I'd ever know before..."

Pausing, he presses his thumb to his lip. It looks as if he's trying to figure out what to say next, but knowing the backstory as I do, I know he's choked up. He takes a breath and a moment before continuing.

"I grew up wondering if I'd ever be so lucky to find someone I felt that way about, or if what they had was a one-of-a-kind thing. Yet here are Shaniya and Tyler, who've proven otherwise. So what does it mean to just...*know*?

"I don't think it means love at first sight, because you can't truly love a person without knowing them. And it's not about fireworks, destiny, a cheeky meet-cute—or all the things rom-coms are made of. I think it's simpler than that. It's knowing yourself and being confident in what you're looking for. Being open to the idea of love, willing to take a chance on that person who walks by you in a crowded bar. Someone who, for whatever reason, reminds you of home. But first, you must believe it can happen."

Clearing his throat, he looks directly at me. I keep my mouth shut to keep my butterflies from getting loose.

"So maybe the phrase 'when you know, you know' isn't the whole story, just the beginning. The moment two people recognize something rare and decide to walk toward it. In the end, the real love—the knowing—can only come in the everyday moments. The way Shaniya and Tyler show us every time they're around each other. Their easy laughter, the way they support each other, how they make each other better people—not by changing who they are, but by letting the other fully be themselves."

He looks to the couple.

"So, thank you, guys, for fortifying my belief in true love. I hope your experience fosters the same hope in everyone here who may still be looking for *their* true love. On that note, I'll leave you with this..."

As he steps away from the podium, Journey's "Don't Stop Believin'" plays over the loudspeaker. Snapping his fingers, Chase does a fancy side-step back to his seat, to the rapt enjoyment of the cheering crowd.

"How's that for winging it?" he whispers to me as he sinks in next to me.

"You just wung that?" I say, half joking, half blown away.

"It's the gift of gab. I can teach you, but first you have to learn how to say 'hoagie' correctly."

He looks at me with the cutest smile. I can't let him know how impressed I am with that speech, so I respond by jabbing his leg. "You totally got that from ChatGPT."

"Nope," he says. "Why would you even think that?"

I look straight ahead. "When you know, you know."

47

Tonight, Ben's asked me to meet him at The Point. According to his text, Leo's been invited to the neighbors' to watch a movie, and Ben is dying for an adult beverage and conversation. I figure this may be a good night to talk about what our future looks like if we decide to step into it together.

I find him at one of the outdoor bars as a reggae band plays in the background. He rises when I approach and hugs me.

"I've missed you," he whispers into my hair. Pulling back, he cups my face and gives me a long kiss.

I wait for the feelings I felt back in law school to reemerge, even the feelings from our date night, but something's amiss. I just can't put my finger on it.

After ordering drinks, he turns to me. "Haven't seen you in days. What have you been up to?"

"Oh, Ben," I say, taking his hands. "I just attended the most incredible wedding."

I tell him about the small personal touches the bride and groom included—keeping it small, writing their own vows, having a simple backyard barbeque reception where we all sat around a firepit drinking beer. How I've never seen two people so in love. I give him the SparkNotes version of the "friend's" speech without identifying the speaker.

"I know you and I have always been anti-wedding, but some people do know how to do it right. I think you would have enjoyed this one."

He guffaws. "Not likely."

I'm a little put off by that, but I ignore the feeling.

"According to Chase, who was with them the night they met, it was love at first sight."

"Do you believe that?" he asks.

"Maybe? I mean, who am I to question people who say they've experienced it."

"I always wonder if it's something people say to romanticize their relationship, as if they're trying to convince themselves of something."

"I dunno..."

"Have you ever experienced it?"

"Hate that I even have this memory, but yeah. Seth. And..." I'll leave it at Seth.

"That's it?"

I take a deep breath, hoping I'm not about to summon Robin to the playground. I think it's high time for some truth. Demons be damned.

"Maybe one other time," I say looking down at my hands, willing them to slap me silly and clasp my mouth shut.

"Who?" His tone is soft, suggesting he knows where I'm going with this.

My eyes slowly rise to meet his, and his expression confirms my suspicion.

"Oh, Kace," he says, taking my hands.

"Did you know?"

"I kinda wondered," he says. Tucking a strand of my hair behind my ear, he smiles. "At first, but we quickly fell into a friendship, and I figured that was it. Why? Was I wrong?"

I give a soft sigh. "By about ten years."

"What?" His tone is hushed, disbelieving.

My heart is pounding so hard I'm afraid I'm on the verge of a heart attack. The truth never felt so physically challenging, but maybe that's because my heart's so badly out of shape for this sport. I half-expect Robin to jump out from behind a palm tree and throttle me for admitting my feelings to a boy before he's told me his.

"Yes, Ben," I forge on. "I've liked you as more than a friend for pretty much the entire time we've known each other."

As scary as it is to finally admit this truth, it also feels liberating.

"Kacie…" He clasps his head with his hands. "Why didn't you ever tell me?"

"I was scared."

"Of what?"

"That you wouldn't like me back. You'd just broken up with your girlfriend and were vulnerable. And then you were with Angi and then she got pregnant, and the divorce…"

He shakes his head. "I just wish I'd known."

"Would it have made any difference?"

His gaze meets mine. "It may have."

He sighs as his dark chocolate eyes melt with regret. "I wish we could go back in time and replay that night in law school."

I'm blown away, hearing his words echo the thoughts I've had all along. This time, I wouldn't push him away, and he wouldn't find comfort between the sheets with another woman, where they'd do something to seal the fate of four lives.

"But then you wouldn't have—"

"Leo," we both say at the same time.

He squeezes my hand. "I guess things worked out as they were supposed to. Because now—" Looking up, he gives me a half smile and a playful shrug. "We're all out of excuses."

I grab his face and pull him to me, kissing him with all the passion I once kissed my pillow, pretending it was him. Only this time, my tongue is met with his, instead of cotton and feathers.

Still, something's missing. Excuses, maybe?

Then I think of Leo wanting a new mom, and I pull away from the kiss.

"Except maybe one," I say, giving him a sad look. "Your son."

He nods. "I was thinking about what you said about Leo and proceeding with caution. I agree, we should set some ground rules."

"Of course. You know me and rules."

He chuckles. "Leo's asked on more than one occasion if we're getting married."

"Oh no..." My heart sinks, but I'm not surprised. I was correct in assuming he understands more than we realize.

"Yeah. I've never been anything but honest with him. I've told him the truth about the prospect of my ever getting married again, and that's...never. Sorry to be blunt, but marriage is simply not in the cards for me. Ever. I hope that's not a problem."

"Oh...okay," I say. Wow, we're jumping right into it. I was thinking ground rules more along the lines of where we sleep, and who makes breakfast in the morning. But...okay.

"No problem."

"Are you sure, Kacie? I saw the way your face lit up when you talked about that wedding. I don't want to promise you something I can't deliver."

"Got it," I say. "Next rule?"

"Your turn. What do you want to see happen between us?"

"We each get our own toothpaste. That way, if one forgets to put on the lid, they're only hurting themselves."

"Fair," he says, laughing.

"I'm not kidding. It sounds cliché, but it's a legit gripe between couples, apparently. What's your second rule?"

He takes a deep breath. "No more kids for me."

"Excuse me?" I say, leaning back in surprise. "I thought you wanted a big family. You always talked about it in law school."

"I've changed my mind."

"But why? You're a great father. Leo's such a lucky boy—"

"I want to keep it that way."

"I'm confused. How would having another child change that?"

"After what we've been through, I want to put everything I have into him. I don't think I can love another kid like I do him."

"I've heard people with one kid say that, but once they have that second, they can't imagine—"

"Can we drop it?"

"Excuse me," I say, flinching. "I thought we were having a conversation."

He's silent for a moment. "The reality is, I can't have any more."

Oh. "I'm sorry, I didn't know."

"I've had a vasectomy."

My brow draws together. "Okay, but I've heard—"

The look on his face tells me he knows what I'm about to say, that vasectomies can be reversed.

"You could change your mind," I say, shrugging. "You shouldn't base your entire future on a decision you made in the midst of a bad marriage."

"I didn't," he says, regarding me with a sheepish expression. "I made it after we were divorced. This spring."

"Oh."

More like...*whoa*. I wonder why. Has he been sexually active? I want to ask, but I can tell he's done with this conversation.

I, however, am not. Before we go any further into *more*, we'll need to discuss this.

"I hope the no-kids thing isn't a deal-breaker for you," he says.

My defenses go up. "When did I ever say I wanted kids?"

"You haven't," he says quickly. "I just feel like, if we're gonna do this, we should be up-front and brutally honest from the get-go."

"Of course," I say sarcastically, snark rising.

"What are you thinking?"

"That you've given me a lot to think about," I say.

Like how this all seems so...unromantic. Not at all like I'd imagined it would be, how it would feel, it if we ever came to-gether. I was the one who suggested ground rules, but this feels like we're negotiating a real estate deal and not a relationship. Old Kacie would've loved this, but new and improved Kacie doesn't. Why can't we let things develop organically and see how it goes?

Again, not saying I want marriage or kids, but...what if I change my mind? Because the one thing this summer is teaching me is this—anyone's capable of changing.

Even change-fearing me.

48

With only a few weeks left of summer, Leo and I are chipping away at his bucket list. So far, we've built a sandcastle shaped like a shark, and he's learning to blow bubbles. He's already halfway to his ticket goal for that stuffed snake, and Ben's going to make his Wildwood Boardwalk dreams come true tonight. In a few minutes, Chase is going to take him up into the lifeguard stand.

As I wait for Leo's surf lesson to be over, I think back on my conversation with Ben, confused at how we ended the night on such an awkward note. Ben laying out his bottom line put a damper on the evening, even though I would have, at any other previous time, agreed wholeheartedly with his plans. But now...things are different, at least for me. I told him I needed to think it over. We agreed to table it for now and haven't spoken of it since.

This may be one reason why attorneys prefer to marry non-attorneys. We have a tendency to make things too attorney-ish.

Since then, I've also thought about something Chase said. Just because you have history with someone doesn't mean they're still right for you. Listening to Ben that night, I wondered where that dreamy boy I once knew went. The one who was full of hope, who believed in marriage and big families. Who gave great romance advice to his female friends and hosted "Pal-entine's Day" dinners for his single guy friends. *He* was a man I desperately wanted, the one I fell in love with, yet the guy I had drinks with the other night was nothing like him.

He's changed, that's for sure. Can't blame him, as I know he's been through some things. As have I. But in my case, I've gone from unhopeful about the future to hopeful. I wish he could join me, but it's not looking…what's the word? Oh. Hopeful.

Regardless of where we decide to take this, I vow to give Leo all the mom-ish experiences he's yearning for this summer while I'm still his nanny, even if it takes me out of my comfort zone.

Leo and Chase come ashore, and I follow them to the lifeguard stand, taking photos as man and boy pose in the stand. Chase shows Leo how to whistle for swimmers to move over, watch for rip currents, and jump in the boat before rowing out for a rescue.

"How was that, little man?" Chase asks as they finish up their mock lifeguarding duties. "Did you do everything you wanted?"

"I guess," he says, sounding disappointed. "Everything but rescue someone."

Chase considers this. "I have an idea."

Reaching into his bag of lost toys, he pulls out a mermaid Barbie.

"This girl is about to swim too far out. I want you to keep an eye on her, and if you think she's in trouble, we'll go in and rescue her."

I giggle as he lifts Leo onto the stand and throws the doll in the surf.

"Oh no!" Chase calls out in falsetto. "I need a brave lifeguard to rescue me!"

Leo jumps from the stand and runs as fast as his little legs can to rescue the drowning girl, who's lying face-down in knee-deep water.

"I'm coming, ma'am!" Leo cries out.

Chase and I laugh as Leo the Lifeguard rescues her from the tumultuous water, dragging her by the hair back to shore.

"We'll have to work on that part," Chase teases.

Still holding her by the hair, Leo dangles her in front of me. "Here's your baby, ma'am."

"Excellent job, my man!" Chase exclaims, giving him two high fives after I take my water-logged mermaid child from him. "You've saved the day!"

"At least *her* day," Leo says, grinning. "Now I know why you do this, Mr. Chase. It feels good to help people."

Chase and I look at each other with watery emoji eyes as our hearts simultaneously melt.

The little dude is literally bouncing off the walls when I take him back to the house after an abbreviated day on the beach. He's proud AF over his daring rescue and all charged up about going to the boardwalk tonight. I make sure he's bathed, dressed, and ready for Ben well before his anticipated arrival time.

"I've never been to Wildwood, but I've been hearing about it my *whole life*," Leo says, splaying all ten fingers for emphasis, even though he's only been alive for half of them. It's hard to keep a straight face.

"It's a fun place, I hear."

"I'm *humongously* excited for it," he continues, employing his word-of-the-day. "Dad says we're gonna get Mack's Pizza and ride all the rides."

"I'm humongously excited for you, Leo."

"Can you come with us?"

His question catches me off-guard. Truth is, Ben didn't invite me. Not that I mind. Spending a night on the Wildwood Boardwalk is tantamount to doing two-to-six in the state pen. In fact, I'd prefer the latter.

"I can't, Leo," I say. "Maybe another time."

Ben is supposed to arrive at 4:00, but when he's not home by 4:30, I start texting and calling him. When I get no response, I'm wondering if I should start calling hospitals. Finally, at 5:00, he calls back. I answer, and without so much as a greeting, he asks to speak to Leo.

"Is it Daddy?" Leo cries out as he races toward me, his face filled with anticipation as he grabs the phone. "Are you here, Daddy? I'm ready to go. I even combed my own hair."

I start putting away his toys, when the silence from Leo becomes deafening. I turn to see his fallen expression, a tear streaming down one cheek.

"It's okay," he says, his chest heaving as if he's trying to hold it together. He nods, defiantly wiping his tear away. "Okay, Daddy. We'll go then."

He hands me the phone with a bewildered expression, his eyes welling with tears.

"Hello?" I ask, expecting to hear Ben's explanation, but he's already hung up.

I kneel before Leo. "What happened, sweetheart?"

"He can't go," he says, his lower lip trembling. "He has to work."

I give him a little pout, and it sends him over the edge. He melts into me, sobbing.

"He's been promising to take me forever," he cries. "But he always has an excuse. I thought it was real this time."

"I'm sorry, buddy," I say, stroking his curls. "I know how much this meant to you."

He pulls back and heaves a sigh. "I looked forward to this more than my birthday party."

I can't bear to watch him go through this. I hand him his iPad, cue up a video game, and excuse myself to use the restroom.

"Where are you?" I hiss from behind the closed door when Ben answers my call. "He's all ready to go. Why can't you take him?"

Silence. Then, "I'm sorry, Kacie. I...can't get away. I'll take him tomorrow."

Anger courses through me. "No, Ben. He's been talking about this all day. You have to make good on this promise and not pull the same shit you did with me. And also, what if I had plans tonight? Instead, you're just assuming I can stay here with him until you decide to come home."

He groans. "Kacie, I appreciate you, I really do. There's—just something here I have to deal with—"

"Deal with this," I snap. "I'm taking him myself."

I hang up. It was one thing standing me up on my birthday, but I'm not gonna let him do that to his kid. Although now I'm wondering how I'm pulling this off without a car. Good thing I know someone who has one.

"Hey, Chase. It's Kacie," I say when he answers my call.

"Why do you sound like you're in a can?" he asks. "Don't tell me, you're in the clink, calling for bail."

"In the bathroom. And not calling for bail, but a bail-out."

"How much is this gonna cost me?"

"Just the use of your Jeep. I'll make sure I fill it with gas when I return it. I'm in desperate need of a vehicle tonight."

"Running from the law, again?"

When I don't answer, his tone shifts from humor to concern. "What's going on?"

I sigh. "Shithead Ben broke his promise to take Leo to the boardwalk. This little guy's been bursting with excitement all day and I can't let him down."

"Wow, that sucks."

"No worries if you need your car tonight. We'll take an Uber—"

"Of course, you can use the Jeep. Under one condition."

"What's that?"

"I go with you guys."

I laugh. "You don't trust me with your Jeep?"

"Of course, I trust you. I just wanna go to the boardwalk. Ride rides. Score some Curley's fries. Win stuffed animals. All the things."

My heart skips a beat. "You sure?"

"Clearly, you've never had Curley's fries. I'm on my way."
I laugh out loud. "Okay. Let me know when you're here."
A text comes through from Ben after we hang up.

So sorry about this. Thank you for keeping him, I really do appreciate it. You sure you're okay to take him?

Yes.

Tx.

Yeah. So thankful, he can't be bothered to spell out the entire word.

I find Leo on the couch, listlessly tapping the iPad screen.

"Hey, kiddo," I say, my voice an octave higher than normal. "I was wondering if you'd mind if Chase and I take you to the boardwalk tonight? I know you wanted to go with your dad... but, um...when Chase found out you guys were going, he begged if we could go. Your dad said—"

"Yes! Yes!" Leo screams, jumping up and down. "A humongous yes!"

He leaps into my arms and I hug him tightly, laughing out loud. It's not that I'm not trying to cover for Ben, I just don't want this kid to know the truth—that work means more to his dad than keeping promises.

Especially from the man who says he *just wants to focus on Leo* this summer.

There was a time when I would've totally understood and even defended Ben's choice. But that was before I realized how much the actions of adults affect these little guys who don't deserve to be shoved aside and put off for the illusion of work's importance. Amy once chastised me for prioritizing work over family because, in her view, "If you die tomorrow, work will find your replacement in a heartbeat. But there'll never be another you for your family."

She was right. Maybe it took losing a job altogether to understand that concept.

"You sure, buddy?" I ask. As mad as I am with Ben, I'm not going to undermine Leo's relationship with his dad.

"I'm *humongously* sure," he says. "Dad's too busy with work, anyway. He'll be on his phone the whole time and won't be as fun as you guys."

Moments later, Chase texts to let us know he's here. Leo bounces the entire way to the Jeep. I strap in the extra car seat Ben keeps at the house in case there's an emergency—like absentee parents.

49

Leo's eyes are bigger than dinner plates as we walk the boards, taking in the sights, the sounds, the flashing lights. It's overwhelming and exciting all at once. He's holding both our hands, occasionally wanting us to swing him forward, which we do.

"It's just like when I had a dad *and* a mom," he exclaims.

Chase and I share a sympathetic glance over his head.

"There's the pizza place," I say as I spot Mack's neon sign. We each get a slice, then go in search of Curley's Fries, which Chase has been talking up as if he's their newest brand ambassador. Then, we take our full bellies to Morey's Pier, where we give Leo his choice of rides.

"As long as I meet the height requirements," he reminds us.

He chooses a kiddie motorcycle ride that only goes in circles. I'm worried about him getting on rides right after eating, but this one looks mild enough.

"Chase, will you go with me?" Leo asks as we join the line. "Dad says motorcycles are dangerous."

"I'd love to, buddy!"

I'm cracking up, watching the two of them. Especially Chase, who I'm surprised they let on the ride. The motorcycle seat is a foot from its base, which means Chase's knees are up by his ears. As he passes me on the first rotation, he throws his hands in the air.

"Weee!" he squeals, and I nearly fall over laughing. Every time he passes, he makes a different face at me.

Next, it's the kiddie airplanes. Once again, Leo invites Chase to join him. After that, it's bumper cars, and this time, Leo convinces me to join them. I'm content to ride the perimeter in my own car to avoid bumping into anyone (#personalinjurylaw) but the two of them think differently. They delight in ramming into me, as evidenced by Leo's outrageous giggles over my for-real screams.

We hit four other kiddie rides, Chase joining Leo on each one. My face hurts from laughing, and my heart swells to see this man screaming like a child with unfiltered delight. There's no doubt he's gonna make a great dad someday.

At the House of Mirrors, Leo grabs my hand. "Chase, why don't you rest while I take Kacie into the mirrors," he says. "She's so pretty, she should see millions of herself."

Chase smiles. "I couldn't agree more, Leo."

After finding our way through the maze of mirrors with "millions" of our doppelgängers, Leo decides to brave the hot-air balloon ride alone. As we lean up against the railing to watch, Chase moves his hand to my lower back.

"Thank you for inviting me," he says. "I'm having the time of my life."

"If I recall correctly, you invited yourself," I tease. "But I feel the same way."

Who would've known such fun could be had on the Wildwood Boardwalk? I can't remember laughing so much.

But here's me, never able to just enjoy the moment. Which is why I say, "You're not wishing you could be here with *Mer-e-dith*?" I slur her name on purpose.

He pulls back and looks at me with an amused expression. "Listen, Jellyfish...or shall I call you Jealousfish?"

"I'm not jealous," I say with a chuckle.

He shrugs. "If you say so."

"So."

"Even if you *were* jealous, there's no need to be." He turns to me as he leans an elbow on the railing. "Let's just say I'd much rather be here talking law than weather. We'll leave it at that."

My heart races and I have to turn away so he doesn't see the forecast displayed all over my face—100 percent chance of swoon.

Rejoining us, Leo announces he's over kiddie rides. He'd been eyeing up a roller coaster and has finally gained the courage to give it a go.

"You sure about this, buddy?" I ask. It isn't the biggest roller coaster I'd ever seen, but it looks daunting for a little guy.

"Yes, Kacie. I'm a very brave boy. Just like Mr. Chase. We're both humongously brave."

"That, you are."

As the ride's about to launch, I catch a glimpse of Chase with his arm around Leo in the car. Leo looks so tiny next to the 6'2" hunk, it's almost comical. From what I can tell, even though I can barely see him over the handlebar, Leo looks both excited and terrified. I guess that's normal for a first roller coaster ride—I wouldn't know, as I wouldn't dare ride one. I watch as they hurl around the track at lightning speed, and I wait at the exit for an exuberant Leo to come bouncing off the ride. But when he emerges, he's subdued and pale as a ghost.

"How was it buddy?" I ask.

I hold out my hand for a low five and he returns with projectile vomit.

"Oh my God!" I scream, as Leo bursts into tears.

I start gagging as Chase grabs the water bottle from my other hand and pours it on my palm. It's the thing I fear the most, someone throwing up on me. Some people get to go through life never being vomited on. Me, twice now.

Chase picks up Leo and guides us to the restrooms, where I hustle inside to wash my hands. Choking back my own vomit, I don't just wash, I scrub to the point I'm about to lose a layer of dermis. When I finally emerge, I find Chase sitting on a bench with Leo snuggled under his arm. The color has returned to the kid's face, and he's laughing at something Chase is pointing to.

Leo leaps up and runs into my arms. "I'm sorry, Kacie. I didn't mean to throw up on you."

"It's okay," I say, holding him at arm's length in case there's a repeat.

"I think I'm ready for a break," Leo says. "Can we go play some games? I wanna win a stuffed animal."

"You sure?" I look at Chase. I was certain a throw-up episode would have brought the night to an end.

Chase must know why I'm asking. "He's fine. Just a little ride reaction."

I wonder how he knows this, but he must be right, as Leo seems totally back to his pre-puke self, jumping up and down with excitement. "I wanna win a stuffed snake!"

Leo chooses a dart game and asks Chase to play for him. It takes several tries, but he finally wins a Major Prize. The snake is longer than Leo is, so we wrap it around his shoulders.

"I'm wearing this snake on my first day of school," he tells Chase.

"Sweet. I bet the kids will love that." Chase turns to me. "Okay, your turn. Wanna shoot some hoops?"

I reluctantly agree, and soon we discover I won't be trying out for the WNBA anytime soon. Having to go to the bathroom doesn't help. I excuse myself to find the restroom while they continue playing games. When I return, I find Chase holding Leo's hand, grinning. His other hand is behind his back.

"We won you a prize, Kacie!" Leo exclaims as he bounces up and down. He's struck by a fit of laugher as Chase pulls my prize from behind his back.

A stuffed jellyfish.

"That's because you love jellyfish!" Leo exclaims, laughing. "Mr. Chase spent forty dollars to win it!"

"For you, Jellyfish," Chase says softly.

My heart swoons as our eyes meet. The look on his face is precious. I can't believe the vicious thing that attacked me comes in such a cute and cuddly form. If only my first encounter was this enjoyable.

Then again, it led me to my new friend.

"Thank you, Mr. Chase," I say, cuddling my prize as we loop back through the ride pier. We're about to call it a night when Leo spots the same roller coaster that made him sick.

"I wanna do it again," he says, looking up at us. "Please, guys? I wanna see if I can do it without throwing up."

I'm ready to say no, but before I can, Chase is agreeing to another ride. As Leo bounces onward, I ask Chase if he's sure about this.

"We have a long drive home," I remind him. "I don't want him getting sick all over your car."

"He's not *sick* sick, Kace. It was just a first-time ride reaction. Judging by how much came out, he probably has nothing left in his system."

I grimace. "How are you so cavalier about this?"

"I teach fifth-graders," he says. "Someone's always throwing up in my classroom. I've even come to know the different types. Nervous puke, motion puke, sick puke—"

"Okay, I got it," I say, waving at him to shut up before power-of-suggestion puke sets in.

He laughs. "I guess when we have kids, I'll be the one cleaning up the chunks."

"Who says we're having kids?" My heart races, but I'm not sure if it's from Chase's comment, or the fear of raising a vomit factory.

"There's a fortune teller across the boardwalk," he says, pointing to a narrow building with a Tarot Cards sign out front. "Shall we go ask?"

"Save your money, dude," I say. "You're gonna have to find some other sucker."

As we approach the roller coaster, Leo asks if he can sit with me.

"But I'm not going—"

"Oh, I think you are," Chase says. "You don't want to let the little guy down."

"Yes, Kacie," Leo pipes in. "Don't let the little guy down."

"Oh, God..."

"It's not bad," Leo assures me as he takes my hand. "I'll protect you."

My heart swells again. There's no way I can say no.

"Consider it a bucket list item," Chase says, his eyes gleaming.

I wonder if he saw it on my list when he picked up my journal that day.

"It's on *my* bucket list for sure," Leo says.

Next thing I know, I'm being strapped into a freaking roller coaster beside Leo, with Chase behind us, stuffed jellyfish buckled in next to him. The ride propels us forward as I say a prayer and offer a silent fuck-you to Amy for including *#8: Go on a boardwalk ride* on my bucket list. As it lurches up the humongous hill, I feel as if I, too, may puke.

Leo reaches over and grabs my hand again. "It's okay, Kacie. I'm proud of you for facing your fears. You got this."

Before I can react, we're being dangled, face down, over the earth. I pray they don't have to unharness my lifeless body at the end of this ride.

And then, we plummet.

Twisting, turning, screaming, laughing...and suddenly, the ride's over. It was the most terrifying thing I've ever encountered in my life. And the most exhilarating.

When the train comes to a stop, Chase asks, "Again?"

We go for another round, this time better than the first.

Leo's still bouncing with joy as we head to the car soon after. "I can't wait to tell the kids at school all about tonight," he says as he skips between us.

"What was the highlight for you?" I ask.

"Throwing up on my own nanny." He starts cracking up. "Biggest highlight ever."

"That's a boy for you," Chase says, smiling at me. "Thanks for being such a good sport."

Leo talks a mile a minute, recounting the night, as Chase navigates our way toward home. Once we're away from the lights and excitement, Leo quiets. Just as we're about to get on the parkway, I hear a little sleepy voice coming from the backseat.

"You guys are gonna make great parents someday."

50

Ben calls the next morning to apologize for missing his boardwalk date with Leo, thanking me profusely for taking him. As he should. He didn't seem super remorseful when we dropped Leo off last night. Instead, he seemed preoccupied and merely took the sleeping boy from Chase's arms, as if he were mad Chase came with us. Like he had any right to judge who accompanied us to the boardwalk.

"There's so much going on at work right now," Ben now explains. "I feel horrible."

"Don't tell *me*. Tell your little boy."

"I already did. He thanked me for not coming. I wasn't sure if I should be sad or relieved," he says, his chuckle giving more sadness than relief. "He said he had the time of his life with you and Chase. I can't thank you both enough."

I'm surprised he's including Chase in the accolades, given how he acted last night.

"Again, thank that little guy for rolling with the punches," I say. "But don't push it, Ben. I've learned firsthand that jobs can be taken from us in a nanosecond. They're never worth compromising quality time with family."

Listen to me talk. The woman who once frequently used work as an excuse to get out of spending time with her own family. And dating. And anything I didn't feel like doing.

Like this conversation we're about to have. I take a deep breath.

"I'm sorry, Ben, I've given this a lot of thought and...I don't think it's gonna work between us. I'm not willing to start a new relationship with such stringent rules for the future. Like no marriage, no kids."

"I thought you didn't want those things?" he says, sounding shocked.

"There was a time I didn't, but I've done a lot of soul-searching this summer. Built a lot of sandcastles with a little guy who's stolen my heart. I'm at a crossroads in life, and my future's filled with possibilities I may not even know exist. I don't want to close the door on any of them right now—in life, law, or love."

After a beat, he says, "Maybe someday…"

"No, Ben. We've had enough *maybe somedays*. I told myself when I came to Sea Isle, this would be the summer I either get with you, or get over you. We're not aligned on what we want for our futures—hell, even the present—which tells me this has to be the summer I—"

"Get over me," he says. "I get it."

The fact that he's so readily accepting what I'm saying, just like he did back in law school, only confirms I've made the right decision.

I'm finally ready to deal with this fact: we were never meant to be anything more than friends. At least we still have that.

51

The day of dread is upon us—the day Typhoon Meredith makes landfall. Fortunately, I've battened down the hatches and boarded up my windows. I'm ready for whatever wrath she has to offer.

What I'm not ready for is the Vine Shrine I walk into upon returning from work today. Featuring Meredith Vine herself.

Somehow, every guy in our house has managed to get to the shore hours earlier than usual—no doubt after hearing Meredith was arriving that afternoon. All seven of them are scattered about the living room in states of dress I'd never seen before. Shorts pressed, shirts new, hair combed. In the center of it all is Meredith, perched on the edge of the couch like she's Jackie O—long legs gracefully bent to the side. All she needs is a two-foot cigarette holder and gloved hands and I'd feel as if I walked into a 1960s movie set.

As I enter, I catch the tail end of a riveting story told by Chase himself, entertaining everyone like he did the other day on the beach. Meredith throws back her head, giving a bubbly laugh, as Chase stands taller, obviously proud of his ability to make this TV icon laugh. It makes me want to puke.

"Oh, here's Kacie," Celeste calls out, sounding sweetly genuine—even though I know better. "Come meet Meredith."

Her smile is pleasant enough, but it doesn't reach her eyes. What does reach them is the invisible middle finger she's waving at me from across the room.

I take a deep breath, smoothing out my voice to cover the snark I'm currently harboring.

"Meredith, such a pleasure to meet you," I say as I cross the room and offer her a handshake.

"The pleasure is mine," Meredith says, sounding genuine.

I hate her already.

Chase removes his duffle bag from the couch. "Here, sit. Join us."

"Maybe later," I say. "Gotta grab a shower."

Or do anything that doesn't resemble hero worship. I make a vow not to treat this celebrity with more fanfare than she deserves. Sure, she's gorgeous, and yes, she's a meteorologist. Whoopdee*freakin*doo. How hard is it to read a teleprompter and banter about barometric bullshit?

Washing my hair, I scrub harder than usual, as though that will rid me of this angst. I can't believe I have to endure this woman being in our midst for the next week. I envision Chase holding court whenever she's around, dazzling her with his charm, trying to win her over. I've seen the rizz emanating from that boy when he's trying to impress someone, having been on the receiving end of his player routine.

But then I ask myself: would a main character carry on like this? No. She wouldn't act like a jealous shrew. *Instead of pulling your hair out, pull yourself together, woman.*

I'm heading back inside from my alfresco shower when I encounter Harry in the driveway.

"Hey, Kacie—this came for you today. I found it in the mailbox."

He hands me what appears to be a message in a plastic bottle with a mailing label addressed to me. Twisting off the lid, I find a furled paper inside, informing me I've been selected as a candidate for a position at Ben's firm. As such, I'm invited to a sunset cruise on August seventh. Ben wasn't kidding when he warned the invite may be a bit cheeky.

"Oh my God!" I exclaim.

"What is it?" Harry asks.

"Basically, a job offer." Even though it's just the first round, I feel hopeful. A first.

"Not what I expected you to say, but congrats."

The first thing I do is call Ben. I figure he had something to do with this.

"Congratulations!" he says. "I had a feeling you were going to be invited."

"Thank you for whatever you've done to make this happen," I say. Even if I'm not 100% sure a law firm job is what I want, it feels good to at least be invited into the process and given an opportunity to consider it.

To show my gratitude, I invite him and Leo to the party we're having tonight. Despite the fact that things didn't work out for us romantically, Ben and I will always be friends. Besides, I need a distraction. Since our boardwalk night, it's been hard to stop thinking about Chase, without remembering that Meredith is here for the week, sucking up all his attention like the award-winning weather vortex she is.

So, Ben and his little sidekick will have to be my entertainment for the evening.

"Leo's having a sleepover at the neighbors' house," Ben informs me. "Is it okay if I come alone?"

"Of course." Although I am a bit bummed little man won't be there.

The party's in full swing by the time Ben arrives. I'm happy to see him. It's been tough watching the Chase and Meredith Show—she seems to follow him wherever he goes. At least I hope it's her following him and not the other way around.

I know I shouldn't care. Being the main character in my own life means not letting some guy dictate my feelings. But it's hard to stave off the pangs of envy I feel over these two beautiful people whose glances seem to linger on one another. I have to admit, they make the perfect couple, beauty begetting beauty.

Maybe Chase is right. I am a jealousfish.

When Ben emerges through the crowd, I act like he's my long-lost love—strictly for the benefit of Celeste, who's standing with Chase and Meredith, not far from me. I want to drive home the point I couldn't care less about Chase, so Celeste can finally remove her claws from my back.

"Hey, boyfriend!" I call out.

Ben does an immediate about-face, looking behind him before pointing to his chest.

I cast a silent "just play along" look as he comes over and wraps his arms around my waist. It's our old bar trick, one we used when someone was coming on to me and I needed to be rescued.

"Hey, girlfriend," he teases in response, hugging me.

I notice Celeste watching us with a raised brow. I also notice someone else's full attention on us—Chase. Watching us intently, a frown marring his handsome face.

"Come on, hunk. Let's go get you a drink." I make sure I say it loud enough for Celeste to hear.

I know you're thinking: *Hey, Kacie...the Golden Girls called and they want you on their show.* You're right, that word gives '80s cougar. Blame Cougar Colleen—apples don't fall far, apparently.

I lead Ben to the cooler on the deck to get drinks. As we uncap our Coronas, Ben gets pulled into a conversation about the Phillies' latest win. We stay huddled around the coolers as the guys discuss players' stats, while I slip into early onset sports-related coma. I have no idea what they're talking about with their acronyms and numbers.

Then Chase and Meredith join us. Yippee.

"Talking about the game last night?" Chase asks as he reaches into the cooler.

"Would you mind grabbing me one, too, Chasey?" Meredith asks.

Chasey...give me a break. She's been on two dates with

the man—hardly enough time to start calling him by a cutesy nickname.

"A gentleman, Chasey is," I joke.

He shoots me a look. "Thanks, Yoda."

"Don't mention it."

Chase turns to Ben. "Boyfriend, how's work going?"

I almost spit out my beer.

"Pretty good, I guess," Ben laughs. "How 'bout you, lover boy?"

Now I do. I double over to catch the beer spewing from my mouth. I love that about Ben. While his humor isn't out there like some, it's understated enough to catch you off guard when you least expect it.

Even Chase laughs and holds out a fist bump. "Nicely done," he commends Ben, who reciprocates.

"What am I missing?" Meredith asks.

"They have a crush on each other," I say.

"True. I've crushed on him for *years*. Right, Kace?" Chase gives me a teasing look. "He's only ever seen me as a friend, until lately. I'm losing my *mind* over it."

"Watch it, lover boy," I warn.

"Just kidding, Ben," Chase says, clasping him on the shoulder before turning to Meredith. "Wanna take a walk on the beach?"

Back, meet knife blade.

"Enjoy your walk, kids," I call out as they turn toward the stairs. "Watch out for the jellyfish!"

"We'll try," Chase calls back. "I've heard they're a real pain in the ass to get rid of, once their tenacles grab ahold of you."

His deadass stare shoots straight across the deck and nearly takes me out at the knees.

"Watch out for the sharks too. They're circling," I say under my breath.

I try not to think about what's happening on that beach walk of theirs, but imagine it'll go much like ours. Twirl around, looking at the sky while Meredith regales him with tales of cumulous clouds and cold fronts. Then, off to the lifeguard stand they'll go, where Chase will tell her all about the constellations before he sticks his tongue down her throat. Been there, done that.

If only I was done *with* that.

The happy couple-to-be returns moments later. Ben goes off to the bathroom while Meredith gets pulled into a conversation, leaving Chase and me alone.

"If it isn't Ten-second Tom," I say. "That was quick."

"What?"

"Your romantic beach-walk-star-watch-lifeguard-stand routine. You've gotten it down to mere minutes."

He gives me a smug smile. "When you know what you want, you go for it."

Back, meet knife twist.

"And what Meredith wants is to keep her feet sand-free," he says.

"What do you mean?"

"She hates the feeling of sand on her feet at night."

I flinch in disbelief—and maybe some relief. "Are you serious? Who doesn't love cold night sand?"

"Right? Major red flag."

"Huge," I say, trying not to smile. "Gonna be hard to make out with a woman in a lifeguard stand when you can't get her out there. I guess you'll have to come up with another move."

"Listen, I don't make out with just anyone in the lifeguard stand."

"That's what they all say."

"No, not all. Just this guy." He gives me a pointed look and raises an eyebrow. "Especially when that can never be duplicated."

He walks away, leaving me with my mouth gaping open. If only the possibilities were as well, but not with Meredith here.

"Kacie, come here!" Speak-of-the-devil calls to me. "I hear you're an attorney. How impressive!"

"Not really," I say. "Any primate can do it."

She and Celeste share a genuine laugh over my joke. It makes me smile.

"I'm serious—you should see some of the baboons I went to law school with."

"I don't believe that for a second," Meredith says. "I tried to get into law school but failed miserably on the LSAT. Turns out, I'm awful at standardized testing."

"That's a shame, because those tests aren't a true measure of a person's ability to research, negotiate, and screw others over, which is at the heart of what you do when you practice law."

"I'm sure it takes more than that," she says.

I'm surprised how down to earth she seems. I don't want to like her, but she's kinda growing on me.

"You and Ben make a cute couple," Celeste says.

I give her the side-eye, checking for signs of snarkiness, but she sounds sincere. And maybe relieved. I guess my little show-and-tell routine has worked, so I don't bother to set her straight.

I notice Ben's rejoined the guys in sports talk, so I go off in search of the girls. I find them inside, where Diane is telling Wendy and Rachel about her wedding plans. I listen in with genuine interest. A first for me. There was a time I would have flung myself off the deck to avoid having to hear someone talk about their wedding. Points added for acting like a grown-up and, while I'm at it, avoiding a neck brace.

After a while, Ben joins us and informs me he's heading home.

"Thanks for tonight," he says as I walk him out. When we reach the sidewalk, he turns to me. "Just curious—does Chase have anything to do with...us?"

My brow draws together. "No..."

"It's just that I've watched you two all summer bantering

back and forth. Is there something going on between you? You can tell me. I won't tell anyone."

I take a deep breath, not sure I want to go there. But Ben is my friend, after all, and friends tell each other about their romantic lives. "Chase and I have had some—things happen. Flirting, a couple kisses, nothing more than that. Good thing too—he's apparently been dating Meredith."

"Lucky guy."

See, didn't I tell you? This is the effect this woman has on all men. I can't compete with that.

"Sorry," he says, "I didn't mean—"

I shake my head to shut him up. "No, I get it. But the point is, he wasn't the reason for my decision about...us. I just made the decision that was best for me."

"Wow, Kacie. I'm bummed, but also impressed. You've changed, and you're much happier as a result. You deserve to hold out for what's best for you."

"Well, when you have a summer bucket list that forces you to do things you'd normally not do, and a career-less summer to do them, change is inevitable."

"Speaking of careers, are you going on the firm's cruise?"

"Absolutely. Like I said, I'm not holding myself back from opportunities until I've given myself a chance to try them on. Kinda like...us." I go up on my tiptoes and give him a kiss on the cheek. "I'm glad we gave it a shot, even if it didn't work out."

"Still friends, then?"

I smile. "Friends to the end."

52

Leo talks nonstop about our boardwalk experience the next time I'm with him. It fills my heart with joy to know it was all because of me. Okay, Chase too, but I was the one who insisted on taking him. Turns out, I may be more of a kid person than I've given myself credit for.

The only thing different about our routine today is that we'd left Leo's prized snake in the Jeep that night, so on our way back from the beach, we swing by my house to get it. As we're heading to the car, we encounter Meredith and Celeste, who've come off the beach for a bathroom break.

"Hey, I know you!" Leo exclaims when he sees Meredith. "You're that lady on TV. The one who talks about the weather."

"That's right, Leo," I say. "This is Miss Meredith. She's a meteorologist."

"A meaty-rolly-jiss," he attempts to repeat. "That could be a word of the day, if only I could say it."

"Hi, Leo," Meredith says, reaching out her hand to shake his. "I'm pleased to meet you."

"Please to meet you," Leo repeats. "My dad was on TV once."

"He was?" Meredith asks, sounding genuinely interested.

"He was?" I ask, sounding genuinely surprised. If he was, it's news to me.

"Yeah. He was at a baseball game once and he got on that big TV thing."

"The Jumbotron?" Meredith asks. "Wow, that's pretty cool. Were you there too?"

"No," he says, shrugging. "He was with some lady."

I scrunch my face, tilt my head. "When was this?"

"When I was at my aunt's house. I remember it because after he showed me the video, I asked if he'd take me to a game." He shrugs again. "I'm still waiting."

"There's a video?" I ask, stuck on that.

"Yeah, I'll show you when we get home."

Back at his house, Leo pulls out his iPad without me having to ask.

"Daddy sent me the video and I downloaded it. Here."

Turning the screen to me, he starts the video rolling. Sure enough, there's Ben in a stadium, wearing a Phillies jersey, hot dog in one hand, beer in another. He's looking around obliviously until his eyes cast skyward. A look of recognition flashes across his face—that moment you realize you're on a Jumbotron—and his smile widens. He raises his beer to the camera in salute, and then...

He leans into the woman sitting next to him and kisses her. On the lips.

Passionately.

My heart stops for a brief second, wondering when this was. From the scoreboard, I see it was one of the games the guys were talking about at the party. One from this summer.

Time stands still as my eyes slowly drift to the time stamp in the corner of the video.

June 23. 7:45 p.m.

The night of my birthday. The night he blew me off.

Hands shaking, I pull up my phone and scroll through Ben's texts, to the one he sent when he told me he was in traffic and wouldn't be able to make our date. It was sent at 8:15 p.m., which means he'd been in the stadium, kissing another woman, thirty minutes before he texted to say he was "stuck in traffic."

My mouth drops open as all the oxygen is sucked from the room. I'm vaguely aware Leo's saying my name, trying to show me something, but I'm transported to that night. I'm hovering above the Deauville Inn like a drone, seeing myself sitting alone at the table in my beautiful dress. Heart full of anticipation, watching the sunset, waiting for the man I've loved for years to join me. My expression falling upon learning he's not going to make it but giving him grace and understanding because circumstances were beyond his control. I'm heartbroken all over again, remembering it.

My first inclination is to run, to leave this house and let this kid fend for himself. But he's leaning into me now, kissing my cheek.

"I love you, Kacie," Leo says as he lays his head on my shoulder. "You look like you need a kiss."

I swallow hard. Pointing to the woman on the screen, which I've inadvertently paused during the kiss, I turn to Leo. "Do you know her?"

"No," he says, and for a brief second in time, I'm relieved.

Until he continues. "But I think that's the woman who was here the other morning. After our boardwalk night."

What? I think back to that night, recalling the way Ben snatched the sleeping child from Chase's arms and shooed us away. I thought he was mad Chase had gone to the boardwalk with us, but...

Oh my God. The fucker must have had someone there with him.

I'm filled with rage over the fact that he was more interested in wining and dining a woman than being with his precious child that night. Or being with me on my birthday. Now, all I want to do is flee and take Leo with me.

For the rest of the afternoon, I pretend to be fine. We put together a puzzle, and as I help Leo fit the pieces together, I'm internally putting together the pieces of this summer in my mind. Late nights working. Missed events. Promises broken.

By the time Ben gets there, my fury has caramelized to the

point it's a slow-moving current of acrid bitterness.

"Hey, guys!" he exclaims as he comes into the kitchen where we're doing our puzzle. "How was your day?"

"Kacie's sad," Leo announces.

Ben looks at me. "Why, what's wrong?"

"Nothing," I say, smiling brightly. I don't want to do this in front of Leo. "Just tired."

As Leo rambles on about the things we've done today, Ben casts glances my way. He knows me well enough to know I'm anything but okay.

When I get up to leave, I hand Leo his iPad. "Hey, kiddo, see if you can draw me a Minion."

"Will do, kangaroo!"

I turn to Ben. "Can you walk me out?"

Ben scrambles to his feet as Leo gets to work on his drawing. We're no sooner out the door than he grabs my arm and gives me a terrified look. "What's wrong?"

I can't help my sardonic laugh. "Why the look of terror, Ben?"

"You're scaring me. What's going on?"

"Where were you the night of my birthday, Ben?"

He looks me deadass in the eyes. I can tell he's trying to remember what he told me.

"This ring a bell?"

I hold up my phone to show him a photo of the KissCam. Of course, I took a picture for evidentiary purposes. I am a lawyer, after all.

I point to the time stamp.

"This was June 23. My birthday, if you recall. In fact, you'd made an eight o'clock dinner reservation for us. Remember that?"

"I don't know—" He stumbles on his words, looking shocked.

"Don't know what, Ben? Okay, I guess we're doing this." I suit up for battle as I pull up his texts. "At 6:15, you tell me you're gonna leave soon, you're running late, and ask me to meet you at the restaurant so we don't lose our reservation. At 8:15, you text to say you're on the AC Expressway in traffic and won't get there in time. Yet at 7:45, you appear on a stadium KissCam. What happened? Were you sucked into the Citizens Park vortex against your will? Did you suffer early onset dementia and completely forget? Or—my guess—you never intended to meet me."

"I did intend—I didn't mean—my boss caught me as I was leaving—invited me to the game. I had no choice."

"Your *boss*?" Like an exaggerating asshole, I pull the phone close to my face and peer at the photo. "Where's your boss? I only see you with a woman."

"I don't know that woman—she's a stranger."

I cackle like a witch stirring a cauldron full of shit. The shit flowing from his mouth.

"If that's the case, how did she end up in your house the night you were supposed to take your son to the boardwalk?"

My heart thumps away in my chest, taking my breath with it as I pray Leo's recall was correct. I have him dead to rights here, and I don't want to assume something incorrectly and lose my advantage.

When Ben's chin drops into his chest, I know I got him.

"You lied to me," I say, seething. "You set me up. You invited me to dinner and blew me off for some rando. And then you turned around and did the same thing to your precious boy."

The last two words catch in my throat as my voice cracks.

"She's not a rando," he says, his voice barely a whisper.

"Who is she?"

He's silent as I stare him down. I know he's trying to weave some fabrication he thinks I'll believe.

"The truth, Ben. I've watched your son all summer long so you could—what—screw around with someone? Blow the two of us off? I deserve the truth."

He deflates before me. Still with his head down he says, "There's history here."

"Apparently."

"Her name is Beth. I've...been with her...on and off...for..."

"For...?"

He sighs. "Years."

I recoil as if he's just slapped me. "How many years?"

"Six," he whispers.

"You were fucking another woman the whole time you were married?" My voice comes out gravelly, as if the devil's speaking through me. "For longer than your son's been alive?"

"Like I said, there's...history."

"I don't give a flying fuck about history. When you love someone, nothing else should matter. Did Angi know about the affair? Oh, Jesus..." Clasping my hands to my head, I walk away, then circle back. "That's why she found someone else. Isn't it?"

His voice is but a whisper. "Yes."

Despite my indignation, I'm surprised how calm I sound on the outside. "You've not only destroyed a marriage—a family, for God's sake—but you destroyed our friendship. You thrust me into a professional nightmare, lying to me as your lawyer, making me fight Angi for custody of your son. Claiming to be the victim, when all the while you were the villain."

His head is now buried in his chest. "I—don't know what to say."

"How about telling me why you've been coming on to me when you're seeing someone else?"

My blood boils as I think of all the grace I've given Ben, holding him in high regard, considering him a safe bet. Someone who wasn't a player, who wouldn't mess with my heart. Goddamn, did I misjudge him.

"She went back to her husband earlier this summer but then they split again. They're on and off. And so are Beth and I, as a result."

Which means nothing about me and Ben this summer was about me and Ben. I bet, if I knew the whole story, I could align every one of Ben's come-ons and blow-offs with Beth's back-and-forth behavior.

"What about that situation made you think it was okay to pull *me* into it? Huh? Into *their* marital tug-of-war? Into your waffling affair?"

"I never intended to do that. I really wanted to explore something with you, Kacie. I meant what I said when I wanted to take you on a date for your birthday. Explore what we could be together. But as I was about to leave the office to join you that night, she came in and told me she'd left her husband again. For me. That she loved me and couldn't stand being away from me. She had tickets to the game and invited me so we could talk about...us...and I thought...you know, you're so easygoing that you'd be okay if I couldn't make it, that I could make it up to you and you'd be..."

He's crying now, reaching out to grasp my hands, but I yank them away.

"I'm so sorry, Kacie. I'm just confused. I've been torn...I know I fucked up..."

I'm done listening.

"You didn't just fuck up," I say, my voice calm as ever. "You *are* a fuckup."

And then, at long goddamn last, I slam the door on history.

53

It's been forty-eight hours since I ended things with Ben. Listen to me—*things*. There were no things, just a farce of a friendship. In that time, he's sent me 103 texts, which I've left on read, and called me fifty-four times, which have all gone unanswered. I'm not ready to talk to him, but out of loyalty to Leo, I know I have to at some point. We need closure, even if it's gonna kill me. Because I know, after we do, I'll never see that little guy again. I need some time to process that I've lost not just one friendship, but two.

I've done a lot of soul-searching in these past couple days. While I feel beaten up, fucked with, and destroyed by Ben, I must lay claim to some contributory negligence. As Amy's pointed out throughout the years, he had his chance to make something happen with me back in law school, but he chose to walk away. And I chose to hang in there, hoping something would change and Ben would make himself available to me. Hoping I'd finally get to have the kind of relationship that would never bite me in the ass, because Ben was a good and safe guy who would never hurt me like that.

What a fool I've been.

Other than that misjudgment on my part, I've been right all along to operate from a place of fear. Turns out, there *are* no safe people. Someone is always waiting to screw you over.

Never. Again.

One of the texts Ben sent was to let me know I was off the nannying hook, and that Leo would be staying with his aunt for the rest of the summer. I was heartbroken for Leo, worried he'd think I abandoned him. But he's five. He'll be with his cousins, and soon I'll be a distant memory. If even that.

The only decent thing Ben's done in the wake of this tragedy is Venmo me all the money I'd have made had I stayed on until Labor Day as originally planned, including payment for the two weeks Leo was at his cousins'. If he was trying to buy my forgiveness, he was wasting his money. I almost returned the funds out of spite, but realized I'd only be spiting myself. I wasn't the one who cheated on their wife, their son, their friendship with me. It wasn't my idea to quit on Leo. He owed me financial compensation for what I should have earned, and I ultimately accepted it guilt-free.

Ben also left a long, rambling voicemail about the firm.

"Please, Kacie, I implore you not to walk away from this job opportunity. You're too good an attorney not to work for this firm, and I think you'll find it to be a dream workplace. If you get the job, you'll be located in a different office in a different part of the city, in a separate area of law. You'll never have to see me if you don't want to. But please, at least go on the cruise, check it out for yourself. I've done some digging, and you're number one on the list as of right now. If you have to slam the door on me and our friendship, I don't blame you. But please don't close a door of opportunity on yourself."

As much as I want to block anything Ben has to say from consideration, I know he's right. If it's true I'm being vetted for this job as a serious contender, I need to move forward with it. I refuse to screw myself by letting something like a broken heart stop me, because then Ben will truly win.

Today's the day of the cruise. I'm about to pack up the shack early to get ready when I hear a small voice behind me.

"Kacie."

I turn to see Leo with a single tear streaming down his face. I crouch down, and he runs to me. I'm hugging him for all I'm worth as tears fill my own eyes. I can't make this any harder for him, so I suck it up and stop myself.

"Hey, kiddo, I hear you've got some exciting news," I say, trying to sound happy. "Dad says you're gonna be hanging out with your cousins for the rest of the summer!"

For the first time, I notice Ben standing way off to the side. He seems relieved I'm not throwing beach chairs and umbrellas at him, although I haven't ruled that option out entirely.

No. I'm taking the high road. Not for you, asshole. For this little boy.

"Are those happy tears or sad tears?" Leo asks as he wipes them away with his thumb.

"To tell you the truth, they're a little of both. I'm sad you won't be hanging out with me, but I'm happy you get to play with kids. You're gonna have a *humongous* amount of fun!"

"I'm glad to see you using my word of the day correctly. Correction—past word of the day."

"What's today's?"

"Remorse. Dad said he's been sad lately because he's remorse. He says it's what happens when you make a mistake and lose something important. But I take good care of my things, so I'll probably never remorse."

I chuckle. "Take care of you, too, little man. Capisce?"

"Capisce." He takes a deep breath. "I'm not sure when I'm gonna see you again. I have to go off to kindergarten after I get back from my cousins'."

The way he says it, it's as if he's going off to war.

"I know, Leo. I'm excited for you. School is fun."

"Dad says I can't take my snake, though."

I refrain from saying what I'm thinking—because the teacher may not be able to tell the difference between your toy and your dad.

Leo places his hand below my neck. "Did you know this is where your heart is? My mom always says, 'I'll be right here in your heart when I'm not with you', so I'll tell you the same thing. I'll be right here in your heart."

My eyes well again. I blink rapidly to keep tears from spilling.

"And I'll be right here in yours," I say.

"Gotta run, honeybun. Aunt Sue's taking us to Hershey Park tonight. Have you ever been to Hershey Park? I hear the whole town smells like chocolate. I can't wait! I love chocolate!"

"Have a piece for me, 'kay Leo?"

"I'll have twenty pieces for you!"

I hold up my hand for a final high five. "Bye-bye, butterfly."

"See you soon, silly baboon."

No, you won't, Leo. I already know how this ends. I choke back a sob and watch as my little buddy skips back to Ben. Our eyes meet, and he mouths, "Thank you."

I simply turn away without response. No middle finger, no shouted obscenities, no umbrella daggers. I know what you're thinking—look at you, Kacie, being a grown-ass adult!

But that doesn't mean I don't duck into the shack and sob. I'm gonna miss that little guy something fierce. The big one can fuck right off.

Back at home, I turn a corner to enter the garage and bump into someone.

A man in a tux.

That's right—it's also the night of the wedding. Chase's big date with Meredith, the reason she's been here all week. Now the tux in the closet makes sense—he's a groomsman in his friend's wedding.

Instinctively, I run my hand down his front in case I transferred sand from my bikini-clad body onto his.

He laughs. "Are you trying to feel me up, Layne?"

"Am I being that obvious?" I joke.

"Humongously so."

The word instantly brings tears to my eyes.

"Whoa! What's wrong?" Chase says, grabbing my arm as I turn to walk away.

"Nothing." I swipe at my tears, but the way he's looking at me, I can tell my secret's safe. "I just had to say goodbye to Leo."

"Goodbye?" His panic-stricken look makes me laugh through my tears when I realize how dramatic that sounds. I haven't told him about the Ben debacle. *Maybe someday.*

"My nannying days are over. He's staying with his aunt from now on when Ben goes to work."

"Aww, I'm sorry to hear that. I know how much you've enjoyed being with him."

He pulls me into a hug, and I rest my head on his chest. It feels good to have a friend's arms around me, knowing I'll never have this again with Ben. The thought makes me cry harder.

"Hey," he whispers as he pulls me away. "What's going on?"

He pulls the pocket square from his tux and dabs at my tears. The gesture makes me laugh again.

"Aren't you gonna need that?" I ask.

"It's for decorative purposes only, until it's called into service."

"What if you need it for your own tears? Weddings have a way of making people cry. In fact, I saw you get choked up at Shaniya's wedding."

"Busted," he says, giving a half smile.

He tries to put the pocket square back but can't figure out how to refold it.

"Now what?" He laughs, waving it in defeat.

"Here." I take it and fold it perfectly before sliding it back in.

"Wow. You're a pro."

"Yeah, somehow I became my brothers' tie-tier and pocket square-folder for family weddings."

"Judging by your prowess, I'm guessing you've had a lot of family weddings."

"An aunt, a few cousins, my older brother and sister...quite a few, actually."

"Does that mean you're next, being the middle child?"

"Yeah, right around the same time California falls into the ocean."

"Could be soon, you know...the way the climate's changing."

"Do you own this badass tux, or is a lease to own?" I ask, as I straighten his lapel.

"It's all mine."

"I *knew* it. You're really a magician, aren't you?"

"Gigolo would be the correct answer. You just never know when you'll have to save someone's birthday."

He perches on a bar stool at the garage bar. "Come, sit. I sense there's more to the story than Leo going to his aunt's."

"Don't you have a wedding to go to?"

"Spill it, Jellyfish."

I sigh, not wanting to get into it, but I feel like I need to tell someone. And who better than the friend who saved my birthday from complete ruin at my other supposed friend's hands?

"You sure you have time for this?"

"We have to be outta here in fifteen, but hopefully that's enough time for the SparkNotes version."

"SparkNotes. Okay. So, remember that night of my birthday, when you showed up looking like..." I gesture to his tux. "This?"

"I remember it well," he says, his eyes gleaming.

"Apparently, Ben was lying when he said he was stuck in traffic and couldn't make our dinner. Because this is where he really was."

I pull out my phone and show him the photo. "A Phillies game."

"Kissing someone else," he says, his expression falling. "How do you—oh. I see the time stamp."

"Yep. To do that to someone who you call a friend? On her birthday? It's—"

"Reprehensible."

"I'm such an asshole to have trusted him."

"No, he's the asshole," he says. He looks from the screen to me with an expression of profound sadness. "Honestly? Never really liked the guy."

"I could tell."

"I'm sorry, Jellyfish." His hands clasp my waist, and he pulls me toward him so that I'm standing between his knees. "You deserve so much better than that. Don't ever forget it."

"Thank you."

I melt into him and he holds me there for a while, rubbing his hand up and down my back. I feel his heartbeat thrumming against my chest.

"Chase, where—" comes a voice. It's Celeste, in a dress, standing in the doorway. "Sorry, I—wondered if you were ready. The Uber's on its way."

"Yeah, I'll be there. Give me a sec."

Celeste's glare lingers on me as she slowly turns away.

"Have fun tonight," I say, pulling back from Chase, trying to sound chipper but instead feeling jealous as hell. He looks so hot in his tux. Meredith is a lucky woman to be going on this date with him.

"You still doing the cruise tonight?" he asks.

My invitation-in-a-bottle was the talk of the house when I received it.

"Yeah. Maybe against my better judgment. Ben's assured me I'm first on their shortlist for hire. If I get it, I'll be in a totally separate section and building and won't ever have to see him. I feel like I owe it to myself to see this one through."

"That's right. Gotta shoot your shot, girl. Otherwise, you may regret it."

"My heart's not in it at all, but maybe a night on the bay with potential coworkers is the kind of night I need."

We head outside, where Celeste is waiting.

"Best of luck, but I don't think you'll need it," he says, giving me a hug.

"There she is!" Celeste exclaims.

We all turn to see Meredith in a sparkling silver gown, gliding down the steps like a princess. She's made up to the nines, her hair coiffed in a French twist.

"Whoa." I can tell Chase's exclamation comes involuntarily, and I can't say I blame him. She is literally stunning.

"Gorgeous, Meredith," I say. "You even take my breath away."

Celeste pulls out her phone. "Let me get a photo of you two lovebirds," she says, pushing Chase toward Meredith.

Chase poses formally, but Meredith rests her hand on his chest as she gazes up at him like a woman in love. All I want to do is pull the pocket square from his tux and wave it in defeat. She wins. As I said, I'll never compete with another woman over a man. With Ben and Seth, I didn't know there was another woman in the picture until it was too late. This time, I do.

"Here, let me get one of all four of you," I say as Celeste's boyfriend comes down the steps.

I snap several photos of The Beautiful People with Celeste's phone before handing it back to her.

"Thank you, Kacie," Celeste says as she slips it into her clutch. "Good luck on your interview tonight."

I don't doubt her well-wishes. They sound genuine. Probably because she knows she and her illustrious cousin have won.

After showering, I head inside to get ready for my own night. For the first time since I received the message in a bottle, a tiny flicker of hope ignites in me. I decide I'm gonna "up-spiral my life" and nail this experience if it's the last thing I do.

54

I'm thankful I had the foresight to pack a professional outfit this summer, just in case an interview popped up. I decide to forgo the suit jacket and just wear the little black dress that goes with it. The dress code is business casual, so it works.

Doing a final mirror inspection, I allow myself to feel excited in a way I usually don't before events like this. Normally, I'd keep my expectations at bay, but the new and improved Kacie Layne knows life's too short not to revel in special moments. Like stepping through a bigger portal filled with possibilities on the other side. Just as Mom described.

After my Uber drops me off, I feel a bit nervous boarding the boat, already filled with people chatting and laughing as they sip cocktails. I'm blown away by the sheer numbers. Ben said they'd received two hundred applications, and I wouldn't be surprised if half of them were here. As intimidated as I am, I forge ahead. On the main deck, a man in a suit approaches, asks my name, and checks it off on his clipboard as a server hands me a glass of champagne.

Damn, this is some level of fancy.

I make my way through the crowd, hoping to see a familiar face. I'm passing a group of people about my age when one of the women waves me over.

"Come join us. I'm Kelly, and..." She leans in and whispers, "Sorry, I forget the others' names."

I introduce myself to Kelly and the others before they resume their conversation about a corporate merger. I understand how Kelly forgot their names—they're boring as hell. I try to pay attention, but it's hard to concentrate when all I can do is wonder about the ratio of people here to positions available.

Excusing myself, I mill about, hoping to find someone else to talk to, but everyone seems deep in conversation. When the boat pulls away from the dock, I lean against the railing, watching the restaurants along Fish Alley, diners waving at us as we pass. It cracks me up how we wave at total strangers on boats but are quick to flip them off in cars when circumstances warrant. The stand-up comedian in me wonders what would happen if we just flipped off boat people instead of waving to them. The thought makes me laugh.

"What's so funny?" a man asks as he sidles up next to me.

"Oh, I'm—" I have no idea who this man is. He's older than me, possibly a hiring partner, so I don't share my thoughts. "Nothing. I'm Kacie Layne. And you?"

"Dave Martin, one of the hiring partners."

Ah-ha! I have a nose for these things.

He shakes my hand. "I recognize your name as one of our top contenders. You resume is impressive."

"Thank you, Mr. Martin. How many of these guests are interviewing?"

"All of them. I'm certain you read the information provided on the back of the invitation about our process."

That would be a no. I intended to but totally forgot. No matter, though—Ben told me all I needed to know.

"You're Ben Steele's friend, right?"

"Yes." Well, was. I pray he doesn't hold that against me.

"Good fella. Great lawyer."

"Yeah." Also, a cheater and a dickhead, but I leave that part out.

"Good talk," he says as he drifts away, leaving me feeling like I've just failed my first test.

"Wait! Mr. Martin?" I call out and he turns back. "How many positions are you hiring for?"

"There are three positions *for which* we're hiring," he says, as if to school me on proper grammar.

I fight the urge to flip him off as I scramble to think of something else to say. Too late—he's walking away.

Three positions? For all these people? Fuck all of us.

After drifting aimlessly for a bit, I end up standing next to a group of men, hoping to overhear what they're saying so I can join in. I need to prove myself to be a good communicator.

"She was something else," I hear one of the guys say. "I walked into court, not knowing what to expect, but I was blown away."

I drift closer, hoping to hear what was so mind-blowing about his opposing counsel. Her legal argument? Her cited case law?

"Biggest bazoongas I've ever seen," he says. "Hu*mong*ous."

The speaker holds two invisible melons in front of his chest. Nope!

Exhaling, I move on. I seem to be the only person not clicking with others. A quick glance at my phone confirms we've only been cruising for ten minutes. We have two hours and fifty minutes left. God help us.

I feel like I don't belong here. Everyone's trying to out-talk each other, out-lawyer each other. Having been removed from this scene for these past two months, it's hard to get back into it. I'd forgotten what blowhards lawyers can sometimes be. Not all, obviously, but as a group we've earned a reputation for a reason.

A text comes through. It's Chase. My pulse quickens.

> How's it going? Have they offered you the job yet?

> Boring AF. How's the wedding?

I wait for a response, but none comes. Of course not—he's at a wedding, doofus. With a beautiful woman. She probably stepped away to go to the ladies' room, and he's texting out of boredom. But now she's back and he's sweeping her onto the dance floor.

Having drained my drink, I head for the bar on the lower deck. Normally, I wouldn't have more than one at a work function, but it's becoming increasingly clear tonight won't end up in a job offer if I don't step up. I need another shot of liquid confidence.

"Total dissolution," I hear someone say as I pass a group by the bar. Ah, something I can relate to. Dissolution is a term used for a no-fault divorce.

"How long was the marriage?" I ask, trying to make my way into their conversation.

They all look at me as if I have six heads.

"We're talking about corporate law?" one of the women says, snarky AF. "Why, are you a divorce attorney?"

"Was."

Everyone gawks at me as if I'd just announced I'm a registered sex offender.

My phone dings with an incoming text. Thank God, saved by the bell. It's Chase again.

> Sorry, had to give my best man speech.

Gasp! I had no idea he was best man. I walk away from the group, more interested in this text than making friends with corporate-law snobs.

> Who would have you as a best man?

> Only someone I could bribe. Is your cruise still boring?

> Yep. Thinking about jumping overboard and swimming to shore.

> Oh no! That bad?

> That bad.

> If you do, stay away from the wake. It's been known to kill people.

> You'll come rescue me, right?

I pause before hitting send. It feels a bit suggestive, but I know I'm safe. Through every conversation and interaction we've had as we've gotten to know each other this summer, he's done nothing but inspired trust, despite me casting him in the role of major player. Talk about a plot twist.

"Hey there, little lady," a voice comes from behind me. I turn to find a man who looks to be in his late seventies, dressed in a leisure suit. I didn't know they still made them. "Are you the sing-ger?"

I look at him, confused. "No...I'm here for the interview process."

"You don't say!" he says, laughing a gravelly laugh, as if he's spent every one of his seven decades puffing on a stogie. "You're a lady lawyer?"

"Um...yes?" I refrain from pointing out that we're pretty deep into the twenty-first century and it should come as no surprise that women have been practicing law for decades.

"Shouldn't a pretty little thing like you be home making babies?"

"Actually, no."

Suddenly, I have all the clarity I've searched for since April as my past, present, and future converge into one. I know what I need to do now.

"I should be right where I am, suing people for sexual harassment."

That's it. I'm done. Bye-bye legal career.

I down my drink and set the glass on the bar, but instead of returning to the party in progress, I head to the stern of the boat and watch as the water churns in its wake. I envision jumping into the frothy water to escape this nightmare.

It strikes me how symbolic this cruise has become. Here I am, supposedly vying for a coveted position with a prestigious law firm, but I'm more interested in texting funny shit to my friend. And why? Because I think I've finally answered the first question I posed to myself in my journal.

I pull the notebook from my purse to confirm. That's right—I now travel with this little diary of mine, the thing I swore I'd never write in. I find the list of questions I drafted at the beginning of the summer to help me consider my career decisions. The first—*Do I still want to practice law?*—can now be answered with a resounding, *Hell no.*

I don't want to spend my life in a constant state of contention, arguing with clients over what's best for them, sparring with the other side, trying to outdo other lawyers. I want to do something positive, something that reflects the new me. I'm no longer a plastic shell of a person like the chest-bangers upstairs, too busy chatting themselves up to realize this boat's gonna sink and take most of them with it. Only three will survive.

I can't believe the next person I'm about to text.

I'm testing to see if she really meant what she said during her impassioned speech about following one's heart, or whether it was inspired by the gaiety of drinks by the sea. I wait for the phone to ring, for my mother to shriek in horror that I'm throwing my life away.

Three dots dance upon my screen instead, followed by her response.

> I think you've been done for a while, sweetie. Congrats on finally realizing it. Go forth and create your ideal life!

My heart soars knowing I have her blessing. I may be thirty-two, but she'll always be my mom, and her opinion will always matter. As will my dad's, but I'll deal with him when I get home. My mom's always been the hardest to impress.

I once viewed my high-powered legal career as my only source of joy, but it took mounting beach umbrellas to realize joy can be found in the most mundane tasks. Turns out, not every job has to be "important," and you don't have to be the best at everything you do. The most important work is what you do on the inside—overcoming fears, battling demons, getting to know your true self, and being willing to take chances on new things. On people. And yes, maybe even love.

I've learned a lot about myself this summer. Like how I was allowing myself to operate under a false set of beliefs, seeing things so black and white, causing me to distrust so many beautiful things in this life. Like love. Marriage. Hope. Even children. All from a place of fear.

Another was not believing I was worthy of healthy love. Maybe it took being lied to by someone I trusted to the core. Someone I chose to love so blindly, I couldn't see the truth... that he wasn't deserving of me, and didn't have the capacity to give me the great love I deserve. Which I do. Or maybe it took someone new coming along who allowed me to be myself, who reflected back all that was good within me—my strengths. Values. A desire to both love and be loved.

I have no idea what comes next, where my life will take me. But that's okay. Now that I've come this far, I know it won't take me much longer to figure the rest out.

I flip to the front page of my journal and look at the bucket list. Eight items have been checked off. The last two remain.

#9 Just say no

#10 Fall in love (with someone who's not Ben).

I pull out a pen and take a deep breath...

...and I check off both.

55

I head to the bow and watch as the pointy front slices through dark emerald water. In the ultimate act of cheesy symbolism, I lean forward like Rose in *Titanic* and revel in the feeling of misty sea spray, wind in my hair, forward momentum. This is what my life will be about from now on—forging ahead, not looking back. I know now that in order to avoid the icebergs, you must face your fears head-on, not hide behind them. Going forward, I won't be afraid to try new things and take chances, because I've learned I'm stronger than I've given myself credit for. I even survived a kid throwing up on me this summer. If I can handle that, I can handle anything.

My stomach drops to my knees as I think of Leo. How that little guy lit up my life, made me question the world around us, see things from a child's perspective. I will miss him fiercely, more than I ever thought was humanly possible to miss a child.

I wish Amy was here right now, so she could see how much I've changed. How I finally learned to *just say no* to things that weren't working for me—like practicing law, and harboring crushes on men who don't deserve my heart. But most importantly, how I've finally achieved number ten on the list, the one I swore to her would never happen.

Fall in love (with someone who's not Ben).

You picked up this book thinking you were getting a romance. And you have. I've fallen in love with the most important person I've ever met. Even if I've just met them.

I pull my journal from my purse, take out my pen, and next to #10, I draw a heart. Inside, I write...
Me.

56

Okay, okay. Relax.

I know you came here for a romance between two people, not just one. And while I may have told you four months ago that you'll never find that with me, I was wrong. Because the epiphany I have on the cruise isn't the end of the story. It never is, is it?

Here's how the rest of the night goes...

I'm still alone at the front of the boat when I hear an announcement over the loudspeaker.

"Folks, we're about to leave the bay and head out to sea, so if you want to catch a glimpse of this beautiful sunset, look toward the stern." He gives a chuckle. "That's the back of the boat, for you landlubbers."

Knowing summer is fleeting, I want to catch every Sea Isle sunset before it's over. I head toward the back again to watch the sun slide toward the horizon, filled with gratitude that this summer has allowed me to slow down and take in the beauty of this amazing planet. The ocean's rhythmic waves, crisp sunrises, swoony sunsets. Cool night sand and the vast beautiful sky. Especially the sky at night, and all its constellations.

Speaking of which...I look skyward in search of Perseus. I need to thank the dude for reminding us how important it is to deal with our fears and slay our demons in order to find love. But it's still too light; I'll have to look for him later.

I open my purse to slip the journal inside, but it snags on the strap. Falling to the ground, it lands open to the bucket list. I pick it up and run my fingers over the finally completed list, smiling at the fact that one of the items has several checkmarks—#2 *Do something completely out of character.*

Starting with leaving my life behind and coming to the shore in the first place. Working at a beach shack. Kissing a stranger. Falling in love with a little boy. And just...falling in love in general. With life. With me. With...

Magic.

I think back to that first night with Chase, when I challenged destiny to bring our paths together, before I knew he was my housemate. It must have been my subconscious telling me this guy was someone special. But instead of opening my heart to him, I did what I always do. I hid my true feelings and desires and used humor and rules as shields, afraid to think that maybe, just maybe, I'd found someone worth the risk.

That's it. No more jokes. No more deflection. I think of my mom's sage advice: *Your life isn't what happens to you. It's what you make happen.* Taking a deep breath, I'm about to add one more uncharacteristic move to make my life happen in a way I'm finally ready for. The biggest of them all.

Telling a boy I like him before he tells me. No more fear. No more jokes. Just truth.

While probably better done in person, I don't want to lose my courage. Nor do I want to take the easy way out and couch my truth in a text. I want him to hear the sincerity in my voice, and my voice to be captured for all of eternity. And what better way to accomplish all that than...*ta-da!* An audio message.

Repeating history, this time with intention, I press record on my phone and start speaking.

"Hey, Chase. It's Kace. Haha, we rhyme! Okay, that's not the reason I'm sending this message. I know you're at a wedding with someone else and this is the most inappropriate and uncharacteristic thing I've ever done. It seems I can't wait until the light of day to tell you what I have to tell you. I've done a lot of soul-searching this summer, learned some new things, made great friends. But the one thing I haven't done is be honest with you. About my feelings. For you."

Ugh. I pull the phone away from my face and stare at the screen. This sounded so much more poetic in my head. And my heart. But I push myself to continue—it's about being honest, after all.

"Um, so, from the moment I met you, I've known you were someone really special. All the joking I've done about house-mate rules was only to hide my real feelings, to keep us from exploring what we could be together, and the story we'd tell our kids one day. Truth is...I like you. I mean, really, *really* like you. I know my timing is shitty, now that you're with Meredith, but I couldn't let this summer end without you knowing..."

All of a sudden, my phone stops recording and the screen goes blank. I push the side button to bring it back to life, but it doesn't respond. Shit. My phone is dead. My heart's pounding as I try to turn it back on, hoping to get just a split-second of service so I can send this text before I chicken out.

Unless...this is a sign I wasn't supposed to do it this way. Of course not—he's at a wedding *right now* with another date. What the hell am I thinking? Thank you, Apple gods. While it's annoying that my phone's unable to hold a charge for a full damn day, you just saved me from making a fool of myself. Imagine the humiliation—me, telling a boy I like him, only so he can turn around and tell me he likes someone else. And is literally in the middle of liking her up at this very moment.

Still, I feel what I feel. As someone brilliant once said, when you know, you know. I finally know...and timing's not going to change that. I'll wait until Meredith and the housemates return to the city, and then I'll gather my courage again and tell him.

I like this plan. I'm at peace. Now let's get this dreaded cruise over with so I can start my new lawless, love-worthy life.

We've come to the end of the Intracoastal Waterway, where

the bay meets the sea. We pass by Townsends Inlet on the left and Avalon on the right, through the rough water I faced as a child on that dolphin-watching cruise. The same churning water I gazed at on my first morning in Sea Isle, thinking how much it reminded me of my life at that time—chaotic, diverging, uncertain.

Finally, we've hit the calm. Which also feels symbolic of my life as it's become after a summer spent by the sea.

Above me, the darkening sky reveals its first twinkling star of the night—the brightest star in the Perseus constellation, the one right near his heart. Like a fated lover, Andromeda joins him.

"Thanks, guys," I whisper to the once-star-crossed lovers. "I did it. I fought my demons."

I'm turning away from the back of the boat when I hear a motor revving. I spin around, afraid we're about to be hit by another boat. And then I hear something else. Someone yelling my name. It's a guy on a WaveRunner—

And he's wearing a tux.

"Sea Isle Beach Patrol! Permission to board!"

Two deck hands suddenly appear and open the gate to a gangplank thingy off the back of the boat. One grabs the WaveRunner and ties it to the side of the boat, as the other helps the man aboard. I stand there, catching fireflies in my gaping mouth.

"Chase, my man," one of them says, giving him a bro hug as if they were expecting him.

"Hey, guys, thanks for the assist." He looks beyond them and gives me that sexy half-smile of his. "I'm told one of your passengers is in need of rescue."

The guys snicker as if they're in on the joke before conveniently disappearing. And then it's just Chase and me.

He stands tall, straightens his jacket and adjusts his bowtie, giving major James Bond.

"What are you doing here?" I ask, stunned by his presence. "Is the wedding over already?"

"No, it's still going on."

"What about Meredith? You didn't just leave her—"

"I absolutely left her. At her insistence. Turns out, she doesn't just read the weather. She also reads people. She told me from the first moment she saw us together, she knew we had something special. She asked if we were dating, and I told her we're just friends. But then she told me I was full of shit."

"Good judge of character," I say, heart racing. "So I guess you got my audio message."

He looks at me confused. "What message?"

He pulls his phone from his breast pocket and taps it to life. "No message here."

"I sent you—" But I don't finish. Of course, he didn't get it—my phone died before I could send it.

Which means...

"I'm here to do what I should have done that first night I met you." With one arm he encircles my waist and pulls me in, hard. "Not let you walk away."

Sucking in a breath, I bite my lip as tears begin flowing down my cheeks.

"When we first met, I told you I'd never settle for less than what my parents had," he says. "I remember my dad once telling me how he felt when he first laid eyes on my mom, like his heart was beating out of his chest, a feeling that only grew stronger over the years. I'd never experienced that—until a marine invertebrate stung this smack-talking lawyer from Philly who, despite all her education, still doesn't know how to pronounce hoagie."

I laugh through my tears.

"Kacie Layne, you're the first woman I've ever met who's made me feel that crazy racy heart thing. You asked why I was single? Truth is—I hadn't met you yet."

Thank God he's holding on to me so tightly, or I'd be puddling at his feet.

"This time, I'm not letting you go. Do you trust me?"

I take a breath, knowing I'm about to step off a ledge I've been clinging to for dear life. But it's time to let go. I'm safe.

"I trust you, Chase."

"Then trust me with this," he says as he takes both my hands. "Take the leap, Kacie. Fall with me. I promise, I've got you. I know you're scared, and you don't believe in love, but let me make a believer out of you. Please let me show you a love beyond your wildest imagination."

Breathlessly, I nod.

He cups my cheeks and leans into me, just like the night of my birthday, when he showed me what it feels like to be cherished. And, like that night, the silvery moon takes its place among a blanket of stars, lighting the night sky with everything that's been missing in my life.

Hope.

Love.

Chase.

Epilogue

"**O**kay, Jellyfish. You take the top, I'll take the bottom."

"*Ooh*, I love being on top."

Chase flashes his eyebrows at me. "You have *no idea* how much I love it."

Oh, stop. I know what you're thinking, and you need to get your mind out of the gutter.

It's November 27, the Saturday after Thanksgiving, six months from the day we met. We're talking about Christmas trees, obvs. Specifically, how to get the tree we just bought from the corner lot to his apartment three blocks away.

Correction: our apartment.

Turns out, my subletting friend was so in love with my place, she begged me to keep it. Chase let my houseless ass stay with him in his apartment in Philly after I returned from my Europe trip at the end of September. Only for a few days, we both agreed.

I haven't left since.

After a few struggles, several jokes, and lots of laughter—the cornerstone of our relationship—we lug our eight-foot tree up three stories—thank you, elevator company, who couldn't come to fix it for two weeks. In case you're wondering, there's a perfect test for a couple's relationship—moving heavy objects into a small apartment. That, and putting together IKEA furniture. We pass with flying colors on both accounts.

Once inside, we set it up in the tree stand I'd already filled with water, thanks to my type-A tendency toward forethought. At least some of my good old habits survived my life's 180.

That, and my killer humor, which I now occasionally share with others at the corner bar's open mic night. That's right—Kacie Layne is finally using her humor for good.

Other than that, I'm new and improved. Which reminds me—I guess there's some catching up we need to do.

For starters, I'm sure you're dying to know what happened after the cruise. No doubt, the Nosy Nellies among you are expecting to hear how Chase and I made mad, passionate love when we returned to the house that night after finally sharing our feelings for one another. But you'd be wrong. We did, however, sneak into my room after discovering Wendy was away for the weekend, unable to wait the extra sixty seconds and two flights of stairs to get to his room. That's how ready we were to act on the passion that had been building between us all summer.

We rolled around on my single bed with our tongues down each other's throats—he in his tux, me in my little black dress. Don't be disappointed, because let me put it this way...there's nothing more exciting than fooling around fully dressed. Talk about anticipation, Heinz has nothing on us. Especially since it would be another two weeks before we finally made love. A perfect amount of time to thoroughly explore each other's bodies in other ways, preparing for the main event. We knew it would be explosive and didn't want to rush it or have others around, especially since most of the housemates had taken off work those last couple weeks to enjoy summer's last fleeting days. In the meantime, we created a bucket list of our own, consisting of all the places in the house we wanted to make love once everyone was gone.

Otherwise, we made it no secret we were together. We paraded around like a couple of lovebirds—lathering each other with sunscreen, clinging to each other in the water, kissing every chance we got. Even in plain view. Turns out when two people are in love, the house rules don't apply. Especially made-up rules, the kind you conjure to keep from opening your heart to love. We later learned there'd been a house bet on whether Chase and I would "get together already." Pockets were lined over that (suffice to say, Celeste's were not).

It wasn't until the Sunday night of Labor Day weekend, after waving to our dearly departing housemates, when we raced each other to the primary suite and he pulled me into him, hard. He kissed me—sweet and slow, with all the light teasing innocence of a first kiss, yet familiar from the many kisses we'd shared since that night on the boat. Intensity mounted as the reality of what we were about to do thickened the air around us—heavy with the promise of everything left unspoken all summer. Stolen glances. Wishful thinking. Lustful thoughts. A season of longing we worked so hard to keep hidden from one another.

As his tongue probed deeper and our kiss intensified, I was orbited to another world until I couldn't wait another second to have him inside me. I pulled his t-shirt over his head and ran my fingertips down the smooth, tan skin of his beautifully sculpted chest—the one I painfully tried to ignore back when we were "just friends." He groaned his appreciation, our lips never parting as we continued undressing each other with increasing urgency, fingers grasping at zippers, tugging, pulling, sighing as we finally melted together, skin against skin, no longer separated by clothing, excuses, rules. Least of all, fear.

If I thought he was perfect before, I clearly had no grasp of the concept. Not until I saw him standing there, naked and fully erect, staring at me with a palpable hunger.

He scooped me up and carried me to the bed, where he gingerly laid me down, crawling toward me as moonlight danced on his bronzed body. I pulled him toward me, and his skin was fire on mine. Our legs intertwined as he dipped his head down and brushed my lips with his before making a trail of kisses to my navel. Our movements were slow, unhurried, savoring the moment we'd been longing for but had been holding back on for three torturous months. There was no rush, just deliberate touches, knowing there was no hurry in our forever.

Coming back up to me, our foreheads touched, breath meeting breath.

"Are you sure you're ready?" he whispered.

Gazing up at him, I nodded, choked with emotion, knowing this was what I'd been waiting a lifetime for. "Yes."

The moment he entered me, I knew I'd never be with another man again.

"Oh my God, Kacie..."

His moan was soft yet urgent as he started moving, every thrust slow and deliberate, his eyes locked with mine, giving me the most incredible pleasure I'd ever encountered. I never knew having someone inside me, someone who filled me up and fit so perfectly, could feel so good. Soon, he became a man possessed as he grunted and picked up speed. I've never been made love to with such fervent passion in my entire lifetime, his eyes never leaving mine except to roll back in his head as we met at the summit.

We came together in one powerful, earth-moving orgasm, the magnitude of which I never knew possible. But it wasn't just about the physical sensation. It was the emotional depth I felt for this man—my hope-filled friend, my old-school romantic, this beautiful man who rescued me in oh, so many ways.

The following day, after fully completing our love-making location bucket list (shout out to my other summer love—the outdoor shower), Chase dropped me off at Philly International for my flight to London to visit Amy. I don't think I've ever had so much fun with that girl, who took three of her allotted five weeks of vacation without anyone blinking an eye, despite the fact that she'd only been in their employ for three months. As stated, some places know how to treat employees, and get that there's more to life than working.

We did it all, starting with the typical London experiences—double-decker bus rides, photos in red phone booths, changing of the guard—before we traveled to Italy, where we spent a whirlwind six days between Rome, Venice, and Tuscany. On another jaunt, we hit up Amsterdam, where Amy dragged me to the Red Light District, hoping to find me a job.

Then, there was Paris. No words needed, especially when you stand at the base of a twinkling Eiffel Tower with your best friend in the world. Well, one of them. The only downer was knowing Chase had a bucket list item involving Paris. And me. *Maybe someday.*

Sitting at an outdoor café the following afternoon, Amy's attention was drawn to something behind me. "Damn, girl. That's *definitely* something you gotta do in Paris."

I turned to see the most handsome man strolling toward me. Black turtleneck, black jeans, five o'clock shadow, long leather coat flowing behind him. If you guessed European model, you'd be incorrect. It was the autumn version of my summer love—my favorite lifeguard, Chase.

Turning back to Amy, my mouth agape, I scrambled to find words to explain Chase's unexpected appearance.

She simply smiled. "You're welcome."

Amy excused herself for the next two days to do a little solo exploring while Chase and I got to enjoy Paris alone at her insistence. We not only kissed at the top of the twinkling tower at midnight, checking off one of his bucket list items, but created a few special memories of our own. I later learned Amy invited Chase not only to surprise me, but to meet him herself.

Finally, I have her wholehearted approval on my man choice. All thanks to her encouraging me to try new things, like that crazy summer bucket list. Which, it turns out, wasn't so crazy after all.

"Let's let the branches fall before we decorate," Chase says, bringing me back to the present. "In the meantime, I have a surprise for you."

He pulls out a small gift. Don't get all excited—it's not a ring box. More like a bracelet box.

"As you know, I'm coaching mini-hoop basketball in January," he says as I eagerly open the package.

It's an ornament—a basketball picture frame with a photo of me in it. With it, a folded piece of paper.

"What's this all about?" I ask, chuckling.

"You'll see."

I unfold the paper, which turns out to be a roster of players' names.

"Is this your way of telling me I made the team?" I joke.

"It's my way of telling you someone has. *Apparently*, a new kid has moved into the district and has joined our rec league. Check out the names."

Breathless with anticipation, I scroll the list until I get to one that stops me in my tracks.

"Leo Steele," I read aloud, as my heart pounds away in my chest. Tears instantly pool in my eyes as I look up at him. "Please tell me this isn't a joke."

"No joke," he says. "I've confirmed it's your little buddy, and I happen to need an assistant. We practice Tuesday and Thursday nights with games on Saturday afternoons. I know with your new job and everything..."

I bite my lip, considering his words, not having to ask what he means by *everything*. To say I'm all booked up is not only an understatement, but a pun. In addition to doing stand-up, I'm also writing a book—a rom-com of all things (I know, right??)

But wait, there's more.

The new job he's referring to is me teaching constitutional law at UPenn—a dream job as an associate professor. All thanks to my housemate and friend, now coworker Diane, who hooked me up. Who also made me realize you don't need ten years to know if someone's right for you. As someone once said, "When you know, you know."

Thank God Chase knew, something he reminds me of every night when we kiss each other before spooning into slumber. I'm so thankful he hung in there, waiting for me to know too.

"What d'ya say, my lovely assistant? Ready to make a *humongous* impact on a little guy's life?"

"*Thoroughly*," I say, laughing through my tears. I'm over the moon, knowing I get to see my little friend again.

He takes me in his arms. "What do you know about basketball?"

"Not a damn thing."

"Perfect, you'll do fine," he says, laughing. "Here, why don't you hang this ornament to make it official?"

I hang it front and center on the bare tree.

"How about this one?" he asks as he hands me another ornament. "I made it for you."

It's a large clam shell on a string, painted in midnight blue, with little white specks to signify the night sky. Along the bottom is a strip of beige, representing a beach, and on it, a tiny white lifeguard stand. Just like the one we sat in the night we met, where we shared our first kiss.

Looking closer, I see that some of the specks in the sky are yellow, aligned in a familiar pattern, just like...

"Perseus and Andromeda?" I ask, dumbfounded.

"Of course."

"But...how did you...?"

I'm so blown away, I'm rendered speechless. After that first night, we never spoke of Pers and Andy again. Nor did I discuss my inner thoughts with Chase, about how their story got to me. How it made me think about the work I, too, had to do if I ever hoped to find love.

"I could see your wheels turning when I told you the story of Perseus having to fight his fears and demons," Chase explains. "I believe that's exactly what you did this past summer. The woman I met that first night was skeptical—dare I say disdainful—about love and marriage. I'm beyond thankful you faced those fears and decided to trust me enough to let me in, so I can show you how beautiful love can be."

I run my finger over the smooth surface of the shell as tears well in my eyes. "It *is* beautiful."

"I painted the constellation so you'll always remember how the stars aligned to bring us together, and that even on the darkest night there's hope."

Once again, I'm without words, but this time it's because his lips are on mine, and as he cups my face and pulls me closer, I thank those lucky stars for leading me to this man. I'm filled with love and hope in a way I've never felt before, showing me that anything's possible.

Anything…

Kacie Layne
and
Chase Maddox

INVITE YOU TO SHARE IN THEIR JOY
AS THEY GET HITCHED

Saturday, May 27 at Sunset
Thirty-eighth Street Beach, Sea Isle City, NJ
Reception to follow at the Sandbar/Ocean Drive

(Shoes optional; party vibe required.)

Epilogue
(Part Deux)

That's right, my friends. One year to the date after we met, I did the unthinkable. Showing up on a beach at sunset, I stood before Chase under a simple arch adorned with jellyfish paper lanterns. With Amy as maid-of-honor, and a little squirt named Leo as best man (who couldn't have looked any cuter in his matching tux), I became Kacie Layne Maddox.

Adjunct professor. Part-time comedian. Friend to some, Jellyfish to one. My husband.

P.S. I also wrote this book[*].

---

[*] I know you just flipped to the cover. Kimberly Brighton's my pen name. Sue me.

Acknowledgments

FIRST AND FOREMOST, I WISH TO THANK THE BOOK PUB-lishing professionals who continue to support me in my author journey. My editor, Emily Ohanjanians, has been with me since the beginning, and for that I'm eternally grateful. It's been wonderful working with you, and I wish you much success and endless joy in your new adventure as author! I also thank my proofreader Shannon Cave for your keen attention to detail. Many thanks to book cover designer, Mary Ann Smith, and interior designer, Jessica Kleinman, for your beautiful work.

If someone had told me I'd one day be the author of not one, but FIVE books, I would have said they were full of shizz. But here I am—100% indie published and proud of it. I'm thankful to those book professionals listed above, and others, who've shared their skills, talents and experiences—including other indie authors, with whom I'm blessed to share this incredibly creative space. I love how supportive and encouraging the indie publishing world is, and thankful we've evolved to this place where *all* authors are welcome to tell their stories. If you have a story to tell, keep writing.

As always, I thank my family for their never-ending support and encouragement. I couldn't do this without you, and I love you all so much.

I also wish to thank my street team and the readers who've embraced my books. It makes my heart full to hear that my humor gives you chuckles, my stories make you swoon, and my books have helped you through tough times. There is truly no better feeling in the world for an author than to hear someone say, "I've read all your books, and can't wait for the next." To those who've shared those sentiments with me, you have no idea how much that inspires me to keep going. You are the reason I want to keep doing this author thang.

To you, individual reader, I thank you from the bottom of my heart for picking up this book. I hope you've enjoyed it.

Reader's Guide

Q&A WITH
KIMBERLY BRIGHTON

BOOK CLUB
QUESTIONS

Q&A with Kimberly Brighton

I OFTEN GET ASKED BY READERS HOW I'VE COME UP WITH ideas for my books. I thought I'd share some of that here.

What was the inspiration for My Summer Bucket List?

If you know my work (and me), you know I'm in love with coastal New Jersey. I'm the offspring of a Jersey Boy from northern parts, and a Jersey Girl from the south, and I've spent a lifetime visiting, vacationing, and even temporarily living in this magical place. In my other books, I shared how I came up with the inspiration for my *Love Actually*-inspired Cape May series, and Hallmark-inspired *Cape May Christmas in July*, so I won't bore you with that here. (If you haven't read them yet, please do!)

While I love Cape May, there's another town I love even more—Sea Isle. Okay, maybe I shouldn't say I love it more. Just differently. I'll explain later.

The bucket list concept is nothing new—a set of lofty goals you've imagined for yourself, whether that be a bougie travel destination, an out-of-this-world experience, or some other self-defined goal. But what if someone else were to design a bucket list *for* you? How different would their list look from the one you make yourself? Sometimes, our loved ones know us better than we know ourselves, including what's best for us.

I thought it would be fun to play around with the bucket list concept and have our brooding FMC's ever-optimistic BFF design a list of challenges to force her out of her comfort zone and, in the process, find a whole new side of herself.

Maybe even a side of love.

I also wanted to explore the almighty friend crush, something I've experienced a few times myself in my youth—that thing that grabs hold of us and keeps us in its grasp, even when we find ourselves relegated to the friend zone. Sometimes crushes work out. Other times, they taint our vision, rendering us unable to see something new and good coming toward us. Maybe it's because we've deemed our crush *that* worthy to forsake all others, or there's something inside us that just won't let us let go. Whatever the reason, we often must shift our focus within before we find the solution to unrequited love. And it's this...

The crush is never the prize. You are.

What's so special about Sea Isle that made you want to set your book here?

As the poem in the opening pages of this book states, once you have slept on an island, you will never quite be the same.

Sea Isle City is a sleepy seaside town twenty-five miles north of Cape May. It's located on Ludlam Island, one of the many barrier islands lining the south Jersey coast. Don't be fooled by its municipal designation—Sea Isle is less city, more small coastal vacation town. With five miles of white sand beaches that truly feel like velvet at night, Sea Isle provides endless summer fun with its seaside promenade, family-owned shops and restaurants, and cool sea breezes.

Sea Isle is where my parents brought us for our first beach vacation when I was four years old. Where my brother and I spent endless summer days boogie boarding and building sandcastles. It's where we had our first run-in with the law, when we played on a lifeguard boat after hours and the cops had to intervene (the childhood version of a 1ˢᵗ degree felony).

In my 20's, I'd flock to Sea Isle on weekends with my two besties, Deirdre and Ellen. After soaking up rays on the beach, we'd do the typical Sea Isle bar crawl, hoping to meet *that guy*. We'd hit no-shower-happy-hours at Ocean Drive and Carousel Bar, sing along to the bands at Springfield or Shenanigans, and finish the night in Dead Dog Saloon. Sometimes we'd mix it up and head to Kix or LaCosta. All still exist, with the exception of Springfield/Carousel and LaCosta. Of course, no night clubbing was without the requisite after-hours Wawa coffee run. We'd sip coffee on the porch of the boarding house where we stayed, being thoroughly entertained by happy people leaving the bars, and placing bets on which ones were hooking up that night.

My family owned a house in Sea Isle for several years, and that's where I spent most of the summer after law school, studying for the grueling bar exam. Later that summer, my law school friends and I rented our own shore house as we awaited our results. Sea Isle is where where my fiancé and I had our engagement photos taken, and where I first dipped my baby's toes in the ocean. Our extended family has vacationed here for years, watching our kids grow from being Sea Isle Baby Parade contestants to being parents themselves. Two years ago, we began the indoctrination cycle again with a new generation. This summer, we'll add two more members to the newly forming Sea Isle Cousins gang with more to come...and so it will continue.

My family's story is not unique. The south Jersey Shore has been where families have settled and vacationed for generations.

So...why Sea Isle? Just ask anyone who loves this place like I do. Their answer will likely be...once you've slept on *this* island, you'll never quite be the same.

How did you come up with the storyline and characters?

Honestly? I just wanted to write a happy love story that took place in Sea Isle. But no romance is without its challenges, its darkest moments, the life lessons characters must learn before they find true love. I needed my FMC to face something that would explain why she was so anti-love and how she was the last person who'd ever come to the Jersey Shore looking for it. What better way than to strip her of the very thing that identified her, in the wake of relationship heartbreak?

Unexpected job loss is something many can relate to. We've either experienced it ourselves or know someone who has. It used to be that if you were good at your job, you never had to worry about losing it unless you did something truly heinous. Today, the opposite is true. No job is ever guaranteed, no matter how good you are at it. We live in an ever-changing, fast-paced world, where family-run businesses have been replaced by corporations, creating a breeding ground for greed and ease. Doesn't make for a pleasant work experience for many of us humans, especially those of us who've spent years building careers we're proud of. While it's arguably Kacie's own doing that causes her to lose her job, I wanted to explore what happens to someone whose identity is so intertwined with their career, they have no idea how to function when it goes away. Especially when that very career has helped shape their life and informed their feelings about life, love, and marriage.

I've also witnessed the "closing a window/opening a door" theory floated by Kacie's mom. So often, when we lose something that matters to us, we do find something much better. Even if we don't know it at the time. I wanted to give hope to Kacie—and everyone who's lost a job, a relationship, or something important to them—that better things await. Of course, you have to keep your mind open and look for those nuggets of opportunity that may pop up, like the kind Kacie was presented with when she was invited to join a shore house.

As mentioned, I had the great fortune of living in a Sea Isle beach house one summer after the bar exam. Neither I nor my friends were independently wealthy, which meant we all needed to find temporary jobs until we learned whether we'd passed the bar. My housemates all sought restaurant jobs, but I'd spent most of my teen years waitressing and was looking for something different. Sitting on the beach one day, I looked over to see a wooden shack where umbrellas and beach chairs were offered for rent.

"I know what I'm doing this summer," I announced to my friends. Like Kacie, I was hired on the spot.

Today, those shacks no longer exist on Sea Isle beaches, but I'm not kidding when I say it was the most fun I've ever had working. Where else can you wear a bikini to work*, soak up the sun, and have days off when it rains? Oh, and the best part— scoping out lifeguards†.

Best. Job. Ever.

I'm also fascinated by the shore group-rental phenomenon, especially after living it myself. In every town along the south Jersey Shore, you'll find college kids living together and working summer jobs in restaurants, boutique stores, ice cream parlors. They serve as lifeguards, beach tag inspectors, summer camp counselors, and more. Beyond college, shared rentals are great investments for single professionals, allowing them to work in the city during the week and flock to the shore on weekends.

When summer begins each year, I'm happy and hopeful for all these housemate groups, knowing the fun they'll have spending a summer by the sea, meeting new friends and making cherishable memories. Some will even fall in love and marry, creating their own version of "The Jersey Shore Romance."

And so, the story continues.

---

* Keep in mind, I was in my twenties then.
† Ditto (or so I'd like you to think)

Like it did for a friend of mine. When we met at a book signing in Sea Isle, she shared her love story with me—how she met her now husband standing in line at the Ocean Drive, but he thought she was with someone else. They parted ways only to reconnect unexpectedly at an outdoor bar at the end of the summer, on a day his golfing outing was cancelled due to rain...

If it sounds familiar, it should. It was the love story of my friends (and book characters) Diane and her husband John. I loved their story so much, I had to include it in this book, with their permission. If you have a great love story you'd like to share, please feel free to reach out to me at KimberlyBrighton@ comcast.net. You never know—it may find its way into a future book.

What would you say is the overarching theme of this book?

There are several. Job loss. Unrequited love. Missed opportunities. Reinventing oneself after devastation.

(Okay, Kacie...how about some positive themes?)

A quaint seaside town as a character. Sunny days, golden sunsets, cool sea breezes. Sleeping on an island. The pure joy a child can sprinkle into your heart, even when they're not your own. But I think the theme that resonates the most is hope. And, of course love.

If you picked up this book hoping for a heart-warming love story, I certainly hope you found it.

Book Club Questions

1. If you could ditch your daily responsibilities and spend your summer anywhere, where would it be?

2. What was your favorite summer job? How about your favorite permanent job? (I include in this question home CEOs!)

3. Have you ever experienced a friend crush? Did you get over it, or did you end up dating, co-habitating and/or marrying them?

4. There are several tropes in this book. Unrequited love (is that really a trope? If not, it should be!) Second chances. Love at first sight. Friends to lovers. Which trope is your favorite (if not one of these, which one?) What is it you like about your favorite tropes?

5. If this book were to become a movie, who would play each of the characters?

6. What's on your bucket list? Amy was gracious enough to share her blueprint for the perfect bucket list here...enjoy filling it out and let me know what you achieve! If you're reading this on an e-reader, you can find a downloadable version on my website, KimberlyBrighton.com.

7. Happy listing!

Create your own bucket list

About the Author

KIMBERLY BRIGHTON IS AN AWARD-WINNING ROMANCE author, incidental humorist, and asparagus enthusiast from the Philadelphia area. *My Summer Bucket List* is her fifth book. She studied satirical writing and screenwriting at The Second City and is the author of *The Shore Blog* (TheShoreBlog.com), a travel website focusing on the Jersey Cape, and *BlaBlaBlog* (BlaBlaBlog.org), a humor website. When not dreaming up swoony romance plots, she spends her time searching for food expiration labels and sitting at red lights. Married for 25 laugh-filled years, she's discovered the key to a lasting marriage: takeout.

To stay in touch and learn more about her upcoming releases, sign up for her newsletter at KimberlyBrighton.com or visit her on social media @KBrightonAuthor.

www.ingramcontent.com/pod-product-compliance
Lightning Source LLC
Chambersburg PA
CBHW060515160726
47991CB00001B/41